Personal connections, and our failure to make and tend to them, dominate this entrancing collection of irony-infused short stories, set mostly in postwar Europe and America. The greatest lure of the stories are the characters. Maitland-Lewis (*Botticelli's Bastard*) sharply limns the foibles of the well-heeled and privileged. The decisions Maitland-Lewis's characters make haunt them forever, and the characters themselves will haunt the readers. Takeaway: The community of characters—the good, the desperate, the greedy—will grab readers' hearts and make them care, story after story.
Great for fans of: Graham Swift, Julian Barnes
–**BookLife** - *Publisher's Weekly*

5 stars (out of 5) Stephen Maitland-Lewis' *MR. SIMPSON AND OTHER SHORT STORIES* include tales that range from droll slice-of-life to high-octane suspense. Maitland-Lewis brings a dry British wit to many of the tales contained in the book.
IR Verdict: Stephen Maitland-Lewis wows with *MR. SIMPSON AND OTHER SHORT STORIES*—a triumph of alternative history featuring humor, action, romance and an eclectic mix of characters, genres, and moods—from an exemplary storyteller with a unique voice. *–IndieReader Review*

Stephen Maitland-Lewis, author of the pulse-pounding financial thriller *Duped*, is back with a collection of suspenseful stories that succeed wildly in chronicling the relentless pursuit of success, status and survival. Prepare to squirm as Maitland-Lewis reveals one dark secret after another. Deliciously ruthless predators rule in this collection of stories about deceit, deception, fraud and power. Highly recommended.
—**BestThrillers.com**

Themes of loss (money, lovers, youth) and unrealized potential weave through the intriguing and wide-ranging stories... *−Kirkus Reviews*

The author successfully reveals that human foibles are universal. Maitland-Lewis' work shows the same variety in its subject matter as the compilation *Fifty-Two Stories* by Anton Chekov. Art enthusiasts, classical and jazz music buffs, lovers of world travel, and those who appreciate the exquisite agony of any creative experience may wish to read this book. **−Heather Brooks,** *US Review of Books*

These stories are wonderfully cosmopolitan. The range of characters really reflects the ways of the world, its successes, and its failures. An up-to-date Somerset Maugham is announced, you might well think. **−David Pryce-Jones** - Author of *Fault Lines, Signatures,* and *Closed Circle*

I admire authors who sit down with their vocabulary and place words in an order that I never could−whether to evoke an emotion, unearth a bygone era, or capture a unique slice of the human spirit. Stephen Maitland-Lewis is one such writer and he accomplishes it time and again in *Mr. Simpson and Other Short Stories.* This book is great. I'm also certain that he knows more words than I do. **−Alan Zweibel,** original *SNL* writer/Thurber Prize winning novelist/All-Around Great Guy

The immaculate attention to both detail and emotional truth makes the reader feel that Mr. Maitland-Lewis was somehow uncannily present in this collection of enticingly varied short stories. A cornucopia of highly enjoyable delights. The pages turned themselves. Witty, immensely readable, and imbued with a warm understanding of the human condition. **−Christopher Renshaw,** Award Winning Director - Broadway and London West End

An entertaining smorgasbord of short stories that pay tribute to the masters of the genre. With an arch sense of humor and a delicious dash of irony, Stephen Maitland-Lewis follows an intriguing cast of characters—including a philandering banker, a blackmailing florist, a failed musician, and a disenchanted spy—through clever plot twists and surprise endings that never fail to satisfy. –**Tom Sancton**, author of *The Bettencourt Affair* and *Sweet Land of Liberty - America In The Mind of The French Left 1848-1871*

Stephen Maitland-Lewis has an unerring ear for character, and characters, and in *Mr. Simpson and Other Short Stories,* he writes about a whole constellation of creations with acuity, poignancy, and wit. –**David Margolick**, Author - *Strange Fruit: The Biography of a Song* and The *Promise and the Dream: The Untold Story of Martin Luther King, Jr. and Robert F. Kennedy*

Stephen Maitland-Lewis serves up a brace of short stories that Somerset Maugham and Graham Greene would have savored. I imbibed *MR. SIMPSON AND OTHER STORIES* with delight. You will too. –**Barry Singer**, founder and proprietor of Chartwell Booksellers–New York City and author of *CHURCHILL STYLE: The Art of Being Winston Churchill*

For me, each story in this book is either an hors d'oeuvre or a bon bon. I'm fond of both. Stephen Maitland-Lewis has created a delicious array of narratives that satisfies a reader's hunger for armchair travels or curiosity about an intriguing personality. Witty, heart warming, this collection is full of characters you'd like to meet. Bravo Stephen! –**Peggy Scott Laborde**–New Orleans based author, talk show host and Emmy Award-winning documentary producer

A marvelous collection of stories penned with insight into the human condition and articulation designed to delight the reader. Maitland-Lewis, an important voice among authors today, brings his unique style and delivers vivid enjoyment with each tale, some touching, some whimsical, some fantastical. Each one a treasure. Unique stories to be consumed repeatedly. –**David Hunt Stafford** - Artistic & Managing Director, Theatre 40 of Beverly Hills

The remarkable storyteller of *Botticelli's Bastard* is at it again with this first-class collection of short stories. Fans of crossing the lines between fiction and history, romance, espionage, royal has-beens, Ivy Leaguers, writers and art dealers, and jetsetters and those who enjoy stories set in London, Paris, New York, Geneva, Munich, and Palm Springs will find plenty to keep them engaged and entertained. Maitland-Lewis' eye for detail, memorable characters, and exquisite narration make each of the stories a genuine pleasure to read. The end result is always, to our good fortune, a reader who wants to come back to the collection wanting more and ready for the next adventure. –**Félix V. Matos Rodríguez** - Historian

In *Mr. Simpson and Other Short Stories*, Stephen Maitland-Lewis delights us with an appealing assortment of intriguing and sagacious tales, told with the elegance and insight of Maugham intermingled with the wit and irony of O. Henry. Each stop in this entertaining excursion into the human psyche in a cosmopolitan world leaves the reader eagerly anticipating the next engrossing and enriching Maitland-Lewis story. –**Angelo Parra**, Award-Winning Playwright, Author, Educator

Having already shown himself to be a master of gripping, long-form narratives in his earlier works, Stephen Maitland-Lewis has now produced a riveting page-turner with *Mr. Simpson and Other Short Stories*. Each bite-sized morsel is perfectly paced and inhibited with memorable characters, surprise twists and turns, and emotions of all varieties. Like one of Louis Armstrong's golden trumpet solos, Maitland-Lewis knows how to tell a story and leave his readers wanting more. –**Ricky Riccardi**, Director of Research Collections for Louis Armstrong House Museum, author of *Heart Full of Rhythm: The Big Band Years of Louis Armstrong*

The diverting short stories collected in *Mr. Simpson and Other Short Stories* concern money—both the lack of it, and what people are willing to do to get it.–**Eileen Gonzalez, Clarion Reviews from *Foreword Reviews*,** Clarion Rating: 4 out of 5

Stephen Maitland- Lewis takes us on a delightful, enjoyable and diverse journey to international destinations, where we meet and become enchanted by some of the most fascinating protagonists we would expect to encounter from one of the most sophisticated and imaginative authors writing today. –**Mike Burstyn,** Award-Winning Actor and Director

A storyteller to the manner born Maitland-Lewis also has the true writer's gift for creating believable characters. Making their acquaintance is the definition of a good read! –**Dan Morgenstern,** Director Emeritus, Institute of Jazz Studies, Rutgers University

Maitland-Lewis' descriptions of his characters are so vivid that it feels as if they are the next door neighbors. –**Howard Storm** - Award-winning director

Stephen Maitland-Lewis' short stories pack a real punch. Engaged in a fully informed way with twentieth-century history and culture—especially the worlds of jazz and high art—these stories are compelling renderings of both individual psychology and social mores. Addictive to read, the collection adds up to more than its individual parts, creating a consistent atmosphere across a group of pleasingly varied stories. I recommend it to readers with confidence that it will provide much pleasure. –**Steven Kruger,** Professor, English, Queens College, CUNY

HERO ON THREE CONTINENTS

"A moving, complex and well-crafted fictional biography... Maitland-Lewis renders the multitudinous cast of characters with marvelous detail ... a touching read, with a fictional character to admire." **–Kirkus Reviews**

EMERALDS NEVER FADE

"A poignant story of two men whose lives are forever altered by a period of history that should never be forgotten." **–Robert Dugoni,** NY Times Bestselling Author

"I couldn't put it down until the end. It is a page-turner – greatly enjoyable and informative. Perfecto." **–Connie Martinson**, TV Host of Connie Martinson Talks Books

AMBITION

"This financial thriller rocks and rolls with sex and skull-duggery and more money than Midas can count. It's un-put-downable. Chilling."
–Kitty Kelley, seven time NY Times Bestselling Biographer

"Ambition creates the excitement of free-fall–it's difficult to put down. Who said financial institutions were dull? A wonderful book and a great reading experience." **–Mickey Kantor,** former United States Secretary of Commerce

BOTTICELLI'S BASTARD

"Botticelli's Bastard is beautifully written and to its further credit impossible to categorize. Part thriller, part intriguing mystery, this book is compulsive reading. Above all, it is a firstclass novel." **–Sir Ronald Harwood**, Oscar® winning writer

"My interest in collecting important art came together with my love of thrillers. Stephen Maitland-Lewis' Botticelli's Bastard is a great read."
–Arnold Kopelson, Oscar® and Golden Globe® winning producer

DUPED

DUPED delivers the excitement of a heist film with the exotic adventure of a globetrotting spy tale. While Maitland-Lewis' dialogue-driven writing makes for fastreading, well-crafted adventures through portions of Africa, Europe and California will please the travel-starved masses. **—BestThrillers.com**

In DUPED, author Stephen Maitland-Lewis has written a novel of high-stake schemes, suspense and sex. A deftly crafted, impressively original, and inherently riveting read from first page to last. **—Midwest Book Review**

Mr. Simpson
and
OTHER
SHORT
STORIES

Mr. Simpson and OTHER SHORT STORIES

Stephen Maitland-Lewis

Hildebrand Books
NASHVILLE, TENNESSEE

Hildebrand Books an imprint of W. Brand Publishing
j.brand@wbrandpub.com
www.wbrandpub.com
Printed and bound in the United States of America.

Cover design by designchik.net
Cover photography: Triff / Shutterstock

Mr. Simpson and Other Short Stories – Stephen Maitland-Lewis first edition

Available in Hardcover, Paperback, Kindle, and eBook formats.
Hardcover ISBN: 978-1-950385-58-4
Paperback ISBN: 978-1-950385-59-1
eBook ISBN: 978-1-950385-60-7

Release date: September 07, 2021

Library of Congress Control Number: 2021907532

contents

NOVELS by Stephen Maitland-Lewis

Hero on Three Continents

Emeralds Never Fade

Ambition

Botticelli's Bastard

Duped

PLAY by Stephen Maitland-Lewis

Mr. Simpson

Photo credit: Nathan Sternfeld

Stephen Maitland-Lewis is an award-winning author, a British attorney, and a former international investment banker. He has held senior executive positions in London, Kuwait, Paris, Munich, and on Wall Street prior to moving to California in 1991. He has owned a luxury hotel and a world-renowned restaurant and was also Director of Marketing of a Los Angeles daily newspaper.

Maitland-Lewis is a jazz aficionado and a Board Trustee of the Louis Armstrong House Museum in New York. In 2014, he received the Museum's prestigious Louie Award. A member of PEN, The Authors Guild and The Dramatists Guild of America, Maitland-Lewis is also on the Executive Committee of the International Mystery Writers Festival. In addition, he is on the Advisory Board of the California Jazz Foundation and is a former Board member.

He has published short stories in various magazines and *Mr. Simpson and Other Short Stories* is Maitland-Lewis' first collection of short stories. His novels have received numerous accolades and his most recent suspense thriller is *Duped*. His other novels include *Hero on Three Continents; Emeralds Never Fade* which won the 2012 Benjamin Franklin Award for Historical Fiction and the 2011 Written Arts Award for Best Fiction; *Ambition* which was a 2013 USA Best Book Awards finalist and won first place for General Fiction in the 2013 Rebecca's Reads Choice Awards; and *Botticelli's Bastard*, a 2014 USA Best Book Awards finalist in three categories and winner of the Bronze Award in Best Regional Fiction (Europe) at the 2015 Independent Publisher Book Awards. Maitland-Lewis' short story, *Mr. Simpson,* has recently been developed as a play and has been performed by noted theatre companies in Miami, New Orleans and Beverly Hills.

In January of 2016, Maitland-Lewis was sworn in as a Freeman of the City of London and admitted as a Liveryman of the Worshipful Company of City Solicitors. In April of 2016, he became a Fellow of The Royal Geographical Society (FRGS). He divides his time between Beverly Hills, CA and New Orleans, LA.

I first got hooked on short stories while at school in England. The love affair began with works by Somerset Maugham, followed quickly by Mark Twain and O' Henry. Over the years, my bookshelves sagged under the weight of the stories of Chekhov, De Maupassant, Edgar Allan Poe, J.D. Salinger, Jack London, Damon Runyan, Ernest Hemingway, Isaac Bashevis Singer, Margaret Atwood, and countless others.

William Faulkner described short story writers as failed poets. Who am I to argue? First and foremost, writers of short stories are observers. Their gift to their readers is something that must be provocative and one that satisfies their needs while on the go, as well as the person who is prone to fall asleep while reading a hefty tome that can trigger frustrations of dealing with forgotten names and characters the next day.

After writing my first short story, so many other scenarios began to emerge in my mind and hence . . . this collection.

Stephen Maitland-Lewis
Beverly Hills, California
2021

CHAPTER ONE

Mr. Simpson

A fictional account of an event inspired by Mr. Ernest Simpson

Ernest Simpson took the service stairs, which allowed him to exit through the basement onto East 76th Street and, more importantly, to avoid the hotel manager. He knew exactly how much he was in arrears; there was no use for either of them in discussing it now. Once outside, he doffed the black homburg he'd purchased in London twenty years before.

Gerry's Barbershop on Second Avenue was four blocks away and Ernest had time for a cut before his two o'clock appointment. He'd taken care with every other aspect of his appearance. His British army regimental tie, thirty years in service to him, was tied in a strategically positioned Windsor knot to mask its frayed places. His suit was remarkably well-kept for having been made for him just before the outbreak of war in 1939 by Huntsman in Saville Row. The immovable wine stains on his shirt were deftly concealed thanks to his foresight in having the cuffs reversed. His black custom-made shoes—perfect. He polished them himself and took care never to wear the same pair on consecutive days.

He'd been a customer at Gerry's since his return to his native New York from London years before. The place was inexpensive. Gerry didn't expect a large tip, nor did he engage customers in barbershop blather. In under twenty minutes, with his silver hair and mustache trimmed, Ernest was out of the door and on his way to the Algonquin.

Getting this appointment had taken three months. Weekly calls to the editor, managing editor, publisher, and two columnists finally resulted in a telephone call from somebody's secretary who told him to expect a call from one of their reporters. A week went by before that call came.

As he crossed onto Fifth Avenue, his moods vacillated between excitement, apprehension, and disgust. Disgusted because he knew he was expected to behave appreciatively—the newspaper didn't carve out time for a cup of coffee with just anyone—even though they needed him at least as much as he needed them, more so when you got down to it. A prestigious publication required a constant blood flow of front-page material, and right now, Ernest was the one who had it.

And they were the ones who could furnish him with the contacts—and leads to the type of deals—that would enable him to settle his rent arrears and buy some new clothes. Already he could envision his schedule filled with lectures, radio and television appearances, and his bank account replenished from a book advance and ensuing royalties. Maybe he would meet a wealthy, fashionable Manhattan widow or divorcee to give him a social life once again.

With the Algonquin lunch crowd breaking up, more people were leaving than arriving. Ernest claimed a small table near the entrance, where someone had left a copy of the morning paper. He picked it up. Nothing of remote interest on the front page. It brought a smirk to his face; if a good offer for exclusive rights wasn't immediately forth-coming, all he'd have to do is mention paying a visit to *The Washington Post*.

The grandfather clock in the lobby struck two. And then two-fifteen. And again two-thirty. His perspiration from the long walk from Gerry's was replaced by the sweat of nervousness. Maybe he should call them. His eyes fell on three nearby phone booths.

At that moment, an out-of-breath man, a youth really, probably just out of college, jogged into the building and then up to Ernest. His rush and the wind outside had left him in need of a comb.

"Mr. Simpson, I'm so sorry to have kept you waiting. The editor convened a meeting and I couldn't break away."

Ernest looked at the young man. Certainly not a day over twenty-five. Was this the best the paper could entrust with his story, and after three months of constant requests for a meeting?

He beckoned to the young man to take a chair.

"I'm Brad Levy. I'm in the newsroom. My editor told me to meet with you. He'd have come too but we're busy with two hot stories and a deadline on one of them. He asked me to have this initial conversation with you."

"What do you mean by 'initial conversation'?"

"Well, you piqued his interest with certain things you said. Like how you should have been awarded an honor by the Queen or Winston Churchill and how you changed the world. He wants me to find out more and report back to him. Then if he wants to have a follow-up discussion, he'll have you over to his office."

Ernest pursed his lips. "He'll have me over." He repeat-ed it. "He'll *have me over*. If you don't mind me saying so, that's the height of arrogance. I may decide I don't want to meet with him and that I'd be better off taking my story elsewhere."

He fixed the young man with a cold stare.

"I'm sorry you should feel that way, Mr. Simpson. That is, of course, your prerogative. In the meantime, do you want to talk to me? If you don't, that's quite alright. I have plenty to do back at my desk."

"That's just the sort of New York arrogance that triggered me to give up my United States citizenship and move to England. Being kept waiting to meet with a low-level rookie is not what I deserve."

"Mr. Simpson, I've already apologized for being late. My editor only told me about this meeting ten minutes ago. I came over as fast as I could. As for being a rookie, this is my second year in the newsroom, and last year I had a page-three article with my own byline."

"Marvelous. One article last year. Tell me, how old are you, Mr. Levy?"

"Twenty-three."

Ernest paused. "And how much do you know about English History? Actually, World History?"

"I majored in English literature and drama. History was not my thing."

"How old is your boss?"

"Thirty, I guess."

Ernest spat *thirty* back at the kid. "Do you think he knows anything about English History?"

"I have no idea whether she does or not."

"She?"

"Do you have a problem with that, Mr. Simpson?"

Ernest remained silent.

"Right now, we are focused on Vietnam, our new president, and the Russians shooting down one of our U-2 spy planes." Brad Levy heard his voice rising. "So forgive us if we don't jump up and down with excitement over some crackpot with a pseudo British accent claiming he saved the world."

Ernest spoke as calmly as he could. "Go back to your office and check out Ernest and Wallis Simpson. And, if you decide you want to meet with me—don't call me. Have a boss call me. Preferably a boss in trousers. Okay?"

They stood.

"I'll tell my boss, Mr. Simpson. You may or may not hear from her."

"What's her name?"

"Stella Ginsberg."

Ernest paused. "Levy and Ginsberg. The British poet, Hilaire Belloc defined New York as 'Shylock's Revenge.'" He smirked.

"Good afternoon, Mr. Simpson."

Ernest stopped off at the corner bar on 71st Street. He limited himself to no more than two drinks a day—normally at night—but he needed a scotch and soda early. Through the window of the damned-near-empty bar, he noticed a movie theater. It was showing *Psycho*. What the hell?

He had met Hitchcock. He could just see the look on Brad Levy's face, and his boss—this Stella Ginsberg—Ernest imagined her to life just so he could also imagine the look on *her* face if they found out how they'd relegated to crackpot status, a man who'd rubbed elbows with Alfred Hitchcock at a pre-war party in London. That was before he'd been socially shunned.

He found the movie disturbing. He couldn't keep from averting his eyes during the shower scene, and the cross-dressing and the psychological inferences didn't help his mood. Still, it had taken up time. Stopping at the market for a sandwich would take up even more, and delay, for that much longer, the moment he could no longer dodge the hotel manager to face his debt. One of his debts. By far not the only one, but the one with the greatest potential to embarrass him.

He always kept his room key with him before entering so he had no need to pause at the desk. It was too bad he couldn't enter the way he had left earlier, but the door into the basement area did not open from the outside without a key.

"Just a minute, Mr. Simpson. You have mail and there have been some messages for you." He took the bundle from the front desk clerk, who fortunately was otherwise occupied with arriving guests. He didn't bother to examine the envelopes; by now he could instinctively discern threatening demands from collection agencies.

He took off his jacket and poured his second scotch of the day. Neat, no ice. He had no refrigerator and he couldn't be bothered to walk down the hall to the ice maker. There was enough left in the bottle he kept on the top shelf of his closet to last him another week.

He hadn't been wrong about the mail. Three collection agency notices; a postcard from a friend in England congratulating him on his sixty-second birthday, three weeks earlier; an offer to buy a complete set of leather-bound *Encyclopedia Britannica*; and the solicitations, one from the Salvation Army and another from Harvard, his alma mater. Then there were the phone messages: two former friends from whom he'd borrowed money wanting to know when they could expect repayment. Phone messages were scrawled on pink memo pads; he'd been through two and he had three remaining, which he flipped over and spread out in front of him all at once. It was like ripping off a Band-Aid. *Get it done and over with.*

One from Brad Levy, two from Stella Ginsberg, each requesting a call back.

With one eye on the clock, Ernest dialed. It was close to seven, but newspaper people worked late.

"Stella Ginsberg here." It was that tone of voice Ernest couldn't stand—arrogant, unfriendly, lacking any trace of charm. Officious. A New York voice, through and through.

"Miss Ginsberg, I'm Ernest Simpson. I'm returning your call."

"Oh, Mr. Simpson. Thank you. Just a minute, please." He heard her shout across the room, "Brad, I have your Mr. Simpson on the phone. Pick up line two."

"Mr. Simpson, Brad here. I want to apologize again for this afternoon. When I got back from our meeting, I spoke with Stella and our managing editor. We would like to meet with you again. How are you fixed to come in at ten-thirty tomorrow morning?"

"I think what I have to discuss merits the presence of a more senior writer. Did you look me up in your archives?"

"That's why my managing editor, who will probably be at the meeting tomorrow, wanted me to call you back. I should point out Ms. Ginsberg is a rising star at the paper. She was nominated last year for a Pulitzer Prize for her article on the Soviet Union, having spent two years in our Moscow bureau."

"Mr. Levy, I don't want a mere rising star. I want a *star*."

"I hear you. And, for our part, I want an assurance from you that until we meet tomorrow that you will not go to any other newspaper with this story."

The happy warmth spreading through Ernest's chest was more than the whiskey. "Ten-thirty tomorrow morning."

"You have our address."

"Indeed. I've been writing and telephoning for the last three months."

He ended the call muttering, "Levy and Ginsberg." Most of his life he would have totally avoided speaking to such people. Now he needed them. He poured himself another drink and then remembered the ham and cheese sandwich in the paper bag.

He left the hotel the next morning promptly at half-past eight. The manager usually came on at nine, so it was safe to leave by the main entrance. It was a long walk down Madison Avenue, but today he enjoyed it. He stopped for coffee on 61st Street and joyfully witnessed the parade of dogs out for their morning strolls. Labradors, Poodles, Shih Tzus, and even Saint Bernards basked in the morning sun as their humans guided them along the sidewalks. When Ernest lived in his country house in England before the war, he owned Labradors and Bloodhounds, but found Irish Setters the best breed for his regular participation in pheasant shoots.

He crossed over to Fifth Avenue and paused to read the notice outside St. Thomas's Episcopal Church on 53rd Street. "From that time on, Jesus began to preach, 'Repent, for the kingdom of heaven has come near.'" He grunted, stepping up his pace. He made it a point to attend services at least one Sunday every month, not because he was in any way religious but because he found it important to demonstrate *belonging*. It was the exact same reason he continued scraping together the dues to maintain his membership of the Harvard Club.

Today, at the newspaper, he was not kept waiting.

On arrival on the fifth-floor, he was met by a secretary who led him to a small conference room, furnished simply with a round table, a coat stand on which he placed his hat and six chairs. He imagined the gentleman featured in the framed portrait to be a former editor or publisher. The table was bare, save for a couple of yellow pads, ballpoint pens and a large crystal dish. Simpson took a seat.

A couple of minutes passed, but not enough to arouse his ire; he had arrived early, after all. Ernest remained seated as Brad Levy walked in the room, followed by Stella Ginsberg.

They took their seats opposite him. The first thing he noticed about Ms. Ginsberg was the sheen of her skin; her taut face was moisturized to the extent that she looked *wet*, as though she'd just been swimming or stepped in from the rain. She was the sort of woman who'd likely never be called fashionable—with chances even slimmer for words like *elegant* and *chic*—but she oozed a sort of sanitized professionalism that masqueraded as power. Ernest Simpson was accustomed to looking for—and seeing through—such gambits; otherwise, he was certain he would have been every bit as intimidated as she hoped he, and everyone else, would be.

"Mr. Simpson, we will be joined momentarily by one of our senior columnists, Martin Woods. He is just finishing a call."

"Martin Woods? Your drama critic?"

"That's him," Ms. Ginsberg replied.

"Would you mind telling me why I'm meeting with a drama critic? I wasted my time with you yesterday." He pointed a finger at Levy. "Am I here to waste more time today?"

When Ms. Ginsberg drew breath, the single-band ring on a silver chain that lay over her collarbone rose and fell. "Mr. Simpson, you should know from the outset that, based on your visit with my colleague yesterday, you are not our most favored visitor. You seem to view Hilaire Belloc's quotation as either vindicating or funny—I'm not sure which, and I don't know what would be worse. In any event, most of us view it as anti-Semitic. It's something you may want to be more careful about in the future, Mr. Simpson, especially in light of the fact that—after you demanded that we research your history—we found that a Mr. and Mrs. Solomons, your grandparents, emigrated from Germany to Plymouth, England where they were amongst the founders of the synagogue in that city. And Mr. Simpson, if you believe you're a novelty or somehow exonerated for your bigotry, allow me to dispel that impression. You are certainly not the first anti-Semitic Jew I've ever met. And you're not the only one who can spout literary quotations to vanquish whoever you disagree with. I believe Mr. Shakespeare trumps Mr. Belloc—wouldn't you agree, Mr. Simpson? I take it you're familiar with William Shakespeare. The man who said, 'To thine own self be true.'"

Ernest sat in silence. *Now* he felt as intimidated as most people probably did upon first seeing Ms. Ginsberg. He was still scrambling to put together a response when Martin Woods joined them.

The man's appearance, while every bit as streamlined and commanding as Ms. Ginsberg's, belied the overwhelming social authority granted him. There was a playfulness—an insouciance, almost—to his blue pinstriped suit and polka-dot bowtie, but anyone who read his columns understood that the mind behind the dapper threads was frequently brutal. From his reviews, one would have to conclude that he didn't actually enjoy Broadway plays half as much as he enjoyed skewering them. It was accepted that a Woods review of a production could make or break its success and the careers of actors, playwrights, and directors.

Woods sat across from Ernest, elbows on his knees, and lit a cigar. He stared at Ernest. Ernest stared at him.

"So, Mr. Simpson. You've been in contact with our paper here for a few weeks . . . "

"Months," Ernest injected.

Woods proceeded undaunted. "So, I don't want to waste any more of your time and I damned sure don't want to waste a minute of mine. I don't know what you can possibly tell us about your divorce and the Duke and Duchess of Windsor that we don't know already. It's now old news. The Duke and Duchess are long-term New York residents. They are held in high esteem. I'm sure any publicity about them would be unnecessarily hurtful, so why drag it up? Why make them uncomfortable?"

"So you have no interest in hearing my story. I believe that I have been unfairly treated by the press. I can provide facts that would certainly suggest that far from being treated as a pariah, I should have received an honor from either the Queen of England or her late father, King George VI."

Woods and his two colleagues could barely stifle their smirks.

"Mr. Simpson, what we have on you is also something that you too would not want us to broadcast, especially in this city."

"Really, what?"

"Do I have to remind you? You renounced your American citizenship and moved to London and became a naturalized citizen of Great Britain. You served as an officer in the British army during the First World War. After the war—and in view of your decision not to return to the United States—your father made you the head of the London branch of his New York shipbroking firm. During your years in England, you hid all references to your Jewish background. During the 1920s and early thirties, when the fortunes of the office you ran were rapidly heading toward insolvency, the Nazis came to power. The situation changed. Through your former wife and her future husband, the Prince of Wales, who had established close links with Hitler's Germany, you were instrumental in handling many transactions that involved the buying and selling of old vessels. These old ships were turned into scrap and used by Krupp, Thyssen, and other German companies active in the armament industries. In other words, Mr. Simpson, you worked against England—the country you purported to love so much it was worth deserting your old country for—to assist the Germans in their quest to re-arm. How many German Panzer tanks, machine guns, and Messerschmitt planes were built as a result of your endeavors? And, heaven forbid, what about the gas tanks in the concentration camps used for the slaughter of Jews who, unlike you, had the strength to *not* hide their identities? How many ancestors of the people you impugn today with Belloc quotes did you help put to death while passing yourself off as a good adopted son of Mother England? Maybe, Mr. Simpson, or should I call you Mr. Solomons, for all this you really expected an honor?"

Ernest shuffled in his seat. He'd thought himself mentally prepared for the verbal onslaught he was bound to encounter. It wasn't as if he was ignorant of his own history, or the reality that any halfway vetted fact-checker at a decent newspaper would unearth most of it. But not all of it—and that's why he was here. He knew things they didn't even know to ask about, these smug, self-proud New York elitists who couldn't decide if they wanted to ignore him or publicly shame him or persecute him more severely. He knew the look in those eyes; he'd been seeing that look for years.

"So? Do you want us to run a story about you?"

Ms. Ginsberg leaned forward and put her hands on the table. "We have on file a report that paints quite the picture of you during the thirties, when your married lifestyle included a retinue of household staff, expensive holidays, large, twice-weekly black-tie dinner parties at home, Rolls Royce broughams, chauffeurs, fox hunting and grouse shoots—not to mention your wife's expansive wardrobe and jewels. You were constantly in debt. Your father refused to increase your salary. But for the business you did with the Nazis and contributions from the Prince of Wales, you would have filed for bankruptcy. We have copies of checks and bank statements on file."

This, unfortunately, caught Ernest off-guard. The incompetence he had witnessed the day before had lulled him into a false sense of security: he hadn't been prepared for them to unearth quite as much as they had. What's more, the picture was becoming clearer and clearer by the moment.

Of course they had no interest in his story. Not the one he'd pitched them—about his life with Wallis and their divorce. He wasn't the venerable source for a favorable article he had hoped they would write. Instead, he was to be the subject matter of a take-down piece. His stomach dropped. He wondered if this was how the pig felt on realizing it was dinner.

"Of course, we've had them for twenty-plus years. Also, you must realize that by accepting money from the Prince of Wales and later the King . . . effectively made you a pimp, on top of everything else." Woods snapped.

Simpson felt the blood boiling in his face.

"To hell with you. You don't know the whole story." His voice rose in anger. "I have letters that you have never seen. They are at my bank. I can show them to you. When you see them, you'll change your tune and apologize. I also have some of the canceled checks that I made out to Wallis and Edward in repayment of loans they had generously extended me during the Second World War when my business folded."

"Tell me, Mr. Simpson, what is the gist of these letters?"

"There's one from the late Queen Mary, mother of the King, telling me I was the only person in the whole saga who behaved honorably. I have another one from Winston Churchill thanking me for my conduct. And I have several letters from my former wife, written before and during her marriage to the Duke, telling me she missed me, loved me, how much she regretted being blackmailed into marrying the Duke and how miserable her life was."

"You have such letters?" Woods asked.

"And letters too from Edward, in his own handwriting. Letters from Edward from back in the thirties, blackmailing me. And from Wallis too."

Woods spoke up again. "We'd like to see these letters."

"I'd like to show them to you. But I'm not bringing them here. I can meet you at my bank and you can see them there. Just say when."

Woods looked at his colleagues, who nodded.

"So, assuming we are satisfied that everything you show us is authentic, would you still wish for us to run a story?"

"I'd like you to run a story that portrays me in a different light. I confess too that I am in need of funds. I'd like to come to a financial arrangement with you if you decide to publish something. An agreement in return for an exclusive."

"So, this is about money. Let me contain my shock."

Ernest ignored Woods's sarcasm.

"So, let's get back to why you believe you should have been honored by the Queen or her late father."

"I've told you already. And God knows how many messages I've left on various answering machines," Ernest said. "I changed the history of the world."

Woods muttered something about delusions of grandeur, but now that Ernest had ignored his derision once, he found ignoring the second time easier.

"It is true I hid my Jewish background. That was easy. I had no Jewish friends. I know nothing about Judaism. I'm told I do not look Jewish. My mother was not Jewish and I was brought up as an Episcopalian. When I moved to London, I attended St. Peter's in Eaton Square."

"So?"

It would have grated on Ernest's nerves were he not hooked into the momentum of his own story now: this way that Martin Woods—whose livelihood depended on his creativity with words and who gleefully scathed performances that didn't meet his mighty standards of creativity—had such a prominent speech tic. *So.* It was the question and declaration and pause at the beginning of everything the man said. *So.* He could imagine it:

You'll be kissing my ass and covering your own when I finish telling you my story, Mister Woods.

So?

If I look down at your pompous New York crowd, it's because all of you owe me in ways you can't fathom. And here's how . . .

So, you aren't a crackpot?

So, you aren't the lying opportunistic hack I thought you were?

So, now I need you more than you need me.

So.

"Don't you see that if I had not hidden my Jewish background and lived in London with everyone knowing of that background, remote that it was, Wallis and I would never have been admitted into London society? Never mind getting within a mile of any member of the Royal Family?"

"So?"

"*So,* Wallis would never have met the Prince of Wales. Unless he found another person as unsuitable as Wallis to be his wife and a future queen, he would have had absolutely no reason to abdicate. True?"

"Go on."

He'd done it. Ernest had broken Woods's broken-record repetition. He took it to mean the man's brain was shifting off autopilot and that he was actually considering things now.

"So the Prince of Wales—either as a bachelor or married to a suitable spouse—would have remained on the throne. Given his pro-Nazi sentiments and the general consensus

in England at the time, England would not have entered
into a war with Germany in 1939. With a grossly underpre-
pared England, Germany would have been met with little
resistance in forcing an alliance with England. Maybe the
two countries would have united—just like Germany and
Austria. The *Anschluss* or political union. In all probability,
Hitler would have made a state visit to London. He and Eva
Braun would have been given an apartment at St. James's
Palace. The swastika would have flown alongside the Union
Jack on all public buildings. Jewish businesses would have
been taken over. Jews would have been rounded up and
shipped to the concentration camps in Europe or sent to
work in Germany as slave labor. There would have been no
Second World War. It is less likely that there would have
been Pearl Harbor and an American war with Japan. German would have become the second language in England."

Martin Woods's cigar had long since burned out; it was
a stump now, rooted in its own cinders in the fine crystal
dish that passed for an ashtray. They all just sat there, looking at him, pencils down. No sidelong glances at each other.
No stalling so.

Simpson continued, "The present Queen of England
would never have become queen and she and her children
would have become minor royalty and would practically
have disappeared from public life altogether." He felt himself smile involuntarily. It had little to do with the content
of his story; it was only that he'd told it. Years of wanting it
off his chest and months of supplicating this haughty paper
to hear him out, and now the bulk of it was said. The air filling his lungs felt thicker than it had just moments before.

"You see now. I changed the history of the twentieth century. For that I should have been honored."

Woods found his voice, even if it did have a creak in it. His crutch had been knocked from underneath him. "You used the word 'blackmail' a few moments ago. Please elaborate."

"I'd be happy to. The Prince of Wales wrote me a letter. You'll see it. In it he pleaded with me to agree to be divorced so he could marry Wallis. He wrote that if he did not marry her, he would commit suicide. So the fate of the British monarchy was in my hands."

"Jesus. And you have this letter? You can put it in our hands?"

"That, and another letter from Wallis saying she felt the same stress and pressure hearing from him similar threats."

"Why didn't you call his bluff?"

"I'm an anglophile." Ernest pronounced the word slowly—as though he expected Woods to be unfamiliar with either the meaning of the word or, at least, its gravity. "I have been my whole life. I love all things English—the traditions, the pageantry, the clubs, life in London and in the country. And what's more, I always liked Edward. How could I have on my conscience that I was directly responsible for the suicide of the King of England? That's one hell of a burden to have on my conscience for the rest of my life. No. I had to agree to what he wanted."

"Do you see them? After all, they live at the Waldorf. It's barely one mile away from you."

"It's better for all of us if I don't. But she writes me a warm and friendly letter, maybe once every month. Sometimes she admits to being trapped in an unhappy marriage and wishes that things could have turned out differently."

"And you write to her?"

"I do."

"You are disappointed not to have been honored. What honor did you expect and what steps have you taken over the years to lobby for one?"

"A peerage. Anything less would be an insult. That way, my son by the wife I married after my divorce from Wallis will have something to inherit. I fear I have nothing else to leave the poor boy. His mother died when she was only forty-two."

Woods appeared momentarily sidelined. His eyes slanted downward, his mouth drifted closed, and his fingers toyed with but did not pick up the neglected cigar. Ernest watched as Stella Ginsberg looked sharply at Woods, apparently hoping to prod him to action. After failing to meet his gaze, she took the lead again.

"And what steps did you take over the years to become *Lord Simpson*?"

"I've written to every prime minister to plead my case."

"What kind of response have you received?"

"Nothing satisfactory."

"Mr. Simpson, if the letters you mention are authentic, yes, we may publish a story. I will need to discuss it with my managing editor. I presume you have a figure in mind."

"Just a few thousand will be helpful. But more importantly, I want to secure a steady income. The assistance of someone to help me write my memoirs. And to help me get radio and television appearances and lecture tours too. I'm available."

"Mr. Simpson, that's not the sort of thing—"

"Tomorrow." The word shot from Woods's mouth as though it were a piece of hard candy he'd spit out when knocked in the back by some blunt force. Alongside the revival of speech came eye contact, a glint in his eye, the making of an ambitious man's smile. "Tomorrow, let's meet at your bank to examine the letters. If everything you've told is true, if you have the documents to validate it, I'm sure we can help you, Mr. Simpson. With whatever"—he looked at Ms. Ginsberg with a sharpness that should have made her proud, as strongly as it resembled her own—"you may need."

The next afternoon, Simpson watched nervously as Woods and his colleagues examined the letters. He'd become an expert at assessing the subtle vagaries of facial expressions over the years. It's what happens when a man becomes a pariah, as he did when the society he'd once taken for granted and had even helped shape, edged him into its shadows. What he'd lost in interaction and honor during his decades of life in the shadows, he had made up in evaluating what went on in people's minds even when their mouths were buttoned tight.

It was how he'd known to write off the blundering Brad Levy they had delegated to meet with him two days before, and also how he knew Martin Woods wasn't half as tough as he pretended to be, and that Stella Ginsberg had retracted her claws; without them extended, her hands carefully kneaded the material in front of her. She tried not to show it, but she was stunned. They all were. Sheet by sheet, they were witnessing the story of their careers—if not lifetimes—unfold.

"Mr. Simpson. I agree we have something here." That's how she worded it. And Ernest understood—she had to look professional. She couldn't exactly jump up and down and whoop and burst the cork on a bottle of champagne, but again, it was there in her eyes: she wanted to. "Please come to my office at six o'clock this evening. I will have an agreement for you to review and upon your signature there'll be a check."

Three months later, Ernest Simpson took a train ride to Washington, D.C. He spent the journey perusing the rough draft chapters from the memoir he was working on with the same ghostwriter who'd penned the stories of TV personalities, a world-renowned restaurant owner, a former first lady of the United States, and an aging rock star telling the tale of how he'd fathered thirteen children by as many women.

His secretary had bundled the pages just as he preferred them: bound with only a rubber band, no staples or paperclips, and tucked neatly inside a plain manila envelope. He couldn't pretend having a secretary of his own was a trivial matter; he adored Sheryl. She arranged calls with David Susskind for appearances on his TV show. She answered the correspondence—no longer any from collection agencies that came to his home office in his suite at the Carlyle.

Sheryl deftly arranged the entire lecture circuit he was now embarking on—after D.C., he'd be in Chicago, then Cleveland and San Francisco. She had hair that glowed like a dandelion in July. She exuded natural energy and professionalism that the likes of Brad Levy could learn a thing or two from, and, perhaps most importantly, she alone had never doubted him.

These had been long decades of silence for Ernest Simpson; he had grown accustomed to being deemed a waste of flesh, a pimp or a traitor, or all three. He had longed for the day when he could surround himself with those who would see him, from their very first interaction, for who he was. Sheryl was the beginning of all that. The glint in her eyes when she glanced up at him—in admiration, eager to fulfill an important man's needs—was the light at the end of a darkness he'd once believed was endless.

She was the one who let Woods know about the phone call from the British ambassador in D.C. She was the one who made his journey to the nation's capital one of multitasking: he would kick off his lecture tour and then he would humbly receive the official confirmation that the Queen of England was going to elevate him to the peerage.

Sheryl was the one who called his remaining family and his rapidly expanded circle of friends to tell them that Ernest Simpson had passed away peacefully on the train to D.C., and also to comfort them—to tell them that even if he hadn't received everything he'd been waiting for, he'd known it was all coming; and if he was the man she knew, that was enough.

.

CHAPTER TWO

The Crochet Dress

The 1970s could not have been a better time for a promiscuous young executive with an unrestricted corporate credit card who was constantly being sent overseas to foster business relationships. It was also a benefit to enjoy easy access to London physicians in case of any delicate issues picked up on the road.

The firm's travel agent had booked Simon into the famed Le Richemond Hotel in Geneva. The hotel was beyond five-star. Its elegance and luxury were without peer. The photographs in the bar of patrons ranged the gamut of popes, sovereigns, celebrities, and world statesmen. Simon's self-confidence was enhanced by being a hotel guest, if only for four nights. But, as he sat in the bar, dined in the restaurant, and meandered through the lobby, he became conscious that he was at least thirty years younger than everyone else, guests and staff alike. He yearned for, in the vernacular of the era, "some action."

After making tactful inquiries of both the concierge and the doorman, he took a cab to the Intercontinental Hotel. An elevator lifted him to the rooftop bar with its magnificent view of Lac Leman. But the horseshoe-shaped bar was dead: just one customer and a bored bartender. Simon sat down on a stool and took in the person sitting to his left.

His eyes rested on her. To avert his gaze, she turned sideways to look out at the view. Simon was brought back to reality when the bartender approached to take his order.

He looked back at her. Black, with long straight hair, magnificent bone structure, large opal eyes, full, sensual lips enhanced with a discreet pink lipstick. Her long, manicured fingers were wrapped around a champagne flute. Her elegant dress was simple strapless white crochet, and she wore a heavy gold pendant necklace with a bezel-set large aquamarine stone the size of a grape that rested on her inviting cleavage.

When the bartender returned with Simon's drink, she turned to face him. He smiled. She didn't. He took a sip, embarrassed by her standoffishness. He looked at his watch. It was early enough to move on to a livelier place.

She must have seen him check the time. She turned, again, to face him. He smiled once more and pointed to the stool next to his, with his other hand beckoning her to join him.

She shook her head resolutely from side to side.

Wasting my time here, he thought. *Time to move on.*

The bartender had disappeared, so there was no way he could get his check. But then, without any change in her expression, she fixed her eyes on him, pointed to the stool next to hers, and suggested, with a mere tilt of her head, that he move.

My lucky day. Maybe.

He carried over his glass. For a half hour, they enjoyed friendly but guarded conversation. She told him she was attached to the Senegal embassy in Paris and was spending a few days in Geneva, where she had been seconded to work at the Senegalese mission to the United Nations. She was staying at the hotel until such time as an apartment rented by the Mission became available for her use. He guessed she was his age, early thirties. He was a London banker, he told her, but refrained from telling her about his wife and two children at home in Kensington.

When the bartender returned, Simon ordered more drinks. He took her hand and kissed it. She did not pull back. Finally, he took the plunge and invited her back to his hotel. She declined.

Disappointed, he gulped his scotch.

"It would be better if you came to my room. Seven-oh-four. But not just yet," she whispered.

His success gave way to a cocky smile.

She tapped her empty glass, which was immediately refilled.

"There's something I must tell you," she spoke slowly and in perfect English, not quite in a whisper but nevertheless softly. "I have nothing to do with the Senegalese embassy. I am a dancer with Le Club Sexy in Paris. I am here for a break and to do some shopping. If I could find a way to cover my expenses . . ."

Simon paused to order another drink. "So how much are we talking about?" he asked, fearful that the amount would be too high for him to conceal within his expense report.

She named her fee. It was high but less than he had anticipated.

"You must stay here," she said. "It would be bad for both of us if we left together," nodding her head in the direction of the bartender now serving a couple who had walked in. "I'll leave now. Come to my room in fifteen minutes." She kissed him good night.

He took time to finish his drink and then paid the check. Before leaving, he went to the restroom. He had the place to himself. From a combination of instinct and experience he took the money for her from his wallet and placed it in a pocket, left one hundred Swiss francs in his wallet, and stuffed the balance inside a sock.

The ride down to the seventh floor and the walk along the corridor to Room 704 was filled with excitement, fear and trepidation as to what lay ahead. Perhaps, she wasn't there. *Maybe she was just playing a trick?* She could have left the building altogether. Someone totally different could be occupying the room and they'd call management to complain. How would it look at the bank if the hotel called the police and had him arrested? Or maybe she was in the room but not alone. Maybe he would be dragged inside by one or more accomplices. And mugged. Or worse.

The corridor was maybe six feet wide. The door had the usual peep hole. She could see his arrival, and an accomplice with her in the room could pounce. Instead of waiting at the door after his single knock, he backed up against the wall opposite to give him some protection just in case the evening was not going to turn out as he had hoped.

She opened the door to its full width, naked, save for a white towel wrapped around her waist. The gold pendant hung around her neck. The room's only light emerged from a small lamp on a desk at the far end of the room. Classical music played softly. She smiled. He was at the point of no return.

He stepped into the room. She let the towel fall onto the floor and closed the door. They embraced. Their tongues danced. Her skin was soft and silken to his touch.

She pulled away gently. "First we must take care of business. Let's get that over with."

"Of course." He had the money already in his jacket pocket. She took it without counting and put it in a drawer. "Now, let's talk about breakfast?"

He was surprised. Overnight privileges were unusual.

"What time do you need to be back at your hotel?"

Simon thought for a moment. His first appointment was at half past nine. He'd first have to shower, shave, and change. "Around eight."

"Then I'll order coffee and croissants for seven?"

She completed the breakfast card and handed it to him. "You're still dressed. Would you put this on the door knob?"

Maybe she'll slam the door while I'm doing this, he speculated. Perhaps this was a trick to lure him into her room, grab his money, and shut him out. He couldn't exactly bang on the door and risk complaints from other residents.

But no. She made no attempt to close the door on him.

"While you're getting undressed, I'll open this bottle of champagne from the mini bar."

Is that included or am I going to be stiffed for that? Perrier Jouet at mini bar prices.

He undressed quickly, being careful when he took off his socks.

What a night of passion it turned out to be. She was as enthusiastic as him. In between, they showered together and finished the champagne, and afterward they slept, contented and exhausted.

Unbeknownst to him, she had set the alarm clock. It awoke him with a start after only two hours sleep.

He was slow to get out of bed. She rolled over and grabbed him, and they made love once more. There was a knock.

"My God. That's breakfast here already."

"Hurry," she said. "I'll open the door."

He grabbed his clothes and ran into the bathroom. He'd *have* to hurry. No time to sit for a leisurely coffee. If he was late for his first appointment—or worse, if he missed it—he'd be in big trouble back in London.

As soon as the waiter left, he called out from the bathroom, "I'll be right in. I've remembered I will be in Paris in ten days. Can we get together while I'm there?"

"Of course. I'll write down my address and telephone number."

"Terrific." It was eight o'clock. He was running late. Dangerously late.

He came out of the bathroom fully dressed. Semi-presentable except he was in dire need of a shave, his hair was uncombed, and his shirt was crumpled; anyone with modest intuitive skills would recognize how he had spent the previous few hours. His mouth was dry and he longed to clean his teeth.

"At least have half a cup of coffee before you run."

He gulped down a cup. Fortunately, it was lukewarm.

She stood, naked, took the paper on which she'd written her address and stuffed it in his inside jacket pocket. He kissed her with the passion of a soldier leaving his sweetheart for the last time before being posted to the battlefront.

The journey back to the Le Richemond took longer than expected due to the morning rush hour traffic. Twenty-minutes to nine. He grabbed his key from the front desk and waited nervously for the elevator. Within thirty minutes, he was washed and changed and ready to leave for his first appointment.

Simon struggled through the meeting in passable Franglais and fought back his exhaustion. When that one ended, he had twenty minutes to get to the rue du Rhône for the next. No time to stop for a coffee, but maybe he'd be offered one at the meeting,

No coffee materialized. Now he was totally exhausted and struggled to keep his eyes open, as he struggled to put two sentences together. Having overexerted himself the night before, he labored hard to speak or understand business French. He knew the bankers were playing with him. They all spoke the perfect English of Harvard and Wharton MBA graduates. It seemed to him they had all conspired to add to his discomfort by ensuring the meetings were conducted in French.

One o'clock. Thank God. His work was done for the day. His last appointment had been just ten minutes from the hotel; a walk in brisk October weather would shake off the cobwebs. He'd order a sandwich from room service and take a long nap before dinner and then embark on a fresh nocturnal adventure. He'd call Claudette when he got back to the hotel to check if, by any chance, she was available for another evening.

"I'm sorry, sir. I need the guest's last name before I can put a call through," the operator said firmly. "But I can confirm that that room is, as of this moment, unoccupied. The previous guest checked out this morning."

Simon was perplexed. His confusion ruled out any possibility of an afternoon nap. He remembered that she had written her Paris address, and hopefully telephone number, on a piece of paper still in the pocket of his other suit.

He opened the closet and grabbed the note. She had written her contact information on the outside of a sealed envelope. Maybe she'd flown back to Paris? The envelope crackled in his hand. He opened it carefully so as not to render her address unreadable. To his astonishment, she had returned the Swiss Francs. Every last one—he counted carefully. His confusion skyrocketed.

If indeed she had left for Paris and had taken a morning flight, she would be there by now.

"I'm sorry, Mr. Murray, there is no such telephone number in Paris. Please check again."

He didn't go out that night, not even downstairs to the hotel's restaurant. Nor was he able to take that much-needed nap. He tossed around on the bed, totally baffled. He remained in a flummoxed mental state for the remainder of his stay in Geneva. He could not get this girl out of his mind.

His week back in London was difficult. His mind was not on business. His wife and even his children got on his nerves and for most of the time he was surly, sullen, and nervous. Forever at the forefront of his mind was the image of this exquisite girl in the crochet dress and the memory of a glorious night of lust. He landed in Paris on a Saturday afternoon. He had flown on a Saturday even though his first appointment was not until Monday morning. The bank turned a blind eye to that sort of scheduling.

After checking in at the Ritz, he showed the concierge Claudette's address and asked him its distance from the hotel. The concierge took out a thick well-worn street directory and opened it up. He took a magnifying glass from a drawer, adjusted his spectacles, and searched. "I'm sorry, sir, there is no such address."

"Are you sure?" Simon asked, unable to conceal his disappointment.

The concierge called over a bellboy and instructed him to ask one of the cab drivers waiting outside on the street if he could throw any light on the address. Simon waited patiently in the lobby awaiting the bellboy's return.

"I'm sorry, sir. My colleague asked two cab drivers and neither of them could assist," the concierge said brusquely as he turned to assist another guest.

Simon's renewed attempts to reach Claudette by telephone were met with the same result as in Geneva. "Sorry, sir, there is no such number."

He idled away the rest of the day with long walks along rue Faubourg Saint-Honoré and the Champs Élysées. There was only one other thing he could do, and that was to visit Le Club Sexy.

The dive was located on a seedy side street off Place Pigalle in Montmartre that hosted several similar establishments catering to the needs of men on their own looking for titillation or more.

Le Club Sexy had a red awning and a storefront window in which were displayed three rows of nude black-and-white photographs of its in-house dancers.

Simon studied the photographs carefully. None resembled Claudette.

A heavyset bouncer in an ill-fitting grey suit, no doubt owned by Le Club Sexy and handed down by his predecessor, approached him. "It seems as if you like the photographs. We have real live girls inside. Only fifty francs admission and a two-drink minimum. Come in and have some fun."

The man was dark-skinned. He didn't appear Parisian.

"Thank you," Simon answered. "I'm actually looking for a girl who works here. Her name is Claudette. She's from Senegal."

"From Senegal. So what's the matter with our white girls? These are the most beautiful you'll find anywhere in Paris."

"But I'm particularly looking for this girl."

"Well, you're wasting your time. There is no one of that name working here. I know all the girls. I've slept with most of them. That's one of the perks of this job. That and an evening meal." He laughed.

"Are you sure?"

"I've worked here for two years and yes, I'm sure. And, I'll tell you something else. No black girl works at this club. The boss has a policy. I don't agree with him but it's his club so he can do whatever the hell he wants. He's making a big mistake in my opinion. He says the white customers are not interested in black girls and the black customers only want white girls. Well, you and I could try to convince the boss he's wrong but he won't listen. He's a damned racist and only likes to hire white girls, though our clientele spans all races. Forget this girl, come in and have a good time."

Simon thanked him and walked on down the street and back to his hotel in Place Vendôme.

He ordered a sandwich and a bottle of wine and spent the night alone.

Who was this girl? Was she a hooker? If so, why did she return the money? Maybe she did work for the Senegal Mission to the United Nations and got her kicks from posing as a hooker?

The mystery of Claudette would forever remain a sort of lidless pothole down which his thoughts, and other pieces of his life, frequently fell.

CHAPTER THREE

A Gardner in Buenos Aires

O n the fifth of every month, for thirteen years, $500 had been wired from a Swiss bank to an account in Buenos Aires belonging to Pieter Mueller. Originating just as the war ended, this arrangement ceased abruptly in 1958, but not before its German beneficiary had received a sum of approximately $80,000 in Argentinean pesos—a small fortune.

A mole in the Zurich bank had tipped off the Mossad, and now the Israeli secret service was keen to find out more about this Pieter Mueller. Not least of all because the particular Swiss and Argentinean banks involved in these furtive transfers were known to be bankers to Odessa, the underground Nazi organization that had bankrolled the escape from Europe to Latin America of former members of the *Schutzstaffel*—the protective echelon—or, as it was more commonly known, the SS.

Certain international banks and the dregs of Hitler's army may have benefited from their connections, but the Mossad was rich with its own. One of its chancier connections, Arthur Gardner, sat at a strategically selected table on the sidewalk of a coffee shop on Buenos Aires' famed Florida Street. The forty-five-year-old freelance private investigator and one-time MI6 operative was trying not to eye the woman at the next table.

He was finding it difficult.

Her allure culminated not only from her silky black hair that spilled over her tanned shoulders and the Ferrari-red polish on her fingernails, but also from the animated way she talked to her friend. Whatever the topic of conversation—it wasn't possible for him to effectively eavesdrop and still pay attention to his assignment—she spoke with a melodic, husky passion.

Gardner was relieved when she got up to leave. After all, he had work to do. He had to track down Mueller for the Mossad.

He looked across at the store that was still closed for the afternoon siesta. It was due to reopen in twenty minutes. He had a clear view of the double fronted shop—an exclusive tobacconist—from where he was seated.

Mossad retained Gardner because the Israelis did not want to create another diplomatic incident with Argentina so soon after their 1960 capture of Adolf Eichmann. By using a retired British major—a long-term resident of Buenos Aires—the Israelis could conceal their involvement.

Gardner ordered another coffee, and was more relaxed than he had any right to be. He'd been assured that if he slipped up—meaning that if they had to clean up another diplomatic imbroglio because of him—whatever joy he derived from his retirement in the land of tango music and the Andes Mountains would be over.

Gardner consulted his watch. Ten minutes until the doors opened.

Buenos Aires was home to more than one Pieter Mueller, he'd uncovered. The present target was number seven on his list of eleven. The search was taking longer than he anticipated. As he was on a fixed fee, this assignment was fast morphing into a profitless endeavor.

After settling his bill, he stood and crossed the pedestrian-only street.

The shop presented its exclusive pipes, lighters, ashtrays, and humidors with an elegance equal to any jeweler's display of diamond rings. Gardner couldn't very well skulk around, interrogate the sales clerk, and then leave with nothing more than a cheap pack of cigarettes—unless he was looking for the most efficient way to arouse suspicion—so he'd decided on a *modus operandi*. He would look to buy a present for a friend.

The door's tinkling bell summoned from the back room an enticing slender woman around his age, conservatively attired in black and accessorized with a chunky gold marine link necklace abundantly dotted with fancy color diamonds. She had the same silky black hair as the girl from the café he'd struggled to ignore.

"Good morning, Signor. How can I help you?"

He picked up and admired a large porcelain ash tray, with a gold painted *fleur-de-lys*. It would sit well on his desk at home. "I'm looking for a present for a friend."

"That is a lovely piece, Signor. I bought it at an auction last month."

"Oh, so this is your store?"

"I'm afraid so."

"You should be proud." Gardner positioned himself so the woman was sure to see his eyes roving over these accoutrements for the high-end smoker, as though he could hardly refrain from an extravagant purchase. "You have some truly remarkable things here," Gardner replied.

"Well, thank you, but—"

"I'm surprised, though." He nodded as casually as possible toward the glass door, positioned at the center of the double fronted store. "I noticed on my way in that the name on the door is Pieter Mueller. I had a friend with that last name once, and you know how it goes. Familiar names always catch your eye." He could see the woman's businesslike smile melting, but he proceeded in his level tone. "Are you his wife? Mrs. Mueller?"

"God forbid," she snapped. "Who are you? What and who brought you to this store? Are you a Nazi hunter or are you with one of the vile organizations in Argentina that gives aid to those bastards?"

Gardner had never developed the smoking habit that so many of his Argentinian friends had, but that's not to say he didn't have his share of vices . . . namely, gambling. Not in the sense of wiling away his nights hunched over a seedy roulette wheel—but more in the sense of taking chances with his investigations. It was simultaneously why the Mossad considered him both a risk and why they relied on him: he was their pinch hitter.

He always knew when he could trust a person, and he could trust this for-now anonymous shopkeeper. There was no use keeping up the ruse that he was shopping for a friend; he was going to reveal exactly who he was. It was just a matter of deciding when.

He started by hiking up his left pants leg, unveiling the tail end of a baby-pink scar. "I've got the limp and chronic pain to go along with this beauty mark."

"Are you Jewish, Mr. . . . ?"

"My grandfather on my father's side was," he claimed. He flashed a crumpled black-and-white picture of man; it looked as though he'd carried it around in his pocket for years.

The woman, still nameless to him just as Arthur Gardner was to her, rolled up her right sleeve. *00157948, Treblinka.*

His eyes traced over the crude branding. "I don't think that it would be appropriate to call me a Nazi hunter." Now his eyes met hers. "But if they fled Europe to come here, let's say I have a vested interest in finding them."

"So you can do what? Turn them over to the Argentinean authorities?" Her scathing tone ridiculed the idea, but her eyes were filling with tears. "You know how I came to own this goddamned store?"

"I'd like to."

Without another word, the woman locked the door, flipped the open sign so its exposed side read *back in a half hour,* and dragged over a stool for him from in front of the case that displayed antique cigarette holders.

Rather than take a seat near him, she opted to lean on the spotless glass that formed a roof over the cigar cutters.

"There is no Pieter Mueller."

Gardner thought this was a hell of a way for her to begin.

"There never was a Pieter Mueller," she repeated.

Gardner had been sure, based on her immediate repulsion at the name, that he'd found the right Pieter Mueller—or the wife, widow, or spurned lover of the right Pieter Mueller, but now he wasn't sure. Four men by the same name did remain on his list, after all. And Gardner was sure there was a Pieter Mueller. Otherwise, who was he chasing?

"I don't understand."

"My sister and I are from Berlin." That part came quickly. She paused for a staggered breath before launching into the rest of the story. The story of how the Nazis had slaughtered her entire family with the exception of her sister and herself; they had survived by miracle, chance, or misfortune—and many days she wasn't certain which.

The sisters were incarcerated in Dachau and then Treblinka until, after the war, an Argentinean relief organization had sponsored them—along with hundreds of others—to come here.

"When you think of it"—she shuddered—"it's remarkable that Argentina has become both a haven for Jewish refugees and a hiding place of Nazis. Here, we are neighbors."

She told him that she and her sister had been adopted by a kind science professor and his wife who gave them the most normal lives possible and even arranged for them to attend the University of Buenos Aires . . . and to meet eligible men.

"I married a dentist," the shopkeeper offered. "He died three years later in an accident."

"You've had a difficult life." Gardner offered it more as a reflection of fact than sympathy. He was something of an expert at detecting people's tolerance for sentiment, and in the professional, widowed Holocaust survivor before him, he saw someone who would only be made uncomfortable by pity.

"My sister met a man at the Opera Society. She always loved musical productions of any kind. The drama and the romance of them. I'd like to think it was the ambience that made her fall in love with *him*."

"So, your sister married also?"

"I never trusted him, but Elsa, my sister, was convinced he was one of these storybook princes come to life. And I'll give you this—the bastard was handsome."

Gardner mused that if ever there were a time to take up smoking, it was right now. An investigation with intense pressure, his capital dwindling, the shopkeeper's story already twisting and turning. The store overflowing with tobacco and means of consuming it in great style. "So there is a Pieter Mueller?"

"Not exactly."

Gardner could not hide his confusion.

"As Elsa found infatuation and lust for Pieter deepening into love, she was relieved when he confessed to her his involvement with the Nazis. One always had to wonder in this place, encountering someone with a German surname and accent. He had been conscripted into military service, he admitted, but he'd always hated the Nazis. He told her that he fled to Argentina not to shirk culpability but out of shame—he was furious and disgusted with Hitler and the whole Nazi party. He was bitterly ashamed for having been sucked into it."

"But you still didn't trust him?"

"Men have a way of hiding who they are when there's something they want from a woman." She did not hide the fact that it was a double-edged accusation. The corner of her mouth flickered with the potential of a smile. "But who was I to deny my sister happiness, after all she'd been through?"

She didn't sit, but she did shift so that her shoulders leaned back against the tall coffee-dark cabinet behind her. Looking at the hazy afternoon beyond her shop window, she lit a cigarette. That she used a blue plastic disposable lighter when she was surrounded by such expensive ones made Gardner smile.

"What do you like best about it here?" she asked him. "The bright murals on the streets? The museums? The *Conservatorio Nacional Superior de Música* perhaps?"

He found something charming about the spontaneity of her non-sequitur. If she'd written instructions for him in the Queen's English, she couldn't have made it clearer that he had to tell the truth about himself if he wanted to hear more about her. If he'd wondered when the right moment to be totally upfront with her would be—it was now.

"I did obtain the scar I showed you from fighting them. The Nazis," he said. "And the limp."

"And the picture of the man you showed me?"

"A prop. It was given to me by Mossad. In case I needed to elicit sympathy." He gestured a polite request for one of her cigarettes. He was engaged in some of the riskiest gambling he'd done in quite some time—he might as well take up a second vice. "Did it work?"

With a stifled smile, she passed a single cigarette across the glass countertop to him.

"So you *are* a Nazi hunter—for Mossad."

"If Pieter Mueller is a Nazi, I suppose I am. Though I hope you'll enlighten me, because if the rumor that I've just heard is true, there is no Pieter Mueller."

Met by her silence at first, Gardner offered a slight smile and responded to her question. "Actually, the food. It's my favorite part of living in Buenos Aires. The *asado*. The place is heaven for a meat-eater like me."

She smiled. Then she told him the truth about Pieter Mueller.

"Pfeiffer," Gardner barked into his phone. He had to yell to be heard over the thumping-turbine sound of the helicopter. On his instructions and without asking questions, the Mossad had sent transportation for him. In less than an hour, he would connect with a sleeker, stealthier means of air transport to ferry him to Mossad headquarters. "P-f-e-i-f-f-e-r."

"Then who is Pieter Mueller?" questioned the voice on the other end—one of the head honchos at HQ in Tel Aviv.

A half-clever fiction, thought Gardner. What he said—or rather, shouted—was, "An alias!"

He did his best to convey the story to the deep-voiced operative whose face he had to imagine, as it was a rare event for him to actually see someone senior in Mossad. Pieter *Pfeiffer* had been tried for his heinous war crimes in Nuremburg in 1947 where he was sentenced to death, but had mysteriously escaped. Pfeiffer charmed a Jewish woman into marrying him—and not just any Jewish woman, but one of only two in her family to survive the Holocaust, a traumatized girl who'd matured into an educated and successful woman—and the union had served as a good disguise.

He would've gone on to shout more details into the receiver—about how Pfeiffer had served as a member of Werner von Braun's team, how he'd also participated in reprehensible medical experiments on children—but the faceless operative stopped him. "We've heard rumblings about Pieter Pfeiffer for years. Does the sister-in-law know where he is now?"

Gardner thought of how much she would've hated that term—sister-in-law.

He boarded the helicopter, taking a seat next to its pilot; in moments, he would lose signal, so he needed to say what he had to say fast. "Men have come to her looking for him over the years. One indicated he might be in Egypt, given that Nasser has offered refuge to German scientists to develop rockets for use against Israel."

Chaotic sounds emanated from the other end of the line: shuffling, chair scraping, furious whispers, drawers being opened, drawers slamming shut. Gardner assumed he had lost the signal. The line went dead. For a moment he couldn't figure out why the silence from an ended phone call would feel so all-encompassing, but quickly it hit him: the pilot had killed the chopper's engine. Gardner knew from past dealings with Mossad that some of their helicopters, cocked for rapid start, could be in the sky within ninety seconds—maximum—from the moment all passengers were seated. The Mossad chose means of transportation that could get them in and out of sticky situations at the speed of light. But this time they hadn't sent one of their quick-escape choppers; this wasn't supposed to be a situation that required a prompt escape. The chopper would take time to fully restart before they could take to the skies.

Gardner watched the man remove his noise-cancelling headset and gesture at his own phone. No one could ever claim the Mossad weren't effective multitaskers—apparently, they'd been communicating with both men at the same time.

"If you need to pack more of your belongings, I can give you one hour," the pilot said.

"Why would I need to pack more?" Gardner asked.

"Didn't they tell you? I'm still taking you to connect with one of their jets, but it will take you to Egypt." The man shrugged. "Looks like you may be there a while."

Gardner briefly considered the contents of the rumpled bag at his feet. There was no use trying to negotiate with Mossad; if they wanted him rushing off to Cairo in the middle of the night, the trip was inevitable. And he preferred getting it over with to going back home to pack additional pants and a lightweight jacket. With a sigh, he told the pilot, "I'm a light packer. Let's go."

In Egypt, Gardner met the Mossad's "man"—their field agent who'd been suspicious for some time of a link between a man now known as Pervas Ghattas and the long-vanished SS war criminal known as Pieter Pfeiffer. Under either name, he'd proven an exceptionally slippery catch: he had few known associates, and it was reasonable to assume that over the years, he had become a master of fooling vulnerable parties into buying his innocence. Now that they knew he was Pieter Mueller as well, they hoped Gardner's findings would highlight something new in the current case.

The Mossad's "man" was Lavi Amado. His businesslike demeanor was exemplified in a permanent vertical wrinkle between heavy brows. He didn't greet Gardner so much as he commanded him to start spilling information: "Tell me what you learned of this Pieter Mueller. How did he operate? How did he convince a respectable Jewish woman to trust him?" Gardner launched into the story of how the man called Mueller had demonstrated acumen for scientific thinking that helped him woo a girl whose adopted father was a scientist. Elsa would've had no way of realizing his knowledge had been honed while working on the German atomic bomb project. Of course, Gardner supplied, Eliana had never truly trusted him.

Lavi Amado paused from cueing up some grainy footage they'd managed to capture of the man they believed to be Pfeiffer/Ghattas/Mueller. "Who is Eliana?"

"Mueller's former sister-in-law." Gardner had nearly left her tobacco emporium that day without learning her name; for so long, she'd seemed determined to keep secret her own identity. She'd waited for him to reveal himself. After telling him everything about Elsa and Pieter, she had said, "Can I assume this information will make your job much more difficult, Mr. . . .?

Gardner had picked up the porcelain ash tray he'd admired upon first entering the shop. He'd opened his wallet to pay for it.

"Arthur. Arthur Gardner. And yes, it does make my assignment more difficult. Not impossible though. And I have to tell you, I'm very curious how he escaped when he was awaiting execution in Berlin. Who helped him?"

"Of course I'm curious about that too, Arthur," she said as she gift-wrapped the ashtray. "Do you think you might find that out on your next assignment?"

He had taken the heavy ashtray, causing its delicate tissue paper to crinkle, and nodded. "I'll definitely give it my best shot."

And that's when she had said it. "Eliana."

He was surprised how, even now, stranded in a manila-colored office with the angry Egyptian sun blazing above, the memory of Eliana's name on her own lips brought a smile to his. He couldn't lie to himself: the thought of bringing her news that would either provide closure about Pieter Pfeiffer or relief about her sister's current state was a motivation equal to his now-desperate need to finish the assignment and collect his much-needed fee.

"She never trusted him," Gardner reiterated, looking at the murky video of a man who did, indeed, resemble the Pieter Mueller he'd been chasing. He watched the man sit at a bistro table in a crowded lunchtime bazaar and shake hands with another man, whose smile glinted like polished ivory under fluorescent lighting.

"She watched him become a violent drunk after marrying her sister, and she didn't trust his so-called military pension of $500 a month. She thought it was a bit too much for a low-level soldier who hated the cause." Gardner waited for an empathetic nod or other sign of life from Amado, but the Mossad's man didn't take his eyes off the screen. "She figured out the same thing I did," Gardner continued. "That his patrons had cut him off out of anger after he'd married a Jewish girl."

Amado surprised him with an indication that he'd been listening after all. "Sounds sharp—this Eliana. She should be working for us."

Gardner nodded toward the screen, at their target's well-dressed lunch companion with the movie star smile. "Do we know who this is? The man he's meeting?"

"We believe he was Atrees Asfour, a high-ranking member of the Hamas terrorist organization. Say—what made Pieter 'Pfeiffer' leave Buenos Aires? I've glanced over your investigation files. It seems he had a rather nice setup for himself there."

Gardner shrugged. "It caught up with him. One day, two men from a Jewish revenge squad came looking for him. Apparently it destroyed Elsa. She got to him before the revenge squad did. She yelled at him, cried. And threw her wedding ring into the trash."

It had been at that point—there in the shop with Eliana, both of them finishing the cigarettes they'd been smoking and crushing the stubs in a marble ashtray—that he'd seen the picture. Eliana had extracted an old photo from her wallet of her sister and herself. Unlike Gardner's "prop photo," this one had not been countlessly refolded and weathered to enhance its impression as an artifact. Eliana had taken good care of this one. It featured two healthy-looking, attractive women, smiling broadly but not giddily, posing but not in a way that made them appear unnatural.

"This is her," Eliana had said. "We were so happy before he came into our lives. She was doing so well." Lighting another cigarette, Eliana had assured him she wasn't normally a chain smoker—it was just that, ordinarily, she didn't have to talk about her sister; if she was being honest, the subject always upset her. After Pieter Pfeiffer had betrayed them, Elsa had nearly suffered a nervous breakdown and then, on her doctor's advice, had left the area. To heal. To forget. To have adventures.

"Somehow," Eliana had told him, "I survived all of these merciless losses of my childhood. And I want to believe that my sister is happy out there, and that I can be happy for her." At this point she had touched her curled knuckles to her breastbone, as though indicating the exact spot Elsa was missing from. "The last time I heard from her, she'd met another man. She talked of him the same way she once talked about Pieter—as though she could see no flaws in him. As though he were a prince from a fairy tale." Her sister had always had a beautifully open heart, Eliana had told him, but by the same token, it made her vulnerable. Vulnerable to a certain type of man. Only then had Eliana's hand dropped from her chest. "I cannot help but fear for her," she told him.

Arthur Gardner knew better than to promise people tidy resolutions—to say nothing of happy ones. His line of work had exposed him constantly to the unexpected and devastating. So he didn't give her his word that he would make sure the Nazi chameleon once known as Pieter Mueller would be brought to justice and that Elsa was happy and safe, far from danger—he promised these things only to himself. This was a part of his job.

Now Gardner looked at the grainy tape of the man he'd been searching for, apparently now striking up a bond with Hamas. He could only feel this put him in near range of the capture he needed, for so many reasons. The Mossad tracked Hamas agents doggedly—surely they were closer than they'd ever been to the man of so many names. But then, before he got too far ahead of himself, Gardner returned to one word that had been uttered by Lavi Amado which had tripped him up.

"You said 'was,'" he said to Amado. "This man—what did you say, Atrees Asfour?—he 'was' a senior Hamas operative?"

Gardner had assumed Amado was simply a dyspeptic man, the sort whose mood couldn't be lifted even by a good plate of *asado* or an ice cream cone, but it was then that he was given a reason for the man's sour disposition. The reason Amado didn't appear as eager as Gardner felt at the prospect of finally closing in on Pieter Pfeiffer, and perhaps from there even leapfrogging to a greater infiltration of the Hamas itself.

"Asfour died recently in a terrorist suicide bombing— taking his wife out with him, and this man"—Amado jabbed his finger at the screen toward the man they had known as Pervas Ghattas—"is suspected to have fled the area yet again. Honestly, I hoped you would tell me this man could never be Pieter Mueller. Now we have bad news on two cases, not just one."

Even as Gardner felt an icy disappointment stealing down his gut, he tried for a silver lining. He needed one. "But at least we know it's a single case now. We can combine forces and follow up on leads faster. I can continue to work on it, but I have to go home first, to Buenos Aires. There's some bad news I have to break in person."

Furthermore, he had to see her again. Before he'd left her shop that afternoon, he had taken the beautiful woman's hand and said, "It's a pleasure to meet you, Eliana. You've been extremely helpful. Before I go, if you don't mind my asking—what's *your* favorite part? Of living here in Buenos Aires?"

Without hesitating, Eliana had answered, "Never needing to run away." And finally, she had given him a full smile. "Though I will say the *asado* may be a close second. Ever since you mentioned it, my mouth has been watering."

Arthur glanced through the windows at the sky, already a deep shade of pink and promising soon to darken into night. He had almost invited her out then, to have dinner with him, but he found that he couldn't in good consciousness. He was in a position to help her put to rest at least some of the demons from her long-haunted past, and it was something he needed to do before he could relax at some celebratory dinner with her.

Lavi Amado was already dismissing Gardner with a wave, while taking another hard look at the file on Pieter Mueller. "That's a coincidence," he muttered.

"What?" asked Gardner.

"You mentioned it before, but I didn't think anything of it. The name of 'Pieter Mueller's' wife is Elsa. That was also the name of the woman who died with Atrees Asfour in the suicide bombing. The name of his wife."

The icy feeling Gardner had experienced previously had at least flowed, in the way of a stream whose texture is just turning to slush as temperatures dip to freezing. Now that ice coagulated. His stomach a solid block of it. He barely managed to get out: "I don't suppose you have a picture of her."

Amado scowled, surely wondering what this could have to do with anything, but he dug out his file on Atrees Asfour all the same. As Gardner looked at the image of Elsa, looking nowhere near as happy and at ease as she had in the photograph Eliana had shown him, his first feeling was one of disgust. It welled up inside him like the first wave of nausea that comes with the flu. Disgust and anger: How could Elsa do this? How could she fall in love with a monster not once but *twice*? And—most importantly to Gardner's way of thinking—how could she do this to her sister, who had already suffered incalculable losses?

Soon enough Mossad, spearheaded by Lavi Amado, would put the pieces together. They would realize that the Hamas had been tracking Mueller as well, hoping to recruit him and make use of his specialized skillset. When they had lost touch with him, his ex-wife, Elsa, had proven much easier to locate—and to charm. There were things about Pieter only she knew: from mysterious passwords she'd discovered on slips of paper around their home to his daily habits, his favorite places to eat, those pastimes he could not pass up. Once her new husband knew these details as well, the Hamas was able to connect with Pieter Mueller.

Elsa had been nothing more than a pawn; when he learned of it, Gardner's feelings would soften toward the woman; he would feel a sympathy for her that, right now, was reserved in its entirety for Eliana.

As he handed the picture back to Amado, Gardner's worries about the fee, the resolution of the case, the spur-of-the-moment international travel and the intrigue that had long adrenalized his life of retirement with the excitement of the old days—all faded away.

The only thing that mattered now was returning so he could tell Eliana the news and hold her afterward, hopefully offering her some sense of both protection and support. They would not wine and dine and celebrate together—not for some time. For now he would simply be there for her. For now, it was time to go home.

CHAPTER FOUR

Anyone for Tennis?

After bidding farewell to his colleagues on the sidewalk outside the Lotos Club on East 66th Street, he turned to walk to his apartment a few blocks away. He glanced at his watch.

Ten o'clock on a humid Friday night. His chums had been generous to host a dinner party celebrating his promotion to the main board, though their hours of heavy drinking had grated on him. As a teetotaler, he knew he was an unusual phenomenon among newspaper people.

Josh had been a long-term member of the club and one of his keep-fit regimens was to time his walks. His record from the club to his home was nine minutes. Tonight, he did it in eleven and felt disgusted with himself. He was tired. It had been a long day.

Back in his apartment, he went immediately for the remote; he'd recorded that day's tennis at Wimbledon. Mixed doubles. Like the mixed doubles that, thirty-five years ago, had changed his life.

After Dartmouth, he'd worked at *The Chicago Tribune*; then onward to Columbia; then, straight out of grad school, he'd gone onto one of the world's most prestigious newspapers. Shortly after, his bosses sent him to its Paris bureau. He translated the pride he felt into mobility, and in no time he'd made his mark. He was where he wanted to be—when other papers tried wooing him, he ignored the offers.

Once a week or so, he and a colleague from the Paris bureau would play tennis before dining at a brasserie then taking the metro to their apartments.

It was June. The Friday preceding a long weekend. With all the courts reserved, the lady in the pro shop asked if they'd mind joining another couple. Though they would've had to be churlish to decline, they still may have done precisely that had they not caught sight of this other couple— at that point, they saw they would've had to be not only churlish but stupid as well.

They were both women, both in their early twenties by Josh's estimate, both wearing the sort of ponytails that looked strong as rope but moved like silk. There was a coin toss to determine partners, but Josh didn't care how it turned out. Chance matched him with Francesca Annibaldi. Their affair would last until she left for a modeling assignment in Milan.

Park benches, patisseries, and tennis courts were all elevated to landscapes by the presence of her artistic form. At first, admittedly, he was compelled solely by the physical: her bold brows that lent a sense of drama to every expression, her skin so smooth it looked and felt liquid, her wavy, gently highlighted blonde hair that forever fell in front of her face if it wasn't bound in a ponytail. But he learned about her, and he appreciated her more with every detail.

Francesca was the daughter of Count and Countess Annibaldi, a distinguished noble family that could trace its lineage back to the fourteenth century. Her father had died in an automobile crash when she was nine and her newly widowed French mother moved back to Paris from Italy.

Having graduated from the Sorbonne, she spoke fluent French, Italian, and English and worked as a freelance model. She had recently split with her boyfriend, the owner of an art gallery on Avenue Matignon. Her deficits on the tennis court couldn't put a dent in her charms. In fact, that first day she'd rendered him a weaker player than herself without trying; though he'd long since mastered the forehand groundstroke and overhead smash, he fumbled both on several occasions.

There were no more mixed doubles. In fact there was no more tennis. They spent every night and weekends together, treasuring those mornings they could lie in bed until midday, take long walks, sometimes even across the river and up the hill to Montmartre, where they would tourist-watch from a table at La Mère Catherine.

One Sunday she told Josh she was going to have lunch with her grandmother, Countess Valeshka Kholovski. She wanted Josh to accompany her; he shrugged a reluctant "yes."

"Actually, she is my step-grandmother. After she divorced my grandfather, she married a Russian Count, Count Sergio Kholovski. That's how she became Countess Kholovski. They were both Russians. They fled Russia in 1917 and settled in Paris. The Count came from a wealthy noble family, but my grandmother was from a middle-class family that also had escaped the revolution. Their paths didn't cross until they were both in their late sixties."

Josh half-listened as he dreamed of, instead, spending that Sunday afternoon making love to Francesca. Any conversation with this aged Russian dame was destined to center on people and places unknown to him—he'd be bored stiff.

"I'll make it up to you. You might even enjoy it." She pinched his arm and leaned to give him a kiss. "Meeting her might be a feather in your cap back at your newspaper."

"How?"

"Wait and see. Actually, I told her about you and she is looking forward to meeting you."

Josh grunted. "Where does she live?"

"She has a suite at the Meurice."

Josh ran his eyes over her shoulders covered by only spaghetti straps, wishing his hands could do the same. "This means a lot to you, doesn't it?"

"I feel guilty." She leaned into his shoulder. "Since you came into my life, I've been neglecting her. She may not be my real grandmother, but I'm closest to her. My maternal grandmother and my mother had a big falling out, so I never knew her. And my paternal grandmother got religion and is in some sort of a convent in Rome."

Sipping his coffee, he glanced at the clock. "Half past ten. What time are we expected?"

"One. I'll go back to my place to smarten up, and why don't I pick you up at twelve forty-five? And look your Brooks Brothers WASP best." She giggled. She'd been trying to convert him to wear Gucci since their third date.

"I'll wear the Gucci loafers you made me buy."

When she next saw him, she approved of his casual, Upper East Side look; her own fashion—a short burgundy Valentino dress—accentuated her natural beauty. On the cab ride over, he said, "I've never seen that necklace before." It was a peacock Tahitian pearl choker.

"A gift from my rich predecessor, yes?"

"Don't be silly. My grandmother gave it to me on my twenty-first birthday."

Fifteen minutes later they walked through the marble lobby and hallway toward the elevators. Josh knew of the Meurice's checkered history, home of the Duke and Duchess of Windsor, Salvador Dali, and others, but also as headquarters of the German SS during the Nazi occupation. It was rumored the basement had been used—through those ignoble years—to torture Jews and suspected heroes of the resistance.

Francesca led the way down the wide corridor on the fifth floor, brightly lit by ornate chandeliers and sconces. A security guard greeted Francesca outside a set of double doors. Josh noted the revolver tucked in his belt.

"*Bon Jour*, Boris."

"It's good to see you again, Miss Francesca. Your grandmother is expecting you." His accent was distinctly Russian. He faced Josh. "And you are?"

The guard repeated "Josh Kendall" twice to commit the name to memory. "Would you mind, please, just spreading your arms?"

Though puzzled, Josh silently submitted to the pat-down. With a grin Francesca said, "I told you that you would have fun today."

"I wouldn't call this fun so much as bizarre."

Boris, satisfied, tapped on the door and then opened it for them to enter.

They stepped into a wide foyer with heavy antique icons hanging from one wall and a large oil painting depicting the Winter Palace at St. Petersburg on the other. It led into a large salon with floor-to-ceiling windows that offered an uninterrupted view of the Tuileries Garden.

On the pale yellow walls hung several family portraits. On a deep pile of dark grey carpet were Art Deco chairs and sofas upholstered in vibrant blue brocade with over-size orange striped cushions. Candles that smelled like fresh pastries burned in a candelabra atop a credenza. On a side table, ash from an incense stick filled a silver saucer. It took a few seconds for Josh's eyes to acclimate to the pano-ply of bright colors and elegance wedged into one space.

"That's my father." Francesca pointed to a silver frame on a nearby table. She whispered, "I think she only displays it when I come. They weren't exactly fond of each other."

He smiled. Families, it seemed, were always the same.

"You're here." A tall figure matching the husky voice emerged from the corridor. While Francesca embraced her grandmother, Josh tried to figure out why the woman looked familiar. As a young man who dreamed of globe-trotting, he'd watched a handful of foreign films from the decades preceding his own era of entertainment—perhaps Francesca's grandmother had once acted.

"What lovely flowers! How kind. Francesca, please find a vase in the kitchen and put them on the dining table. Thank you again."

Francesca did as she was bid.

"And you are Josh, the great tennis player who has taken up my granddaughter's entire time. I should hate you for that, you know. But you have made her happy and that's all that counts. Ignore the protective and possessive feelings of an old lady." She kissed him on both cheeks. The warmth of her welcome took him by surprise.

Her full, green velvet dress mostly concealed her pink slippers. Her face, free of makeup but clear and unblem-ished, was on full display with her grey hair pulled back in a bun. Deep green, it appeared, was her color—for today at least. Her earrings and bracelet both prominently featured emerald, the color's omnidirectional effect highlighting the green in the woman's eyes. It was something she had in common with her step-granddaughter, in addition to being tall, slender, and surprising.

"Josh, will you bring in a bottle of champagne?" Glasses had already been placed on a corner table set for three. "And you'll see some canapes in the refrigerator as well."

Francesca pointed him toward the kitchen. Josh only hoped he'd been sent on the errand so the grandmother could express her approval to Francesca. He returned with an open bottle of Dom Perignon.

"So tell me, young man, about yourself. Francesca has told me you are employed by the New York newspaper and that you were at Dartmouth and Columbia. Excellent credentials."

He smiled. "I'm here for several months unless the paper decides to keep me here longer, although it may be better for my career if I did go back to the States in due course."

"I haven't been to America since just after my divorce."

"You lived in the States?"

Her smile had the same captivating quality of her granddaughter's. "So I take it you haven't told this nice young man anything about me?"

"No, Grandmother. I left it for him to ask and for you to tell."

"After lunch. I've ordered *blinis* and caviar to begin, followed by chicken Kiev and for dessert, *vatrushka*. An authentic Russian meal. But no vodka. I must be the only Russian who ever lived who is allergic to that damned drink."

Turning to Josh, "New York, Josh. Oh yes, I lived there for many years. I have the keys to the city, given to me by Mayor La Guardia. I also have an honorary degree from your alma mater, Columbia."

"You *do*?" He hoped there was nothing insulting in his tone; he was simply surprised—happily.

"And one from Cornell too. There was a blizzard the day I received it. Terrible weather. Just like I remember it in Moscow."

Who the hell was this woman? Josh flirted with the theory that she was a nutcase—that this was all fantasy.

"Francesca, tell them to hold the lunch for a half-hour. Let's get my saga over with so we can all relax and enjoy our lunch in peace and talk of other things, like you and your young man."

After Josh, at her request, refilled their glasses, she began. "If either of you interrupt, we'll be off on a tangent. Better to save all questions until lunch. Okay?"

They agreed in unison, and from that point, Francesca's grandmother paused only to sip her drink.

"I was born Valeshka Petrov in Moscow in 1899. That makes me eighty-two. My father served in the Imperial Navy and then in some capacity, I never understood what exactly, in the Winter Palace. In 1917, we fled Russia and came here, to Paris.

"Our first years in Paris were difficult. We were middle-class and not part of the wealthy White Russian clique that led more comfortable lives. To support my mother and me, my father gave bridge lessons and contributed articles to White Russian periodicals. He scraped by to make a living. And my mother, who had never worked before, became a seamstress and worked for various couturiers. At eighteen I started making money as a model. Soon I was making more than my parents combined—not to mention attracting some rich boyfriends. You might imagine I received quite a bit of jewelry, and I sold most of it to help my parents."

Josh looked at her. She was still a beautiful woman. He imagined she would have had no difficulty in attracting men. Was it possible that desperate times had led to prostitution? When he caught Francesca's gaze, she reminded him of his pledge with a finger to her lips.

"One day I was approached by a handsome and most distinguished gentleman my father's age. He became my paramour. He held a senior position in the Russian Communist party. We talked politics and I developed a great deal of sympathy for the Bolsheviks, even though they considered me a traitor for fleeing Russia in 1917. As though I had any say in the matter. Times were different then. Children obeyed their parents."

Francesca laughed.

"Anatol persuaded me to emigrate to the United States, where I could continue to work as a model. He arranged for me to be set up in an apartment on Madison Avenue and to be paid a generous monthly sum that would be sent to an account for me in Geneva. In exchange I was to infiltrate New York society and meet as many prominent people as I could and report back to a contact person *matters of interest*."

Josh could no longer help himself. "You were recruited to be a spy?"

She continued as though the question hadn't been asked. "I left for New York in 1923. It was very exciting. The crossing in a first-class stateroom on the *Mauretania*, the music, the dancing, and the black-tie parties every night. What a glamorous time. The people I mixed with suffered no inconveniences on account of prohibition. Booze flowed. The Charleston. Gershwin, Cole Porter—these were the golden years. See the photograph there of me with Gershwin? What a lover. He was very much in love. Unfortunately, it was with himself, not with me."

Josh's penny began to drop, as did his jaw. He looked again at Francesca. She nodded.

"During these years, I met Jack Butler. He'd divorced the previous year and had just become mayor. He made millions from construction. No matter what people say, any man who makes millions during a time like the Wall Street crash, based on the misfortune of others, is not a nice person. And Jack Butler was definitely not a nice person. It took me a few years, though, to fully realize just how nasty he was."

"Jack Butler, who was . . ."

"I was, as they now say, his trophy wife. That echelon of society considered a Russian who could converse in English and French exotic. I gave up modeling, of course. He installed me in a townhouse on East 63rd, a few yards from Fifth Avenue. And I can't say it was all bad: he showered me with jewelry and furs. But his eyes were on bigger things. He'd profited so richly from connections with underworld figures and unions, yet being mayor of New York would never be enough for him. But President of the United States—surely it was impossible. That's what I told myself. A pipe dream. But to accomplish it, he insisted that we marry. He did not believe, and in this he was correct, that a divorced man whose mistress lived with him would sit well with the electorate. I was bribed with a significant sum, and I agreed. We were married.

"My employers at the Russian Communist Party couldn't believe how well this turned out for them. I'd not only been the mistress of the mayor of the most important and dynamic city in the world, but I was close to becoming the First Llady of the most powerful country on the planet. They tripled my monthly income and gave me a multimillion-dollar bonus. And, young man, that was in the thirties when a million dollars was a million dollars."

Josh understood why she'd postponed lunch; any meal in front of him would've gone cold while he listened to her, unmoving and nearly unblinking. Could this possibly be the mysterious woman once married to the President of the United States, who had been out of the public eye for more than thirty years?

"And then—would you believe it—in spite of all the adverse publicity and his well-known business shenanigans, he was elected. Off to the White House we went. My bosses in the Kremlin were thrilled. Now they had an agent in bed, literally, with the President. The only thing better they could have hoped for was the President himself. And soon enough they had him as well."

"Wow."

"Within days of Jack being elected, millions were deposited into my Swiss account, and my monthly pay quadrupled again. But I earned it. Not only did I have to sleep with the swine, I had to mine for information and then pass it on to my handler, Pierre Martin. He was my hairdresser—he came to me every morning, weekends included, at half past eight. We feared cameras and microphones may have been installed in the salon, but we had to take the chance. These were frenzied years. The Cold War, McCarthyism, the Rosenberg trial."

Francesca excused herself to fetch another bottle of champagne from the kitchen.

"Then something happened which really gave me enormous power over Jack. By now I had come to hate him. He was drunk most nights, and ate nothing but junk food. He must have gained thirty pounds during his presidency. He was a ruthless bully, a racist. He had affairs, used prostitutes, and even forced me to have threesomes with the wives of several of his friends. He was embroiled in tax problems. He blackmailed two senators. He was a monster.

"In the middle of all this, he was in default on some big loans. What a scandal that would be. He couldn't raise the money. I wasn't going to lend him a dime. Thank God he didn't know about the millions I had hidden in Switzerland. I negotiated a loan for him of fifteen million from the Russian State Bank, on the condition that Jack would keep me informed of developments on United States atomic bomb manufacturing capabilities. A loan of that size, interest-free . . . how could he refuse?

"So, yes, I was a spy. And think about it. Jack's conduct was treasonous. Imagine the President giving me most secret classified information relating to atomic bombs. I had information denied to most of the cabinet. Every day I would pump him for information and let him know that if he didn't come up with it, his loan would be in jeopardy. And, if that wasn't enough, I had a contingency plan."

Certainly she had been breathing this whole time—Josh as well—yet her delivery and his reaction seemed so breathless that when she now paused, it felt to Josh as though he'd rocketed up from the ocean's depths to break the water's surface and fill his lungs again. He hadn't even noticed Francesca return with fresh champagne. He certainly hadn't noticed her pour him a glass. He hadn't noticed his own sweaty fingers automatically reach for it and grip the glass stem. Sipping his drink, he nodded for her to—please—continue.

"The contingency plan was that my handler would arrange for me to be spirited out of the country to Russia. Once back in Moscow, I would go public with my story. The resulting scandal would likely end in the President's suicide. What other solution could there be?"

"Wow." Typically much more eloquent, Josh now seemed able only to repeat these monosyllabic expressions of amazement until they threatened to become a chant. "Wow, wow, wow."

"Of course, I never had to resort to that plan. But what leverage I had! Naturally, he hated me. The power I had over him was all-encompassing. We agreed there would be no divorce until after his presidency. Clearly, there was no way he could stand for re-election. So, I had another eighteen months to endure. I have to say this about Jack—he put up a good face. No one, I'm sure, knew what had been taking place. Maybe after we were divorced. Some people, especially J. Edgar Hoover over at the FBI, had their suspicions.

"So we divorced. That attracted a lot of publicity, but that died down after a month, by which time I had returned to Moscow for protection. And after six months, the KGB agreed it would be safe for me to move anywhere I wanted— except, of course, back to the States. They agreed to give me lifetime armed security. Boris, who you met when you arrived, has been with me for seven years. My other guards are Dimitri and Ivan.

"I even got a generous settlement in the divorce. He offered me a lump sum payment or the income for life from a building he owned in New York. It was tempting to take the income, but my lawyer advised the lump sum. If it ever came out that I'd spied, the United States would block my income from the building.

"I had to agree never to write my memoirs or go public about my marriage with Jack. Second, I had to promise that I would never set foot again in the United States as long as I lived. It was easy to agree to both conditions."

"Please, Countess, forgive me for interrupting, but I must ask you something."

At his side, Francesca sat in silence. Her grandmother nodded; apparently she'd softened to questions at this point.

"You've lived in Europe for over thirty years. You are a former First Lady. How come you have avoided the press all these years? Are you a prisoner here at the Meurice? Do you live a normal life—do you have friends? Do you go to restaurants, art galleries, plays, concerts?"

"Of course. I lived a normal life in Rome with Francesca's grandfather, and then I moved to Paris after that divorce. I disappeared from view. People lost interest. There was a new President of the United States with a young, glamorous wife. No one gave a damn about me, and probably not about Jack either. He died a couple years after our divorce and no one has found him interesting enough to write his biography. There's no Jack Butler Library. A couple of journalists have tried to interview me over the years, but I refused to give them any time. They left me alone."

"But why are you talking to me? After all, you know I work for a major newspaper."

She hesitated.

"I'm an old woman. And, despite what you think, I'm not in good shape. Francesca knows. She's my only heir. She'll inherit the lot, and believe me: it is a lot. Seeing as she's given me a good report on you, I would like to help you in your career."

"That is very kind. So what do you suggest?"

She proposed that over the next several months, Josh would spend as much time as he needed interviewing her. He would write whatever he wanted; it would be an authorized biography. But she intended to spend her final days in peace and knew she couldn't achieve that with the rest of the journalism community beating down her door. So the one condition she imposed was that nothing—neither the book nor any articles—appear in print until after her death.

"And that," she assured him, "will be within nine months."

"Oh, Grandmother, don't be such a pessimist."

"And you don't get sentimental, Francesca. You were with me when the doctor laid out the facts."

Francesca rose from her seat to kiss her grandmother.

Josh was stunned. Fortuitously at that moment Boris admitted the waiter with their lunch. They took their seats at the round table.

"Of course, I will instruct my attorney, Maître Dujardin, to draw up an agreement between us. I'll see if he can come tomorrow to take my instructions."

"I don't understand, why do you need an attorney, Grandmother?"

"Several reasons, my dear. This young man is going to devote himself to interviewing me and writing my biography. I am sure Josh wants the security of an exclusive right to all this. And I don't want to be sued by Jack's estate for disclosing anything that years ago I had covenanted to keep confidential. Oh, and there is something else. Any publisher's royalties that Josh receives are to be shared equally between Josh and you, Francesca."

"Oh Grandmother. That is so kind. You have already given me so much."

When the old lady began to tire, Francesca gave Josh a wink and nodded toward the door. In silence they returned to his apartment. All he could say when they arrived back was, "This is amazing. I'm in shock. I can't thank you enough."

During the sleepless night that followed, he thought of the time issues that would arise from attempting to complete this in a matter of months—never mind the interviews necessary for promoting the book—while still employed at the newspaper. He would have to disclose to his editor what was going on in his life. People in New York might not be cooperative. And then what? Could he trust the head of the Paris office not to steal the story?

Once he had a copy of the signed agreement, he telephoned New York and requested an urgent, confidential meeting with the publisher and the editor. He told the Paris office that he had to go to New York unexpectedly on family business but while there would look in at the office. That preempted anyone in New York from telling the Paris office that he was in town and thus cause a problem for him on his return.

The editor and publisher received him cordially but with confusion. When he recounted his meeting with the Countess—and former First Lady of the United States—they could not hide their incredulity. Only after Josh produced from his attaché case a copy of the agreement, along with a couple of photographs taken by Francesca, did they express delight and utter amazement. Even congratulations.

"Josh, this is a scoop. Well done! How do you want to play this?"

He'd given it a great deal of thought. "I'd like you to give me a twelve-month leave of absence, at my current salary, to write this book. I'll need to stay in Paris but to write from my apartment and not from the office. And I'll need you to continue to pay my rent and expenses."

"Agreed. But who is going to own the book's copyright?"

"I am. The newspaper will have exclusivity on all interviews and a percentage of royalties—from the book and from any deal on a movie."

When Josh arrived back in Paris, he saw a note under his door from Francesca. She would be away for a couple weeks on a modeling assignment in Milan. He had to admit his disappointment was tinged with some relief—he had a lot of work to do.

Francesca's couple weeks in Milan turned out to be indefinite. Working at least fifteen hours daily, eating sandwiches at his desk, and seeing no one except the Countess, Josh had no time to miss her. And given her vested interest in the royalties, it was in her own interest not to disturb his progress on the book.

As the Countess's health deteriorated, Josh had to cut working days down by several hours; in his new spare time, he edited and prepared questions for the next meeting. Francesca sent him a card now and again from Italy but provided no way for him to contact her. The Countess had the same complaint. *Where was she?*

The months ticked by. Josh's manuscript was almost complete. He'd conducted three lengthy interviews with her, accompanied by professional photographs, for publication.

And then, almost to the day of her nine-month prediction, the Countess died quietly in her suite at the Meurice. The hotel contacted Maître Dujardin, who in turn notified Francesca. She was the only one with whom she had kept informed of her life after she left Paris months earlier.

Maître Dujardin made arrangements for the Countess to be buried at the Père Lachaise Cemetery. A handful of people attended. It was a cold, dry November morning, and the pathways were covered with dead leaves. Two other burials with larger swarms of mourners took place nearby, leading Josh to wonder about those deceased. Surely their lives hadn't been as sensational as the Countess's.

The Meurice sent a delegation including the general manager and Astrid, a concierge whom the Countess was fond of and had included in her will, along with Maître Dujardin and his secretary. Also in attendance were Boris and three elderly men—two of who were pushed in wheelchairs by their caregivers—and who were likely White Russians. No representatives from either the United States or Soviet embassies. At the cemetery, Josh looked around for Francesca.

After the coffin was lowered into the ground, and as Josh was leaving the cemetery, Maître DuJardin approached. "Just a second." He unbuttoned his overcoat to take from an inside pocket an envelope addressed to Josh.

"This is from Francesca. She asked me to give it to you after the Countess died. I know its contents. Read it carefully and think kindly of her."

Josh was in no rush to get back to his apartment. He stepped into the first bar he could find on leaving the cemetery. It was still only eleven o'clock. With an hour or so before the lunch crowd descended, he ordered a beer and moved to a table.

He looked at the envelope and recognized Francesca's handwriting.

Dear Josh,

I asked Maître Dujardin to give you this letter on my grand-mother's death. I shall go to my own grave ashamed that I have not been in touch with neither her nor you these last few months. I stayed away from Paris deliberately. I was pregnant. She would have been horrified to have seen me that way and might even have cut me out of my substantial inheritance. And my shame is compounded because you may have been the fa-ther. I will never know. As soon as I arrived in Milan, I began an affair with someone. He could have been the father too. I'll never know. The baby died. It was a boy.

Please forgive me.

Good luck with the book!

Au revoir,

Francesca

To this day, he kept the letter as a bookmark. It marked some indiscriminate passage; it remained where he'd blindly tucked it years before, in the body of his book on the astonishing life of a countess spy and the one-time First Lady of the United States. For thirty years, he had touched neither letter nor book.

With a sigh, he looked at the television. The mixed doubles match was still in play.

CHAPTER FIVE

The Author

Bronwyn Tasker, flanked by Princeton's librarian emeritus and her literary agent, was escorted by a young summer intern along the long narrow corridor on the twenty-seventh floor to the book-lined conference room of Larkin & Forrest's Manhattan office. She took her time, pausing frequently to stare at the portraits of the firm's Nobel- and Pulitzer Prize-winning authors. Finally she found the one for which she had been searching. Arnold Lincoln. The brass plaque on the frame stated his name and the years 1879–1950. At ninety-six, she was now exactly twenty-five years older than Lincoln had been when he died. The young intern interrupted her thoughts. "Mr. Larkin is waiting for you, Ms. Tasker." She continued to stare at the portrait for several seconds before moving on. Her only thought, as she was rushed along, was that he had a kind expression.

They entered the conference room. Mr. Theodore Larkin did not stand to greet them. With him were two dour and expressionless middle-aged women and a young man who bore a distinctive resemblance to the elderly Mr. Larkin. *Maybe a grandson,* she speculated. They remained seated, two of them continuing to sip from their elegant coffee cups, barely giving her a glance. No coffee was offered to either Professor Tasker or to her two companions.

"Ms. Tasker, I haven't much time so let's get to the point. I'll be frank. I only agreed to meet with you because of Lloyd Cape, here. As a Princeton man myself, I have known of Lloyd for many years. He has a well-deserved reputation as one of the country's most eminent librarians. How he comes to be involved with you made me curious. And as for your agent"—Larkin paused to stare at Hyman Shapiro— "we have never published any of your authors and I doubt we are going to make an exception in the case of Ms. Tasker." He pushed his cup aside.

Fixing her with a cold stare, he continued, "Larkin & Forrest has never, in its hundred and forty-three years, published anything written by a convicted criminal, so why have you come to see us?"

"Mr. Larkin, I want someone to write my biography. I'm ninety-six. I cannot write my own autobiography. If someone writes my story, I may not live to see it published. I need a successful biographer to take this on. Someone skilled. It cannot be third-rate and trite. I want a major author. Someone like Kitty Kelley."

"Oh really," Mr. Larkin snickered. His three sycophants joined in with a cacophony of giggles and guffaws.

When the mirth evaporated, Mr. Larkin spoke. "And what makes you think the world's preeminent biographer would want to give you the time of day, Ms. Tasker?"

"Because what I have to say will be the biggest bombshell in publishing in centuries."

More snickers.

"I have a non-negotiable demand."

"And what is that?"

"I need to generate one and a half million dollars from this book. The full amount is to go to Princeton's library, not one dime to me. Revenues over this can go to you and the writer as you determine. As long as Princeton gets one and a half million dollars."

Mr. Larkin looked at his watch. Then at his colleagues. After a few seconds, he broke into a grin and laughed. His shoulders shook. "I am beginning to enjoy this nonsense, Ms. Tasker. Before you start, however, I want you to make your own case for your book. There is no need for your agent—whose name I've already happily erased from my mind—to remain. Similarly, I'm not sure that Mr. Cape wishes to besmirch his good reputation by being present. After all, he is not pitching the merits of this questionable opus."

He paused. "I suggest the two of you wait in our reception area. This won't take long, I assure you."

One of the women stood to refresh hers and Mr. Larkin's coffee. The other one escorted Mr. Cape and Mr. Shapiro back to the reception.

"Now," said Mr. Larkin, "I have approximately ten minutes to spare, so go on—please. Amuse me."

"I assure you, Mr. Larkin, your attitude will be different when you have heard my story."

"You have ten minutes. Not one minute more."

"I graduated from the University of Aberdeen in Scotland."

"I know where Aberdeen is, Ms. Tasker. Please make this quick."

"I graduated in 1949. My studies were interrupted by the Second World War. I graduated in zoology, but during my studies I developed an interest in puffins and decided to research for a doctorate. The university awarded me a scholarship to study puffins and to spend a year photographing and observing them for my thesis. This necessitated a move to the Faroe Islands."

"Puffins?"

The table again broke into lampooning laughter and sneers.

"Yes, Mr. Larkin. Puffins. So I went to the Faroe Islands, which, as you may know, are to the northwest of Scotland halfway between Norway and Iceland. The islands are an autonomous country within Denmark with a population of around 50,000. Very rugged, windy, and wet. It's a wonderful place to study puffins. I settled in a small village, Hosvik, that had barely 300 inhabitants."

"Get to the point."

"It was there that I met Gerald Mustell."

"Our author, Gerald Mustell? The Nobel Prize winner for literature?"

"Yes, that Gerald Mustell."

"Go on."

"His mother was Danish, as I'm sure you know. That's why he settled in the Faroe Islands. He spoke the language fluently. After you published his first book and it became a huge success, he became reclusive and moved to Hosvik, where he lived in a modest cottage. It was remote. No telephone. No neighbors nearby. And there he wrote, never having to deal with interviews, book signings, and all the other things that successful writers have to do. He lived totally alone, never saw a soul. Just him, his writing, and his model airplanes. Did you know he built model airplanes?"

"So you met him and then what?"

"I met him one day at the general store in Hosvik. We had a lively conversation about puffins and the trials and tribulations of living such a solitary existence. We began to take daily walks together along the coastline and to neighboring villages. I used to go to his cottage and cook for him from time to time. And he fell in love with me. He was much older, but that was never an issue between us. After a time he asked me to move in with him. I did."

She paused.

"So you were his muse?" Mr. Larkin raised an eyebrow.

"You can call me what you like. Muse. Girlfriend. Mistress. We made each other happy. We lived together until he died."

"He died in Stockholm when he went to receive the Nobel Prize for Literature."

"I was with him, Mr. Larkin. He died in my arms at the hotel when we were getting ready to leave for the award ceremony."

He refilled his coffee cup. "And you're telling me your life in the Faroe Islands was exceptional somehow? Book-worthy?"

"It was simple. Every day after breakfast, including Saturdays and Sundays, Gerald would disappear into his office until around one o'clock. The only sound I heard was of him banging away on his typewriter.

"Meanwhile, I'd converted a small room off the landing into my office. It had no window, as it had been a storage closet. It was in that tiny cubbyhole that I worked on my doctorate.

"We would meet up in the kitchen around one, have soup and a chunk of bread I'd warmed up, and then we'd go for a long walk. Sometimes we'd walk for two or three hours. Less in the winter months, as we wanted to be home before it got dark. We'd have simple dinners, usually stews, listen to classical music on the radio, and then go to bed. As I said, we were happy. That is until Gerald was notified that he'd been awarded the Nobel Prize for Literature. At that moment, he changed. Life became hell. What should have been a most joyful moment in our lives became an absolute misery."

"In what way?"

"He started to drink heavily. We always had a vodka before dinner, but an entire bottle every evening became the norm for Gerald, with me just sticking to one small glass. He would walk a mile to the only shop in the village that sold liquor and buy as many bottles as he could carry home. God knows what they thought."

"Do you know what triggered this?"

"Yes, he was scared stiff. He'd been out of the public glare for so long, suddenly being thrust into the spotlight filled him with panic. Frequent vomiting, sudden rages, insomnia. He even lashed out at me and blamed me, for goodness sake. Why did he blame me? For helping him get the most distinguished prize in literature. It was madness."

"I agree."

"First he wanted to decline the award. I used every argument under the sun to persuade him to accept. Finally he agreed. Then he refused to travel to Stockholm to be honored. And that created more rows and violent scenes. Every day, I had to put two empty bottles into the trash."

A secretary came into the room with a fresh pot of coffee. No one indicated wanting more.

"Then the speech. I reminded him that he needed to make an acceptance speech. I thought war had broken out. Shouting, screaming, more abuse. He even struck me. I fell onto the kitchen floor. And he kicked me mercilessly. Oh how I wished we had neighbors, but we lived well over a mile from the closest."

"Did you help him with the speech?"

"I offered, but he refused. Whenever I asked how he was getting on with it, it led to more screaming and shouting. I asked to see the speech countless times but he always refused. It was a nightmare living with him during those weeks, believe me."

Mr. Larkin looked at his watch.

"We flew to Stockholm and someone came to the hotel to fit him for formal attire for the award ceremony. Gerald gave me money to buy a dress suitable for the occasion. After all, I never had a reason to wear a formal evening gown in Hosvik. It was long, black, and most elegant. I've never worn it again, not after that evening.

"We were two days in Stockholm before the night of the ceremony. We never left the hotel suite. It was as if he'd lost his voice. He wouldn't speak. He walked around in a daze. After all the hell I'd been through with him since he was notified of the prize, I guess I should have been relieved. But it was scary. He was so different."

"Did he appear ill?"

"Not physically, but obviously there was something wrong with his mental condition. The afternoon of the ceremony, Johannes came to give us the final instructions and to say that he would pick us up at six o'clock. Johannes had a position with the Nobel organization."

"Johannes Svensson? The man you murdered?"

"Yes. He deserved to die."

He repeated words he had used several times, but now with less impatience. His was a coaxing tone as he said, "Go on, Ms. Tasker."

She watched as he sipped his coffee. She craved some herself.

"Johannes arrived on time, at six. We were ready to leave with him. We were dressed, and if I may say it myself, we looked good. Elegant, he in his white tie and tails and me in my new black evening gown. Gerald said he needed to go to the bathroom before we left. That was no surprise. He'd been having prostate problems and had to go frequently. We stood waiting for him. We heard a loud thud. He'd obviously slipped. We rushed into the bathroom and there he was on the floor. I bent down beside him and cradled his head in my arms. Seconds later, he drew his last breath."

"Quite a shock?"

"Johannes ran back into the living room and called for a doctor. Then I heard him talk to someone else but I couldn't understand Swedish and I had no idea who was at the other end of the line.

"Some medics arrived as well as the hotel manager and God knows who else. The room suddenly became hectic. Poor Gerald's body lay on the bathroom floor and I couldn't hold back my tears. No one spared me any notice."

"And then?"

"Well, when Gerald fell onto the floor, and I took his head in my hands, I noticed a piece of paper, folded in half, slip out from the inside pocket of his tails. I guessed—correctly, as it turned out—it was the speech he was due to give."

"And what did you do with it?"

"Something told me to keep it. If Gerald wasn't going to deliver it, no one else would. I took it from his pocket and slipped it under the bathmat. Seconds later, three people came into the bathroom to take Gerald's body away. Just like that. They left me on the floor, crying. Ten minutes later, everyone had left. The doctor had asked me a few perfunctory questions and said that a coroner might have other questions for me but that it seemed to him, at first examination, that Gerald had had a heart attack."

"And that was later confirmed, was it not?"

She nodded. "Imagine the callousness of everyone. They had left me alone. I got up from the cold tiled floor and walked into the empty living room in a state of shock. The next morning, I read in the English-language newspaper that someone had given a speech to honor Gerald and announce his death. There was no one to either receive the award or give the acceptance speech. I then remembered the paper under the bathmat. I went to retrieve it. When I read it, I was stunned."

Mr. Larkin stretched to pick up a telephone on a side table. "Hold all calls," he ordered the operator.

"Johannes arrived to present me with Gerald's award around ten that morning. I was still in my evening dress from the night before. Johannes knew that Gerald had no family and that he and I had been together for close to thirty years. He assumed—incorrectly, as it turned out—I was his only heir. He asked me if Gerald had a speech prepared for the award ceremony. I lied and said no. The last thing I wanted was for him to see Gerald's typewritten speech. But there it was lying next to me on the sofa.

"'What's that?' he demanded. I hesitated. Again, he shouted, 'What's that?' He ordered me to give it to him so that he could release it to the press. That was the last thing I wanted. 'Well at least read it to me,' he ordered. I hesitated still. He shouted again, and in my vulnerable and shaken state, I feared he would strike me. So I read him the speech. He looked at me in disbelief. He said he would come back later to discuss this with me but, in the meantime, I was not to say a word to anyone. Well, he didn't come back later that day, or the next. It made no sense for me to remain any longer in Stockholm, so I flew back to Scotland. I took the ferry the next morning to get on with my life in Hosvik."

"Did you go to Gerald's funeral at least?"

"No, Mr. Larkin. As you know the Nobel people notified Gerald's agent, who got in touch with his attorney here in New York. He had Gerald's will. He wanted to be cremated and his ashes dropped into the sea. Any sea. He was an atheist so there was no religious service. I was a beneficiary and within a short time I began to receive a substantial monthly check out of the estate."

"What about your PhD? Did you continue with your research on puffins?"

This time no one snickered at the mention of puffins.

"Yes, I had been awarded my doctorate years before but had done nothing with it. After Gerald's death, I returned to the workplace. I moved to London and joined the faculty of King's College.

I'd been living in London for about six months, and out of the blue, the doorbell rang at my Bloomsbury apartment. It was Johannes Svensson. At first, he was pleasant, but after about an hour, he began to blackmail me. He demanded money. Fifty thousand dollars. I should have refused but I didn't. I asked him to give me a few days to arrange this, which I did. This became a pattern. Every six months, he flew to London to demand money. Each time, he came he demanded more. First it was fifty thousand, then seventy-five thousand, and then one hundred thousand. He became more and more unpleasant and abusive. Finally, I couldn't stand it anymore. My nerves were shattered, so I went to my bedroom to get my gun. I came back into the living room and shot him. I have no regrets. None whatsoever."

"How come you had a gun?"

"I'd had one since the day I went to the Faroe Islands. With the wildlife there, it was prudent to have one for my own protection living in an isolated place as a young single girl."

"So you had just shot him."

"A neighbor heard the shots. There were two. She called the police. I was taken off in handcuffs to the police station. I was charged with murder. I pleaded guilty."

"Why didn't you tell the court that you were being blackmailed?"

"I didn't need to. Blackmailed over what? I wasn't ready to deal with that. Anyway, it wasn't necessary. Prior to me firing the shots, he'd hit me, broken my nose and my jaw and given me a black eye. It was a clear case of self-defense. I was sentenced to twelve years imprisonment for man-slaughter. I was released after seven for good behavior."

"And then you moved to the United States. How were you able, with your criminal background as a murderess, to obtain a visa to come here, let alone settle permanently?"

"That was no problem, Mr. Larkin. I'm an American citizen. I was born in New York."

"Oh."

No one spoke for at least a minute.

"And you think that your life story, interesting as it is, merits the attention of a major author like Ms. Kelley."

"Yes, I do."

Again, silence. One of the two dour women rose from her chair to whisper something to Mr. Larkin.

"Quite. Quite," he murmured. "Tell me, Ms. Tasker, about Gerald Mustell's acceptance speech. Where is it?"

"I have it here in my purse."

"Please may I see it?"

"I will be happy to read it to you."

"Please."

She opened her purse and took it from an envelope. She began in a firm voice that displayed no emotion.

"Your Majesty, Mr. President of The Nobel Committee, distinguished ladies and gentlemen. This is a great honor, but not one that I can accept. My life has been one big fraud. Please allow me to give this short speech and then disappear into oblivion for the remainder of my years. After I graduated from college, I took a summer job with the great writer Arnold Lincoln, working as his general factotum and helping him with his research. That summer job lasted for fifteen years. He paid me well, and I enjoyed my life with him at his home in Connecticut. He died suddenly. Before I left his household, I stole seven of his completed and unpublished manuscripts that he wrote between 1910 and 1922, many years before he became famous. I knew that they were good. I moved to Hosvik and began to retype the manuscripts. I submitted them, one every few years, under my own name, and I gave them new titles. They became best-sellers. Apart from the title changes, every single word had been written by Arnold Lincoln. I am a thief and an imposter. Simple as that. Arnold left his entire estate to Princeton University. I have bequeathed my estate to Princeton too, in honor of the man who should be here today to receive this award. My only request is that a generous allowance be granted for her lifetime to my muse, Bronwyn Tasker, who knows nothing of my criminal activities and whose love for me, I know, will be forever lost as a result of this confession. Please forgive me. Good night."

"Good God," Mr. Larkin said, a look of bewilderment crossing his ashen face.

Practically in unison his colleagues echoed similar sentiments.

"Now, you will understand why I want Princeton to get one and a half million dollars. Any earnings above that are for the author."

"Now may I see the speech?"

"Yes."

Mr. Larkin rose, crossed the room, and stood behind Ms. Tasker to study the speech. "And you mentioned not being his only heir?"

She gave a wistful shrug. "Gerald was a mystery."

He walked back to the telephone and asked for someone called Candida, whom Ms. Tasker presumed was his secretary.

"Tell the chef Professor Tasker and her friends are staying for lunch. Meanwhile bring in a couple of bottles of champagne. And get Ms. Kitty Kelley on the telephone."

CHAPTER SIX

The Gap

"You must be Faversham." The man was tall, unshaven and tanned to the color of a saddle, wearing black jeans that blended into his black boots and a hat whose brim made for a comically wide sunshade. "Recognized you by what I was told. A snotty-nosed English kid, son of a fucking bishop, planted on us for a few months." The hot Auckland sun made the man's red shirt all the brighter. "God help us."

Just one week before, Tony Faversham had graduated from what many would have called England's finest boarding school for boys. Though especially respected within the British Empire for its values, academic results, and rugby stats, it was famous throughout the world. The highest ranks of the army, navy, foreign office, judiciary, colonial office, and—in particular—church were filled by former pupils.

Before graduating with honors, Tony had been captain of the cricket, rugby, and debate teams, not to mention captain of his house. In addition, he held a post tantamount to the Americans' student body president—here referred to as school captain—and he had lorded it over a student body of eight hundred. Friend and hero of the boys, he served, as well, as confidante of his teachers, the headmaster, and the school's two chaplains. Folks from the village admired him too: his good looks, his fine physique, and the way he strutted down the cobbled lanes in his black tailcoat, top hat, and bright red paisley satin waistcoat. This admiration, however, was pittance compared to the pride—the excitement—they felt when he took to the sports fields. He was, truly, the village hero.

Or had been. Now he was in New Zealand, spending the first five months of his gap year working on a sheep farm in exchange for board, lodgings, and a weekly allowance of twenty dollars. It wasn't that Tony wasn't excited about the farm—from pictures sent by the owner, Angus Whitehead, he gathered it was idyllic, and if nothing else, it was a chance to get out from under his father's thumb—but he was jet-lagged and more than a little confused by this welcome. He said nothing. He extended his hand, but the gesture was ignored.

"Yes, I'm Tony Faversham," he filled the discomforting quiet. "And you are?"

"Your boss. Greg Russell. Follow me."

Tony picked up his two bags and followed Russell, in silence, through the terminal and into a parking lot a distance away. Every couple of hundred yards, he had to put his bags on the ground for a momentary rest. Russell made no attempt to offer to carry one.

"Here's my truck. Throw your bags in the back."

Tony struggled to lift the cases enough to transfer them into the vehicle, an old rundown Toyota with dents in both sides. A spare tire had to be pushed aside to make room. Tony was still settling into the passenger's seat when Russell reversed from his parking space.

"So what's your connection with Angus Whitehead?"

"None at all, really. He's a friend of an old friend of my father's."

The friend Tony referred to was a retired clergyman in New Zealand. The wide spectrum of his father's connections had long ceased to dazzle Tony. It was believable that Reginald Faversham, an in-demand orator for speeches and sermons around the globe, would be closely connected with everyone from a sheep farmer to an attorney in Los Angeles, California, who fought First Amendment defenses in the courts. In fact, via his indirect association with the attorney, Tony would spend the second half of his gap year in L.A.

As usual, Tony fell somewhere between grateful for, and weary of, his father's influence. Reginald himself had served—as his father and his father's father—as captain of school, just like Tony. Reginald had followed up his starring role at Oxford by climbing the ladder of church leadership with impressive speed. It hadn't hurt his ascent that he'd married the daughter of a former archbishop of York and that his favorite uncle had been the dean of Westminster Abbey.

Tony understood from Russell's whole demeanor and his sparse response to Tony—nothing more than a grunt—that he would have no use for the boy's family lineage. And as put off as Tony felt by this dispatch from the Welcome Wagon, he was glad not to recount his father's many accomplishments. When being the only son of a bishop wasn't an embarrassment, it was a bore.

"How far from here is the sheep station?" Tony made sure to use the right nomenclature. He'd been advised it was *sheep station*—not *sheep farm*.

"Ninety-six miles. Be there in a couple hours. Whitehead is in France. His wife is French. I'm in charge while he's away. You ever worked on a farm?"

"How long will he be gone?"

"Few months anyway."

Tony couldn't help but scowl, wondering why Angus Whitehead's sabbatical hadn't been mentioned to him.

"No," he answered. "I haven't worked on a farm."

"Christ."

"Isn't this an odd time for Mr. Whitehead to be away?"

Russell laughed as he might have upon being asked, by a preschool child, didn't he think it was odd there were no crackers to go with the big cheese moon. Just before Tony could ask what was so funny, Russell said, "Boy, what sorta special 'time' you think this is for Whitehead to be gone? I take it you been told we need help in July, but I can tell you, kid, you must be here just 'cause somebody owed your dad a favor. Shearing season ended in April—you missed it by a mile—and lambing season don't start 'til on into October. Means you'll *just* miss out on being the slightest bit of use to us."

Tony also couldn't help but wonder why he hadn't been briefed on who would be greeting him—and moreover be his supervisor. He could've braced himself. He could've even, if necessary, reconsidered his options.

"Well, let's use this time constructively. I'm going to tell you all about what is expected of you while you're here and the arrangements for your food and board. Got it?"

Stifling a yawn, Tony summoned the courage to answer, "I've just come off a twenty-plus-hour journey and I'm feeling a bit groggy. I'll try to stay awake."

Russell, it would seem, appreciated neither the courteous wording nor the courage behind them. "Listen hard and pay attention. I don't expect I'll have to repeat anything. First, I'm your boss. Never forget that. If you ever do,

I have full authority to put you on a bus back to the airport and you can fly back to wherever you came from."

Tony resisted responding that he'd be happy to return to the airport immediately. Save them both the time and trouble.

Russell told Tony there were twelve barns total, three of which he would be responsible for. "The Finnish boys will work the other barns."

Tony nodded, curious about his coworkers but not willing to interrupt Russell to ask about them.

"Your main job is feeding, grooming, and maintaining the grounds for the ewes. Get used to it, we'll move you to working with the rams too. Whitehead prides himself on having his beasts' area spic and span, and since you're here, you can be goddamned sure you're earning your keep. That means the sun's up, you're up. Normally the sheep sleep outdoors, but the sick ones stay in stalls, and you're responsible for those too. Cleaning shit out of the stalls, putting out fresh bedding, spraying the area to keep the flies from bothering the ewes. When you've done all that, then you got to feed 'em, give 'em fresh water."

Now it was Tony's turn to grunt. It was all he could muster in response to such a barrage of information when all he wanted was to arrive at their destination and shut his eyes.

"If you do everything properly—and by Christ, you'd better or else you'll be on the next flight back to England— you'll have been working for about four hours. Time for breakfast. I'll show you your quarters when we arrive."

"Will I be living with the Finns?" Tony was hopeful that, at least, the shared hardship of his and the other farmhands would amount to some camaraderie.

But Russell informed him the Finns kept to themselves, adding, "They don't speak English and they're ugly drunks. None of 'em's sober after six o'clock. Stoners too. God knows where they get their supplies." Tony was looking for a way to ask if the boss had a problem with this—debating whether to word it *doesn't Mr. Whitehead mind* or *don't you mind?*—when Russell helped him out. "It doesn't interfere with their work, though. That's all that matters."

There was a pause in the conversation as Russell overtook a sixteen-wheeler.

"I'll work with you for your first two days. Then, I'll expect you to work on your own. The sheep will have to be fed again at four-thirty. You'll have to monitor a section of the fences and repair any breaks as soon as possible. Field work too—growing the crops needed to feed the sheep when the pasture is scarce. You'll need to be checking all the time for sick animals. Whenever you see one, first you separate it from the others and second, move your ass and notify me."

"Is there a break for lunch?"

Russell gave a snort. "Just make sure you have a big breakfast. The working day should end around seven but there's no set hours. I'll tell you later about your evening meal."

"Will I be having that with the Finns?"

"No way. Stay away from them."

"What day do I have off?"

"Day off," Russell sneered. "This is a job, kid. Not a holiday camp."

Tony did a mental calculation. A hundred-hour week at twenty dollars. Twenty cents an hour. It was akin to slave labor. *Were there no laws against this exploitation?* Still, he said nothing; but he imagined five months of this and thought, *Oh God.*

Russell turned off the highway onto a narrow two-lane road and, after a couple of miles, turned into a driveway with a wooden sign carved that read "Whitehead Sheep."

"Well this is where you'll be for the next five months unless you screw up beforehand. We generally lose around four men each year your age due to incompetence or drunkenness."

"I hear you," Tony mumbled, thinking either sounded like a fine ticket out.

"It's exactly one and a quarter miles to the main house. These pink dogwoods you see on both sides, boss's mother planted 'em. As we round this bend, you'll see in the distance the barns and stables, well out of view of the boss's house. 'Bout half a mile down on the right, there are cottages. My wife and I live in one, Finns in another, and the other permanent hands live in the big one."

"And where will I be living?"

"I'll show you your quarters in a few minutes."

"Where is the nearest village? I like to go to church on Sundays."

Russell shook his head. Tony's naïveté, it seemed, was overwhelming to him. "Ain't no village. Few miles off at the crossroads, there's a general store, a pub, gas station, post office, and the bus station."

"Is there a church anywhere nearby?"

"Look, kid. Think you're already forgetting what I said about this not being a vacation camp. That goes for Bible vacation camp too. Long as there's ewes needing tending to seven days a week, that's how many days you're working."

Even as sirens blared in his head, Tony was pleased to find his courage hadn't abandoned him entirely. "Funny that the person who got me this job is a retired clergyman, a friend of Mr. Whitehead's."

"I know nothing about that. If you want to pray, pray. On your own by your bed every night," Russell snapped. "Jesus Christ. I have a hunch you are going to turn out trouble."

"Someone drives once or twice a week to the general store. Usually my wife. Give her a list of what you need and she'll buy it for you and it'll be docked from your pay. Payday is on Fridays."

He slowed down and made a turn into a paved stable yard with an electric gate that Russell opened from a remote in the truck. A long brick building came into view, with twelve individual stable doors and eave windows that indicated an upstairs.

"We have eight horses here. The boss and his wife ride two of them. The others, the senior farmhands and I use for getting around the ranch. This is where you will be billeted. Of course you'll have some yard work to do."

Tony learned that he would share with the standoffish Finns the responsibility of mucking out the stalls, preparing the feed, cleaning and filling water containers, cleaning the tack, and reporting to Russell if any cuts or scrapes were found.

With that, Russell brought the truck to a halt. "Time to see your living quarters."

En route to the place, Tony's lack of enthusiasm had turned to dread and now took the form of extreme fatigue. As though he'd already endured months of torture at this place—as though it had already whipped and broken his spirit—he trailed behind Russell to a whitewashed door at the end of the building.

"This is the tack room. At the other end of the stables is where we keep the hay. The horses are all out now but they'll be coming back within the hour." He glanced at his watch. "The Finns and one of the other farmhands will be seeing to them."

He led the way through the tack room to, at one end, a narrow wooden staircase.

"Follow me."

The staircase shook as the two men climbed up to a large open space, a square room with a wooden floor and a low ceiling from which hung two raw lightbulbs.

"This will be your digs."

Tony looked around. A sink, a wooden table, two chairs, a microwave and an old fridge and a pine chest of drawers. There was no wardrobe; in place of one, there were plastic coat hangers on nails driven with no apparent pattern into one of the walls. A radio, unplugged, sat on the table.

"You have an electric kettle and in that cabinet over there, you'll find tea, coffee, bread, cans of soup and beans and some knives and forks. Everything you need. In the fridge, there are eggs, butter, and milk." Russell pointed out the pad and pen where Tony could write down any extravagances he wanted outside of what was provided—the items Russell's wife would go into town for and dock from Tony's pay.

"Where's the bathroom?" he asked. "And where do I sleep?"

"The bathroom is downstairs, off the tack room. And there's the mattress with a couple of blankets and a pillow."

Tony's father and mother had both gifted him a buffer of $500 each before he left, his mother advising him not to disclose her contribution to his father. Other than that, he'd been sent off with the lean luggage thought necessary for life on a farm along with a note from his father. In his abiding message to his only son, the missive meant to encapsulate his feelings and his wisdom for his son as he embarked on the adult world for the first time, the bishop had written that Tony was to behave—antics on his part would reflect poorly on the bishop—and that he was to be useful. And he was, of course, to attend church on Sundays. Tony had read it on the twenty-eight-hour flight, over and over, until his eyes felt gritty as sandpaper. If he couldn't stick it out these five months, he knew his father would be livid.

"Well, it's six o'clock. I'll see you in the tack room tomorrow morning at five. And wear your proper work clothes and boots. If you brought some, that is."

Over the next five months, as opposed to developing any sense of kinship with the animals, he came to view them as aggressors—enemies. He was once kicked in the stomach by a horse while raking out its stall and twice bitten by sheepdogs. The swollen clouds released a cold rain almost daily.

While he saw the Finns on a daily basis, they didn't get beyond nodding. The other farmhands had their own cliques and, like the Finns, kept their distance. The only people with whom he had daily contact were Russell and his equally loathsome wife. If he'd expected any compliments for work satisfactorily performed, he would have been disappointed; there were, instead, insults and abuse.

Twice a week, Mrs. Russell left a shopping cart containing his provisions at the foot of the staircase in the stables. These never varied: a loaf, butter, eggs, canned beans, sardines and tuna, cheese, tea bags, and, not surprisingly, some lamb chops. When he needed toilet tissue, toiletries, or candy bars and cookies, he'd write down his list and she would collect that later in the day.

She would deliver these items to him with the next drop off of provisions and at the end of the week, on payday, Russell would hand him an envelope containing in cash his wages for the week, with the cost of the items listed and deducted together with a deduction of a three-dollar service fee for shopping. When he needed to use the washing machine and dryer in the tack room, he was obliged to feed it coins. Washing powder too had to be purchased with coins from a vending machine on the wall.

After three weeks of not leaving the ranch, he asked Russell if he could take a few hours to visit the village.

"No one's going today. You'd have to walk."

An old motto from his school occurred to him. "The severe thing is the true joy." *Like hell it is,* he thought.

While feeding the sheep one morning, Russell approached him. "Mr. and Mrs. Whitehead came back last night. If you see a well-dressed couple in their fifties around the place, look smart and introduce yourself. Chances are you'll see them when they come to exercise the horses. And"—he dug deep into a pocket of his jeans—"a letter came for you yesterday."

Tony recognized his mother's handwriting on the envelope.

"You can read it later on your own time, not during work hours. And, if you reply to it, just leave it with the list of what you need and my wife will take it to the post office on her next trip into the village. A stop at the post office will incur an extra two-dollar service fee, plus postage, of course."

That night, and after making himself some fried eggs and a cup of tea, he read his mother's letter. She wrote to tell him how much she missed him but how happy she and his father were to know that he would be having a wonderful time in New Zealand and that she hoped he had an opportunity to do plenty of sightseeing as she understood that New Zealand was a beautiful country.

He couldn't bear to read any more. Lying back on his mattress, he considered how to respond. Should he write back and tell them the truth or should he whitewash the whole ordeal? And, if he did write the truth, who knows whether Mrs. Russell, the bitch, would open the envelope, surely triggering her bastard of a husband to make his day even more of a living hell.

Tony had brought just one book from England. Churchill's speeches. He was now reading it for the third time. He couldn't trust Mrs. Russell to bring back from the village a book that was worth reading, that was assuming there was any reading material to be found at the general shop—he hadn't seen so much as a newsstand in the place. In the five months he had the displeasure of working for Mr. Russell, Tony must have read some of Churchill's speeches in full twenty times. The radio that had sparked some hope in him upon his arrival proved to be broken, and Russell had responded succinctly to Tony's request that it be fixed: "What the fuck do you want me to do about it?"

Russell's one redeeming quality had seemed his utility around the farm, and even that was apparently extremely limited. He couldn't fix electronics and wouldn't see to it that someone else did.

Frequently throughout the months, he'd hoped for some company from the Finns. He started making a game of trying to break through to them—he'd go crazy with no more variety of subjects to think about than how much of

Churchill's speeches he had memorized and how much he'd grown to detest sheep. He tried variations on their standard brief nod of a greeting. One day he would nod upward and with a slight smile, but they would respond in the way they always had.

One day he would pass one of them while he mucked out stalls, and would offer an enthusiastic half-wave. The Finn would respond as all of them always did, with a nod.

One day he would see another of them as he shouldered an enormous bag of feed; not having his hands available for waving, he instead would say, in the most cheerful voice he could muster without sounding foolish, "Good morning!" And the Finn would nod, as all of them always did.

If he were being truthful with himself, it wasn't just a matter of trying to break up the monotony. Part of him had hoped his overtures would initiate a friendship between them, and that these substances he'd heard they had access to would be shared. It was true, the extent of Tony's forays into anything capable of altering his alertness had been a couple of beers he sipped slowly the day he'd graduated. He had enjoyed two in as many hours as he waited on his father to finish up a meeting with the board of trustees so they could leave the place, so that his future could begin in earnest. Mostly, he'd drunk them to celebrate the fact that he could openly do so now that he was of age—but he'd found that even two beers made a pleasant haze descend over the worries that had been brewing in his gut.

He remembered—as he sat alone on his bed, wondering what sort of merriment the Finns were up to at that very moment—how nervous he had been that afternoon at school. Excited, certainly, but also fearful of what it would mean to leave school, where mastery of his tasks and the social scene had come so easily to him. He supposed he knew now: what came next was eating budget beans and drinking milk while sitting on a threadbare mattress at the end of a day of working, in isolation, in the cold weather that was always as damp as spit, for twenty cents an hour—minus expenses. While somewhere on the same farm, the only people who could've potentially alleviate his loneliness and nerves wouldn't go beyond simply returning his nod.

But at least the end of this long terrible adventure was in sight. As the date drew nearer, Tony grew more and more like a weary traveler who could finally see the lights of his own home sparkling, albeit blearily, in the distance. He didn't know what the second half of his gap year would bring, and part of him warned the rest of him not to get excited—what if it was *worse*? But Tony allowed himself to dream. His fantasies—of driving to get whatever he wanted himself, of eating food that didn't come from a can, of sleeping on a mattress with springs rather than knotty floorboards underneath it—gave Tony a revived lease on hope.

Until the day of feeding the dogs.

Tony had fed them what felt like a million times before, more than once limping away from the overeager beasts, but he'd fed them in the normal way, out of bags and cans, the same way he ate these days. Perhaps Tony had allowed himself to look too optimistic; at least that's what he reasoned afterward. He'd betrayed some emotion that wasn't abject misery, and that tyrant, that bully, that prison warden Russell had decided to squash it immediately.

Tony had just finished a routine part of his job; he ferried a sheep with an injured, perhaps broken, leg over to

Russell. He'd then turned to go—he was never invited to watch the veterinary measures that brought the farm's prize animals back to health—but he was stopped. Russell handed him a knife.

Not since his father had informed him sheep farming would be on the agenda for his gap year had Tony felt at such a loss. Was he to arm himself? Was trouble from the Finns or some rival sheep lords anticipated? Even as Russell traced his finger across his own throat and nodded to the sheep, the truth was slow to dawn on Tony. When it did, he felt queasy. He felt a cold sweat cover him.

"You can't expect me to—"

"Can and damned well do. Any reason you're too good to do the parts of your job that ain't pretty?"

"I, I don't under—"

"Only thing for 'you, you'"—Russell imitated Tony's stutter in a dreadful high pitch—"is this ewe's no good to us like it is, be stupid to let it go to waste, and it's your job to take care of it."

Tony could barely get the words out. At first, he thought he said them only in his head. "Couldn't somebody else . . . "

His boss crowed. "You think the others don't do this? Listen, Bishop Boy, the Finns kill the sheep when we ask 'em and don't say nothing about it. Certainly don't go through all this fuss like you. Now it's your job." Russell's face drained of all merriment. "Do it."

Perhaps if he hadn't been so close to the end, Tony would've fought it harder, telling Russell to whistle for his ghastly wife so she could take him back to the bus stop and he could get the hell out of here. But he was so close, and now he had the feeling it's why Russell was having him to do this. To try to break him when he was nearly at the finish line.

The sound of him swallowing down his own spit seemed to echo off the rafters. He'd just positioned himself near the sheep and tightened his grip on the knife, now slippery with sweat, when Russell said, "When you're done slitting its throat, you'll slit the whole thing open. Then you'll skin it."

It was a haze. A haze of blood-curdling bleats followed by blood itself, everywhere. On his hands, his wrists, the shoes his father had insisted he buy and pack for this work, this man's work, blood seeping into the floor, dying the sheep's wool the color of brick. Through the rest of it, his hands shook as though his whole body were being pounded by the wind. The moment he had finished, he watched the knife slip from his hands. He promptly vomited then fainted.

When Tony came to, he was given his next job—to feed the dogs.

He went through it numbly. For the remainder of the day he felt nothing, not even when the Finns broke their long code of silence and demonstrated their grasp on English vernacular all at once, yelling at him from a truck rumbling by, "Pussy!" One miming his retching, another his fainting. Word certainly traveled fast.

Tony didn't bother changing out of his gore-soaked clothes. It made him a target, even more than usual, for the dogs, but he didn't care. He didn't care enough to change them when he climbed up to his room and sat calmly on his mattress.

On the day he was to leave, Russell said that he, rather than his wife, would be driving Tony into Auckland. After inspecting his room, and sighing in apparent disappointment that Tony had tidied it up well enough that he wouldn't be able to deduct a clean-up fee, he handed Tony an envelope containing a reference letter and his final week's pay. It was five dollars—fifteen had been docked for the ride Russell was providing.

Along with that, he handed over the boy's last piece of mail: a letter from his mother, expressing her disappointment in his lack of communication and reminding him to thank Mr. Whitehead for the useful experience he'd gained on the job.

On the twelve-hour flight to Los Angeles, Tony enjoyed his first lengthy conversation in five months. His neighbor in the next seat was an American backpacker returning home after vacationing in New Zealand. Tony listened to the man's account of all the places he visited in both islands and the fascinating days he spent in a Maori village. Tony was too relieved to be leaving the damned sheep ranch and too excited about the next five months to be envious.

The plane landed on Friday at ten-thirty in the morning, and by one o'clock, he had checked into his hotel in Santa Monica. His view of the ocean was like a portal into heaven itself. After months of having adjusted his eyes to the cardboard-colored view in his meager room at the sheep station, he could've stared at the ocean for hours. Hell, watching the sunlight reflecting off dimples in the water and dancing around his room would've been entertainment enough. When he'd gazed at the ocean long enough to feel certain it wasn't going to suddenly vanish—some cruel mirage dreamed up by a mind that had been defeated by the drudgery of sheep farming—he fell backward onto the mattress. He wasn't sure whether the place he'd just left was hell or simply purgatory, but he knew he'd made it to a more celestial kingdom now.

Finally, after unpacking, he found the telephone number of the attorney to whom he was due to report after the weekend.

"Welcome to California, Tony." The man's voice was as warm as the weather.

"Thank you, sir. I'm looking forward to meeting you."

"The first rule is that you don't call me 'sir.' I'm Dick. And hey"—Tony could hear the laughter burbling in the man's voice—"some say I *am* a real dick."

Tony laughed. Dick Bradshaw had probably used that line a million times, and a million times it had broken the ice.

"Why don't you relax over the weekend and come to my office in Century City on Monday morning. I'm clearing up a few things there as I'm now installed in my new place in Palm Springs. Come around eleven. And bring your bags with you. We'll drive down to the desert—I have a place for you near my new office. I have a car ready for you too."

It crossed Tony's mind that Dick Bradshaw was his reward for surviving Mr. Russell. He'd have dwelled on the severe contrasts between the men longer, but there was no room for thoughts of Russell in this place. He had his father's credit card, which he hadn't used once since leaving England, and now he had room service to order.

After breakfast and a much-needed haircut the next morning, and given that he hadn't had one since the start of his travels, he took a long walk on the beach. At that moment, he could imagine no wealth greater than the feeling of the sunlight on his face. He smiled at everyone he passed—the surfers, joggers, cyclists, sunbathers—and they smiled back. Many waved. Some even gave him a carefree, "Hey, howya doin'?" Along with the horror of Mr. Russell, the unresponsive Finns faded away.

He strolled the boutiques on Third Street Promenade, where a flirtatious sales girl easily sold him two pairs of designer jeans, a couple of sports shirts and a pair of sneakers. He looked in the mirror in the fitting room. He was pleased. He looked the real McCoy . . . a California native.

After breakfast on Monday, he dressed in one of his two formal suits, white shirt, and navy polka dot tie, and hailed a cab to Century City to meet his new boss.

He took the elevator to Dick Bradshaw's office on the seventeenth floor. He stood to marvel at the view of the ocean and the blue cloudless sky. A tall man—athletic build, tanned with jet-black hair—approached him, pausing only to have a quick word with the receptionist. Tony guessed, moreover hoped, that this was his new boss. White jeans and shoes, tie-less black shirt, with a long heavy gold chain and crucifix dangling from his neck. The sight of the crucifix was a jolt. A reminder, though not a particularly favorable one, of Bishop Reginald, his father who had arranged his five-month nightmare in New Zealand. He was determined to compensate for that by the only way he knew that would piss him off . . . the frequent use of the credit card intended only for emergencies.

"I'm Dick. You must be Tony. Welcome."

"Come to my office and relax. Bring your case." The man had a wide grin. "Look at you. Look like you're going to a funeral. I hope you've got some casual clothes in that case of yours."

Tony followed him to his office along a long corridor with floor-to-ceiling windows that offered the same ocean view.

"I share these offices with some other attorneys. Or *did*, I should say. Today's the last day. Already got my new digs set up in Palm Springs. In fact, soon as I wrap up a couple things, we can go. Why don't you get out of that suit and be more comfortable. It's a hundred and one in Palm Springs—dress accordingly."

Tony could hardly contain his excitement seeing, parked in a reserved spot near the elevator, the bright red Ferrari. "This is *some* car."

When Dick accelerated on the freeway, both men smiled at the roar of the engine.

"I'm very excited about the prospect of working for you, Dick. Thank you again for the opportunity. Since it's your specialty, I've been reading up on First Amendment work."

"And what have you learned, specifically?"

Tony recited perfunctory facts—some of the landmark challenges to the First Amendment, its biggest wins and losses. Dick had a way of smiling where half his mouth put in all the effort and the other half relaxed. It was a smile that said, "Everything's going to be all right" and was comforting even when you weren't aware of needing that reassurance.

Feeling slightly more relaxed now, Tony asked his own question. "Why did you move your office from Los Angeles to Palm Springs?"

"I have some clients in the desert, mostly in Studio City, and it's often easier to get to them from there than from Century City. Plus, I'm a member of a tennis club in Palm Springs, play there several times a week." To Tony, those reasons sounded like plenty already, but Dick wasn't through. "I already have a home there. Small group of friends. One or two girlfriends." He looked meaningfully at Tony as he mentioned this final benefit.

"Those sound like good reasons."

"Now, I own a house close to my office. Five-minute drive, tops. There's a spare room and bathroom there. You can live there. It's a large house with a pool and a Jacuzzi and you'll meet some fun people who'll make sure you are well-looked after. *Very* well-looked after, I must add. I'll take you there to introduce you to your flat mates later."

"That's very kind. Thank you."

"I have a car for you. You'll enjoy using it. It's a Mustang. Just try to keep within the speed limit as the cops will sure as hell ticket you if you go over the limit."

Tony grinned again.

"Here wear these." Dick opened the glove compartment and took out an extra pair of sun glasses. He turned on a classical CD and kept one eye on the rear view mirror to watch for the California Highway Patrol—the infamous "CHP." "The bastards have ticketed me for speeding on this stretch of the freeway twice in the last twelve months."

After close to an hour and a half they pulled into Palm Canyon Drive, Palm Springs' main shopping street. Scantily dressed tourists filled the sidewalks, pausing at a plethora of T-shirt and souvenir shops. Once off of the main drag, Dick made a sharp turn into a large parking lot.

"The restaurant over there—the Oaks—is where I lunch most days. My office is in that building." He pointed to a two-story building at the far end of the lot. It was built in Mediterranean style, with columns, balconies, and smart boutiques on the first floor and offices above.

Dick parked the car behind the building and led the way up a flight of tiled steps toward his office.

"So this is it. Take a look around, and let me introduce you to Jill, my assistant. Jill, meet Tony. He's going to be with us for a few months."

Jill was in her mid-twenties, and exquisitely tanned with long blonde hair. She wore cut-off jeans and a white unbuttoned shirt, exposing her assertive breasts and bare midriff. She gave Tony a smile and held out her hand.

Wow, Tony thought. *This is how an attorney's secretary dresses?*

"Sit down, Tony. Jill, give him a beer and I'll take him over to the house in a while to introduce him to the girls. Give him the keys to the Mustang and tell him where it's parked."

An hour later, Tony pulled up in the Mustang directly behind Dick in front of a house hidden from the road by a tall wall covered in pink bougainvillea and white oleander. A heavy antique door opened into a paved, Mexican tile courtyard and a circular swimming pool.

"Hello ladies," Dick shouted across the courtyard. Two women were in the pool and another two, naked, were spread out on inflatable mattresses. "Come and meet Tony."

The four women giggled as they approached Tony. "Do we have to get dressed?" one asked.

Tony could barely hide his embarrassment.

"Shouldn't you be working?"

"No, Dick, it's only four o'clock. We're on at five o'clock today."

"We haven't had lunch yet. Order in pizza for us and one of you show Tony to his room. By the way," Dick continued. "Where's . . . ?"

"Up in her room." The brunette who answered pretended to pout. "She outswam all of us and now she's showering for work."

As they walked away, Tony could hardly keep his voice deeper than a whisper. "Is this where I'll be living, Dick? Really?"

"You bet. Go easy when you write to your father. I'm sure he wouldn't be too thrilled."

"You're not kidding."

One of the bathers approached Tony. She wrapped a towel around her waist and smiled. "Come on, Tony, let me show you to your room."

He followed her into the house. She pointed out the kitchen and the living room and toward the back and to a downstairs bedroom. "This is your room. We're upstairs... but if you ever feel like some company, don't be a stranger." She giggled. "We'll give you a real California welcome. Dick told us to take good care of you."

He smiled but was unable to conceal his embarrassment. He had been at all-boys schools all his life and had no experience of socializing with women, let alone naked ones.

She left him at the threshold of the door to his room and with one hand stroked his face and with her other, his leg. She leaned forward and he breathed in the fragrance of her suntan oil. She kissed him on the cheek and giggled as she walked off to rejoin her friends outside in the courtyard.

Tony entered the room. A large room, all white, a Mexican tile floor, white painted walls with two large movie posters, *La Dolce Vita* and *Deep Throat*, and French doors that led into a small cactus garden with a wrought iron table and chairs. Apart from the king-size bed, there was an armchair, a television, and a small desk and chair. One door led into the bathroom and another to a closet.

By the time the pizza arrived, everyone had left for "work." Tony could only speculate as to what that meant.

"Okay, young man," Dick said to him as they dived into the pizza. "Now this is the story. My specialty is First Amendment. But not the highfalutin elegant stuff that you've been reading up. In a nutshell, my clients are based in Studio City and they are producers of adult movies. Porn, in other words."

Tony tried, unsuccessfully, to keep himself from gasping.

"I represent them in all their contracts with directors, cameramen, actors, deals with distributors and so on. I'm their go-to attorney for all legal work."

"And the First Amendment comes in . . . ?"

"It also covers freedom of expression. Obscenity is something else. Obscenity is the issue. When a porn movie crosses the line into obscenity, a state may forbid its distribution within that state. What is or isn't obscenity varies from state to state. Each has its own criteria. If a state goes against one of my clients for distributing a hard-core movie, I am usually called in to appeal that decision. That type of work is my bread and butter, and it takes me to Texas, Arizona, Virginia, Florida, and Georgia."

Tony wanted to know what counted as obscenity in, say, Texas.

"I'll give you some DVDs to look at. On the boxes, I've made notations like 'okay for Texas but not Virginia.' You'll get the hang of it. Try not to watch them with the girls here." Dick laughed. "You'll get too turned on."

"And I get paid for this. For watching dirty movies?"

"That's just one part of your job."

"And the other?"

"I own a strip club close by. It's open from twelve noon every day until two in the morning. That means two shifts, each of seven hours. For each shift I have a manager, a bouncer, bartender, a server, and stage manager who works the music, lighting, and the curtain. Then there are the performers."

"The . . . women . . . is that where they work?"

"Yes. Today we are opening at five because we are having work done on the air conditioning.

"So what will I be doing?"

"Managing the women. You are to be in charge of this house. There are five bedrooms. You have just seen yours, of course, and they each have their own."

"So what am I to do exactly?"

"You are to visit the club at odd times during the day to keep an eye on everything. You're to take the cash every day and deposit it at the bank. And see that everyone is paid. And—this is important—the women are not allowed to bring any men back to this house. The last thing I want is to be prosecuted for operating a brothel. They all understand that, but once in a while there's been trouble and I've had to pay off a few people in the police department. No men ever in this house apart from you, me, and a workman should we need to call one in. Understand?" Dick's normally buoyant voice had gone firm.

"Got it."

"Now as for you . . . If ever you want to enjoy yourself with any of them, go for it. I do. But no money is ever to change hands. Ever."

"Of course."

"I suggest you spend the afternoon relaxing, unpack, watch some of the DVDs I've given you and I'll come by to take you to the club later."

It didn't take Tony more than three days to fully adjust to his routine; it wasn't a hard gig, and he was no fool. And as grateful as he was—no, grateful wasn't even the word—as stunned, as overwhelmed and appreciative and ecstatic as he was—he couldn't shake the feeling that he was walking through a museum, viewing displays from pivotal moments in time but in no sense a part of them. Forbidden, by what he couldn't say, from touching anything.

The first time he'd entered the strip club, he wasn't just a kid in the candy store. He was that kid except every piece of candy is unwrapped, every jelly bean dispenser is open and the sugar's flowing freely. It was too much. All the women flirted with him: they touched him, ran their fingers through his hair, tugged at the hem of his shirt, and let him know in no uncertain terms that if he was interested, they were available later, back at the house. Or at least he thought it was all of them. When the crowd of them finally dispersed, he noted someone standing back from the others, watching him. They were all wrapping up their shifts for the night and the customers had been cleared out, so she had to be one of the dancers. Under a mop of straw-colored curls, she watched with thoughtful eyes and a Mona Lisa smile.

On his third day, he stood slightly off from the stage, waiting for the manager who would hand off that night's deposit to him—and he stared down at his feet—when he noticed a pair of high heels join his sneakers.

It was the someone who'd eyed him while the others had fawned over him and pawed him, treated him like a morsel that doesn't mind being tasted. He couldn't help but stare at her. Which wasn't saying much—he couldn't help but stare at all of them, but with her, it wasn't simply that she was a beautiful woman flashing more flesh that he'd ever seen outside of fantasy; it was that she intrigued him.

As he waited for the deposits and generally "kept an eye on things," he felt her eyes on him, and he wondered what opinion of him she was forming behind that patient, pensive gaze.

Now here she was, close enough he could breathe in the scent—oranges and orchids—that clung to her. He swallowed, remembering, with an unpleasant jolt, the last time he'd felt so nervous. It had been before he slaughtered the ewe that was to become dog food.

"Are we that scary?" Her voice was a husky whisper.

"What? No . . . I'm . . . "

"Scared." Her eyebrows gently leaped as she shrugged; it was a gesture that set him at ease, though he couldn't have explained why. "You're scared and it's okay. Lot to take in, huh?"

"It's, it's, it's—"

"Relax." When she placed a hand on his shoulder, a peaceful warmth penetrated him to his very spine. Enabling him to stand up straight. To look her in the eye.

"I'll try."

She laughed. "You'll get the hang of it. And once you do, don't forget to take advantage of the perks o' the job. I'm sure you know the girls would be happy to have a little, uh, playtime with you."

What he was hearing was the fulfillment of wishes he hadn't dared consciously wish for, yet something in him made him concentrate on the one part that wasn't cause for celebration.

"The . . . wait . . . " He knew she understood that he was truly asking—"Not you?"

Before she left—to get prepared for her set, stripping before strangers—she ran a finger over his cheek. "Somebody's got to have the heart of gold in this set, right?"

With a wink, she was gone.

A full week later, Dick was still finding it necessary to tell Tony to dress casually for god's sake—this was Palm Springs. He always said it good-naturedly, and Tony always obliged. Even he couldn't understand why he kept reverting to his stodgy way of dress, nor why he so often felt not simply breathless but as though he were choking, as though there wasn't enough air for breathing with all the beautiful women in the house, with all the people wearing bright coral and turquoise and looking for a good time in gorgeous Palm Springs.

They were standing in Dick's kitchen, all the white tile sparkling under the sun streaming in through the skylight, when Tony made his report: "I've watched the videos you gave me. I think I'm starting to get the hang of it. What Texas deems obscene versus what, say, Georgia deems obscene."

Dick laughed as he poured himself a tall glass of orange juice. The sun made it appear . . . fiery. *Everything* was brightened or in some way heightened in this ever-present sunlight. As though it were an afterthought, Dick added a splash of tequila. "Tony, you sound like you're giving a book report."

"Is that a bad thing?"

He laughed again. Answering required, apparently, a long pull of the spiked juice. "Nah. Means you take your work seriously. Take yourself seriously. It would make you a good lawyer."

"You think I could be one?" He stopped himself from adding "Like you?"—it would make him sound like a little boy looking up to an action hero, though it would be an accurate representation of how he felt. He also stopped himself, as he did all the time, from adding "sir." Dick was not the sort of man who wanted to be called sir, at least outside the courtroom.

"Are you kidding? I learned all about you before I agreed to this little internship sorta deal. I know you've got the brains. But that's the easy part—half the world's got the brains. They just don't have what you really need."

Tony squinted. He felt as though he were being asked to work an equation with a deceptively difficult answer. "The heart?" he finally offered.

With a shrug, Dick downed the last of his juice. Either Tony's stab at an answer or that last tequila-soaked sip at the bottom had brought a smile to his face. "That too I suppose," he answered. "But the real thing is the grit. See, when we fight for the First Amendment, we're not up against feeble little mom-and-pop joints that are going after somebody who lifted five hundred bucks from the cash register. We're up against people who think whatever our clients are saying or whatever they're doing—however they're *expressing themselves*—is a threat."

"A threat to their way of life?"

"Exactly. And a threat to decency itself. When they come at us, they believe they're fighting the good fight and we represent the devil. People like that, they're gonna come at you with everything they've got—all their money, all their time, all their legal resources. It ain't always pretty." Dick glanced back at the refrigerator, likely considering pouring himself one more before it was time to start the day, but apparently deciding against it. "Sometimes we lose. Sometimes we get shit on and mocked, and sometimes crowds are outside the courtroom clapping when we do lose. And if you're ever going to make it in this sort of law, you have to be able to take it and keep on going."

Tony could only nod. He could feel something he wanted to say welling up inside him. Something about how he'd spent the first half of this mercurial gap year, but Dick interrupted his thought process.

"Tell you what, Tone. I think you need a night off."

Tony shook his head fervently, not wanting Dick to believe for a minute he wasn't up to the challenges of this line of work. Besides—who would need a night off from *this*?

"Relax, relax, relax," Dick said, echoing the dancer, the one who stripped and lived in this mansion with him but whose name he still hadn't learned. "You're doing fine, trust me. But for tonight, forget you have work. Just go be a kid. And hey, if you're trying to emulate me, keep in mind—I act like a kid every chance I get."

That night, with the veritable hedonistic delights of Palm Springs open to him, plenty of cash in his wallet, and a Mustang at his disposal, Tony went to the same place he now spent much of his working days. The strip club. On his way in, Alicia, Melody, and Francine waved and blew kisses, probably all assuming this was just another work day for him.

He had to look around hard—he was noticing for the first time how truly dark the club was—but soon enough he found her. She stood toward the entrance to the girls' dressing room, lassoing her mountainous curly hair into a ponytail. She looked up at him. "Hey, kiddo."

"What's your name?"

If she was taken aback by his question, or the boldness behind it, she didn't indicate. She only gave him a half smile. "Cheyenne. Like the city. What's yours?"

"Tony. Like the tiger."

When she burst out laughing, the tension Tony had felt in his shoulders, perhaps since weeks before he graduated, began to melt away.

"Well, Tiger, why the sudden change in confidence? Since when do you go up and ask strange women their names?"

"Since I've got a night off work."

She pulled one twisting tendril of hair from her ponytail, winding it and winding it around her finger. "You mean to tell me you're not here on official business?"

"I'm here because Dick thinks I need to have more fun. I think it's because the job is so demanding, and can be discouraging, and since that's the case you need to take every chance you get to have—"

"Sh-sh-sh." When she placed her finger on his lips, her skin felt like a rose petal. "So Dick thinks you need to have more fun . . . What do *you* think?" When he couldn't answer—and suddenly could no longer look her in the eyes, the adrenaline that had gotten him this far having plummeted—she helped him out. "Go 'head and ask me."

"Do you do private dances?"

"As a matter of fact, I do."

"Could I . . ."

He didn't have to finish his question, a fact he was most grateful for, as he had no idea what words would've come out of him. The room for private dances was draped in gauzy plum-colored fabric. The half-moon-shaped bench had a thick pillowtop and was velvety to the touch. When he was stationed in place, he observed, or at least thought he did, her first moment of shyness. He took it to mean it was his turn to help her.

"So, how do you usually get started?"

It worked: the amused, knowing smile returned to her face.

"Well, I usually start by telling the guy my name."

"So that's all I had to do to find out? Buy a dance?"

"All you had to do was ask." She made a face at him. "But it's not quite that easy. I never give them my *real* name."

Already his heart was thudding like the wings of a caged butterfly. "Well, don't give me special treatment. Who are you, miss?"

"Cherry." She slid her hand into his for a shake but stagnated, her hand momentarily just holding his, as she sidled up to him so her legs were on either side of his. When she let go, it was all at once, as though she'd just remembered herself. She batted her doe-like eyes. "And who would you be, big fella?"

Naturally, he had nothing planned; he simply went where the moment took him. In his best Montana-ranch-hand voice, he answered, "Just a lonely sheep farmer, miss."

"What *fascinating* work."

The tracks had just changed, and there was no denying this one had the perfect tempo for Cheyenne's variety of dancing. He watched with bated breath as she started to gyrate, from her fluid hips up to her neck and down to her braceleted ankles.

"It's not really." Already he was fumbling with the accent, struggling to keep his character intact. But he felt he needed to keep the spoof going for a bit longer; it was putting them both at ease, and he wasn't here simply because he wanted to be closer to her flesh. Certainly there was a thrill in that alone. He wanted her to come away from tonight wanting him. After months of enduring experiences no man should have to, he was ready for at least one experience the world regarded as integral to being a man. So far, he had felt paralyzed by the dazzling sea of possibility around him—it didn't matter which door you picked because pleasure was behind every one—but he was taking his boss's words to heart. Moreover, he was extracting the true message from what Dick hadn't said but had surely intended to convey: there was a time to be dead serious, and then there was a time to . . . not be.

"It's the most lonely, boring, horrifying work in the world," he mumbled, as his eyes feasted.

"Horrifying, honey?" She was keeping her "character voice" as well—she was still Cherry the stripper. "Now how could it be horrifying working with precious little sheep all day?"

As she moved her hips toward him and away, toward him and away, he felt the bottom of her thighs brush the top of his, gently at first and then with more pressure. Now he almost wanted to drop the character bit altogether, but his mind was a jumble. He'd been asked a question, and before he could stop himself, he was answering: "Sometimes you gotta put one of 'em down. Sometimes their blood gets all over you."

At first, she appeared angry. She stopped moving immediately, stepped back from him as far as she could without bumping into the enormous cushioned ottoman behind her. They'd been playing a game, and he'd taken it down this needlessly brutal route. Then, perhaps observing the faint line of red around his irises, how heavily he was blinking back some emotion, she softened. "Tiger? What's wrong?"

While she didn't resume her dancing, she did sit down beside him. He tried not to look at her, but the fruit-and-flower scent of her combined with her warmth made too magnetic a presence. "I'm sorry," he whispered.

"Don't be," she whispered back. "Is this real, Tiger? You, working on a sheep farm?"

And with that, he told her. He handed over enough money for five back-to-back private dances in this room that felt like the inside of a genie bottle, and Tony told Cheyenne all about his time in Auckland, how he'd worked for pittance, how he'd felt lonely and sometimes afraid, how the closest thing to company had been the Finns who called him a pussy after hearing he couldn't slaughter a ewe without vomiting.

When he was done, she gently stroked his forehead. "So you always heard these Finns had the good stuff, but the assholes wouldn't share, huh?"

He laughed, grateful to her for picking up one of the lighter threads in the horror he had just shared. Then he nodded.

"Well, Tiger, there's not much I can do to help you erase that awfulness, but maybe I can show you what you were missing."

She meant pot—the thing that had helped keep the Finns sane in New Zealand—which she rolled into a joint for him, lit for him, popped into his pursed lips, and instructed him how to smoke. If he hadn't already been falling in love with her, he was sure that seeing her beautiful face through a cloud of sweet-smelling marijuana smoke would have done it. And later, back at home, she showed him everything else he'd been missing.

Afterward, as she lay in his arms, he either wasn't able or wasn't willing to keep his hands off her naked shoulders, back, thighs, stomach. The scant amount of her that had been hidden behind the strip club's uniform was as breathtaking as he had imagined.

Rolling onto her back to gaze at the ceiling, Cheyenne said, "I think Dick was right. You needed to have a little fun."

You got that right, Tony thought. "You think he was right about the other thing he said too? About how I'd make a good lawyer?"

Now she turned her head to look at him. "God, yes. And I'm not just saying that because you paid me $100 to not dance for you." They both laughed, and then she continued. "But I'm serious, Tiger. You know what makes Dick such a great lawyer?"

"He's a great legal mind."

"Yeah, yeah. And I'm sure you've already heard his spiel about how half the world's got the brains, yadda yadda. He is smart, but the real thing is that he really cares about what he's doing. This First Amendment stuff—he can joke around about it, but in the court room, he acts like he's fighting for his life. And the life of everybody who's in the industry."

He kissed her right shoulder, currently finding it much easier to see the good side of "the industry" himself.

"Well, I'm glad you have someone like him to fight for you." It was Tony's turn to look at the ceiling—the vaulted ceiling that appeared to be inlaid with gold—as though he were searching it for an answer. "I wish I'd had someone like him in New Zealand." His eyes returned to her. "That's what I kept thinking the whole time I was there: it can't be legal to treat people this way, to treat them like slaves."

The look on her face was even more contemplative than usual, her mouth pulled into a delicate bow of a smile. "You know," she said, "maybe you could be that lawyer for somebody else. Stick it out here, learn from the best. Go out into the world and fight hard for the little guy." As she wrapped her arms around him, she kissed his ear and then went lower. Down to his neck. His shoulder. His chest. "And along the way, maybe relax and live a little."

CHAPTER SEVEN

Flowers by Raffi

Y ou would think he'd been born into the flower business. For twenty-seven years, he'd unlocked the Madison Avenue floral shop at five-thirty every morning. It was perfect timing: it gave him fifteen minutes before his assistant pulled the van up to unload cases bought that morning from the flower market. If he got started any later, Justin would never find such a prime parking space.

The weeks between Thanksgiving and New Year's Eve were always hectic with deliveries all day. His three-man team of floral arrangers would arrive by eight; Lydia, his deputy manager, would start taking telephone orders at the same time while he attended to the stream of customers that flowed steadily once the shop opened at eight-thirty. Perry inventoried the boxes as Justin wheeled them into the back of the store.

At sixty, Perry still had no problem with the brutal hour of his morning routine. It was everything else that was getting to him. The routine itself. The daily pressures. The demands and histrionics of his Upper East Side clientele.

After all, he wasn't a *born* florist. He'd had a successful career as a window dresser for one of the major department stores before he met Rafael, proprietor of Flowers by Raffi. Before Perry had become a florist, he and Rafael were a couple. After a quarter century of running the shop together, the only thing left of Rafael was his nickname incorporated in the store's name.

When the van was finally unloaded, Perry locked the door once more and then picked up the previous day's mail, which he had left untouched on the counter the night before. He stepped into the room at the back to turn on the coffee. He'd received a postcard from friends in Portofino, in Genoa.

Rafael had introduced him to Portofino shortly after they met, and the pair visited every year until Rafael became too ill to travel. While their official purpose was visiting friends, they mostly enjoyed strolling through the fishing village—the living, breathing representation of the postcard he'd received. For two men who spent their daily lives taming naturally beautiful flora so their clients could display arrangements that would dazzle their friends, there was something that felt pure—more honest, in a sense—about the artistic side of this harbor commune. While its prominent natural resource, the Italian Riviera, was breathtaking, it was the manmade art that stood out most of all. The brilliant buildings that flanked the water, the canvas art spawned by the many prestigious or outright famous people who journeyed to Portofino for the explicit purpose of being inspired, nudged to create something new. It's exactly what Perry wanted now: inspiration.

How many times had he dreamed of selling the business and his attached apartment and moving there? First with Raffi, but even in his absence; in fact, the dream had grown stronger since he'd been gone.

Besides the postcard, three letters awaited his attention. The first envelope bore the return address of the landlord's disagreeable attorney. *Now what?* He ripped open the seal.

The letter reminded him that his lease came to an end on March 31, and that as of April 1, his rent would be . . .

Perry gulped.

The rent is going up from $25,000 per month to $50,000.

He put the letter back in the envelope. How could they do this? Doubling the rent was unconscionable. He would have to double his prices—and he'd lose every customer he had. He'd gone through a similar increase before—$12,500 to $25,000—and all attempts to negotiate had proven not only futile but humiliating.

It was easy enough to put the problem behind him for the day; the phone calls never stopped, nor did walk-ins asking questions about the orchids and roses for which Flowers by Raffi was known.

"Perry, it's Mr. Garnham. He insists on speaking to you."

Perry sighed. Garnham was a good customer. He spent at least $800 a month on flowers.

"Good afternoon, Mr. Garnham. How can I help you?" He grabbed a pencil and pad. "Of course, we'll deliver for you this evening." He looked at his watch—twenty minutes to six. Why the hell couldn't he have called earlier? A silly question. Perry knew exactly why.

"The usual note, Mr. Garnham—'Love from Terry and thank you for a wonderful afternoon'? Of course, Mr. Garnham. Always happy to take care of your special orders."

"Has he got a new girlfriend?" Justin shouted across the shop. "Or is it still the redhead?"

"You are going to deliver to Tiffany Keyser on Park."

"She's the redhead. Doorman in her building says she's a former porn star."

"Such a shame. Mrs. Garnham is a true lady. She's on the board at the Met, you know."

"As soon as Polly has finished putting it together, I'll drive over and drop it off."

"Thank you."

After closing the store and totaling sales, he set off for home. He enjoyed the walk and sometimes stopped off at a bar on 61st for a scotch. This night he certainly needed one. Sitting at his corner table, he found himself thinking of Garnham, and his other clients like Garnham. There was Evans, the CEO of the largest insurance company in town; Monk, the speaker of the House; Smythson, the newspaper publisher; Sagesmith, the head of a television network; and Stellman, the Broadway producer. Half his business, now that he thought of it, was dependent on the adulterous she-nanigans of New York's elite.

What a thing! And the notes that accompanied those orders—notes such as: "How can I live without you?" "One hour of ecstasy with you is worth a lifetime." "You are the love of my life." "Thank you for a glorious time this after-noon." It was rare that a customer came up with anything original.

He ordered another scotch at the bar and then remembered the letter in his pocket from the landlord's attorney. Long-established businesses all over Manhattan were suffering from the same fate: forced out by unsustainable rent. How would Raffi have reacted? He would probably have soldiered on.

A wealthy man who loved the business, Raffi would have happily continued to work like a slave, even at no profit. But Perry was tired. He wasn't cut out to run the business alone. His only qualm would be leaving the place so steeped in memories of Raffi.

Well, that and the fact that he wouldn't know what was next. After estate tax, difficulties with an IRS audit, and having to put a new roof on the house he shared with Raffi in East Hampton, he was cash-poor. He didn't love the business as Raffi had, but he counted on it.

The next morning, around half past nine, Perry stood on the sidewalk gazing into the store, checking on the window. Dressing the window was his favorite aspect of the job—after all, it recalled his original line of work. When charged with a design, his creative spirit took over. Once he'd established a picnic scene in the window, flowers adorned the tabletops, polka-dotted the fake turf, even dangled from the ceiling like floral rain. And speaking of rain, he had once created an umbrella display by weaving the sea-colored roses around a wire mesh frame. There had been bicycles (their baskets spilling over with orchids), boots used as planters, and long, spiraling windchimes with flowers braided into them. Today it was dressing dummies, the partywear they displayed had knitted roses in shades of champagne. The task was a small thrill, but he would take reminders of that old sense of inspiration whenever and however he could.

As he looked over his work, he felt a tap on his shoulder. He turned. It was Kate Ingram, the travel agent with an office on the second floor. She'd been there for as long as Perry had worked downstairs.

"Morning, Perry. How are ya?"

"Not so good, Kate. Did you get a notice about the rent increase?"

She nodded. "I don't know what I'm going to do, tell you the truth. The bastard wants us out, that's for sure. My business is in a slump. The days of independent travel agencies are long gone. With the internet came all the Expedia types, and all the hotels and airlines have their own websites. Why do clients need us? The large corporations have their own in-house travel coordinators."

He listened attentively as she went on. Hers wasn't a problem he could say he faced; customers still tended to prefer seeing and sometimes handling their flower arrangements—not to mention that his clients, at least, appreciated knowing their florist. Knowing, specifically, that their florist was discrete.

Still, in a very real sense, he and Kate were in the same boat.

"If I showed you my books, you'd see I'm barely in the black. I have a few loyal clients but I need more. If it were not for the fact that adultery is alive and well and thriving in this city, I'd be out of business."

With that, she opened the door to the right of Perry's window that led to the narrow corridor and the staircase to the upstairs offices.

Kate was a good neighbor. She'd handled Raffi and Perry's travels over the years, their romantic trips to Portofino included. He let her have her flowers at cost and she was always generous to Justin whenever he delivered her orders.

Tuesdays were always quiet. Fewer walk-ins and Lydia took care of all the telephone orders. It gave him time to sit and think, but this time all he could think of was the letter about rent burning a hole in his jacket pocket.

"Kate, it's Perry. What are you doing after work?"

"Going home. Drinking too early. Stewing. Why?"

"I have an idea. Meet me at the bar on 61st?"

She took a seat at the corner table and waited while Perry carried over her usual gin and tonic and his scotch.

"So what's your idea? How we can assassinate the landlord?" she chortled.

"Tempting thought, but I've got something different in mind."

"I'm all ears. Go ahead."

"I thought about something you said this morning. If it weren't for cheating spouses, we'd probably both be out of business."

"That's true. Today, I booked one of my lowlife husbands and his girlfriend a week in Paris. His wife had his baby just three weeks ago. Got another bastard taking his mistress to Marrakesh for Thanksgiving while his wife spends the holiday with her family in Maine."

"You and I have secrets like doctors and attorneys."

"Or priests taking confession. So what's your idea?"

Perry looked around to see if anyone might overhear them. In a low voice he continued, "Kate, neither you nor I can possibly afford to stay in business at these new rents. So we have to improve our business. We can't increase our prices and remain competitive—but we can increase our volumes."

"Well you can do that with flowers, but I don't know how I can do that in the travel business."

"Let's send a joint invitation to all our bastard customers to a party telling them that it is crucial for them to attend. We will tell them that we are facing ruin and may have to close down. That is unless they can help us out."

"And how would they help us out? More to the point— why the hell should they?"

"Very simple. I have the names and addresses of all the women to whom they've sent flowers over the years, women who were neither their wives, sisters, nor daughters. And, additionally, I have the salacious give-away wording of the notes that accompany the deliveries. I could hang them with those notes."

"So, you're gonna blackmail them?"

"I'm going to 'lean on them.'"

"And they're gonna, what, fork over a bunch of money?"

"Not directly. I want them to agree to increase their expenditure with me by fifty percent and to agree to a service charge of seventy-five dollars per order, inclusive of delivery. I did a back-of-the-envelope calculation, and based on what fifteen of my lowlife husbands spent with me last year, if I could get them to agree to that, I'd be able to pay the increased rent."

"So if they don't agree, are you planning to out them to their wives, for God's sake?"

"That would be too crude. Just a hint that I will have to do what I have to do to stay solvent."

"Where do I come in?"

"Look, Kate, you've said that margins in your business are rotten and that the competition is eating you alive. Putting aside percentages, in actual dollars, what does that mean for you in a rent increase?"

"Bout ten grand."

"Very simple. Let's say you have ten clients who are cheating on their wives."

"I've got twenty, easy."

"Do what the doctors do. Simply charge them a 'concierge fee'—thousand bucks a year. You'll cover the rent with plenty left over."

"And how the hell do I justify this?"

"Simple. You have all their travel details. Copies of the hotel bills. Double rooms and suites, first-class flights. Car services doing pick-ups and drop offs at the women's addresses."

They sat in silence for a minute, interrupted only by Perry walking over to the bar to refresh their drinks.

"Okay, I'll go for it, but I think it would be more effective if we approached each of the bastards separately, not altogether at one gathering. I mean, chances are they know each other but not necessarily what each other are up to. Can't very well address their privacy concerns by outing them all at a party."

"You're right, Kate. I think this could get us out of a hole. If I can sign a new lease and stay in business, I'll have a viable business to sell, and then I can retire. At last. Portofino beckons."

"I'm going to try this out on one of my beauties. Provided he doesn't rant and rave, I'll work my list."

"I'll do the same. Let's compare notes by the end of the month."

"You've got it. In three weeks, we'll know how we stand."

"Mr. Gaffney can see you now."

Perry followed the receptionist with the tight, plum-color pencil skirt along the corridor with its floor-to-ceiling windows, pausing momentarily to admire the view of the East River from the thirty-third floor.

Perry was more than a little apprehensive about how he would begin the conversation and how Gaffney would respond. Would he argue? Would he throw him out or would he cave? He'd chosen Gaffney because he promised to be the toughest nut to crack. Born and raised on Staten Island, he'd started working at sixteen on Wall Street in the mail room of a firm generally reviled as a no-holds-barred stock trader whose clients, as well as the firm's partners, were "connected." After military service in Korea, he established his own trading company in midtown, married, and commuted daily from his home in Old Westbury—except for those nights when he stayed in his apartment on Central Park West.

Still on the phone behind his desk, Gaffney beckoned Perry to take a seat at the round conference table on the other side of the room.

Perry felt perspiration bead on his forehead. What was the worst that could happen? He could be thrown out of the office; Gaffney could take his business elsewhere. There was no shortage of florists in the city. And then what would Perry do? Would he really follow through with blackmail, maybe anonymous letters to Gaffney's wife? And if he did that, with Gaffney's connections, he'd probably end up at the bottom of the East River. He looked across at the view from the conference table. Suddenly the East River didn't look so appealing.

Gaffney ended the call.

"Perry, good to see you." Gaffney took his own seat at the conference table. Well over six feet tall, he had a perpetual tan from overuse of sunbeds and a full head of hair too black to be natural. Perry had seen, while waiting in the reception area, a photograph of a much younger Gaffney standing over an opponent he'd knocked out in a boxing match.

Gaffney continued, "I believe we've been doing business for, must be, ten years or more, and this is the first time we've met."

Perry nodded.

"You sounded worried when you called yesterday. What can I do for you?"

Perry cleared his throat and spoke of the many years that he and Raffi had numbered Gaffney as one of their best clients. But now, the business was in peril because of the upcoming rent increase.

"And I wonder how you could help me, Mr. Gaffney. It would, of course, be in our mutual interests if you could."

This was the phrase that he had conjured up and upon which everything depended. *It would be in our mutual interests.*

Gaffney got the message. "So specifically, what would you like me to do? Of course, if I can help, I will. You have always given me good service. I am confident you've always handled my business with the utmost discretion."

"Certainly, and I will continue to do so. But I need help."

"Be specific."

"First, I'd like you to spend more money. Let's say a minimum of two thousand a month, and I'd be obliged to increase the delivery fee."

"Two thousand is a lot. How about fifteen hundred plus the delivery fee?"

"Mr. Gaffney, you are a gentleman. That would be helpful. Thank you."

They shook hands and then Perry left. The entire discussion had taken no more than five minutes. Back at the store, he took from his desk drawer the notepad on which he'd listed target clients, more or less in descending order of difficulty. He'd figured Gaffney for his most difficult case, but Jay Swift was a close second. Married into one of New York's premier old families, he had fathered a child by a girlfriend he'd shipped off to Florida. *Allegedly.* His present girlfriend was married to a former mayor.

Buoyed by his first victory using that winning phrase—*in our mutual interests*—he put in a call to Swift. And within forty-eight hours, he had his second deal. Two down, fourteen to go.

Several days later, he bumped into Kate as she was slipping across the road to the coffee shop.

"How's it going, Kate?"

She grinned. "This is unreal. I thought the bastards would at least put up a fight, but they couldn't be more accommodating. Haven't got a no yet."

"It's your feminine charm, my dear," Perry teased.

"Don't be silly. These scumbags just know what they stand to lose."

Perry gave her a report of his progress; with only three names remaining on his list, he, like Kate, hadn't encountered a refusal yet. They agreed they were as good as home free.

Perry scheduled a meeting with his accountant, Bill West, who had handled the store's tax returns for more than twenty years. At the end of a busy week, he sat in the back room with a glass of wine and a cigarette—he allowed himself three a day—while Justin minded the store. Perry was daydreaming of selling the business when Justin hurried in.

"Perry, there's a man in the store. He doesn't want to buy anything, but he insists on seeing you. Frankly, I don't like the look of him. I lied and told him you were in a meeting. I don't think he believed me."

"Okay. Tell him I'll be there in a minute." He finished his cigarette and flicked the stub into one of the large bins the arrangers used to discard the surplus leaves and stalks. Through the glass pane on the door, he could confirm that he didn't like the look of the man either.

He was in his fifties, stocky, and dressed in a dark blue overcoat and a black fedora. He carried an attaché case and stood staring out of the window watching the buildup of late-afternoon traffic on Madison Avenue.

"Good afternoon. I understand you want to see me. I'm Perry Spark. And you?"

The man ignored Perry's outstretched hand.

"Peter Beynon. Place we can talk in private?"

"Not really, I'm afraid. We close at six and it's only four-thirty. I have my arrangers working to fulfill orders that need to go out tonight, and if we have any walk-ins . . ."

"I see. Maybe we could slip across the road to the coffee shop on the corner."

"Very well," Perry replied, making no attempt to conceal either his curiosity or displeasure at the disruption.

Once settled at a table at the back of the coffee shop, Beynon began.

"You don't recognize my name, do you, Mr. Spark?"

"Should I?"

Beynon paused. "I suppose not, but I have bought flowers from you over the last couple of years."

"I hope we've given you good service. Thank you for your business. So . . ."

"Does the name Jerry Holland mean anything to you?"

"Jerry Holland, I don't think so. Is he a client too?"

"No. He's the president of the corporation that owns your building. I take it you only deal with our law firm."

Perry shuffled nervously.

"Jerry is retiring in a few weeks. As of January 1, he'll be living in Florida. Since his wife died, he's been eager to leave New York."

"And what's your connection with Mr. Holland? Right now, I have to tell you, he's not my favorite person. I've just received notice that my rent is going to be doubled."

"I'm connected to him two ways. First, as of January 1, I am taking over from him as president of the corporation, so effectively I will become your landlord. Secondly, Jerry is my father-in-law."

"And?" Perry sounded bolder than he felt or appeared. He looked into his coffee cup. He couldn't say Mr. Holland's son-in-law was in the running to become his favorite person either.

"I know you have been in contact with my brother-in-law, Neil Buxton, with regard to a sensitive matter. Neil has discussed this with me. I too need to reach an agreement with you that would be to our *mutual advantage*, given that Neil and I have a lady friend whom we, if I may be blunt, share."

Perry relaxed to such an extent that he had to suppress a smile. His sweat cooled in the breeze of the pendulum swinging back in his direction.

Beynon continued. "I know you received a letter from our law firm about your lease and the rent increase. I propose that we give you a new five-year lease at the same rent you are paying at the moment and that you can tear up that letter."

"Mr. Beynon, make it seven years and we have a deal."

"Good. Agreed."

"There is one other thing. One of your other tenants, Kate Ingram, has a travel agency. There's no way she can stay in business with that prohibitive rent increase. Offer her the same as you've offered me. She's about to have a nervous breakdown over this."

"I understand. I'll go and see her as soon as we leave here."

"Thank you."

They walked back together and shook hands outside the store and Beynon went through the door and up to the offices above the store to meet Kate. Half an hour later, a jubilant Kate stepped into the flower shop as Perry was turning off the lights and planted a kiss on his cheek.

"Mr. Beynon on the line for you, Perry," Lydia called out from her perch at the back of the store.

Perry's heart skipped a beat. *The bastard's changed his mind.*

"Perry, here." He hoped Beynon wouldn't hear the nervousness in his voice.

"I'm sending you the new lease for you to sign. Seven years at the same rent. Get it back to me as soon as you can. Also, when I was in your store the other day, I felt it could do with freshening up. Outside too. I'd be happy to send over my painters if you'd like. At no charge to you, of course."

Perry tried hard to stifle a laugh or any other expression of joy.

"Mr. Beynon, that is most kind. Thank you. And I presume you . . ."

"If you are asking about Kate Ingram upstairs, yes, she's my next call. I think her office could do with a fresh coat of paint and some new carpeting. Her lighting could be improved too."

"You're very kind. I never experienced this level of generosity from your father-in-law, Mr. Holland."

"That's because he never had the same recreational pursuits as I enjoy."

This time Perry didn't bother to suppress a laugh.

"By the way, there's another small office suite becoming available on the second floor, with windows facing Madison Avenue. You may know the suite. Silvano Moretti, the tailor, he's retiring. It will become available at the end of February, if you know anyone who needs space."

"What's the rent?"

"Depends who the tenant is."

"Let me think about it, Mr. Beynon. I'll get back to you."

Two days later, over drinks at the bar on 61st, Perry and Kate toasted their success.

"You know how long I've wanted fresh carpet in that place? Something nicer than that concrete-colored Berber? It just didn't seem worth doing. Now the place is gonna look brand-spanking-new."

"And I've told my accountant that I don't know, now, whether I want to sell the business. He thinks I'm crazy. He even thinks he has a potential buyer. But with my projected revenues plus seven years of rent at a bargain, I could get a terrific price for the business. But you know what, Kate? All this has suddenly given me a new lease of life. I'm not so sure I want to retire to Portofino."

When life had been nothing but a routine with nothing more but more years of the same forecasted, he had dreamed of the fishing village constantly. But now he couldn't help thinking of how quickly he'd grow bored. His art was in making arrangements, not riverscape painting. And the memories of Raffi he had there were a faint zephyr compared to the memories of him here. He didn't even know the damned language.

"I think it's because you're getting greedy. Me too. We're both going to see significant increases in our cash flows. God, I love thinking of it."

"Kate, I have another idea."

"Well, if it's half as good as your last one . . ."

"Beynon tell you that Moretti's space is becoming available?"

"*I* don't know anyone who wants to take it. You?"

"I'm taking it."

"What for, for heaven's sake?"

"He's letting me have it seven years at ten thousand a year, and he's going to do the same for me as he is doing for you, a total refurbishment of the space."

"What are you gonna do with a flower shop with no street presence? What are you gonna do with *two* flower shops?"

He leaned in. He smiled. Over the last couple weeks, his confidence had reached a lifetime high.

"We, and I do mean we, are going to open a new business.

"For God's sake."

"Spark and Ingram, The Private & Diplomatic Jewelry Company."

He paused to let her take this in. "Don't you see, Kate, we'll have covered all the aces—"

She said it for him. "Flowers, travel, and jewelry."

"We've already got our customer list, primed and ready. What do you say? Partner?"

She laid a cigarette pack out on the table; shortly she'd slip outside to enjoy a rare smoke. She would even cajole Perry into abandoning his three-a-day rule—it was really more of a guideline anyway. After all, weren't business celebrations the time for making exceptions, for breaking the rules? Didn't she and Perry have a booming and soon-to-expand client base for that very reason?

"Go get me another gin and tonic," Kate said. "And make it a double, partner."

Mangoes

I've known many fascinating women over the years, but I will never forget one in particular. Josephine.

I met Josephine forty years ago at one of those luxurious boot camps where affluent Londoners go to lose weight. I checked in one Sunday afternoon and met her, a fellow inmate. Within a few hours, we were in bed together.

Josephine had no weight to lose. She was a few years older than me, which she denied. She had long, straight, waist-length red hair. She was captivating. Attractive, yet not quite beautiful, she still oozed sex appeal. She was divorced and had a young son who was away at boarding school, and her ex-husband had custody of the boy. She lived alone in a prestigious apartment building. She had no reason to go to a health farm other than she was, in a nutshell, a nymphomaniac. Josephine accurately deduced that men who checked in at these places, deprived of food, cigarettes and liquor for a week, would be able to satisfy their sexual urges with greater regularity and enthusiasm than after a hard day's work at the office, given there was little else to do. I heard from one of the masseurs there were rumors that she had been blacklisted at certain similar fat farms.

We had a wonderful ten days together. The mornings were taken up with exercises, massages, saunas and jogs. After the daily lunch of a half grapefruit with a prune stuffed in the center, we would spend the afternoons in bed, only to rise, dress and go downstairs for the other half of the grapefruit. The other residents surmised what was going on and shunned us. No doubt they had also heard from the staff that she had a history. We didn't care.

She told me that she was in a long-term relationship with Brian, the managing director of a well-known company located a hundred miles from London. His routine was to drive up every Friday night to spend the weekend with her. I didn't know or care whether he knew about her exploits.

I continued to see her in London after we checked out of the boot camp, once or twice every month for three years. It was ideal. I would take a cab to her apartment after work and we would spend a few hours together. Then I'd get dressed and go home to sleep comfortably in my own bed. She didn't smoke, drink, or do drugs, and I rarely saw her eat. She considered the dating custom of dining in restaurants as foreplay to making love to be a waste of precious time. From my perspective, it was a perfect arrangement.

After a couple of years, she began to make certain demands, such as, "On your way over, could you pick up a few bottles of Dom Perignon from the liquor store on the corner? I have friends popping in."

Or, "When you next pass Harrods, Patricia on the tea counter has some tea set aside, and I've told her that you'll pick it up." That sounded like a bargain compared to a half case of expensive champagne, but it turned out that it wasn't plain old Lipton's tea. Oh no. It was a particularly rare leaf from the foothills of the Himalayas, which is only harvested three weeks of the year and is supposed to have formidable healing benefits. It cost close to $1,000 for just one pound. Similar requests were hurled at me for ludicrously priced face creams, and for theater tickets that were only available on the black market at exorbitant prices. The timing of these demands always coincided with my twice-monthly early evening frolics. And if ever I neglected to meet her demands, the quality and duration of those frolics suffered. I tired of it all and withdrew.

Four years passed before I saw Josephine again. I was vacationing in the South of France at my family home in Grimaud. I drove down the hill one afternoon to Saint-Tropez to meet up with friends who had an impressive yacht moored in Antibes. We had arranged to rendezvous at Le Gorille, a well-known bar on the quayside.

I arrived early. My friends had left a message for me with the bartender, advising me that they had set off from Antibes later than expected so I had a couple of hours to kill before they arrived.

I sat alone at an outside table sipping my Campari. I spotted an attractive woman walking off a yacht berthed in one of those highly visible spots especially reserved for the largest and most ostentatious vessels. Heaven knows how much the owners had to tip to secure such prestigious docking privileges.

She was dressed in perfectly tailored white slacks, with a navy striped silk shirt and a floppy hat. Her large dark sunglasses made her unrecognizable, but so alluring. She was striking, and I wasn't by any means the only person who watched and admired her.

She walked straight past me along the sidewalk. It was a purposeful and sexy walk, not a window-shopping or people-watching stroll. I speculated that she had a rendezvous with either a suitor or a hairdresser. She knew that she was being watched. After she passed me and walked on a few yards, she suddenly turned on her heels and came back.

"Good God, it's you, Simon. What the hell are you doing here? I haven't heard from you in, what is it, four years? You disappeared, just like that."

Truly, I did not recognize her behind those dark glasses and the huge hat, but the voice was unmistakably Josephine's. I stood to kiss her on the cheek and stammered something meaningless, riddled with clichés and untruths, about how delighted I was to see her again.

I was slow in inviting her to join me for a drink, not for any reason other than that the shock of seeing her threw me. However, without waiting to be asked, she sat and ordered a freshly-squeezed orange juice.

We exchanged routine questions about how each of us had spent the years since we had last seen each other. I hoped she would move on before my friends arrived. I had been assured that they would be bringing a spare girl with them to meet me: an Italian model about whom I had heard wonderful and promising things, and the last thing I wanted was Josephine hovering around.

"And how's Brian? Are you still with him?"

"We're married," she replied. "Three months ago."

"My God. I'm amazed. I never thought you were the marrying kind after your last one."

"We don't live together. It's still the same old routine. He comes up every Friday and goes back late on Sunday nights."

"So why did you get married, for heaven's sake?"

"It was like this. It's a long story but I'll make it as short as I can. In any case, I've only got twenty minutes, so don't interrupt. And don't be judgmental."

I breathed a sigh of relief. She'd be well-gone before my friends were due to arrive.

"Brian had been knighted for services to British exports. He deserved it. I won't take that away from him. He cashed in some of his stock options, and it dawned on me that he was one helluva good catch. I wasn't getting any younger, and I fancied being Lady Webster. The time was right to get him to marry me."

I nodded, seeing her point of view.

"So you proposed to him. Is that what you're telling me?"

"Shut up and listen."

Here we go again. Still the same old bitch.

"He was never going to propose. Never. We'd been together for thirteen years and never did it occur to him that I might have wanted him to propose. I suppose he feared I'd reject him. Over the years, I actually did propose to him on several occasions. I was always rebuffed."

I resisted saying anything to the effect that Brian, despite his contribution to British exports and his undoubted management skills, was clearly a first-class oaf to have put up with her and her shenanigans over so many years.

"My Portuguese maid, Maria. You may remember her?"

"No, I don't. She was always gone for the day when I arrived at your apartment."

"Well, she's been with me forever. Her daughter is pregnant. Maria is excited, as it will be her first grandchild. This is what I cooked up. Maria is a wonderful person but not the sharpest knife in the drawer. I told her that my doctor is able to determine the sex of an unborn baby from a sample of a pregnant woman's urine."

"Is that true?" I asked.

"Don't be such a blithering idiot."

Here we go again.

"I told Maria to bring me a sample of her daughter's urine and I would take it to my doctor and he would determine the sex."

"Josephine, that's terrible. You were taking advantage of this woman's simplicity and her affection for you."

"I don't know why I'm bothering to tell you this. And I told you not to be judgmental. So listen. I have to leave in ten minutes anyway."

"Okay, okay. So get on with it."

"A couple of days later she came with the urine. Fresh from that morning. After Maria left, I went to lie down. And at six, Brian arrived after his long drive, exhausted as usual, after a busy week. He found me lying on the bed, moaning and groaning and feigning illness. Fever, stomach ache, nausea, and all of that.

"The poor chap was concerned and genuinely sympathetic. I told him that my doctor had gone away for the weekend and I really needed to see someone.

"He agreed. I asked him to drive me to the clinic in Harley Street and that there'd be a doctor on duty there who would see me."

"But there was nothing the matter with you? You might have been able to fool Brian, but how the hell were you going to convince a trained doctor that you were ill?"

"Listen. When we arrived at the clinic, I signed in at the front desk and showed them my insurance card and all that. They told us to stay in the waiting area and that I'd be called in a few minutes. Fortunately, they weren't busy so I didn't have to wait long."

She paused to sip her juice. "Sure enough, a nurse came over after a few minutes and took me down a hallway to a small examination room. Brian wanted to accompany me but I told him to stay where he was."

"He always did what he was told."

"You can cut out your snarky comments."

I raised my eyebrows and glanced at my watch.

"The nurse was jolly. I told her that I thought I was pregnant. Before she asked, I took the test tube containing Maria's daughter's urine from my bag and handed it to her. She smiled and made some comment about how she wished every woman was as prepared as me. She went away and said she'd be back in about fifteen minutes, and did I want to go back to join my husband?"

"So you were married?"

"No, of course not, but the woman assumed I was."

We both paused to admire a glamorous couple who strolled into the bar. They were greeted warmly by the bartender and waiters, as well as by several customers. They were probably local celebrities.

"I waited patiently for the nurse to return. Fortunately, someone had left a magazine, and that occupied the time. Finally, she came back to give me the good news. I was pregnant."

"You really are something, Josephine."

"The nurse said I could re-join Brian and tell him the good news. 'Better still, why don't you call the front desk and have him come and you tell him,' I told her."

"Why?"

"Much more authentic if it came from the nurse's lips and not mine."

Mata Hari was an amateur compared with this bitch.

"Brian came quickly, concerned of course that the news was bad. And when the nurse uttered the words: 'Your wife is pregnant,' he almost burst into tears. He came over to me. I was lying down on the bed and he embraced me. He drove me home, overcome with emotion. I would have won an Oscar for my performance, believe me. Anyway, to cut to the chase, he proposed. I accepted. And a week later, I became Lady Webster."

Some 'lady,' I thought.

"But, Josephine, you weren't pregnant. How did you deal with that as the weeks flew by?"

"You are so naïve. I had a miscarriage, didn't I? And here I am on the Riviera staying with Giovanni on his yacht, recuperating."

"And what did you tell Maria about the baby's sex."

"I said it would be a girl. So if it turns out to be a boy, then what the hell?"

I stared at her and took in a deep breath.

"I must go now. I'm having my hair done around the corner. Giovanni and I are giving a party on board tonight. I'd invite you, but I can see you don't approve of me."

She stood, smiled and left the bar. I never saw her again. I have no idea what became of her. But, it reminded me of an old saying that I'd heard along the way: "Women are like mangoes. They are either green, ripe, or rotten."

CHAPTER NINE

An Artistic Dilemma

L ooking in the foyer mirror of her Park Avenue apartment, Ulrike Fischer tightened her Gucci scarf before giving her standard poodle a pat and a reassuring, "I'll be back soon," which even Bijou, the dog, knew was a lie. Thankfully, the housekeeper and the dog walker would be arriving soon—facts that were of comfort to Bijou as well as assuaging any guilt Ulrike felt.

Typical of November mornings, this one was cold and wet; she opted for the Burberry coat she'd purchased the previous winter. As she adjusted her thick blonde hair around the collar, she thought—not for the first time—that one of these days she must get a cut. She had begun to think that at her age, long hair wasn't simply impractical, it was inappropriate. Shoulder-length would be so much easier.

The door swung open letting the brisk morning air brush her face. "Good morning, Miss Fischer," came the familiar voice of Jared, the young doorman. Unbeknownst to her, Jared and his evening-shift colleague wagered a casual bet as to which of them would score first with the forty-year-old divorcee a week after Ulrike's husband had moved out. Their peculiar career afforded them every chance to discover details about the beautiful woman that others surely would miss. They saw the artwork she either ferried in the building herself or assigned to be carried by people the doormen assumed to be hired help. They often overheard her in a flurry of conversation, speaking of artwork in a way that went beyond aesthetic appreciation to include numbers, dollar figures. They figured her for an art dealer. A German one by the sound of the language they sometimes heard as she rushed past, always offering them an enticing smile.

It was the coming and going of men at all hours—men of various ages, sizes, and ethnicities—that convinced the doormen to scrap their bet. They'd both lose, they agreed; they didn't stand a chance against the clear signs of wealth they saw parading through the lobby.

If this doorman, the baby-faced one named Jared, knew that Ulrike fancied him too, he may have tumbled out of the very door he held open, falling flat onto the chilled pavement. Ulrike continued smiling to herself as she headed out. Better he didn't know; she hardly wanted to be responsible for the boy getting hurt.

The first step onto the sidewalk caused her entire body to go rigid, an instinctive reaction to the bitter low temperature, it couldn't be higher than the thirties. This combined with the glittering sunlight pulled her back in time to skiing in San Moritz. Dancing from evening until the sun rose over the slopes, splashing colors in a way even Monét would envy. Still, she always managed to be on the slopes a mere seven hours later.

She quickened her pace to cross Park Avenue before the light changed; from there, it was four short blocks to her gallery. She avoided a puddle on the sidewalk, not wishing to see her black, thigh-high Saint Laurent boots muddied.

When she had nearly reached her office she passed a heavy-set, helmeted worker. What an anachronism the fellow was; a true caricature of his job as he wolf-whistled *and* called out to her, "Nice legs, lady!" Had she been less coy, she may have called, "You're welcome!" to him, assuring him that, yes, those long sleek calves belonging to a woman fifteen years her junior *were* for the gawking at, and yes, she had left her top coat unbuttoned over her tight miniskirt on purpose. Her slender waist and perfectly voluptuous hips drew the attention she so desired. As it was, she didn't call out, but she did assure him of these things in her own subtle way, with a grin.

Ninety percent of her clients were men, a fact that enabled to charm and sleep her way into many negotiations. The reality that most were married seemed to be of no consequence.

She paused to look into the window of one of her competitors. "Bastard," she mumbled. He was showing the Vlaminck she had tried to buy a few months ago from that shyster estate attorney. She was certain he'd have sold it to her if she'd accepted his invitation to spend Labor Day Weekend with him in the Hamptons.

"Good morning, Ulrike. You look divine as usual. Coffee is made. You've had three calls already. The messages are on your desk."

Ulrike had never once regretted poaching Anna, the gallery director, from an auction house when she had established the New York branch of her Munich gallery five years earlier. Not even during the days of Anna's short-term affair with her ex-husband. Ulrike was certainly not about to lose a good director over Stephan's lust for any halfway attractive woman.

Ulrike sat down at her glass-topped desk and glanced at the messages. The first was from Stephan. She knew what that was about. He wanted to discuss reducing his monthly alimony payments, as he'd lost his job at an investment bank; now that she was making a name for herself in the art world, he knew she was doing well. To hell with him.

The next was from Stuart Butterfield, the real estate broker in Connecticut. She'd met him three weeks earlier when she had gone looking for a weekend home in Litchfield County. He'd shown her the perfect property. Priced correctly at just under a million, it was not too big, not too small. Three beds, two baths. Three-car garage on the side, pool in the back. A landscaped garden with majestic trees and a manicured lawn and the all-important white picket fence. The wide brook at the lawn's edge was every bit as enchanting as the squirrels and rabbits that occupied the garden. It was being sold by two gentlemen who had been in business together as interior designers in Manhattan; thanks to their efforts on the eighteenth-century colonial, she wouldn't have to sink a dime into restoration.

Yes, she'd fallen for the property and had made an offer that the sellers accepted. This left her having to put down a hefty deposit to begin the purchase formalities. And therein was the problem. Writing that damned check.

She tried to justify the purchase of the house, known for two hundred years as "Nightingale Cottage," as being good for business. The Hamptons had a surplus of art dealers and a deficit of collectors, whereas Litchfield County, Connecticut, was still relatively virgin country as far as collectors were concerned.

Stuart, the broker, was becoming a pest. He'd offered to drive down to the city to pick up the check and get her to sign the purchase agreement. She'd managed to stall him. He told her that the sellers were getting nervous and were demanding he continue to show the property to other potential buyers. But could she believe that?

Yes, it was becoming embarrassing. After all, what was the difference between a real estate broker eager to close on a sale and an art dealer trying to do the same thing? She'd stall a bit longer. The third message was from one of New York's major collectors, Gerald Lawson, the scion of Manhattan's Lowenstein real estate corporation.

Across the past thirty years, and two divorces, Gerald had amassed a considerable collection of modern masters: Georgia O'Keefe, Jackson Pollock, Milton Avery, Willem de Kooning, and Mondrian. The walls of his Fifth Avenue duplex left barely any room for additions to his collection.

Gerald spotted her from across the room at a Sotheby's sale and invited her for a drink at his apartment, a five-minute stroll from the auction house. Of course, she had heard a great deal about him but they had never met. That he wasn't her type was of no consequence: He was a collector. In aggregate, his collection was worth millions, and she hoped that despite his shortage of wall space, he might still be in an acquisitive mindset. The very thought was adrenalin in her veins. *His* call she would promptly return.

That night, not long after the second bottle of Dom Perignon, he led the way to his bedroom. As she lay beside him the next morning, she went for the jugular. "Have you ever considered buying an Old Master?"

Well, he hadn't. But at the end of the day, when she was back at her gallery and him at his office, he called to say he'd given some consideration to an Old Master painting, but instead of buying it for cash, he'd prefer to exchange it for one of his paintings he'd grown tired of.

She smelled the deal.

Over dinner that night at Lutèce, he boasted of his sailing prowess and invited her to join him and his friends on his new ninety-foot racing boat, which he kept at a Connecticut marina. Although she offered a coy smile at his invitation, her mind was thoroughly consumed by her plan that she would put into action that night.

When they arrived at his place she strategically suggested a glass of wine, which she nonchalantly carried to the very place she intended to hang the Old Master.

"I think you should have a Dutch Old Master here. A marine scene to manifest your love of the sea and sailing," she purred. He squeezed her hand.

"You're right. In the foyer, directly opposite the door so it will be the first thing people will see when they visit."

"A perfect place for it," she agreed. "I'll measure the space tomorrow morning."

Sexual activity with a three-a-day cigar smoker like Gerald Lawson was an ordeal, but it was the price she was obliged to pay if she could finally sell the Willem van de Velde the Elder painting she had on consignment from one of Stuttgart's nouveau riche, Wolfgang Muller. Wolfgang was the one who liked her to beat him with a riding crop. He wanted $4 million for the painting.

She hurried out of Gerald's apartment at dawn and, once back at her gallery, telephoned her director in Munich.

"Dieter, I think I may have someone for the van de Velde. Finally. Please have it crated and shipped to me and be sure to notify the insurance company and Wolfgang. Send me all the documentation, the X-rays, ultra-violets, expert's authentication, and provenance. The lot. Be sure to take copies."

Four days later, amid dodging more calls from the Connecticut realtor, and after two more tortuous evenings with Gerald Lawson in his smoke-infested apartment with cigar ash falling from his naked torso onto hers, the wooden crate containing the van de Velde was delivered to the gallery.

She unpacked it with Anna's help. Fortunately, even with the heavy gilt frame, it was neither too large nor too heavy for the slender duo to move.

"Gerald, I have the perfect painting for you. It's just arrived. I had it shipped from Munich. I have all the accompanying documentation for you to review. May I bring it to you this evening?"

Expedited shipping of the painting, insurance, clearance at JFK customs, and its delivery to Manhattan, had run her a few thousand. If she couldn't secure the deal with Gerald, she'd be obliged to send the painting back to Munich, doubling her expense.

When Gerald opened the door of his apartment a few hours later, it was impossible to tell whether his undisguised excitement had to do with the painting or another lustful night with her.

"You're not to look at the painting until I hang it where I think it will be best displayed," she said playfully. "Fix me a drink? I'll call you when I'm ready."

As soon as he left the foyer, she took from her bag a hammer, a picture hook, a pencil, and a folding wooden ruler. She had perfected the delicate technique she was about to enact yet again: clutching a sizable painting in one hand while, with the other, making a small pencil mark on the wall where the hook would go. She positioned the painting on the wall and then stepped back.

"Can I come and look?'

"Not yet." The painting, like a beautiful actress, deserved proper lighting. "Bring me that floor lamp from your study."

A minute later, he stepped into the foyer.

"No looking. Go back and I'll call you once I've plugged in the lamp and adjusted it."

Obedient in the way men were when they anticipated sex, he set down the lamp and withdrew without peeking.

She struggled to find an outlet, then, having turned on the lamp, experimented with angles. "Okay, I'm ready," she called. "Come and look at it."

He rushed back into the foyer, bearing two champagne flutes. He turned to face the painting. He moved toward it, so close that his nose almost touched the canvas.

"Well, the paint is dry," he smirked.

"Don't be so ridiculous. It's undated but the experts believe he painted it in 1687." She reached down to her bag to take out a file. "Here's all the documentation. Provenance, expert authentication from three renowned European art professors, ultra-violets and X-rays." She repeated the phrase she'd used when requesting the documentation. "The lot."

He stepped back and took the manila file from her, without looking at it. His eyes remained affixed to the painting.

Her breath hitched in her throat as she waited. "Well?"

"Ulrike, I like it. How much?"

She knew negotiations could be rocky; Gerald's reputation as a pit bull in Manhattan's business and social circles hadn't materialized from thin air. But still, she could hardly temper her enthusiasm. She could almost smell the wet ink on that check she needed to write. She could almost feel, too, the air around her clearing when she parted ways with Gerald and his cigars. "Five million," she said.

"That's ridiculous. There's no way I would pay five million for that painting," he snapped. "But we'd talked about a swap."

"Well, tell me what you've got."

"How about the Mondrian in my study?"

"Gerald, I don't know anything about Mondrian. I've never sold one. I'll take a look at it and any documentation you have. Tomorrow morning I'll take it to my gallery and call in a couple of experts to advise me. I'll leave you the van de Velde. How's that?"

"If we can do the transaction as a straight swap, I'm on." He slipped her flute of champagne into her hand, finding it necessary to first lift that hand from her hip. "Now let's polish this off, order in from the restaurant downstairs, and go to bed."

The next morning, she put the Mondrian, to which she gave only a fleeting glance, into a garment bag that Gerald loaned her, and he accompanied her to her gallery. She had no doubt that it was not for *her* protection. There had been a spate of muggings again on the Upper East Side.

He left her as soon as she unlocked the door and was safely inside. She went straight to her office. Anna wouldn't arrive for another hour. Ulrike listened to her telephone messages. There were three from the Connecticut real estate broker, each one expressing disappointment that he hadn't heard back from her and repeating first that he needed a check and second that he would drive into the city to pick it up. Her girlfriend, an interior decorator who had visited the house with her, also called to say that the house was fabulous and she had some terrific ideas for how she would decorate it; she wanted to come over to discuss them.

The next message was from a landscape designer in Litchfield who had heard from the broker that she was buying the house. He had driven over to take a look and had some thoughts on how she could redesign the patio to make it more appealing. Oleander or bougainvillea would work very well at the front of the house, he promised.

The next message was from the building inspector asking if she had any questions on his report. He was, he said firmly if politely, awaiting her check.

There was no avoiding the fact that she loved the house and was excited about buying it, she had made offers on paintings both in New York and in Munich, if any of them were accepted, those were more checks to write. That fast, she'd be in the hole. If she could only swing this Mondrian/van de Velde deal, everything would work out.

As soon as Anna arrived and made coffee, Ulrike called to ask her dear friend Terry, from one of the auction houses, how he would go about finding a buyer for a Mondrian, given that this was not her area of expertise.

"Two names for you," her friend answered. "The first is Felix Mancia. He's bought and sold two or three Mondrians over the last few years. He has a client in Geneva and another in San Francisco who I know are serious collectors. The second is Lawrence Tibbett. He retired last year from the Museum of Modern Art. He's the one who is usually called to authenticate Mondrians. His word is treated as gospel. You have their numbers?"

"I'm sure Anna can get them. Lunch sometime?"

"That would be great. When I get back from Tokyo, I'll call you."

She nodded. "Tokyo." He had been cultivating the Japanese for a few years, and as much as Ulrike wished he would help her open doors in the Far East, she knew he wouldn't—or couldn't. He feared his wife would throw the book at him. She'd never forgiven him for sleeping with Ulrike, even though he'd been single at the time.

Within an hour, Felix Mancia's eyes were inches from the Mondrian. He examined it as he examined all paintings—with both the stillness and silence of a sculpture; it gave one the impression of artwork examining artwork.

"What's the provenance, Ulrike?"

"It's been in the same private collection for several years. The collector bought it at auction here in New York."

"How much? Dealer-to-dealer price?"

"Five and a half."

"Phew. How negotiable?"

"I have no room. Maybe I could do it for five and a quarter, but seriously, not a dime less."

Felix looked at the painting again. "Will you give me an exclusive on it for a week so I can speak to my client?"

"Felix, I'm sorry. I can't. I really need to know now whether you want it. I'm told on the grapevine that you have two avid Mondrian collectors. This is a transaction that I must close today."

"Can you at least give me until this time tomorrow morning?"

She looked at her watch. "Nine-thirty tomorrow it is."

"I'm pretty certain I'll be buying it. I have had several Mondrians pass through my hands over the years, and certainly this is one of the finest I've seen. The quality is astounding, and it's in perfect condition. Can I use your phone?"

"You'll have privacy in Anna's office."

"Thank you. I want to check on what it went for when it was last sold at auction and I'll try to reach one of my clients right now."

The moment he was out of the room, Ulrike picked up the phone to call Dieter.

"Dieter, drop everything. Call Wolfgang Mueller immediately. I may have a buyer for the van de Velde. See if he will take three million seven hundred and fifty thousand for it. Christ, it's almost ninety-five percent of what he's asking—and I'll drop our commission by half, to ten percent. So, bottom line, he'll end up with . . . " She paused to calculate on a Post-it note. "Three million five hundred sixty-three versus three million six. Wolfgang will never do better. Call me back right away."

Anna brought in a cup of coffee and raised her eyebrows. "I sense something good is in the air."

"Shush. No jinxes."

Felix rejoined them. "Okay, we have a deal. Five million two hundred and fifty thousand. Give me a couple of hours to study the documents and I'll messenger over a certified check." They agreed that he would pick up the painting and the bill of sale the next day.

"Thanks Felix. Let's hope we'll do lots of business like this in the future."

"Of course."

"He's cute," she said aloud but to herself once he was out of earshot. She picked up the list of telephone calls that she needed to return. Most of them connected to the house— her dream house. As long as the deal went through, and it would, the house was hers. She would have to take care of Terry, of course. One way or another.

"Yes, Dieter?" She knew it was him calling. "What did Wolfgang say?" She paused to await the answer. "Terrific. Well done. With a bit of luck, I'll be able to wire the funds to him tomorrow. Find out where he wants them."

An hour later, Anna showed into Ulrike's office an elderly man, tall with snow-white hair and rimless glasses. Professorial appearance, black corduroy trousers, grey herringbone jacket over a navy vest and open-neck white shirt. He gave one the immediate impression of a tour guide in a museum.

"So, my dear. You have a Mondrian to show me. Where is it?"

Ulrike pointed to the back of an easel with the painting out of view. Professor Tibett maneuvered around Ulrike's desk to examine it. After twenty seconds, he let out a cry.

"Oh my God, this fucking fake again! Please, don't waste my time. I looked at this painting years ago when it came up at auction, and I told the auction house it was a fake then and they wouldn't believe me. And some poor idiot ended up paying a fortune for this piece of crap. Believe me, it's worthless." Without so much as a goodbye, he stormed from the gallery. His parting words, "You damned crooked dealers" echoed through the gallery.

"Oh my God," Ulrike whispered. *Now what?* She had one dealer telling her it was among the best he'd ever seen, and he was certainly nobody's fool, and within the hour, she had an expert declaring it was a fake.

Among Anna's countless talents, making a coffee brew both strong and smooth was something Ulrike cherished about her, but the coffee wasn't going down easily now. She sensed her potential paths forward unfolding, but selecting one was no easy task—and not solely because of her payment on a dream house hung in the balance. If she told Felix he was wrong about the painting, taking that bastard Tibbett's word, she would lose him—as both a business connection and a potential bedmate. She would essentially be telling him he wasn't the aficionado and expert he fancied himself; he'd never want to look her in the eye again.

And what about Gerald? Would he have a case against the auction house that pawned off a fake? The doctrine *caveat emptor* swam through her thoughts—let the buyer beware.

"Mr. Lawson is on the phone for you," Anna called out from the next room.

"Shit."

"Ulrike, do we have a deal?"

She paused. "Just a moment, Gerald. Let me call you back."

At that moment, Anna came in with an envelope. She saw from the return address it was from Felix Mancia. She leaned forward to take her letter opener and carefully slit the envelope. There it was—a certified check for $5,250,000. Accompanying the check was a Post-it on which he'd scrawled confirmation that he would pick up the painting and bill of sale the next day.

She looked at the check. Citibank, New York. Certified. $5,250,000. Less what she had to wire to Wolfgang her net would be $1,687,000. That would cover the total purchase price of the house, plus all the landscaping, furnishing and decorating of it. She could even buy for herself the sapphire bracelet that she'd seen at Harry Winston. She still would have money left over.

One more long sip. Then she picked up the phone.

"Gerald. We have a deal. The van de Velde is yours. A straight swap for the Mondrian. I'll have all the paperwork for you to sign. Let's have lunch and"—she added in an attempt to preclude questions or further discussion— "spend the afternoon together doing what we like to do best." She promised herself it would be the last time she'd have to go to bed with him.

"Anna, bring me a gin and tonic, please."

"It's a bit early, isn't it?"

"Maybe, but I need it. Make it a big one."

"Mr. Butterfield is one the phone for you," Anna announced.

Ulrike took a long sip before she picked up the call.

"Is that my favorite real estate broker?" she asked him, turning on her flirtatious voice.

"Yeah, Ulrike. It's good to hear your voice. Finally,"

And yet he didn't sound happy. He would though, in moments. "Nice to hear your voice too." For the moment, he sounded like a man exhausted, accustomed to dashing from one pastoral Connecticut property to another.

"I have good news for you." Men and women alike were astounded at this unique skill of Ulrike's—how she could purr when her words contained no rs, no traditional feline sound.

"You have the check ready?"

Ulrike smiled at the happy uptick in Stuart's voice. Imagine the poor man: always making other people's homesteading dreams come true, probably fraught with nerves constantly from dealing with well-to-do trust-fund babies and Hollywood starlets and their flighty, occasionally deceptive, ways. Maybe she would find a way to help him relax.

She got out her checkbook. She sniffed that subtle aroma of wet ink she'd imagined earlier, hovering the tip over the long black line for *amount*. "You *did* say you could come into the city and pick up this check, didn't you?"

"I, I . . . " The poor fellow was attempting to make sense of her tone; she knew the signs.

"Could you come to my apartment?"

He was stuttering through his yes, and she was drawing those first delightful looping numbers in the cost of her down payment when Anna poked her head in, rapping softly on the doorframe. "Sorry to bother you." She mouthed the words.

Ulrike smiled. Nothing could bother her now.

"Felix Mancia's on the line for you. It sounds important."

CHAPTER TEN

The Light Went Out

Mrs. Thelma Brewster was one of the stalwarts of the New York charity that had been established years before by her late mother-in-law to raise funds for research into ailments connected with the one part of the anatomy for which no foundation had yet been established. Since becoming a widow a few years earlier and chairman of the family's charitable trust, she had been able to dispense substantial funds at her sole discretion. There was hardly a charity on the eastern seaboard that did not court her. She was a soft touch for animals, symphony orchestras, and opera societies. Orphanages, veterans, and religious organizations had a much harder time reaching out to her. Police and fire departments stood no chance.

She would have preferred to stay home that evening to watch, yet again, Gloria Swanson in *Sunset Boulevard*, but her old friend Emily Peacock cajoled her into attending that evening's annual gala. Emily always supported her pet projects, so she felt obliged to reciprocate by attending in full force, with her twin stepsons at her side.

The elderly, black-tie attendees were gathered in small groups in the reception room adjacent to the ballroom where dinner was to be served, either sipping pre-dinner cocktails or browsing a vast array of assorted items displayed on tables filling the entire length of the three walls.

Two groups cleared the vestibule so Mrs. Brewster and her stepsons could make their entrance. She received a smile or two as she passed onlookers, heading toward the silent auction offerings. Most turned away. She was happy they did. She had no time for meaningless chitchat with people she neither knew nor wished to know.

Mrs. Brewster, not yet sixty, was a tall woman of muscular build, an artifact of her years as a renowned tennis player and golfer and, previously, her college days of captaining Vassar's lacrosse team. Her late husband had enjoyed an easy popularity among their social circle; *her* booming voice coupled with a dearth of grace, humor, and charm generally led to her being avoided—except by those sycophants targeting her for charitable donations, always willing to sacrifice pride and succumb to third-degree interrogation and humiliation in the hope of catching her in a generous spirit.

She wore a long-sleeve black dress and a simple, vintage Cartier diamond necklace and bracelet, but barely any makeup or nail polish. Her grey hair was cut like a man's, short and straight, and her earrings were small diamond studs. She stopped to greet someone she knew while her stepsons hoped a waiter would soon pass with a champagne tray.

Hugo and Cameron were identical twins. They were thirty years old, unmarried, well-educated, polite, and pleasant company—all traits inherited from their father. Overall, *quite* eligible. And though they hadn't inherited her genes, they were, like their stepmother, tall, broad-shouldered, athletic, and expensively yet conservatively dressed. They were always immaculate, clean-shaven, and tanned.

A serious skier, Hugo spent three months of every year at the family chalet in Klosters. Cameron had been captain of his college tennis team. The boys shared stewardship of an eighty-five-foot racing yacht they kept at Martha's Vineyard. As regular competitors in international yacht races, they had, that August, sailed across the Atlantic to Cowes in the Isle of Wight, won two trophies, and then traveled south to spend three weeks on the Mediterranean before returning to Massachusetts via the Azores.

Cameron waved across the room to a friend and left his stepmother and brother. Mrs. Brewster and Hugo elbowed their way in to look at the display. The usual array of auction items beckoned the crowd, including gift vouchers for restaurants and stores; costume jewelry; some sculpture and ceramics; weekends in the Hamptons; a week's stay at a Corfu villa; a day at a tony spa. Hugo paused to look at a baseball bat, allegedly signed by Joe DiMaggio, and wrote down his bid of $750. He didn't care whether he won it but felt obliged to bid on something. Mrs. Brewster carefully appraised a computer guru's offer of a six-week course in learning basic computer skills. The $500 reserve was well worth it. She hated to be dependent on others and was tired of asking her stepsons to repeat their explanations of fundamentals even a five-year-old could handle blindfolded. After writing down her bid, she moved to the next table, with Hugo still at her side.

A few watercolors, placed on table-top easels, were pleasing enough but not special. Two seascapes and a handsome golden retriever. And behind on a screen, three portraits. A woman with a King Charles Spaniel and another woman with a baby. And then her eyes turned to the third painting. She froze.

"My God," she whispered. "Hugo, look at that painting."

She grabbed his hand and he felt her tremble. "Hugo, what do you think?"

"It's her. It's Arabella."

"I know. It has to be. Look at the eyes. Look at the hair. Her smile. And those pearls. That's the necklace I gave her on her twenty-first birthday." In a shaky, whispering voice, she addressed no one in particular. Her eyes watered. "Who's the artist?" she asked. "Go and see."

Finding a break in the row of tables, Hugo navigated around and back to the painting. His examination turned up only one identifying mark: "HC 2011."

He carefully removed the painting from the wall to see if there was anything on the back of it that would identify the artist. Simply a small label suggesting that, at one time, the painting had been sold by Taylor & Comer, a Boston gallery. He replaced it and looked across at his mother, whose eyes had not diverted from the portrait.

"Are the other two paintings by the same artist?" she asked. "Find out."

The other two, he found, had been properly signed by a woman artist. He walked back around the table to rejoin his mother.

"Go find Cameron. Say nothing to him. Let him see the painting and we'll watch to see how he reacts."

She glanced down at the sheet on the table. There had been no bids for the girl's portrait, but the reserve was the same as the computer course she just bid on. She picked up the pencil next to the sheet and wrote $5,000. Her eyes returned to the painting.

The two boys soon joined her.

"You'll never guess who I've just been talking to," Cameron said. "Lucas Tindall. You remember him, don't you? We were at school with him. He got expelled for selling drugs."

"Cameron. Shut up. Just look at these paintings."

"Very well," he answered with little enthusiasm.

He picked up one of the seascapes and then the other. "Very nice. You see stuff like this at every gift shop on the Cape. What's the big deal?"

"Look on the wall."

His brother and stepmother waited in silence.

"Jesus Christ," he said softly. "That's Arabella."

Hugo and Mrs. Brewster nodded. "No doubt about it."

"Those are the pearls you and Dad gave her on her birthday, I think," Cameron said.

"People are moving in to take their tables in the ballroom," his stepmother replied. "Hugo, you stay here until they close the silent auction. If anyone places a bid over mine, go up, scare them off. Go up in increments of five thousand. Stay here until the silent auction is closed. Cameron, let's find our table."

Hugo nodded. He knew better than to argue.

"In fact, stay here for the rest of the evening. Just in case there are any shenanigans with people placing bids after they announce the auction is closed. It wouldn't be the first time. I'm not taking any chances. Cameron can swap places with you every half hour."

Mrs. Brewster did not enjoy the rest of the evening; she had nothing in common with the man sitting next to her, a professor of mathematics at Columbia University. Cameron was so overwhelmed by the painting that he was oblivious to the lukewarm tomato soup, tasteless chicken breast, and chocolate gateau. The speeches and the live auction sucked the breath from the room. Mrs. Brewster sat motionless, her face drained of color. Her wine glass remained untouched, as did the food on her plate.

Hugo came over to the table and whispered something in her ear, his eyes lingering longingly on her uneaten dinner. When she pushed him away, he slunk back to his post to see if anyone had topped her bid for the painting. No one had.

As soon as the silent auction ended and just before the entertainment began, Mrs. Brewster nudged Cameron, and they rose without a smile or wave good-bye to the other eight people at the table. As they passed through the ballroom to join Hugo, the loud screeching of a heavily tattooed and tanned singer, sporting a bright green wig and a strapless, barely-there white sequined dress, propelled them to walk even faster.

Ignoring the protestations of a volunteer, Cameron removed the painting from the wall as his stepmother favored the charity of the night with a $5,000 check. With the painting tucked under Cameron's arm, they left the hotel to walk the single block up Fifth Avenue to their co-op apartment.

Cameron carefully positioned the painting on an armchair across from where his stepmother sat.

"Pour me a cognac," she snapped. "And bring me tonight's program. Let's see if we can determine who donated the painting."

Hugo did the honors.

"She would have been twenty-seven now"—Mrs. Brewster tugged a drink of brandy—"had that bastard not murdered her." She wiped away a tear. "I can't believe he got away with it."

"It was tough on all of us," Hugo offered, referring to the loss of a father and then, not three months later, a kid sister.

"Don't I know it?" she answered.

"Looks as though the painting might have been donated by a gallery in Tribeca. McGrail and Foster," Cameron said, turning over the pages in the program.

"I'll call them in the morning. I'm going to bed. This has been an emotionally exhausting evening, to put it mildly." No one slept well that night.

"Why the hell don't art galleries open at an acceptable hour? Ten-thirty," she snarled as she looked at her watch. "That's not for another two hours, for God's sake." She put down the telephone after leaving a curt message demanding a call back.

Her stepsons loitered at the breakfast table. They knew better than to comment. After a lifetime of observing how her moods of mild irritation could quickly turn into temper tantrums, they had mastered the art of keeping their thoughts to themselves.

"I'll call Emily Peacock. Maybe she can shed some light on the painting's provenance," she mused. "Fancy Emily not being there last night after she badgered me for weeks about the damned event. But I'm glad I went. After all, Arabella's portrait . . . " She sipped her coffee. "And what are you two dilettantes doing today?"

Cameron stretched. "Meeting at the yacht club to discuss putting together a team for an upcoming race."

"It must be terrible to be so overwhelmed with work," she answered with undisguised sarcasm.

"Well, did you find out anything, Mama?" Hugo asked as he poured himself a pre-dinner cocktail. Neither Hugo nor

Cameron liked calling this woman mother. On top of that, they doubted she enjoyed hearing the maternal moniker any more than they liked saying it. But before his passing, their father had made it clear he expected them to act like a family—and that meant addressing his bride as though she'd given birth to them.

"Absolutely nothing. Emily has pneumonia, or so she says, and that's why she wasn't there last night. She hasn't the first clue about how Arabella's portrait ended up as an item in the silent auction. I took a cab to Tribeca to visit the art gallery. They were most unhelpful. They refused to give me any information whatsoever about the artist."

"How did they get hold of the painting? Did they at least tell you that?"

"No. All they said was that if I left my name and telephone number, they would let me know if another painting by the same artist came in."

"So, I suppose there's not much more we can do," Hugo said.

"Nonsense. After I left the gallery, I came straight back here and telephoned Bill Field, our attorney, who suggested I call David Hudson, who is supposed to be a tip-top private investigator. I met with Hudson at his office on 57th, and I've retained him to find the artist. He charges a fortune, but I have every confidence he'll come up with something."

Cameron set down his own cocktail. "Say how long it might take him?"

"Not exactly. He told me to be patient and that it might be three months before we hear anything."

"I hope you're not paying him a daily rate for his services."

"Cameron, that's none of your business. I'll pay whatever it takes to find this man."

Hugo and Cameron found their stepmother seated at her desk in the library of her forty-room mansion in Newport staring out the window at the harbor. The brothers had been interviewing crew members for their upcoming voyage to New Zealand and were not pleased with her summons for this immediate conference.

"You certainly took your time," she hissed.

"We're sorry but we were in the middle of something. What's so important that couldn't wait until dinner?" Hugo replied.

She paused to sip the first of the evening's gin and tonic and waited until John, her butler, brought the boys their usual cocktails.

"It is three months to the day since I retained David Hudson to ascertain the identity of the artist who painted Arabella's portrait." She beckoned to the wall where the painting hung far from the window to avoid the fierce sun that during the summer months could be brutal.

"So what has he come up with? Anything?" Cameron asked.

"I'm not so sure that what he has come up with has been worth close to $1,000 a day, but it's a start."

Hugo set his drink aside. "You've invested $90,000—already?"

"Don't worry. It's my money and not a dime has been paid from your trust."

"So tell us what he's found out."

"In a nutshell, Hudson believes that the painting is by a man called Edward Peterson."

"Well, that's bullshit before we go any further," Cameron insisted. "The initials on the canvas are HC."

"Cameron, be quiet."

"Okay, Mother, go on."

"Edward Peterson's seascapes sell quite well in Boston, Portland, and Connecticut. He has a representative who promotes his work with mid-range galleries on the coast between New York and Maine."

Since Cameron, having been shut down, now seemed content to stare at the drink he swirled in his hand, it was Hugo's turn to object. "So, here we have you in search of an artist who painted a portrait of Arabella who signs his works 'HC' and you've spent $90,000 and have come up with an artist called Edward Peterson who paints seascapes. Not a good investment, if you don't mind me saying so."

The brothers sneered.

"When you let me finish, you'll wipe that grin off your face."

"Okay, okay. Go on."

"HC stands for Hallowell City, a small town in Maine on the Kennebec River. That's where Peterson was born. And, it's barely five minutes from Augusta."

"So?"

"Have you forgotten that Arabella had a friend in Augusta she would visit often? A girl who was her roommate at college."

"That rings a bell," Hugo admitted.

"And what did the artist paint after the initials 'HC'?"

"The year Arabella was murdered . . . 2011."

The boys looked at each other, stunned.

Cameron risked speaking up again. "So where do we go from here?"

"We pay Mr. Peterson a visit."

"Did your Mr. Hudson come up with an address?"

"Sort of. As a child, Peterson spent many summers lobster fishing. He developed a love for the sea and he excelled at art in school, hence the seascapes. And then he joined the navy."

"Is he still in the navy? How old is he?"

"Hudson believes him to be in his early sixties. He retired early from the navy and, like many ex-sailors, got a job as a lighthouse keeper."

This pulled Cameron's attention fully away from his drink. "That doesn't make sense. There are hardly any lighthouses anymore that are manned. They're all automated—they're equipped with machinery that can be controlled from land."

Not one to gracefully withstand correction in any matter, nautical or otherwise, Mrs. Brewster sniffed. "Anyway, he's a lighthouse keeper. That's what Hudson told me."

Hugo thought out loud, "It's possible. There are still some lighthouses that are manned. What a lonely job. One would have to be extremely self-sufficient to take on something like that, after the camaraderie to which he would have been exposed during a long term career in the navy."

"And remember, he liked to paint."

"But how would he have met Arabella, for God's sake?"

"That's something we're going to have to find out. Remember Arabella mixed with a rough crowd—heavy drinkers—and the way that girl dressed sometimes. Well, your sister could look and act like a tramp at times, you know that. Maybe this Peterson was a dealer and she met him because they were both addicts. Who knows?"

Cameron, however, had another theory. "Do you think he killed her because he was after her money?"

"Unlikely. When we went through all Arabella's papers and bank statements, there were no noticeable withdrawals. And, according to Hudson, Peterson sold about one painting every month for between three and five thousand—that, added to his salary and navy pension. Not to mention he lived a frugal life on a rock in the middle of the Atlantic with just one long weekend break every month."

"Arabella was killed on a Saturday night."

"That's right, Hugo. How could I ever forget that telephone call the next morning?"

"We're just assuming Peterson's the murderer."

"He *is* the murderer. Of that I have no doubt. And there's another clue."

"Go on." Even as Hugo compelled his stepmother's discoveries, he glanced toward Cameron, to gauge his reaction. Was Hugo alone in his concern that Mrs. Brewster sounded overly conclusive about details that could be coincidence, or his concern over what the old woman would *do* with her newfound information? Cameron returned to inspecting his drink.

"Hudson managed to find out—and don't ask me how, because he wouldn't tell me—that every month, he'd withdraw $1,000 in cash. What did he do that for? Why did he need cash when he was the only person in a damned lighthouse?"

"You have a good point, Mother. I wouldn't know."

"That is because you are a halfwit. He was paying off someone to keep his mouth shut. He was being blackmailed."

"I suppose that's possible," allowed Hugo, always the quicker of the twins to recover from their mother's stings.

"This is what we're going to do. Next Tuesday, we'll meet in Montauk. We're going to pay the murderer Peterson a visit. You sail there and I'll meet you at the marina. After a quick lunch, we'll take a little trip to the lighthouse. I'm told it's about seven miles out at sea. Bring the small boat. No need to sail in that ostentatious thing you blow your trust income on."

"How are you going to get there?"

"Eric will drive me."

The brothers bristled at the name of their stepmother's chauffeur, her former gardener who, soon after he began sleeping with her, was promoted—first to chauffeur and then effectively to the majordomo at her Rhode Island estate.

Hugo and Cameron set off the following Tuesday, at seven o'clock, from Newport to pick up their stepmother, in Montauk. "You think she'll actually get on the boat?" Hugo asked his brother as soon as they were underway. It wasn't an unreasonable question. She hated sailing, and she wasn't very fond of their company either. Her own preferred means of travel between Rhode Island and the Long Island peninsula was by limousine, and now that Eric was on the scene, road trips were her only means of travel.

Cameron hoped the realization that she could not similarly take a chauffeured car to the lighthouse would encourage her to board the yacht without complaint. However, this was merely hope and not an expectation.

The twins each privately anticipated their stepmother's slights and grievances as soon as she stepped aboard, no doubt to plant herself at the starboard bow, where she would complain about the ocean spray as the sailing yacht skipped spritely along, urged by the day's brisk winds. She wouldn't correct the problem by going aft or burrowing herself in one of the boat's two comfortable sleeping cabins. She wouldn't relax and trust her stepsons' years of sailing expertise. If anything, she would grumble to them that this yacht, at an ample forty feet, was nothing compared to the eighty-two-foot, $5 million-plus yacht with its twenty-foot beam and four sleeping cabins, which the boys used for transatlantic crossings. She was the sort to vacillate between finding *that* boat gaudy and superfluous, and thinking it was the only vessel good enough to transport her.

Within a few hours, they arrived at the marina in Montauk, and there she was waiting for them, her mouth set in a thin, grim line.

After they secured the boat for what they hoped would be its short berth at the marina, Hugo alighted the yacht and started, "Hello, Mother. We—"

"This is why I don't like boats," she greeted them. "It's too unpredictable trying to time your arrival. Do you know how long I've been standing here waiting for you two? Do you *care*?"

It was—as always—respect for the memory of their late father that helped Cameron stifle the response he was tempted to give, to say instead, "Sorry you had to wait. Is there a bag I can help you with, Mother?"

"Well, I can't lug the thing out of the trunk and onto your rickety boat by myself. And Eric has hurt his back."

"Very well. Where is he? Is he joining us for lunch?"

"No. He's gone inside to use the restroom. He knows you two dislike him, and he can't stand the sight of you, either. This mission is hard enough for me as it is without having to witness the hatred in everyone's eyes across the table."

Then she added, with a rare chuckle, "It would spoil my lunch."

"Cameron"—she pointed toward the limo at the curb, its glittering onyx exterior in sharp contrast with the marina's mostly brown, beige, and tan tones—"Eric will wait for me back here. I'm hungry and I won't be getting on that damned thing with an empty stomach. Your brother and me will go in and get a table."

"Your brother and *I*." Cameron corrected her grammar in the same way he expressed most of his sentiments about her: under his breath. He then struggled to unload the cumbersome kitbag from the trunk of her car. Was she carting hand weights out to the lighthouse? He finished quickly, joined Hugo and their stepmother for a tense meal of lump crab cake (which she found offensively spiced), bourbon-glazed salmon (which she found too smoky), grilled asparagus, and pan-roasted mushrooms (which she didn't even touch).

After lunch, they boarded quickly. Mrs. Brewster checked twice to ensure her heavy kitbag had been loaded, and she revealed no humor when asked about its contents. "I'll be right here," she announced, planting herself starboard bow as predicted. "It's the only spot on this thing where I can stand and not get seasick."

The voyage lasted only seven nautical miles, but it felt much longer to the twins.

Fortunately, the sea was calm and the wind was light. A colony of seagulls led the way to the lighthouse. As they approached, they saw a tall, tanned man wearing a sailor's cap and a blue nautical pullover with dark grey trousers. He tinkered with an outboard motor on his small boat moored on a short jetty that stretched out from the rocks.

"Take a good look at that swine," she ordered the twins.

The man glanced up and waved. It was less a hospitable gesture than a perfunctory acknowledgment of their approach. Between prescribed hours, lighthouse keepers were obliged to extend a welcome to visitors. To many, such visits were delightful interruptions that broke up the monotony of the day. To others, they were intrusions. Seeing that these seafarers were intent on stopping for a visit, he put down his tools, stepped out of the boat, and walked to the end of the jetty, where he beckoned to them to approach.

"Welcome to my home," he said with a forced smile. "Throw me your rope and I'll tie you up."

Mrs. Brewster picked up her bag and stared at him.

"Cameron. Get off first. I don't want to touch this man's hand if he offers to help me get off this damned thing."

He obliged.

"I don't get many visitors, especially this time of the year," he announced. "So welcome. May I invite you in for a coffee or tea, perhaps?"

"That would be nice," Hugo volunteered, assuming this would fit into his stepmother's undisclosed plan.

"I'm Edward Peterson. And you?"

"I'm Emily Carlton," Mrs. Brewster rushed to reply. "These are my nephews, George and Terry English."

The boys looked askance at her deception.

They followed Peterson from the jetty and along a stone pathway and around to the other side of the lighthouse to a heavy door that opened up to a spiral staircase.

"There are three floors. Upstairs, on the first floor, I have my kitchen and living room, my bathroom and bedroom is on the floor above, and then there's the actual light and all the paraphernalia that goes with it."

Mrs. Brewster paused at a couple points along the steep staircase before reaching the open kitchen.

Cameron—briefly wondering if he was supposed to be George or Terry—wanted to confirm a thought he'd previously expressed. "Most lighthouses are automatic these days, aren't they, Mr. Peterson?"

"Yes, there are just a few of us keepers still around. This one will be automated next year, and then I'll be pensioned off. Twenty-five years in the navy and this is my nineteenth as a keeper, so I'll be ready to retire."

"How many times do you have to go up and down these stairs every day?" Hugo had determined his best role in this subterfuge was to keep things affable, asking the questions he figured a passerby named George or Terry would ask. "It's quite a workout."

"It is. Now, please step inside and I'll put the kettle on. It's tea or coffee. Only instant, I'm afraid."

Mrs. Brewster paused to take in the almost round room, sparsely furnished with a basic kitchen, a square wooden table with four chairs, and a well-used brown leather sofa and armchair. To the right of the kitchen counter was an easel on which stood a canvas with an outline of a girl's face etched in pencil.

"I can't offer you anything other than some chocolate brownies. Picked them up when I went over to Montauk last week to get a few provisions. I try, weather permitting, to get over once every month. Mostly a day's trip. Anything longer than that, I need to make sure I get a relief keeper, but that's becoming harder by the year. More and more are leaving the service."

Mrs. Brewster was silent. Her eyes were affixed on the walls. Seven portraits. All in oil. Each painting the identical subject matter. The same colors. The same features. Por-traits. Each one unquestionably Arabella. She cleared her throat to gain the attention of the twins and nodded in the direction of the walls. They turned to look.

"How do you like your coffee, Mrs. Carlton? I only have powdered milk, if that's okay?"

He bent down to open a cabinet under the kitchen counter.

The zipper on Mrs. Brewster's bag issued a menacing whine as she ripped it open. The lighthouse keeper—and artist, and murderer—turned his head toward the sound but neither turned around nor stood fully straight again. For someone who'd had to catch her breath on the stairs, she now demonstrated lightning reflexes. The speed of a skilled executioner. She retrieved her lady's pistol, bought years earlier when she'd taken lessons at a Manhattan rifle school, and aimed.

Peterson arose with the container of powdered milk in hand. And the guest he knew as Emily, shot him through the chest.

The twins' eyes went from the man, blood oozing from his chest onto his navy pullover, his bewildered expression pleading for explanation, to their stepmother. Both boys felt numb, leaden, and could only watch as she sauntered even closer to Peterson's slumped body, which lay on the floor beneath the kitchen counter and the wall.

"Just to make sure," she spat out viciously, as she fired one more shot directly at the dying man's head.

"Jesus Christ, you've killed him!"

"How very observant of you, Cameron. Hugo, open that window. Do as I say. I have this all planned out."

Hugo's limbs seemed to move involuntarily: freighting him to the window, opening it as she had commanded.

"The two of you, I want you to throw the body out of the window, okay? Then, go to the boat and bring out the kitbag and put it alongside the body. I have some work to do here. Now move."

Cameron may not have moved at all were it not for the sight, amid this sudden gale of chaos, of his brother struggling with a chore. If the task itself was gruesome—trying to lug the deadweight of a murderous and murdered lighthouse keeper to the window—Cameron's instinct to help his brother with whatever needed doing was familiar. Together they managed it. Then, together, they exited without further instruction.

Alone in the lighthouse kitchen, Mrs. Brewster mumbled, "Thank God I remembered to wear gloves," as she retrieved a rag and began to mop up the few drops of blood on the floor and to put the unused coffee mugs back in the cabinet, the brownies back in the tin.

Standing at the window to wipe away any fingerprints, she peered out and saw Peterson's body crumpled on the ground. And the twins, looking out to sea.

"Okay," she said as she approached them. "Put the body into the kitbag. You see the blood on the path. Grab that watering can over there, fill it, and wash away the blood. When you've done that, stuff the can in the bag too."

She watched them as they obeyed her, less in the manner of children honoring a parent than robots responding to code.

Minutes later they were aboard and on their way back to Montauk. A couple of miles into the journey, she spoke again, for the first time. "Toss the kitbag into the water now. The weights will ensure it doesn't float and goes down to the seabed. Okay?"

Neither twin had yet broken free of his spell; in their shock, they had become like so many modern lighthouses—automated. They did as she said. They tossed the kitbag.

On the way back from the lighthouse to the marina, the seven miles felt longer still. Every choppy wave they cut across sent a jolt through Hugo's spine. While he manned the helm, Cameron wandered—aimless and wide-eyed—into the sleeping cabins sequestered below deck. When he reached one of the beds, his knees gave out, and down he went.

He knew his brother had seen what he had: their stepmother murdering the lighthouse keeper. And now she was on their boat. They were, in a sense, her getaway drivers, albeit in a sailing yacht rather than a fast car with its windows tinted dark enough to match lightless alleyways and the dead of night.

She was up there right now. With his brother. With Hugo.

The thought propelled Cameron from his seat up the stairs, toward the large wheel his twin brother clung to with white-knuckled fingers. After seven rugged, stomach-turning miles at sea, they dropped her off back at the Montauk marina.

Her composure after murdering a man—the way she stepped off the yacht and onto the dock with her accustomed air of disapproval for everything that surrounded her—made both boys wonder if, to her, this was nothing new . . . if it was just another day.

She waved to them, dismissively, without a glance backward.

Cameron couldn't speak, but Hugo managed a few words. "Good-bye . . . Mother."

The twins' own journey back was gruesome. Sailing conditions had changed from good to severe within a few hours. It was as if the sea responded to their new status as accomplices to murder by visiting on them rough waters and heavy winds and pelting rain. Instead of sailing back to Rhode Island, they opted to hug the coastline and sail back to New York, where they had a mooring at the New York City Marina on West 79th Street. Nevertheless, it was after midnight before they were back at their apartment on Fifth Avenue. They had barely broken their silence since leaving the lighthouse several hours earlier.

A few days later, Cameron telephoned his brother from his gym.

"You'll never believe this," he whispered. "The Coast Guard reported Peterson is missing and they're conducting a search. It was Peterson's brother who was the murderer and he's on the lam. Evidently, Peterson has been paying off his brother's blackmailer all these years. "

"My God. She killed an innocent man."

"Meet me near the entrance to the zoo in Central Park, half an hour."

Hugo sat stone-faced as Cameron approached. Since receiving his brother's phone call, he had purchased that morning's newspaper; waiting on the bench, he'd read and reread the three-paragraph story on page five describing the lighthouse keeper's mysterious disappearance.

"Have you spoken to that bitch of a stepmother?" Hugo asked.

"I called the house immediately after I called you from the gym."

"And?"

"Day after the murder, she flew to London with Eric. God knows where they are now."

"My God."

Cameron pulled his cell phone from his jacket pocket. "It's Janet," he said, "housekeeper at Rhode Island. Yes, Janet?" He listened attentively. "I'm with Hugo. We'll go to the marina right away. Thank you."

Hugo didn't have time to ask before Cameron explained: "We've got to get over to the marina immediately. Janet had a call from Rod at the marina, who's cleaning out the boat. Something's up."

Within ten minutes they approached the marina. Two police cars were already parked together with a truck that bore the markings of a bomb disposal squad. Someone had already alerted the media. Photographers and reporters wielding microphones swarmed the scene like locusts.

A detective approached Cameron and Hugo as they got out of the cab.

"Is this your yacht, gentlemen?"

Hugo found his voice first. "What's going on?"

"Your man, Rod, found a shoebox under one of the bunks. He heard ticking. He had the common sense to call 911 and our guys discovered a time bomb in the shoebox. Was set to go off several days ago, last Tuesday to be exact, at eight o'clock in the evening. Where were you that night?"

The twins looked at each other.

Cameron spoke not to the police officer but to his brother. "My God, we were on the boat, sailing from Montauk to Rhode Island but because of the storm, we decided to hug the coast and sail down here."

"Who do you think put the bomb aboard? Any ideas?"

They shrugged.

"And I guess the bomb was to be activated by a remote and because of the storm there was no signal. That storm saved your lives." The police officer whistled. He had that demeanor unique to emergency responders: able to sound lighthearted in the face of bombs and sinister schemes and near deaths. "We need to discuss all this with you at length, gentlemen. Be at the precinct in an hour?"

"Of course."

They walked back onto 79th Street to hail a cab. "It must have been Eric who put the bomb aboard while we were having lunch," Hugo whispered. "So she wanted us dead too."

"Jesus Christ." It was all his brother could say.

"We better call an attorney."

CHAPTER ELEVEN

No Good Turn

S cott Mathews glanced at his new gold Patek Phillipe that he picked up the day before from the watch shop on Zurich's *Bahnhofstrasse*, newly engraved with his monogram. The first-class lounge at Zurich's airport was quiet. Never many travelers on Christmas Day. He looked out of the floor-to-ceiling window that overlooked the runway. There was snow on the ground. That did not bode well for a prompt departure. It was one of many possible unfortunate events that caused him concern whenever he traveled.

He'd been in Zurich for merely three days, and rarely ventured out of his hotel suite, opting to order his meals from room service. With the exception of two visits to his bank, two visits to buy the watch, once to choose and pay for it, the other to collect it, and a daily trip to *Sprüngli* for coffee and ice cream, he'd spent practically the entire stay watching television and reading the English and Spanish newspapers.

He had another hour to wait before boarding the flight to Madrid, then a four-hour flight to Bogota and another layover before his flight to La Paz. A shorter route would have been via Miami but that didn't suit. Too risky.

La Paz had been Scott's home for seven years. He had a suite in one of the grand hotels in the center of town that overlooked the Plaza Murillo with a view of the Presidential

Palace. He spent his days walking around the city, dropping in at neighborhood coffee shops and restaurants, reading, attending music recitals, and whenever the snow conditions afforded him the opportunity to ski, he would hire a car and driver to take him to Chacaltaya, Bolivia's only ski resort, a scary hour's journey from La Paz. He kept to himself most of the time and had little contact with the expat clique. His circle was exclusively the local Bolivian community. His late mother was Venezuelan and he had been brought up bilingual, which made fitting in easy for him. He played poker once a week with the chief of police, was a frequent guest of the city's mayor and his wife, and was well in with the Archbishop as well as other local dignitaries. When he went skiing, he was often joined by the editor of the local newspaper or a judge with whom he shared a passion for strong cigars and Glenlivet Scotch Whisky.

Scott chose Bolivia because it had worked well for that Nazi monster, Klaus Barbie, until those damned Klarsfelds succeeded in getting him extradited. Even though there was an extradition treaty between Bolivia and the United States, thankfully, there were sufficient officials who had their hands out who could delay normal legal processes forever. Fortunately, he had sufficient resources available to ensure that those outstretched hands would always be generously greased. Hence the need for his annual trip to Zurich.

He glanced admiringly at his watch again, and got up to walk to the restroom. Fortunately, he had it to himself. He looked in the mirror and straightened his heavy tortoiseshell glasses which sat slightly uneasily over his nose since he had follow up cosmetic surgery a few months earlier. Years before, people admired his thick head of straight grey hair that reached his shirt collar. But, he had it all shaved off and now, every few days he ran an electric razor over his scalp. He'd also taken off his Groucho Marx moustache and since he'd arrived in Bolivia, was down sixty pounds from a high of two-hundred-forty. The mayor had introduced him to his tailor and he now had a wardrobe that emphasized his new-found, trim build. He took great care not to splash his watch as he washed his hands, even though it was waterproof. He grabbed a handful of napkins to wash his face, and some liquid soap squirted onto his shirt and dripped over his monogrammed shirt pocket. He went back to his seat in the lounge and looked out at the snow. The tarmac was now a white carpet.

"Excuse me, Mr. Mathews."

Mathews looked up at the young tall man, in his immaculate, dark blue airline uniform. He had impeccable manners and spoke with a heavy *Deutscheschweiz* —a form of German spoken by many Swiss natives.

"I'm afraid, I have both good news and bad news."

"Christ," Mathews said to himself. "Tell me the bad news first."

"Sadly, your flight to Madrid has been cancelled. The plane could take off from here, but the weather in Madrid is much worse. They are having heavy snow right now and it is expected to get worse as the day goes on. This means that your plane could not land in Madrid."

"Shit."

"Well, that is the bad news. The good news is that we have transferred you to another flight, and actually it's a better one. This flight will get you into La Paz four hours earlier and will only involve one change of plane. Your baggage has already been transferred to the new plane."

"Well, tell me about the new itinerary."

"Instead of flying to Madrid to Bogota and finally to La Paz, you are now on a Swiss Air flight direct to Miami and from there a direct flight to La Paz."

Mathews went quiet. He nodded.

"Here are your new boarding cards and baggage claim. Your flight will board in an hour and your layover in Miami will be just two and a half hours but you won't have to change terminals or go for another security control. Your baggage is checked all the way through to La Paz. The flight to Miami is just under eleven hours."

Mathews nodded and took the boarding cards. "Thank you," he mumbled. There was no point in making a fuss. Any other traveler would be delighted by the switch in flights. He leaned back in his chair and felt a few beads of perspiration flow from his brow and at the back of his neck. He looked around, just a handful of people, no more than a dozen and probably not all on the same Miami flight. He closed his eyes and dozed off.

"Your flight is ready for boarding, Mr. Mathews. Please allow me to take you to your gate. It's close by." The young man reached down to assist him out of his seat and to take his attaché case.

The flight attendant gave him a warm smile as she took his overcoat and jacket to hang in the closet by the galley. He took his seat in the second row. He would have much preferred his original routing via Madrid but had no option. It would have been just as uncomfortable to spend another night in Zurich to take a flight the next day as to have a layover in Miami.

"Just a glass of water, please," Scott said, taking a sleeping pill from his small silver monogrammed pill box. He suspected that one pill alone would be insufficient to help him relax, let alone put him to sleep, so he left the box on the tray alongside an Agatha Christie paperback he'd picked up at the airport. He looked across the aisle at an attractive woman—maybe forty-five—as she rummaged through her handbag to find something, growing more exasperated that whatever it was, wasn't there. She looked up and caught his stare. He smiled. She didn't.

He told the attendant that he wanted to sleep and would skip dinner, and declined her offer of anything other than Perrier.

Miami. My God! The last thing he wanted was to be diverted to Miami. He remembered the last time he was there. That was about ten years before under very different circumstances to attend a convention. Andrea had accompanied him. Poor Andrea. She couldn't take the scandal and shame and committed suicide. They had seventeen years together. Fourteen of them had been bliss.

Time for the second pill.

He looked behind before he pressed the recline button. No one in the seat. The attendant passed and offered him a blanket, which he accepted. *How long is the layover in Miami?* he asked himself. *Two-and-one-half-hours*, he remembered. He looked at his watch. Another eight hours until landing. Finally, he fell into a light sleep, waking up with each bump, every announcement and each time an attendant brushed his elbow as she hurried toward the galley.

After a couple of hours, Scott was awakened by a shriek from behind. A woman's voice. An attendant hurried to the scene. Mathews was too slumped in his seat to turn around. The captain or some other officer was summoned by another attendant and soon came down the aisle from the cockpit.

"Is there a doctor aboard?" The captain announced.

Mathews closed his eyes.

A minute passed.

"This is the captain again, a passenger is sick. Is there a doctor on the plane?"

Mathews closed his eyes firmly and wrapped the blanket tight around his shoulders.

"Again, please, is there a doctor aboard?'

To hell with it. He threw off the blanket and tossed it aside, put the seat upright and stood. He looked back and saw two attendants and a woman hovering and looking down in the direction of the window seat three rows behind his. He put on his glasses and padded down the aisle, not bothering to put back on his shoes.

"I'm a doctor. What's the problem?" he asked, with a slight hesitation in his voice. It had been a few years since he had identified himself as a doctor.

One of the attendants was the first to speak.

"We think this passenger may have had a heart attack." She and the others moved away to allow Mathews to move toward the passenger.

"That's not my area of expertise, I'm afraid. But I'll do what I can. Unfortunately, there is not much that one can do on a flight." He turned to the woman who he correctly surmised was the wife.

"Does your husband have a pre-existing heart condition?" He took the man's pulse, loosened his tie, and unbuttoned his shirt to feel the man's heartbeat before ordering an attendant to bring some aspirin. The man appeared to be around forty-five and had a slender build. His eyes were wide open and he was alert.

"Are you in any pain? Chest pain?" Scott asked.

"No, Doctor."

"Have you been drinking any alcohol?"

"No. Just coffee."

"Your heartbeat is very fast. How much coffee have you had?"

"My husband is a coffee addict. He's never without a cup."

"That's true. I've been serving him coffee and nothing else ever since we took off." One of the attendants volunteered.

"Do you smoke?"

"Yes, but only a few each day."

"That's a lie, Doctor. He goes through at least a pack a day."

"When did you last see your own doctor?"

"About three weeks ago?"

"And what was that for?"

"I have an irregular heartbeat. I am on medication that requires monthly blood tests."

"So you're on blood thinner?"

"Yes."

"Do you sometimes have dizzy spells?"

"Yes."

Mathews stood and turned to the wife and the attendants who were hanging on his every word.

"Please understand I'm not a cardiologist. I don't believe he is under any immediate danger but, I think it would be best for the duration of the flight if I took the seat next to him. He pointed to the wife to take his seat. "And I'd like him to have no food or drink, other than water. Plenty of water. And a couple of aspirin. Call the airport in Miami and have an ambulance meet the plane when we land and rush him to the nearest hospital to run the usual tests. Okay?"

He surprised himself with the way he had assumed control and in such an authoritative voice. Just like the old days.

"Thank you, Doctor. We are very grateful," the wife said. She was a mousy little woman with her brown hair in a bun and no makeup. "How can we ever thank you?"

"It was nothing. I'll keep a close eye on him until we land."

She held out her hand. "I'm Phyllis Carlton. My husband, Dick Carlton, is president of The Whitbread Bank in Florida. We're just returning from a bankers' convention in Switzerland."

"And I'm Philip Mur . . . Ur." *Fuck*, he whispered. "Scott Mathews."

Shit, how could I have made such a slip? Maybe no one noticed. It must have been the effects of the two sleeping pills and being back in the doctor's mode. Oh my God. This is the second time in seven years I've slipped up. The first time, the others were so drunk they didn't notice. But these flight attendants are wide awake. Scott Mathews is on the passenger list. My monograms on the shirt and pill box back on the table . . . The wife is ditzy and nervous, and she wouldn't have noticed, but maybe the attendants noticed. Hell. They did look at each other when I started to give my name. But, maybe, I'm imagining it. Oh my god.

Every half hour one of the attendants came by. "Is there anything we can get for Mr. Carlton, Dr. Mathews?" *Did she hesitate before saying my name, or did she say it in a knowing, sarcastic way?* While his patient relaxed and conversed normally to discuss Switzerland, politics, and banking, Mathews stared ahead, panicked.

How could I have been so careless? he kept asking himself as his patient dozed off. There was no way he could do the same. His fear didn't lift, either, when the attendant came to hand him his monogrammed pill box that he left on the table at his original seat. Scott took a sip of water and the ice in the glass fell onto the crease in his shirt by the green soap stain that had splashed and left a mark that highlighted that monogram.

Mrs. Carlton came back every hour to check on how her husband was faring and remained, not caring that she was blocking the aisle, to renew her repetitious expressions of gratitude. The airline magazine held no interest, and the Agatha Christie book, which had also been brought to him, required more intensive concentration than he was now able to give.

Little over an hour before landing, the final meal of the flight was served. The captain's announcement woke up the patient.

"For goodness sake, don't have coffee," Scott told him. "Stay with water."

Carlton nodded.

"Doctor," the flight attendant said, "when we land, before taxing to the gate, we're going to make a brief stop. An ambulance will be waiting on the tarmac to take the Carltons to the University of Miami Hospital. The paramedics will need to talk to you when they come aboard."

"Of course. As long as I am not required to go with them to the hospital. I have a connecting flight."

"Understood," she replied before hurrying back to the galley.

They started the descent. Once the plane broke through the clouds, Mathews leaned across Carlton. Seven o'clock in Miami. There appeared to be heavy traffic on the freeway. The headlamps on the cars lit up the landscape.

"How are you feeling?"

"Much, much better, Doctor. Thank you."

"When we land, I don't want you to try to retrieve any baggage in the overhead locker. The flight attendants will help you with that. An ambulance will take you to a hospital for a check-up just to make sure you are okay. And you should be sure to contact your primary physician."

Carlton nodded in agreement.

The captain made the usual announcement about preparing to land, and added that there would be a short stop before taxiing to the gate. Scott heard the wheels unlock. The flight path on the screen showed an altitude of twelve hundred feet.

"Oh my God," he whispered. "Miami."

Thud. Landed. Another damned announcement about keeping seat belts fastened. The plane came to a halt. Mathews leaned across to look out of the window. There was the ambulance. Three paramedics stood on the tarmac and next to them stood a man, not in a uniform, no doubt a physician. A stairway was wheeled toward the plane. As soon as the door opened, the co-pilot and one of the flight attendants hurried down the steps to confer with the paramedics. Mrs. Carlton left her seat to rush to her husband and hold his hand. He smiled back at her.

"I'm okay, honey, I feel fine."

There was a hush on the plane. The other passengers remained silent and no one seemed impatient to get off. Some, like Mathews, would also have connections, but there was a calmness that was spooky. No one felt this more than Mathews. Two of the paramedics carried a stretcher and followed the flight attendant and co-pilot back on board.

"Now then, Mr. Carlton. We're going to take good care of you. How are you feeling?"

"Great. Thank you. The doctor here has been taking excellent care of me."

"That's good. Now are you okay to walk or do you want us to take you down to the ambulance on the stretcher?"

"I'm fine to walk, thank you."

"When we're in the ambulance, we're going to give you an EKG, check your vitals and transport you to the University of Miami Hospital for a thorough examination. Okay?"

"Yes, of course."

"Your wife will be coming with us in the ambulance and the airline will ensure your checked-in baggage will be delivered to your home."

"Doctor, would you have a problem coming with us to the hospital?" a paramedic asked.

"Actually, I would. I have a connecting flight."

"I understand. Well, before we say goodbye to you, please would you give us just a quick account of what happened?"

Scott gave an accurate rundown as to how he responded to the "is there a doctor aboard" announcement. His prognosis was that Carlton experienced a reaction to excessive caffeine in his system that exacerbated his irregular heartbeat, but that he hadn't had a heart attack.

"Thank you, Doctor. Now if we need to get hold of you, how can we reach you?"

Christ that wasn't a question I had anticipated, he cursed to himself.

"That's going to be difficult. I have a connecting flight to La Paz and then in a couple of days I'm flying to Lima, Peru," he lied, "and then onto Caracas."

"Busy man."

"Yes, medical conventions."

"Well, thank you. What was the name again? I'm sorry."

"Mathews," he remembered.

It took several minutes for Mr. and Mrs. Carlton to leave the plane, escorted by the paramedics and the co-pilot. Mathews shut his eyes. The sight of the co-pilot talking with the paramedics and the man in the dark suit was scary. What more was there to talk about? *Just get the bloody Carltons to the hospital and get this fucking plane to the gate.*

Minutes later, another announcement came from the cockpit that they were now taxiing to the gate. While Mathews had his eyes closed, he did not see the man in the suit come aboard and take his seat . . . the one that that Mrs. Carlton had just vacated.

"Thank you," Mathews said as the attendant brought him his jacket and coat. The plane came to a halt. Passengers jumped from their seats to retrieve their items in the overhead bins. Mathews stood slowly, exhausted and frightened. He took his time to put on his jacket and stepped into the aisle to walk the few feet down toward his original seat to collect his attaché case and put on his shoes.

As he stepped off the plane, he nodded at the attendants as they stood wishing the passengers well and thanking them for their business.

Now what do I do? Do I leave the airport now, or do I continue to La Paz? Oh my God. Do I go to the gate for the next flight, or do I go to the lounge?"

He opted for the lounge.

So did the man in the suit.

He followed the overhead signs, passed the concessions, and made a brief stop at the rest room. A couple of hours layover . . . maybe he could relax in the lounge. All he had to do was to keep his eye on the board showing departure time and gate information. He already had his boarding card. The woman at the desk, he felt, gave him a weird look as she examined his boarding card and directed him to the seating area behind her desk. He threw his overcoat onto a chair and sat down beside it. A waiter came. He asked for a Perrier.

It didn't take long before it happened.

The man in the suit who had followed him approached with two uniformed police at his side. Mathews stood.

"Okay, I know," he said softly.

He ignored the stares of the others in the lounge as he was cuffed and led off and out of the lounge and through the terminal into the open air and pushed into the back of a waiting police car.

"This is Federal. Otherwise we have a holding cell here at the airport, but we have to take you to downtown HQ."

"Whatever," he mumbled.

Half an hour later, Mathews was taken into a small room at the police headquarters where he faced three uniformed policemen and a plain clothes detective. They read his rights and asked him a few cursory questions to which he gave perfunctory answers. He was asked if he wanted to speak with his attorney. He no longer had one, but he did not waive the right to be represented by a court appointed lawyer at a hearing. There was a warrant out for his arrest, and it was now compounded because he jumped bail seven years earlier. A hearing would be a waste of time.

"We'll have to keep you here overnight, of course," one of the officers said. "Until we know what to do with you. Being Christmas, the jails are full of drunks and other low-lifes and we're short-staffed. Anyway, it's marginally more comfortable here."

He led the way down a well-lit corridor towards an elevator.

"I left my attaché case on the table upstairs," Mathews said, suddenly remembering that it contained his address book, false passport, the receipt for the watch, close to $20,000 USD, and the key to his deposit box at the Swiss bank where he left his bank statements and details of the transfers he'd arranged for his friends in Bolivia who were guaranteeing his non-extradition.

They'll get me on the overseas bank account, of course, he thought, *on top of everything else.*

He was no longer panicked. Resigned and relieved would best describe his mood. At seven the next morning, he woke on hearing the heavy steel door unlock. A police officer came into the cell with a small tray.

"Here's a coffee and a donut for you. I've also brought you a copy of today's newspaper. You made the front page."

"Thank you."

He got off the bed and went over to the table. Without looking at the paper, he took a few sips of coffee. It was the worst he'd had in years. The donut was wrapped in cellophane and it was hard to open. He bit a corner and took out a stale, tasteless dough ball that had been baked well before Christmas. He grabbed the paper and sat down at the side of the bed. There it was.

DOUBLE DRAMA AT MIAMI AIRPORT

Last night, two passengers disembarked off Swiss Air's flight from Zurich. The first, 45-year-old Richard Carlton, the popular president of Whitbread Bank, Florida's fourth largest and fastest-growing Miami-based bank with ninety-seven branches throughout the state and with offices in London and New York. Mr. Carlton took ill on the flight and a mystery man responded to the captain's announcement asking if there was a doctor on board. The man was traveling under a false name and passport. He identified himself as Dr. Scott Mathews, but he is actually Philip Murdoch, a former Michigan plastic surgeon who was sentenced, in absentia, to twenty years imprisonment in 2009 for charges that included mail fraud, filing false tax returns, and billing health insurance companies for unnecessary procedures. Murdoch pleaded guilty to all charges. The Court stated that it found Murdoch's fraud was in excess of forty-five million dollars. Murdoch fled the United States under a false passport, and law enforcement authorities have been searching for him for seven years. He is now in police custody, and is expected to be transferred to a high-security prison to begin his twenty-year sentence.

Meanwhile, Mr. Carlton has undergone a thorough medical examination and has been discharged and plans to return to the office on January 2nd. Mrs. Carlton, who accompanied her husband on the flight, thanked the Swiss Air personnel for the wonderful and efficient manner in which they took care of her husband. As for Murdoch, Mrs. Carlton said, "I felt he was strange from the get-go. I didn't trust him. There was something about him that was weird. Anyway, he really didn't do anything to help my husband. All he said was "lay off coffee and drink lots of water. That was the extent of his involvement. Anyway, my husband is now going to stay at home over the Christmas holidays and we're going to have a quiet time, relaxing with our children."

Murdoch put the paper down.

"No good turn goes unpunished," was his only comment.

CHAPTER TWELVE

The Tattoo

Williiam Elliott—formerly Wilhelm Eisenbach— climbed uneasily into the black Mercedes parked outside Munich's main railway station. It was a particularly cold, wintry December. The heavy snow that week had turned into an ugly slush that formed deep puddles on the streets and sidewalks which had remained unrepaired since the end of the war, two years earlier.

William Elliott left Germany for all the obvious reasons in 1933, and this was his first visit back in fourteen years. It was a trip he dreaded, but as a senior executive at a major Hollywood studio, he couldn't refuse when his boss, a legendarily ruthless and crude mogul, gave an order.

Elliott tightened his scarf around his neck, buttoned up his long, black trench coat, and pulled the rim of his fedora over his face to fend off the cold, blustery wind.

"How was your journey, Herr Elliott?" the driver asked in German.

Elliott had vowed never to speak German again. So many memories. He already knew that his parents and sisters had been killed at Auschwitz along with friends, uncles, aunts, and cousins. Knowing was *not* the same as accepting. He was one of the lucky ones who got out. The lure of Hollywood made it an easy decision to leave. The others decided to weather the Nazi inferno, believing it would be merely short-term madness.

"Very good, thank you," he found himself answering subconsciously in German. "I understand you are originally from Munich, Herr Elliott. Welcome home."

Elliott paused. *Home,* he thought. *How could this place ever be home again to me? So many memories. So much tragedy. I have no home. Hitler succeeded in making Germany a dirty word.*

"I was wounded in the war," the driver continued. "After I was invalided out of the army in 1943 I became a driver for one of the directors of The Dresdner Bank. Last year, I was hired as chauffeur to Wolfgang Lendner and his wife. We are *en route* to Mr. Lendner's office for your meeting. I will wait for you there and then I'll take you to your hotel."

"Thank you."

Lendner was an interesting man. Elliott had never met him before. He had emerged out of nowhere in 1945—after spending several years in concentration camps where he met his wife, another inmate—to become one of the major post-war movie distributors in Europe. Within just two years, he became a force to be both respected and feared within the motion picture industry. Elliott's boss, of similar character, was eager to establish a business relationship with Lendner. To Elliott's discomfort and reluctance, his boss thought him the best qualified executive to make a deal with Lendner.

It took twenty minutes to drive through Munich's war-torn streets to Lendner's office in Schwabing. Elliott got out of the car, straightened his coat, and followed the driver—

whose name had neither been offered nor requested—to the front door of a nondescript, grey stone building.

"Mr. and Mrs. Lendner live on the top two floors. You should go to the door at the end of the lobby. Ring the bell and the secretary will let you in. I will be outside whenever you are ready."

"Thank you."

"Oh, Mr. Elliott, I forgot. Don't be surprised if Mr. Lendner shows you his tattoo. He's very proud of it." He chortled and turned to leave the building.

The door to Lendner's office was open and Elliott walked straight in. The secretary, an attractive middle-aged woman, looked up from her typewriter. Before she could speak, there was a roar from an office. "Is that you, Wilhelm Eisenbach? Come in."

Elliott followed the roar and found himself in a large office on which every wall was smothered with posters of movies of the 1930s starring Hans Holt, Ilse Petri, and Franz Weber among other successful German actors of the era.

The room reeked of cigar smoke. Behind a large untidy wooden desk, cluttered with open files, stood Wolfgang Lendner. He struck an imposing figure. Maybe forty years old, at least six feet tall with broad shoulders and a full head of blond curly hair with a prominent beer belly that bulged over his belt. His red tie was covered with cigar ash, as were the lapels of his blue jacket.

"So, Wilhelm Eisenbach, it's good to meet you." He waved for Elliott to take a seat.

"No one has called me by my original name in fourteen years. It seems strange."

"I understand. Have a cigar." He pushed across the desk an ostentatious silver humidor. "And how about a cognac?"

Elliott pierced and lit the cigar but declined the cognac. "You have some marvelous posters here. I'm impressed."

"Thank you. Like you, I'm hopeful that your company and mine will be able to do good business together."

There was a round table next to Elliott's chair that displayed a large, silver-framed photograph. Before he could say anything, Lendner injected, "That's my wife on our wedding day. January 2, 1946. We were married here in Munich."

"A lovely woman. Is she from Munich too?"

"No. Berlin. We met in Auschwitz."

"I heard you were in the camps. It must have been a terrible, terrible ordeal. My family all perished."

Lendner removed his jacket. Elliott watched in silence as he rolled up his shirt sleeve. He then came around from his desk and stood directly in front of Elliott and stuck out his arm, almost defiantly, to show Elliott his tattoo, as if it were a medal for valor, to confirm his incarceration at Auschwitz. "I was lucky. Like you, I survived. Now let's talk business."

For the next hour, they each described the business activities of their respective companies. Elliott listened to what was basically a monologue. He was impressed by how much the man had accomplished in merely two years. They agreed to meet again the next day to further their negotiations.

The driver opened the car door and looked at Elliott strangely. "To the hotel now?"

"Yes, thank you."

Elliott was in no mood to enter into any conversation. From photographs he had seen of liberated, emaciated concentration camp inmates, Mr. and Mrs. Lendner, in

January 1946, looked to be in robust health, even perhaps overweight.

The route that the nameless driver took to the hotel was not direct and wound through streets that were familiar to Elliott. He was curious but said nothing. The driver went down one side street after another, down narrow, unlit alleyways before coming to a halt in an industrial area outside a modest store sandwiched between a shoe repair shop and a used tire dealer.

"I thought, Herr Elliott, you should see this."

Elliott shrugged his shoulders. *Why not? I'm in no hurry.* He got out of the car and walked toward the store. It wasn't possible to see inside on account of a dark green curtain, so he looked back at the driver, who pointed to a sign above the store.

"Hildegard. Tattoo Artist. Discreet."

The meeting scheduled for the next day with Herr Lendner did not take place.

CHAPTER THIRTEEN

Hubris

In November 1988, Sir George Nigel had what he considered to be a lucky break. A forced retirement from the army at age fifty-five coincided with the news that Edward Heatherton—who currently headed the struggling merchant bank Davenport's—had fallen terminally ill.

The board of directors consisted of Heatherton; Arthur Lincoln, a retired stockbroker; Tubby Fortescue, a Gloucestershire farmer; and the fourth member, an unimpressive and financially strapped member of parliament. The board decided to put out feelers for the bank to be acquired when a felicitous coincidence occurred. A chance encounter at the bar at the Athenaeum between the unemployed Sir George Nigel—fourth baronet within the Davenport-Lockwood lineage—and Tubby Fortescue. Within the month, Sir George was named chairman of the board and Davenport's new managing director.

The fact that he knew nothing about finance was irrelevant. With his army pension, and the modest salary that Davenport's was able to pay him, he could cover the rent on his newly acquired, rent-controlled studio apartment in Covent Garden. The living expenses for a lifelong bachelor were minimal; the salary covered his club membership dues, and—initially—he found this sufficient.

The bank had certainly enjoyed more storied days. Established in 1805 in Manchester, it prospered as a merchant bank that specialized in financing imports of silk from China, cotton from Egypt, and guano from Latin America under the management of Sir George Davenport-Lockwood, the first baronet.

In 1830, Davenport's moved to a building it acquired on Throgmorton Avenue in London, close to the stock exchange. Granted authorization by the Bank of England, it took its place among the ranks of merchant banks active in overseas finance and trade during England's Industrial Revolution. Whilst never matching the clout of Rothschild's or Barings, it became successful enough that George Davenport-Lockwood and his family enjoyed living quarters in London's Belgravia, country estates in Gloucestershire, racehorses in Newmarket, and an oceangoing yacht moored at Lymington.

Contrary to many of its rivals, Davenport's employed practically any family member who needed refuge from domesticity between the hours of ten and five. For Davenport-Lockwood offspring, life was a carnival of fox hunting, golf, and horseraces at Ascot and Goodwood—and of course, the Chelsea Flower Show and Wimbledon tennis.

Never an institution to advance merit over blood, Davenport's rarely employed—and less frequently promoted—unrelated workers. Consequently, the city's talent found opportunity elsewhere. To describe Davenport's as a bank run by dimwits would be too cruel, but certainly the boardroom was occupied by lazy incompetents whose consuming interests and passions lay many miles from the city of London.

While other merchant banks were harvesting their fortunes by the time of the Boer War in 1901, Davenport's, while not insolvent, was a sleeping dwarf. On the outbreak of the First World War, several of its remaining indispensable staff were conscripted, and by war's end, the days of the bank's overseas trading activities had come to an end. The bank suffered a further significant loss upon the death at the Somme of Sir Nigel's grandfather, the last of the Davenport-Lockwoods to play an active and reasonably constructive role in managing its affairs.

Under the stewardship of a distant cousin named Edward Heatherton, following the Great Depression and the outbreak of the Second World War, Davenport's focused solely on extending small unsecured loans to members of the military and the police. Execution of this venture required only three elderly, low-paid clerks. Unable to afford any promotional campaign to enhance its business, the bank relied on small classified advertisements in trade journals. Not that the bank needed to solicit business—borrowers tended to roll over their loans. It could coast; it simply couldn't expand.

For many, a history of private school and service in the army might have contributed to a personality that was aloof, even arrogant. Sir George Nigel, however, had attended the former from age six to eighteen and had engaged in the latter for the next thirty-seven years, and his resultant character was simply independent—fiercely so. He did not need companionship, male or female. In fact, he became so immersed in his own world that even a friendly greeting from a neighbor or the lady in the coffee shop sometimes struck him as an intrusion.

While his appearance would not cause any passersby to stare, he was tall and reasonably good-looking with a full head of hair that was only beginning to turn white.

He had played tennis and golf in his younger days but only when it would have been churlish to decline. Fly-fishing he enjoyed; it was a solitary sport. His superior officers had never complained about his performance, agreeing with his peers that he was simply an *odd bod*. No doubt if he had been more sociable, he would have risen and maybe even become a brigadier.

But Sir George had no regrets; his choices had led him to the opportunity before him now. With Davenport's, he reasoned, he had the chance to garner the company's wealth and, in so doing, gradually increase his own—but this was secondary. While it was true he'd never cared much for socializing, in taking the helm of this institution, withered though it may have become, he felt he'd acquired the exact sort of companionship he'd unknowingly searched for all his life: he'd joined the heritage of overseers of an important name. The name Davenport.

Through the dimmest of Davenport's struggles, its formal recognition as an authorized bank remained essential to staying in business. Under normal circumstances, this legitimacy would have been lost by the beginning of the twentieth century, but old-school ties and social connections ensured that, however fragile the bank's condition, it still remained in good standing with the Bank of England.

Ownership of the bank was another issue. It was founded by the first baronet and his two younger brothers, each with a one-third stake. By 1991, the bank had more than one hundred shareholders. The largest shareholding, two percent, was owned by a sheep farmer in New Zealand who'd never set foot in England. The other shareholders—all descendants of the original founders, were mostly scattered between Australia, Argentina, the United States, and South Africa—not one lived within a hundred miles of London. With the exception of three—a retired school teacher in Edinburgh, a vicar in Cornwall, and a diplomat in Cairo—none had ever complained of never having received a dividend in more than twenty years, or had even made any inquiry as to the bank's condition.

The bank's premises were housed in a four-story house built mid-nineteenth century. On the outer door of its ground-floor office, a brass plaque read, "Davenport's, Merchant Bank, established 1805." Three upper floors were occupied by a law firm and an insurance brokerage. The City owned the house, and Davenport's lease had another four years to run. The board had seemingly given little thought to the question of what would happen next.

Apart from Sir George, the staff consisted of just the three clerks who handled the small loan business, one bookkeeper, a secretary, and an office boy. Paint—once white but now greying—peeled from the walls; burned-out bulbs remained in their fixtures like the flying bugs that followed the light's siren call and died there; and there was mustiness about the large, one-room banking hall and Sir George's office, which led off it. One of the clerks smoked a pipe and no one had the nerve to ask him to stop. Apart from the seventeen-year-old office boy and Sir George, at fifty-five, the youngest staff member was sixty-three. Practically a pensioner.

The majority of the bank's assets covered its walls in the form of paintings acquired over the two hundred years of the bank's existence and transferred from previous locations. No one knew exactly how or when they'd arrived at St. Mary Axe. The only time they may have warranted comment was when, after the office cleaner made her weekly rounds, one hung crooked. It was believed that the cleaner disturbed the paintings deliberately to ensure her visit had been noticed.

Sir George was a man of routines. Choosing his suit for the day was easy. He owned only two, both acquired twenty-five years earlier and both, to his credit, still appropriate for his frame. Likewise, just three polka-dot ties, his regimental tie, and one black one reserved for funerals. His white shirts were beginning to be frayed at the cuffs and his black shoes were in need of new heels.

If weather precluded walking to the City, he preferred the bus to the underground. A hasty cup of tea and a scone at the coffee shop on the corner preceded his arrival at the bank. He would come upon the staff already at work. Ms. Bourne, the spinster secretary, approached his desk with the morning's *Financial Times*, which he barely read, and the *Times*, which he found similarly uninteresting, apart from racing news and obituaries. He lunched once a week at the Overseas Bankers Club, charged to the bank; otherwise, he had a cheese sandwich and coffee at his desk. Before returning to his studio apartment, he'd drop off at the Flying Messenger, the pub closest to home, for a beer and a sausage roll. Once a week, he enjoyed dinner at his club.

Weekends were for long walks, visiting his club to read newspapers and watch television, as he hadn't one at home. When he still had the cottage in Hampshire and gone fly-fishing on the River Test and golfed at the Army Gold Club, there had been a few men with whom he'd spent time. Had he married, his social life surely would've been broader, but he spared the lack of a wife no thought. His last relationship had been thirty-three years ago; now she was a dowager duchess living in Scotland.

Following the horses constituted his only real pastime. Hardly a day passed when he didn't place a few bets. His wagers were relatively small but so were his earnings. He wanted to take a loan from the bank to clear his overdraft at Coutts & Co. and to settle his account at one of his book-makers, as well as buying a few new clothes, but the board did not agree. The board unanimously informed him that they found it impertinent of him to even apply for one, given he'd been at the bank only three weeks. The board's refusal was humiliating.

Apart from the chimes of the grandfather clock that had been a fixture for most of the bank's existence and the clatter of Ms. Bourne's typewriter, sounds during the workday were rare—especially the sound of human voic-es. The clerks worked in silence; necessary conversations were conducted in whispers. The one consistent human noise was the cough of the elderly pipe-smoking employ-ee who sat close to the sealed window.

As Sir George sat at his desk—the same desk occupied by his ancestors—he entertained the ideal curiosities he sometimes did. What if he'd stayed on in the army until he turned sixty-five? What if he'd made passage to Aus-tralia in the 1950s and started a new life there? What if he'd returned to Kenya, where he had happily served? He didn't romanticize the army life, but at least there had al-ways been a well-subsidized Officer's Mess when he served.

Sir George had been with Davenport's for a few months when the Bank of England summoned him to a meeting. News of Edward Heatherton's death had found its way to one of the officers at the Bank of England who was respon-sible for supervision of banks of Davenport's size. There was concern about Sir George's lack of financial experience, the small number of outside depositors, and the limited scope of the bank's activities. Without going so far as to threaten withholding the all-important Bank of England authorization, Sir George was informed in no uncertain terms that Davenport's needed an injection of capital of at least two million pounds and the appointment of a new managing director—one who had the experience he lacked.

The Bank of England had a proposal though: a merger with another small bank—Gillespie's. Established in 1900, Gillespie's had prospered unlike Davenport's, but never made it to the big league. They had sent a team to examine Davenport's books. Whilst Davenport's was not insolvent, the price Gillespie's put on the bank was an insult. But there was little time, and fewer options. The Bank of England made it clear that if the board of Davenport's declined the merger, it would lose its cachet of being an authorized bank.

For Sir George, the blessing of the situation was evident—Gillespie's agreed to keep him on at his same salary and as a nonexecutive chairman—but, less evidently, there was a curse.

After more than two hundred years in business, and under his watch, the name Davenport's would vanish from the city of London. That is, unless it was content to be stripped of its authorized status, to become another lowly, moneylending outfit treated with contempt and derision. As he contemplated this, he stared at the same portrait he'd idly gazed at in the previous months: a dark, somber portrait of an unattractive female ancestor. A brass plaque attached to the wooden frame identified her as Martha Davenport-Lockwood, the widow of one of the three founding partners.

Underneath the portrait was something to which Sir George had not previously paid attention. The name of the artist. Edward Burne-Jones.

Sir George knew nothing about art, but the artist's name rang a bell. He decided to visit Westminster Public Library that weekend. His findings pleased him. The artist was indeed one of the most celebrated English painters of the nineteenth century. Further research informed him that paintings in good condition by this artist could fetch at auction one million pounds and more, depending on the subject matter, size, and condition.

As for subject matter, Martha Davenport-Lockwood was certainly no beauty. And size, he grabbed a ruler and measured that the framed piece was thirty-six inches square. Regarding condition, hopefully it only needed a good professional cleaning.

He went back to his desk and pulled out from a bottom drawer the previous year's balance sheet. The bank's artwork was listed at ten pounds. Who would know if he were to remove it? He'd sat across from it, sometimes looking directly at it, for months and only recently could he have described its subject. To cover the blank space on the wall, he would bring in a picture from home.

He had just the thing: a still life so dark it was almost black, depicting a group of people sitting around a table. He'd inherited it with a collection years before from an uncle he despised. The painting was even duller than the man who'd bequeathed it to him—it was ideal for blending in, for never being noticed.

His research at the library remained at the forefront of his mind for two weeks. Apart from once, forty years before, when he passed a bad check to cover gambling losses, he had never committed a felony or misdemeanor. But Coutts was still breathing down his neck. Litigation over unpaid debts would dissolve whatever future remained for him at Davenport's—and it was more official now than before that Davenport's was in no position to bail him out.

He swapped the paintings in early December; he would do nothing with the Burne-Jones pending the New Year. If no one commented on the still life during the three weeks before New Year's Eve, he would proceed to sell the Burne-Jones. If anyone did notice, he would simply say that he'd borrowed the Burne-Jones to display it for family members at a Davenport-Lockwood family reunion over Christmas. He would imply his intention to return it when business reopened after New Year's.

The backup plan proved unnecessary, however; no one averted their eyes from their own routine to even notice it. And while Sir George did not display the painting for any non-existent family reunion over Christmas, he used his holiday break to pick out an art dealer in St. James's who represented himself as an expert in nineteenth-century British paintings.

He telephoned the dealer, Cornelius Busby, and inquired whether he would be interested in acquiring a Burne-Jones. The answer was positive. Any qualms or suspicions that Mr. Busby had about the provenance were dispelled after Sir George identified himself and informed him that the painting was of an ancestor. Embarrassed about inviting Mr. Busby to his modest apartment, he suggested they should meet at his club on Sunday; no one except Shelby, the doorman, would be there.

On the day of the meeting, Sir George wrapped the painting in a blanket, and in spite of his frugal existence and the need to avoid any extravagance, he took a taxi to his club. Cornelius Busby was already waiting him, sitting in a dark leather chair in the foyer.

"Sir George," he said as he stood. "How good it is to meet you."

"And you too, Sir. Thank you for coming." After hanging his overcoat on an antique brass hook, he led the way toward the club's Maitland Room, named after a former member and hero of the Napoleonic Wars. While a log fire warmed its immediate proximity, the rest of the room retained a chill accentuated by the fact that, this being the weekend, no lights had been turned on.

Sir George displayed the painting against the back of a sofa upholstered in a floral pattern commingled with decades of red wine and port stains.

Mr. Busby had readied himself—he had a magnifying glass in his jacket pocket. He said nothing while he examined Martha. Sir George's heart raced as it had in his days patrolling in Kenya for Mau Mau fighters.

"Sir George, I think this is a genuine painting, but I need to examine it more closely. Would you allow me to take it back to my gallery? I'll have an answer for you tomorrow?"

Sir George hesitated.

"I'll give you a receipt—of course."

At that, Sir George led Mr. Busby over to a writing table so that the dealer could write out a memorandum of receipt on club letterhead. Only after they'd parted company did Sir George realize that he would be without his only blanket on that cold January night.

The next afternoon, true to his word, Busby called. He would buy the painting for fifty thousand pounds. While it was far less than he'd expected, Sir George needed a quick deal—certainly not a sale by auction —and he'd never learned the art of haggling.

By the end of the year, Sir George resigned from the bank, but only after Gillespie's had relocated Davenport's to their much larger premises in Gresham Street. In the course of relinquishing the St. Mary Axe office, they donated its contents to the Salvation Army, save for the grandfather clock, which was sold at auction with the artwork.

And at the auction, the hammer went down on Sir George's still life. Which was, it so happened, a Velazquez. It sold for fourteen million pounds.

CHAPTER FOURTEEN

Where There's A Will

The large convoy of cars leaving the cemetery after Matthew Carter's burial proceeded at its customary respectful speed along the oak tree-lined Greenwich, Connecticut avenues and past the grand estates built before the First World War for the city's professional and business leaders. Days before, the death of fifty-nine-year-old Matthew Carter, from a heart attack during his morning commuter train ride into the city, shocked the many people now leaving his funeral.

He was not known to have any medical issues. He'd just returned from a Mediterranean cruise, and as many noted, with his new tan and his salt-and-pepper hair recently rewound to a shiny black, he'd never looked better.

His legacy was perhaps best examined by a peek into the cars at the head of the procession now winding its way toward Weatherby Lodge, where a kingly spread awaited his mourners. His widow, Gwen, had the event catered. Hiring caterers was a specialty and a hobby of hers.

Inside the third car sat Matthew's firstborn, Samantha, and her husband, James. Samantha gazed out of her window not just because she was lost in thought but because she was trying to ignore James' counterfeit sadness. Over on his own side of the car, James knew he should take his wife's hand but could barely fight off the urge to wave to curious passersby as though he were royalty—a visiting sultan, an oil magnate, a famous movie star. Anyone other than the man his father-in-law wished his prize daughter had never married.

The cause of Matthew's distaste for his son-in-law had never been obvious. It was true that James' accomplishments didn't quite match Samantha's, who was an honors student at an Ivy League school where she had been admitted to the bar as the youngest in her year. However, like his wife, James *had* recently joined one of the city's most prestigious law firms.

James and Samantha both knew, as everyone did, more or less—that James's parents were the reason Matthew stifled expressions of the disapproval that clearly boiled in his veins. His father was dean of medicine at Samantha's alma mater and his mother was, well, a dean's wife; they were connections more than they were in-laws, but they wouldn't have stood for their son being treated as a leper or a flunkie.

Not that James thought any better of *his* in-laws. Gwen was a simpering wuss, a woman whose personal ambitions started and stopped with home décor. Matthew, at the opposite end of the spectrum, had been a ruthless despot who'd amassed wealth and enemies in equal measure. Many of his adversaries had sought satisfaction in the courts, where Matthew was well-known in legal circles as a vexatious litigant. James figured this was brought about by his unfulfilled ambition to be an attorney himself. He loved the game, the fight, the whole *milieu* of attorneys, judges, juries, and courthouses. It was no coincidence that

Samantha pursued a legal career. When notice of her birth was announced in the local newspaper, some twenty-five years earlier, it might as well have read: *To Matthew and Gwendolyn Carter, an attorney.*

James had little enthusiasm for the law. He would have far preferred life as a musician (he played an acceptable jazz stride piano) or as an art dealer, specializing in pop art. But to abandon the law now after so many years of study and excruciating examinations and finally securing a place—albeit at the bottom rung of the ladder—at a premier law firm, would have wreaked havoc on his marriage and on his relations with both his own family and Samantha's.

Finally, James did hold out his hand to Samantha. She ignored the gesture. She looked out her side window still, thinking mostly of how all major family decisions would now fall to her. Her mother had never signed a check, paid a bill, or been concerned with anything other than keeping a well-stocked refrigerator and pantry.

In the next car was Samantha's younger sister, Paulette, a high school dropout whose twin passions in life were looking at pictures in fashion magazines—without reading the accompanying articles—and shopping. At a time when a dollar was a dollar, she spent upward of one hundred thousand annually. Her boyfriend, Trevor, had twice been ousted from casinos for counting cards.

Back at the house, Gwen, accompanied by her sister, left her guests and went to her bedroom to cry about the loss of her husband. Samantha and Paulette disappeared into another bedroom to console each other. Trevor sat in the kitchen, watching a sporting event which no doubt he had money riding. That left James to mix and mingle with the others, who ate from the buffet and drank from the bar as if food rationing and prohibition were just around the corner. He had to refrain from sneering whenever he approached two or three "mourners" standing together, laughing, swigging vintage cognac or Dom Pérignon. When he neared, they would don their most soulful expressions and adopt the standard funeral *patois,* only to revert to jollity the second James moved onto the next group. He picked up on anxious whispers as he circulated.

"How on earth is Gwen going to manage without Matthew?"

"At least she has Samantha to take care of everything."

"What about Paulette? How will Gwen cope with that nightmare?"

"I hear things aren't exactly rosy with Samantha and that husband of hers."

After the funeral, the atmosphere around the house assumed a new normality. Samantha hunkered down in her father's office. Paulette went on another shopping bender. Gwen sat in the breakfast room, talking with the housekeeper and the gardener, wading through her daily two packs of Marlboro and half bottle of Chivas Regal.

And James visited the art museum and galleries and read up on Jasper Johns, Roy Lichtenstein, and James Rosenquist. He'd recently had it in mind that he and Samantha should emigrate to France. On his visit a few weeks earlier, he'd seen a bar for lease at the harbor in Saint-Tropez; he dreamed immediately of converting it to a piano bar with local artists' work hanging on the walls. Taking inspiration from the movie *Casablanca,* he'd call it Jim's.

However, when he'd taken the plunge and mentioned it to Samantha—before Matthew died—she'd asked if he'd gone stark raving mad. And that had been the calm before the storm of her main remarks. Next she exploded: "I married you because I wanted an attorney as a husband. Looking at you now, that was my first mistake. And if you think I'm going to decamp so you can run a third-rate bar on the Riviera, you're sorely mistaken." She had no desire, she made it clear, to play Ingrid Bergman to his Humphrey Bogart.

And true to form, she did not delay in reporting James's thoughts to both his parents and hers. It had resulted in the expected Armageddon.

James and Samantha were due to go back to the city on Sunday. Over breakfast on Saturday morning, Gwen announced that Brian Marshall would be coming for a drink that evening to talk about Matthew's will. "I want you all here." She hesitated before adding, "That includes you, James." Instinct told him to nod and say nothing.

Now in his early seventies, the Honorable Brian Marshall was the second son of a prominent member of the House of Lords by his second wife, a prominent New York socialite. The firm at which he served as senior partner had represented Matthew Carter in his various real estate and commercial dealings as well as instituting on his behalf or defending him in a constant flow of legal disputes. Matthew had thought that rubbing elbows with Brian would transfer to him, by osmosis, the trappings of aristocracy. He paid less attention to the fact that Brian Marshall was not the sharpest knife in the legal drawer; the man's primary tactical move, in fact, was subcontracting work to attorneys whose skills exceeded his own. Matthew's will and family trusts, however, he handled himself.

By midmorning, James felt claustrophobic. He was trapped with a distant wife, an inebriated mother-in-law, and a sister-in-law cutting out images from her magazines with both the focus and selectivity of a kindergartener making her first collage. Samantha, ever penurious in tending to family affairs, had cancelled her father's newspaper subscriptions within forty-eight hours of his death, so James announced he was going out to get the *Wall Street Journal*. In truth, he was going out to listen to jazz on the car radio and spend as much time as possible away from the house.

The Honorable Brian Marshall arrived promptly at eight. He had not been invited to stay for dinner and no one felt like dining out. However, it seemed to everyone present as though the man had already drunk his dinner when he arrived. And judging by the creased khaki pants and polo shirt he wore in place of his customary dark suit, they could deduce he'd drunk it at his golf club. But getting sauced ahead of time was just his way of applying the same ritual to which he accredited all his legal success to the important matter of a long-term client's will.

"Now, Gwen, let's get down to business. I assume you've spoken with Samantha already about what we discussed on the phone yesterday and that she's on the same page as us?"

"Actually, I'll leave that to you." For a moment her cheeks flushed with the pleasure of again, however temporarily, having a man to whom she could leave things. She ushered him toward the dining room. "Come, it will be more comfortable in here, especially as I believe you have lots of papers."

"Just copies for everyone of poor Matthew's will."

Everyone—including James, who'd returned after sitting in his car as long as he dared—followed Gwen through the double doors into a large dining room, with walls of dark green striped wallpaper and still life paintings that hung between brass sconces. The windows on the opposite wall looked out on the immaculately manicured lawn and rose bushes, that surrounded a circular pond with a fountain.

Fourteen upholstered chairs were positioned around a highly polished antique mahogany table. At its center sat a silver fruit bowl that had never housed fruit.

"Brian, you sit at the head of the table, where Matthew always sat," Gwen said in a tight voice, blinking back tears.

Before sitting, he opened his attaché case and took out a thick sheaf of papers.

Gwen took a seat to the attorney's right and Samantha to his left. Paulette drooped into the chair beside her mother, pouting to protest the fact that James was here while her Trevor had been excluded. She had not been persuaded by her sister's argument that a recently acquired gambler boyfriend was not on equal footing with her own lawyer husband. James sat at the far end of the table, directly opposite the lawyer, notwithstanding the empty chairs between himself and the others.

"Let me begin," Marshall said. "I have here the original and four copies of Matthew's will."

Samantha took the four copies, each consisting of twenty-five stapled pages, and walked around the table to distribute three of them. Her heels mimicked the quick tick-tock of a metronome as she walked all the way down to her husband and then, after dropping the papers in front of him, all the way back to her seat.

"You have before you Matthew's last supposed will and testament. Please take a few minutes to read it before I tell you the situation. The first few pages and the last are standard boiler-plate paragraphs that relate to all wills and particularly to the duties and obligations of the executors. As you know, I'm one of the two executors, and Samantha is the other."

Gwen smiled at her elder daughter. She couldn't replace Matthew, but the take-charge nature she'd inherited from him was a blessing.

James quickly turned over the pages until he came to the bequests. He knew that his father-in-law, despite his ruthless reputation, was charitable. He had no idea just how charitable.

Hundreds of thousands of dollars had been left to distant relatives around the world: England, Australia, Brazil, and Spain. First, second, third, and maybe fourth cousins; nephews, nieces, great-nephews; employees, both long-term and those who had worked for him for under a year—people whose names the man had never mentioned before—were all now beneficiaries of sums greater than twice their annual salaries. Also honored were the Episcopalian church where he and Gwen had married, the Roman Catholic Church where his mother had been a stalwart, the synagogue whose rabbi was Matthew's bridge partner, a local orphanage, a city library, the Botanical Gardens, and, somewhat ironically, the Heart Foundation. Pages of bequests that ranged from $10,000 to upwards of two million.

Curious of the grand total, James thought of whipping out his pen for some quick back-of-the-will arithmetic, but that would have been too gauche.

Neither Gwen nor Paulette made any move to look at the documents in front of them. Both gazed out onto the garden. Samantha was focused on those pages that related to her fiduciary role as one of the two executors.

Minutes ticked by. The silence in the room was interrupted only by Gwen standing to pour Marshall another scotch. And to refill her own glass.

"I take it you have all had time to scan the will?" Brian softened his accustomed loud bluster for this part. "Are there any questions?"

No one spoke.

"Well, this is what I have to tell you. You will see the pages that list all Matthew's bequests. It's a testament to Matthew's generosity." He flashed a smile that seemed to claim partial responsibility for his client's benevolence. "In fact, a rough calculation of his estate would be in the region of twenty million dollars, of which this will contains bequests of around nine million. Excluding legal fees and estate duties, the balance would be approximately nine million for Gwen and four and half each to Paulette and Samantha. Of course, this house is in Gwen's name, as is Matthew's business."

The only elements of surprise in James's mind related to the amount his father-in-law had willed to individuals and organizations outside the immediate family—and that Weatherby Lodge and the business were in his mother-in-law's name.

"But now comes the part that changes everything."

Gwen looked down at the table, Paulette blinked at her fingernails, and Samantha stared at the lawyer. James couldn't tell whether she knew what was coming. He assumed that his mother-in-law did.

"This will is invalid. Matthew died intestate. Excluding fees and estate taxes, Gwen will inherit, under the rules of intestacy, thirteen and a half million in round numbers, and Samantha and Paulette close to seven million apiece."

Having already splurged her energy on dissecting magazines and hating James, Paulette had none left over to suppress her smile. And though one couldn't argue that she'd spent any tact that day, she had none of that remaining either.

James went to the signature page of the will. It appeared properly executed by his father-in-law, dated and witnessed by someone called George Lyles, a CPA with a firm's address in the same building as Brian Marshall's.

"I don't understand, Mr. Marshall. Why is this will invalid? It seems as if my father-in-law signed it and that it was properly witnessed. Each of the twenty-five pages bears Matthews's initials."

"Check the date of the will. You will see that it was signed on August 10. That was ten days before Matthew and Gwen left on their cruise. Matthew insisted that this will was temporary, only to take effect if he died while on vacation. We agreed that we would meet on his return from the cruise and he would then make a new will. And that new will would be his final will and testament and that it would incorporate any changes which he had pondered about while on vacation."

James squinted at Brian, both because the man was truly far enough away to blur and because he couldn't yet see his point. "But he didn't die on the cruise. He died on the train when he was back in this country."

James saw the hostility in his wife's and mother-in-law's eyes as they stared down the table at him.

"You are right, James. But as far as I'm concerned, he was still on vacation. The law will support me on this. Yes, he was back home, but he had not yet returned to his office. Any reasonable person would construe that until he had his feet back under his own desk, he was still on vacation."

"Mr. Marshall, with all due respect, I think that is quite a stretch. First, I don't see the word 'temporary' anywhere in the will—it clearly reads 'Final Will and Testament'—and second, he'd been back in this country for a few days before he died. And he died on the train going back to his office."

Marshall took a deep breath, which he forcefully transformed to a chuckle. "How long since you were admitted an attorney, son? Two years, three maybe? Oh, I know how it goes with you young attorneys—you always know everything. You're always spotting the details and the loopholes nobody else spots." Then the amiable tone sloughed off to reveal not simply a sigh but a growl. "Let me remind you that I am seventy-three, I've been in practice for close to fifty years, and I'm the senior partner in a *highly* respected and *long*-established law firm. I also chair a Bar Association Committee on probate law. And you have the nerve to challenge me?"

"James, apologize to Mr. Marshall immediately!" Gwen shouted. "You should be ashamed of yourself. You're a cocky upstart. What's got into you?"

If anyone had expected James to tremble upon being shrieked at by an in-law and berated by an old lawyer, they clearly didn't realize he was accustomed to both. He looked toward his wife with a shrug. "Sam, surely you see my point?" And then to Mr. Marshall, "I don't mean to be rude. I just question whether a court would uphold this will as invalid."

"Don't you see that this will never get to court?"

"How can you be so certain? If any of the beneficiaries get wind of this will . . . "

"Well they won't." Marshall picked up the original from the table and, in a theatrical gesture, tore it in half and then in half again. "I suggest you all do the same."

And they did. James too, still in a state of bewilderment.

"Now, I'm waiting for you to apologize to Mr. Marshall," Gwen insisted.

"Let it drop, Gwen. I'm sure James meant no harm. You should hear the arguments I have with my own son, a junior partner in my firm. And as far as the beneficiaries are concerned, you can always make them gifts at your own discretion."

James followed a procession of emotions similar to the one Brian Marshall so recently had manifested: first he sighed, then he chuckled, then he was flooded with anger. If Matthew had been partially redeemed by his charitable nature, the same characteristic did not redeem his wife—none of the beneficiaries would see a dime.

When he returned from escorting Mr. Marshall to his car, he found the women talking in whispers in the kitchen.

"I hope you apologized when you took Brian to his car," Gwen snapped.

"Actually, I didn't." He had, but he wasn't about to tell her that. And he'd made sure his apology sounded as hollow as it was. "It seems like a shyster move to deny the legitimate rights of Matthew's beneficiaries to inherit what he clearly intended them to receive."

"You really are a smug piece of shit," Gwen slurred as she downed the last drop of Chivas from her glass. "Matthew wasn't all wrong about you."

"Well, tell me this. Matthew's will was over twenty-pages long. Why would he go through the motions of drawing up a will of that length and in that detail shortly before leaving on a cruise, only to make a new will, as Brian alleged, on his return two or three weeks later?"

"I don't know why you give a damn. You aren't in the will, anyway. I'm going to bed," she replied as she stormed out of the kitchen.

"Me too." James looked across at his wife. Samantha ignored him. "Unless you want to drive home tonight?"

"In the morning," she snapped. "I'm tired."

Later that night, James looked across at Samantha as she slept. He couldn't sleep; he was contemplating how Brian and Gwen, and maybe Samantha too, were in cahoots to defraud the beneficiaries. Of course the will was valid. A man who considered himself an honorary lawyer, as Matthew did, would never make such foolish omissions.

Hungry, thirsty, and remembering the cheesecake in the refrigerator, James tiptoed downstairs in his robe. The doors to Gwen's and Paulette's bedrooms were closed with no light shining underneath, which made sense; it had to be two in the morning by now.

When he passed the open dining room door, his eyes fell on those wills that had been torn up but not discarded. After he had cut himself a generous slice of cake and put the kettle on for a cup of tea, his mind returned to the dining room table.

In front of where Mr. Marshall sat lay the original of the signed copy of Matthew's torn-up will. And there lay the torn photocopies in front of where Gwen, Samantha, Paulette, and he had sat. He stared at the five sets. James skimmed back over the largest shreds as he ate his slice of cheesecake, then pocketed the original will. If Gwen asked where it was, he would tell her Brian had taken it, though he found an inquisition unlikely—Gwen, like Brian, had appeared too drunk to focus on where all the papers lay.

James stuffed the torn sheets in his robe, tiptoed out of the dining room, through the back corridor to a door that led into the outside and to his parked BMW. He opened the trunk and stuffed the sheets of paper into the concealed compartment that held the spare tire. He returned to the kitchen just in time before the electric kettle began to whistle.

A few hours later, he woke up to the sound of Samantha getting out of bed to go to the bathroom.

"I want to hit the road," she said. "I don't think my mother is in any rush to see you this morning. We can always stop for a coffee on our way back into the city."

"Suits me," he replied.

By the time he was showered and dressed, Gwen and Samantha were already in the kitchen. Paulette had either spent the night with Trevor at his place or was still in bed and unlikely to stir until midday.

"Coffee's made, if you want some," Gwen said, pointing to the carafe.

"I'm having one so you might as well have one too," Samantha said. "It will save us from stopping on our way home."

James sat down at the table as an unsmiling Gwen set his mug before him in a less-than-gentle way.

"Thank you. How very kind," James remarked.

Before they left, Samantha found one last situation that she needed to take charge of. She gathered the torn shreds of wills from the dining room table—the absent copy was not mentioned—and solicited advice on how best to destroy them.

"Why not light the fire in the living room and burn them?" James asked.

"Why James, what a good idea." And, though her tone was drenched in sarcasm, she did exactly as he'd suggested.

Within two years, Samantha had joined Brian Marshall's firm and made partner. She'd also moved out of the apartment she had shared with James and into one within walking distance to her office.

Having been yelled at by one too many lawyers cut from the same gin-soaked cloth as Brian Marshall, James had quit law.

Divorce proceedings were well under way.

James knew he should have been mourning the end of his marriage, but he wasn't. James knew he should have done, said, and felt many things over the years that he hadn't. He shouldn't have married a woman who was trying to both please and rebel against her father all in one choice of husband. He shouldn't have slept with other women, no matter what Samantha was doing with Brian's son. And he shouldn't feel so relieved—exuberant almost—while being permanently and legally severed from his wife, especially in light of the letter his lawyer had recently received from hers.

Citing irreconcilable differences, which apparently he alone had failed to reconcile, she was seeking a financial settlement and alimony far beyond his capabilities. And far beyond what she could possibly need, given both her salary and her inflated inheritance.

He should hit back with charges of her adultery, which had started before his and involved a more prolific span of partners. But it wouldn't be enough. And besides—he was a gentleman.

He should feel as cowed and penitent and nervous as he should have felt the day Brian Marshall yelled at him for questioning his deceased father-in-law's will. He shouldn't, quite to the contrary, be sitting in a café, sipping coffee and fantasizing of how it would feel when he opened the doors of his piano bar on the Riviera. Sure, the old location had long since been snatched up, but he'd found another. A better place even, and one he could certainly afford now.

It was a grey and drizzling afternoon, but nothing could get James down today. When the waitress came by, he ordered two coffees, one to replace his rapidly emptying cup and one for his lawyer, who would be meeting him shortly.

Glancing down at the large chunks of paper reassembled into their original formation, the waitress said, "Looks like you have been working on a puzzle there."

James only smiled. *Actually,* he wanted to tell her, *I solved this puzzle quite some time ago. I've just been waiting for the right moment to reveal it.* And now, with the promise of freedom from the Carter family and emigration to France just around the corner, the time was right indeed.

CHAPTER FIFTEEN

Thirty Days Left

"George, please take care of yourself. Write often. Please. I love you. I will miss you," she said, sobbing as she hugged him. He felt her tears against his cheek. "Oh hell. Why are army uniforms so rough against the skin?" She forced a giggle as she pulled away to scratch her bare shoulder.

"It won't be long. A year at most. And of course I'll write. You write too, okay? I want to hear all the news, and don't forget to send me the clippings from the paper about the Cleveland Browns."

"You and your Cleveland Browns," she replied with another vain attempt at lighthearted banter.

Not long before, they had stood in this same place, an envelope littering the floor between them. He remembered that his thumb had covered the Department of Defense seal in the upper left corner of the letter, and that after he'd finished reading, a thumbprint of perspiration distorted that noble image of the eagle donning a shield.

Neither his familiarity with the letter's layout nor his expectation that a deployment was coming could stop his heart from racing. The canonical numbers and date following ORDERS; his name in reverse: *Erickson, George L*. The message:

You are deployed on a One-Year Temporary Change of Station (TCS) assigned to: Gao, Mali. His heart sunk and Julie cried aloud when he read the words. *Where was Mali, for God's sake?* His purpose was listed as *Deployment In Support of United Nations Peacekeeping.*

What do I care about a United Nations peacekeeping mission? Let the people of Mali sort out their own problems. He bet even his African-American friends couldn't point out Mali on an atlas. Feeling numb with disbelief, George gently placed his arm around his fiancée's trembling shoulders while he read the details of his mission: his starting date, his security clearance, and his travel voucher instructions.

His enthusiasm for the post hadn't grown a bit since that day.

"I better go downstairs. They're picking me up to take me to the base. I fly out tonight. The jeep should be here by now."

She glanced at the kitchen clock. "Yes, and I'd better get ready for school."

When he looked at her quizzically, she said, "Ms. Saunders is out on leave, remember? I'm subbing for at least this week, maybe longer."

"Maternity leave?" he asked.

"Life as a substitute teacher is almost as bad as being in the military," she mumbled.

"At least you don't have to face bullets."

"True, just adolescent pupils, bastards all of them, a lecherous principal, backstabbing teachers, and a hostile PTA—not to mention having to fend off advances from some of the parents, both the mothers and the fathers."

He picked up his kit bag and kissed her once more. A long, lingering kiss interrupted by the sound of the jeep's horn out on the street.

Forty-eight hours later, after multiple stops, he stepped off the plane at the Gao International Airport and, along with several other soldiers, was driven in the back of an army truck to base. The primitive barracks were stripped of any amenities other than water, electricity, and the pure basics, and housed men from France, Germany, Holland, Finland, Australia, and Kenya. A Dutch corporal showed him to his billet, a miserable hut with one window, a ceiling fan, and six beds.

"You'll be sharing with fellow Americans. That's the way we like to do it here," the corporal announced. "We try to keep citizens of the same country together. It minimizes possible conflicts and language problems. You'll find not everyone speaks English as well as I do," he added with pride.

After staking his claim to one of the two vacant bunks, George unpacked his kit bag and noticed that his comrades had stuck photographs of their wives and sweethearts on the individual magnetic clipboards on the walls of their lockers. He removed from his wallet a photograph of Julie, taken on a Florida beach several weeks earlier, when they'd gone for a last romantic getaway before his deployment. In it she wore a tiny white bikini, and her long, straight blonde hair contrasted with her dark tan. Her right hand rested just inside her bikini and a finger from her left hand, phosphorescing with a new diamond ring, pressed against her lips. A provocative pose, and maybe too much for a military barracks—it could give rise to salacious comments from the other guys. He knew he couldn't handle that. He put the photograph back in his wallet and pulled out another, taken at his brother's wedding the year before. Much more suitable.

He settled into a routine that, after a couple weeks, spelled unparalleled boredom. On most days, he spent a few hours in an armored vehicle with three colleagues, machine guns at the ready. Just in case. Three basic meals a day in the mess where the men sat at long tables, nationalities keeping to themselves with no manifestation of basic comradeship. And the scenery well, just think of an African safari but without the wildlife.

There wasn't even the sound of any military conflict in the neighborhood to break the monotony. And George couldn't decide which of the two warring factions was the enemy.

This is the problem with peacekeeping, he wrote in one of his first letters home to Julie. *I don't give a fuck who wins.* He wanted to fill his letters with more than complaints, but he had little news to share. He settled for telling her of the one burgeoning friendship he'd found among his so-called colleagues.

So there's a guy in my barracks named Chuck Granger, and guess what? He's from Strongsville, Ohio. What's that, like seven miles from us? Hell, we might keep in touch when I'm back home. That final simple word created fumes of emotion in him. *And it can't come soon enough.*

After three months, he'd neither fired a single shot nor seen a single soul with a gun pointed in his direction. Nevertheless, a couple of weeks before George arrived, three United Nations soldiers were killed and five others seriously injured when an explosive device had detonated as they escorted a convoy traveling between the towns of Anafis and Gao in Mali's volatile north. The team was constantly reminded by the post's commanding colonel that there was no room for complacency, and that 'round-the-clock vigilance was the key to survival.

Mail was the highlight of the week. The letters would be collected and driven every Monday to the capital, Bamako, where under an arrangement with the Swedish embassy, they would be flown in the diplomatic pouch to Stockholm and from there mailed to the recipients. On Sundays, the men would find a quiet spot, usually in the canteen before the evening meal or in their billets, and finish writing their letters started earlier in the week to be sure they were completed before the truck left the next morning. The truck usually arrived back at camp around ten that night, and by eleven, the commanding officer had sorted their letters. George always tried to be first to see if Julie had written. He was never disappointed.

Sometimes she sent photographs of Lindsey, his brother's first child, who was born shortly after George left for Mali. She kept her promise and sent him clips from the *Plain Dealer* about the Cleveland Browns.

As much as he enjoyed these mementos, he most anticipated her letters themselves, written in large looping handwriting, usually in dark blue ink on light blue stationery. In one of her early letters, she wrote:

Guess who's taking off the rest of the year to be with her baby, and guess who's subbing for her for a couple months? I mean, I wasn't crazy about it at first but, you know, I thought hey—it keeps me from sitting around too much thinking of how you're sooo far away and how I miss you like crazy!

I have to tell you all about these needy nutjobs I work with. I told you they're a pack of letches, right? We all roll our eyes about the principal because he's this sad, ancient guy and he hits on all of us women—and like half the dads do too! Married or not! Ugh.

Anyway, I have made one friend, kind of. It's this art teacher named Mr. Benedetto and he's at least nice. He feels bad for me that you're deployed, and he said to tell you thank you for your service! He's fun to talk trash with about everybody.

Her letters—long, chatty, gossipy—tended to go on for nine or more pages, and George's fingertips seemed to absorb a certain warmth as they traced over her paragraphs. He was embarrassed he couldn't make his letters as interesting as hers. There were limits to how many times he could write about how terrible the food was, how boring each day was, the heat, the humidity, and the absence of anyone he could strike up a meaningful friendship with. Well, except for Chuck.

Chuck and I play dominoes a lot, he wrote to her. *A lot of the guys do. That or poker or backgammon. It's that or watch movies in the mess on this old, rickety projector. That's assuming the one corporal who knows how to work it is here. It's too hot in there if the ceiling fan's off, but if you put it on, the breeze shakes the whole screen.* Mostly because he could picture Julie's face upon reading this—she'd probably be envisioning scenes from *Casablanca* or *Love Actually,* her own favorites, leaping in the hard fan gusts—George chuckled.

Chuck had on his clipboard a large sheet of paper numbered 365 to 1 and would record the number of days remaining in his posting to Mali. He was down to 253 before he would end his term of duty and return home to Ohio. George calculated that this meant he had about 220 days still to go. His release date and Chucks's were approximately one month apart.

Well, Lindsey's growing like crazy. I'll try to get a fresh picture of her from your sister-in-law next time and send it. And your Cleveland Browns are doing well, from what I hear. I'll also remember to cut out their latest and greatest news and send it to you next time.

I got some exciting news yesterday! Ms. Saunders is thinking about not coming back. Period. She wants to stay home and be with her baby for a couple of years or something. Well you know how I was already considering finishing up my full teaching certificate? They said if I do I can stay on! And teach these annoying kids full time!

I am actually excited about it, even if the kids are annoying. I just don't know though. Wish I had you to talk about it all with. There are just other things I have going on right now. Raymond—that's Mr. Benedetto—he said he really, really thinks I should go for it and fulfill my dreams and . . . blah blah blah. I think you'd like him and he'd like you.

Her letter went on for another five or so pages, and still, her words seem to imbue his fingers tracing over them with a sort of wane heat much more pleasant that the scorching sort he was accustomed to in Mali. He just wished her letter was longer, but he also understood she'd gotten busier with her job.

While he couldn't say he was any busier than normal, he had even less to report now, so many months into what seemed an eternal assignment. He wrote that Chuck had promised to teach him chess if he had time—and if he didn't, perhaps he would teach him back home. He wrote of dreaming of the three weeks' leave he would have upon his exoneration from Mali, how he'd thought of a thousand places he wanted to take her and asking her to suggest a few places of her own. *If we haven't set our wedding date for sure while I'm over here in hell,* he wrote, *maybe we can make our plans then.*

I decided not to do the teaching certificate thing for now. Just too much else going on, you know. Her letter had fallen out of the envelope lightly into his hand. The front and back of a wide-ruled page; where it had been ripped from the spiral of a notebook, its edges were torn in varying formations, reminding him somewhat of ragged snowflakes. The very thought of it sent a chill through his fingertips. *Sorry I didn't remember the picture of little Lindsey or the Browns article. Just so, so busy right now. Plus, I've been feeling pukey lately. And so tired. Anyway, everybody asks about you and wishes you the best and thanks you for your service.*

In all the days left to go, not much happened for George. He watched movies he'd already seen that hopped like Mexican jumping beans on the screen. He learned the first steps of chess, but Chuck's countdown was nearing single digits, and George didn't know if any of his remaining fellow soldiers would be able to teach him once Chuck was gone. The Finns maybe. They seemed more intellectual and looked more intelligent than everyone else.

A lot happened in Cleveland in that time, though.

So, the Browns are having a GREAT season. Really wish you were here. You'd love the hell out of watching them.

Bunch going on right now. Most of it just depressing as shit, and sorry about that—wish I had better news to send you. Remember the old high school principal? Mr. Pickering. Or Mr. Pickling like everybody used to call him? 'Fraid to say he died.

And your old girlfriend, "Vanessa the Undressah"—she died
too. Overdose.

That little mom-and-pop ice cream joint you liked because
they always had that weird banana and cherry combo you dug,
closed. So we can now get yet another McDonald's around here,
because THAT's just what the world needs.

And finally—remember that old movie theater, the one on
Maple Street you used to love so much? I hate to tell you, but a
bunch of gentrifying bastards came in and razed the thing to
put up a new shopping mall. Didn't Millennials supposedly kill
malls? Who even goes to those useless eyesores anymore? Your
fiancée maybe, but nobody else.

How is she anyway, man? Nobody ever sees her anymore.
Sue has given her about a hundred pictures of Lindsey to
send to you, hope you're getting 'em. Anyway, bro, I'm proud
of you for making it through this bullshit assignment, not
everybody could do it. Can't wait to see you back home.

Thirty-four days before his posting was due to end, he
was excited to see a letter from Julie. It came in a large envelope, so his immediate assumption was that it contained
a longer letter than he had been receiving over the previous weeks. Maybe she had included some of the hundreds
of pictures of Lindsey she'd been given? To his horror, she
had merely scribbled a brief note on a yellow Post-it affixed
to a ten-day-old copy of the *Plain Dealer* referring him to
read about the upcoming mayoral election. As if he gave a
damn who'd become mayor of Cleveland. He hadn't cared
even when he'd lived in Ohio, so why did she imagine he
would have any interest while posted in Mali?

Only four days later, after dinner in the mess, he sat
down with Chuck at the back of the room and played dominoes; it was one of their last chances before Chuck flew

back. They had given up on chess—at least until they were both back home.

"Mail's arrived," someone yelled as one of the non-commissioned officers began to lay it out on a table. George stood waiting to see if there was one for him. He was lucky. He took it and opened the envelope. Chuck remained at the table, not expecting any mail.

George read the letter slowly and then folded it, placed it in his shirt pocket. Instead of walking back to the table to rejoin Chuck, he left the mess.

A week later, Chuck parked his mother's Chevy outside an apartment building in Tremont, one of Cleveland's trendy neighborhoods. He checked the address from an envelope in his jacket pocket. He was at the right place—a four-story complex. Apartment 23 was on the second floor. The door to the building was unlocked.

The elevator was out of order so he walked up the stone stairs, two at a time. He stopped to take a breath and walked down a short corridor to the apartment. He paused at the front door. He heard a woman's voice, a child crying, and then a man's voice, with an Italian accent. He rang the bell.

A woman came to the door. It was eleven in the morning and her short black negligee was visible underneath the flimsy robe she'd clearly thrown on to answer the door. Behind her, a man, shirtless and wearing jeans, held a baby.

"Yes," the woman said.

"I'm going to keep this short, but it won't be sweet."

"What do you mean?" the man asked at the same time the woman was asking, "Who are you?"

"I'm a friend of your late fiancé."

Chuck turned and left, but only after throwing Julie's paragraph-long letter on the ground. He was gone before he could watch her, gasping and stumbling, lift it to her face so she could read her own words—*Sorry, but you know, I'm proud of you and we had a good run and I know you'll be just fine when you're back home*—in the same spot where, approximately one year before, he had read the words Gao, Mali and she had wept for him.

CHAPTER SIXTEEN

Every Employee's Dream

I hadn't slept well—never did the first night in a hotel—and now I was awake, thanks to the midtown Manhattan traffic, its racket building to a crescendo even on Sunday morning. I looked at my watch. Seven-thirty. But then I realized noise from the street hadn't roused me. The telephone had. And the damned thing sat on a desk facing the window. Hell, why couldn't they put it on the nightstand? I got out of bed but didn't make it in time. *Shit.* Probably one of my kids, thanking me for yesterday.

I'd flown in from Los Angeles on Friday night with the aim of spending the weekend with my eleven-year-old twins, Kate and Tommy, and then flying back home on Tuesday. I'd have Monday to myself to do the rounds of the bookstores and art galleries and have some alone time. Some people may think a divorced man with no one special in his life would hunger for a break from alone time, but mine was a precious asset that became all the more precious when I was away from home and could explore without consulting. That had been the plan. After I'd bought my nonrefundable ticket, however, my ex told me I could see the kids only on Saturday; she and her lawyer husband had plans for Sunday. So here I was, with an additional day of solitude.

We'd had a pleasant enough day together. After Gina dropped the kids off, I took them to breakfast at the Waldorf. From there it was Saks Fifth Avenue for Kate (I bought her a dress and shoes) then FAO Schwarz for Tommy. While he ran loose through the toy store, I caught up—well, as much as a father can catch up with his preteen daughter who's learned the art of guarded answers. I tried to navigate the topic of how she was getting along with her mother and her new stepdad with delicacy; we weren't past it being a sore subject, if we ever would be. When the subject involved Gina moving, kids in tow, when the lawyer she'd been having an affair with relocated to New York, the soreness wasn't going to be easily rubbed out.

What did I want though? The guy was a better bet than me. Younger, more successful. Plus, "lawyer's wife" had a better ring to it than "wife of an underpaid, overworked human resources director of a midsize publishing company." It boasted an underpaid payroll of around 250 discontented employees spread between Los Angeles, San Francisco, and Sacramento. And the head of the company? Labor laws were promulgated because of people like him.

In fact, perhaps the thing I missed most about Gina was how she would console me, and be on my side when I complained about the guy. I could vividly remember the evening I'd come home, nodded to my family, and headed straight to our room to sit on the bed in the dark. I remembered Gina joining me; she knew to ask what my boss, Gerard Pepper, had done this time.

"You remember Babs and Judith?" They were sisters in their sixties, and they'd worked for the company from the time they finished high school until, for Babs at least, the end of her life."

"Babs died?" my wife asked. "Poor Judith."

I could tell, though, she was confused about why the woman's death would hit me so hard. And truth be told, it hadn't. Not directly.

I told Gina how Gerard had caught me first thing when I'd arrived at work to tell me Judith had taken a whole week off to mourn her sister and housemate—the two had lived together in the same house where they were born. I told my wife how I'd somehow mistaken his line of questioning at first, how I'd responded by asking if anyone had attended Babs's funeral or sent flowers.

"That's not the point," he'd told me. "Our employee manual clearly states that for the death of a sibling, an employee is entitled to take off two days. Judith has taken five." The way he said *five*, he made it sound like six months.

When I'd expressed my opinion that surely we could be flexible in light of the circumstances, Gerard had shaken his head the way a retired-athlete father might upon watching his son swing the bat so hard and inaccurately that he falls backward on the catcher.

"You're to see Judith and you're to ask her how she wants us to treat those extra three days. Does she want to be docked for them or does she want to have them treated as vacation days?"

Gina's jaw had dropped in disbelief as I'm sure my own had at the time I heard it. She'd then put her arms around me and mused for the thousandth time about how nice it would be if I could quit that awful job. It had become a game of ours to speculate about how life would be if we stumbled into millions, the same way it had become an ongoing habit for my friend John and I to purchase weekly lottery tickets. That evening, Gina and I had evoked some of our go-to fantasies: we could eat at the best steakhouses and cruise the waters to remote, romantic villages. Sell this house and buy a bigger one and fill it with art, hardwood floors with a jewel-like gleam, racks of the finest wines. And best of all—I'd never have to see Gerard's geriatric, yet intimidating face again.

But that shared dream, like the promise of my wife's comforting arms to come home to, had expired long ago. Now I was in an average New York hotel for a weekend visit that had been shaved down to a one-day visit. Now my kids were off with her and her lawyer-husband and I was peering blearily across at a light flashing on my telephone.

The call that I had missed—whoever it was left a message.

"Larry, it's John. Call me urgently. Good news." He sounded out of breath with excitement.

John was a terrific guy, always smiling, always happy. Together we'd been playing the lottery every week for years. We always rolled our winnings—the largest so far amounting to forty dollars—over to the next week. Everyone at the hair salon where John worked scoffed at our pursuit of "The Big One" with endless reminders that the odds were stacked a trillion to one against us. But they couldn't deter us. We had the faith.

"Larry? Are you sitting down? We won last night. Don't hold me to it, I'll find out tomorrow, but it looks like we won twenty-three million. Finally." I couldn't tell whether the noise he emitted was laughter or tears. But it was a noise. I listened, stunned, and my hand that held the phone began to shake.

"Are you sure?"

"Pretty damned sure."

"What happens now?" I asked.

You'd think that with the importance this weekly ritual had taken on for the two of us over the years, we would have a plan for what to do if, one day, it worked.

"I'll get the claim form online tomorrow. Then we go to the office with the ticket and file it. They'll have to check that we don't have any legal claims against us—taxes, child support, that sort of stuff. Since there are two of us, they recommend we get a lawyer to draft a trust deed." I felt only gratitude that John knew what to do. He sounded confident about each step; no doubt he'd been at his computer, toiling through lottery forums, from the moment he saw the numbers line up. "And then we wait. We already know we're going to take it lump sum." That was true. It was the only sign—beyond the negligible financial investment in weekly tickets—that we had ever believed winning to be a real possibility: we had agreed in advance how to collect the money. "They deduct the taxes. Unless I'm mistaken, we should each receive about around six million. But don't start spending yet. Apparently, it's about three months before we'll see any money."

"Fucking hell. I'm not complaining about six million. I can't believe our luck."

"Start believing. Start believing." I'm sure he didn't recognize that he did this: repeated himself when the statement held some gravity. "When are you flying back?"

"Tuesday."

"I'll handle the claim tomorrow."

We made arrangements to meet Wednesday afternoon and celebrate. My idea of a good celebration was a hearty meal at one of L.A.'s premier steakhouses washed down with a bottle of the best. John's idea leaned more toward vegan platters complete with couscous and green tea. No matter. We'd compromise.

I lay down on the bed. Heart racing. Mind rioting with emotion. *What the hell would I do with the money?* The lottery-winner fantasies I'd shared with Gina flashed through my thoughts, and it was with a tinge of sadness that I realized I needed independent dreams now. On the other hand—and this thought caused a smile—being divorced, I didn't owe her a cut. Meaning, I wasn't doomed to imagine what she would buy for herself, and the man who'd replaced me, with *my* money. *Of course I'd make sure part of it went to the kids, but what about me? What would I do?*

First and foremost, I would tell that Scrooge of a boss to go screw himself. That was one scenario that transferred smoothly from Gina's and my fantasies to mine alone. After basking in the incredible pleasure of that, maybe I'd take a world cruise and plan my future. Forty-four was too young to retire. Would I stay in Los Angeles or would I move closer to the children on the East Coast? Jesus Christ. Within a ten-minute span, the whole country—if not the world—had opened up for me.

Although it was still early and I had the day to relax, I couldn't go back to sleep. *Why the hell had I told John I would be flying back on Tuesday? Why not tomorrow—or today?* The office didn't expect me back until Wednesday, but nothing was keeping me here. *What the hell?* Another decision—and another option. I was now in a position to fly first class, charter a plane and not give a damn about the lousy fifty or so dollars to change my flight. *Calm down, Larry.* John had said it could take three months before I saw a dime. I had a few thousand tucked away, but it may not be enough to sustain me until the winnings rolled in if I did what I wanted to on Wednesday: tell Gerard Pepper to go fuck himself. No, I'd stay in New York and fly back as planned on Tuesday.

I ended up taking a long walk around Central Park. It was a beautiful, sunny day with a picture postcard-clear blue sky and lots of dogs to watch. I'm a dog lover. Always have been. I'd have enough to buy a house somewhere in the countryside with big back yard and I'd have four. Four rescue dogs. And maybe a new car. With four dogs, I'd need something like a Range Rover.

Sunday and Monday passed slowly. Unable to concentrate on newspapers or the paperback I'd brought with me, I meandered through one of the world's biggest, most booming cities but felt only restlessness. Not even the sommelier-recommended wine with the five-star meals I treated myself to could calm my nerves. I told myself to relax—to luxuriate in these first days of life beyond a shoestring budget—but my gut wouldn't listen.

Tuesday morning. The day of my return. My flight was at two o'clock. Plenty of time to pack, have breakfast, and get to JFK.

Except that Tuesday morning there wasn't time. For anything. That Tuesday, a black hole opened in the sky and New York City fell through it. Tuesday, September 11, 2001. Staring at the TV through glassy eyes, I believed the carnage reels to be cinema. A spoof, perhaps, of Orson Welles's famous *War of the Worlds* radio broadcast. But that fantasy fast erupted. *It was real.*

The traffic and sirens in the street below flew by. Announcement after announcement. There were no answers for the *whys, whos,* and *what the hells.* None of which prevented the talking heads from glutting the airways with their soundalike expressions of bewilderment. The death toll would be unimaginable. The largest terrorist event on American soil in history.

All flights cancelled until further notice.

I hesitated about taking the elevator in case of an outage. Instead, I reached the lobby by way of a service stairwell. To be greeted, at my destination, by bedlam and confusion. As the city was now blocked off, pretty much, there'd be no new check-ins. Just lines of people who needed, like me, to extend their stays. JFK was closed, as were the bridges and tunnels. Those at the front desk were as helpful as it's possible to be when hell has overflowed onto earth. I went back to my room and made a coffee. Thank God I had a coffee maker as the line for a table or counter seat at the hotel's coffee shop was endless.

I had three calls to make, and landing open lines to place them took the better part of an hour; on a normal day, I'd have zipped through them all in five minutes. On a normal day, of course, I wouldn't need to make them. First I phoned Gina. She and lawyer-husband lived far from the site of destruction—their jobs and the twins' school at safe distances as well—but I had to check. Everybody was checking on everyone. All phone lines knotted with New Yorkers' desperate efforts to find each other.

Second, I needed to notify the company that I couldn't fly back as planned and that I'd be in the office at the first moment I could, no longer tomorrow but certainly before the end of the week. I couldn't be more precise. Except that Tuesday morning there wasn't time. For anything.

Finally, I called John. When I got hold of him, it wasn't quite six in the morning.

"What's the matter, can't you sleep, Larry? Too excited about the money?"

"John, turn on the TV right now!"

"Good Popeye cartoon on?" He laughed. "By the way, I filed the papers yesterday. And I've got an attorney lined up. Twenty-three million it is."

His calmness and good humor starkly contrasted my panic.

"Oh my God," I heard him cry out as the images on his screen echoed mine three thousand miles away. "Oh my God," he repeated.

"I'm marooned here in New York," I told my friend. "The airports are closed. There's no way I can fly back today. I'll keep you posted."

"Please do."

Never mind not being able to fly back today—I wasn't inclined to leave my TV set. Apart from a trip back down to the coffee shop for muffins and a Danish, and to the gift shop for Cokes and chocolate bars, I barricaded myself in the room. While I doubted housekeeping would come around, I hung the *Do Not Disturb* sign anyway.

The news got more grim by the hour. Thousands dead. Twin Towers—destroyed. Smoke, fire, stench. Ambulances, sirens, frantic families, heroic firemen. The usual talking-head pundits. And of course, center stage, the hard-hatted mayor.

The next day was the same. My only venture out of the room was to stock up on junk food; staying otherwise glued to the screen. Finally, the news announced flights were leaving from JFK on Thursday, September 13.

I left the hotel at six-thirty that morning to rejoin a stunned city. With no traffic, I rode in silence. What was there to discuss with the driver?

Despite the long line growing even longer at American Airlines check-in, no one pushed and shoved or displayed the slightest whiff of impatience. The agents, shell-shocked as everyone else, tried hard to find flights for passengers who had been unable to travel these past forty-eight hours. And who knows whether they too were mourning, not just a general mourning for what was thought to be the six thousand dead, but for specific friends, neighbors, colleagues, and family members.

Finally, my turn came. A six-hour wait for a flight to Chicago, and a three-hour wait in Chicago before my connection to Los Angeles. Pretty grim, but it was the best the woman behind the counter could do, and I was happy for that.

I arrived home that evening exhausted and drained. I was so worn out that, believe it or not, I was no longer thinking about my lottery win and what it would mean to my future. I collapsed on my bed in my small apartment in Hancock Park and slept solidly until the alarm clock woke me up at seven the next morning.

Eight-thirty was the usual time I arrived at my office downtown. I knew I'd be late, but that didn't worry me as it normally would. I still managed to park my car in the company's parking lot in front of the grey stucco two-story building by half past nine.

As I walked through the glass front door, Bridget, the friendly receptionist, gave me a smile. "Welcome back, Larry. We've all been worried about you. We knew you were in New York." There was a perennial kindness about Bridget; God knows how she maintained it in this atmosphere.

I looked to my right and left. Everyone was in their booths, working or pretending to. Some gave me a half wave; others remained absorbed by their screens—whether they were composing articles, preparing monthly reports, or, more likely than not, watching the news out of New York.

The first thing I noted when approaching the wide staircase up to the second floor was that the area around the staircase and up the steps was littered with an array of plants. My initial thought, from a distance, was that someone high up in the company had died. An outpouring of potted foliage like this is often the response of a mourning community. In fact, I wondered for a moment if someone besides me had been in New York, and maybe hadn't made it back. Though if a colleague's death hadn't triggered the whole community to send flowers, I didn't know whose would.

Besides, as I was drawing closer I was realizing these were no funeral flowers. These were plants from around the office along with bushes—bushes from outside. While normally three or four people could have passed by without bumping into each other, these plants had reduced the walking space to accommodate only single-file passage. I had to wait until a couple came down.

No sooner had I entered my office and put my attaché case on the floor than I spotted a large piece of paper scotch-taped to my monitor with a handwritten message in large red ink ordering me immediately on my arrival to report to Gerard Pepper. I recognized the handwriting as Dorothy's, Gerard's wife. A nice enough woman, but she, as the rest of us, lived in fear of her tyrannical husband. She had been director of Human Resources before me but now had a roving brief that no one quite knew exactly the specifics. What everyone did know is that Dorothy patrolled the two floors every morning at eight-thirty and at six o'clock every evening with a clipboard to see who had arrived and who had left. What only I knew, being the HR director, was that she, her damned husband, her son by a former marriage, and one of Gerard's sons—just four people in total—took out more than sixty percent of payroll. I use the term took out as opposed to earned because earn would describe an action that didn't apply to this crowd.

Gerard's door was open. I gave it a gentle tap and walked in.

Dorothy was sitting in a hard-backed chair facing her husband across the desk, watching as he was speaking on the telephone. She gave me a nod and a smile, which I returned, and she beckoned me to sit in the chair next to her.

I watched Gerard—in his late seventies, never a hair out of place—as he wrapped up his conversation. His tan indicated he'd spent the weekend pursuing one of his passions, gardening. His other passion was a friend's Vietnamese wife, something known to me and probably half the firm after an employee had spotted them at the Santa Anita Racetrack. He was practically bald with a shiny scalp and with white hair at the temples and sides. He always wore a white shirt and tie under a colored cashmere V-neck vest. That day it was salmon pink.

Finally, he finished his call. He shuffled some papers aside and fixed me with a cold, long stare. Even though I knew I no longer needed the job, I still felt the same fear and trepidation about sitting in that chair as every other employee felt when summoned into that room. I made myself return his stare. He would've made a fine SS officer.

"Good to see you," he snarled. "*Finally.*" No questions about New York, the terrorist atrocities, the mayhem, the deaths, the destruction of the Twin Towers.

"We have a few things to cover, before you contact the broker who handles our medical insurance to see if we can get competitive quotes. Let's try to trim the costs. I'd like to see higher deductibles. That will reduce our premiums. We need to do that."

I nodded. I knew that providing medical coverage to everyone was a bee in his damned bonnet. It wasn't as if we offered it to spouses and family members. Just the employees.

"Next, now that you have finally arrived"—he caught my eye, making sure I hadn't missed his second, none-too-subtle *finally*—"you will have seen we have assembled something like a hundred potted plants and even some trees. Well we've had them for years. They've outgrown the place. It's become like a jungle. So we're selling them to the staff. Dorothy has put price tags on them. Cash only. You're to keep records and take the cash and give it to Dorothy at the end of each day."

My jaw must have fallen. I turned to look at Dorothy. She turned away from me.

"Shouldn't we just give them away either to the staff or to a local hospital?"

"I've told you what I want done with them," he snapped. From experience I knew there was no point in getting into an argument.

In less than a week, I had won the lottery *and* lived through a terrorist attack on American soil, and Gerard Pepper could still shock me.

"Next, this thing that happened in New York the other day. A great many members of staff did not come in that day or if they did come in, they left early."

"But from what I heard and saw on television, parts of downtown were evacuated and even First Street was closed off for a time. There was concern that the terrorists would strike here."

"Well, the terrorists didn't strike here and there were plenty of places where people could have parked within walking distance. I was here. Dorothy was here and so was the office manager." Everyone knew the office manager, stupid sycophant that he was, took backhanders from the people who operated the vending machines and from the office clearing and security companies.

"To make your job easy, Dorothy has the list of the no-shows and the ones who left early. They are to be docked one day's pay. No option to take this as a vacation day. Got it? Shoot them all an interoffice e-mail telling them."

I shook my head in disbelief.

"Now you. You took an extra day off too. Don't think you're immune. You'll be docked as well."

I'd had enough.

"I wasn't exactly enjoying myself. I was stuck in New York. All flights were cancelled. I couldn't get out."

"Of course, you could. You could have rented a car and driven somewhere and flown from there. Boston maybe? Anywhere."

I couldn't bring myself to look at his wife again. I stared at him and nodded. I also counted up to ten and took a deep breath.

"You know what Gerard. You can go fuck yourself."

Dorothy turned to face me in shock. This time it was Gerard's turn to be gob smacked. He tried to respond but no words came out.

I stood and left the room, walked down the stairs to the parking lot and started up my car. For the past week, it had been hard to tell if I was really awake; my life had been os-cillating between dream and nightmare, none of it feeling real. But here—leaving this loathsome office while the sun was still out and Gerard Pepper's jaw was still somewhere around his knees—I knew none of this was a dream. It was real. It was my life, and I was about to get on with it.

CHAPTER SEVENTEEN

House Seats

Max Dawson enjoyed the afternoon walk from his hotel to the theater where he was starring in a revival of a Noel Coward classic. The exercise was good as was the usual stimulation of street life. He was content. The play was a success and its run had been extended.

"Good afternoon, Sir Max," Len, the stage doorkeeper, greeted him cheerfully. Len was a legendary figure on Broadway. He'd had this job forever.

"Your assistant had to go out on some errands. She'll be back before curtain. She's left a pile of photographs for you to autograph. Also a letter from an old friend wanting house seats."

"Thank you, Len." He passed through the backstage lobby and along the narrow brick-walled corridor toward his dressing room. "Some dressing room," he muttered. "My closets at home are twice the size."

He turned on the light and looked in the mirror. Sixty-five years old, full head of hair, and he was the same weight he was at twenty.

"Now let me see who this cheapskate is who wants house seats." He sat down at his desk and picked up the letter. "Michael Holman. For God's sake. After forty-odd years."

He read the letter two or three times in moods varying from disbelief to disgust to anger. He opened a drawer and took some writing paper from a drawer. "Six house seats. What nerve!"

Michael, I have received your letter advising me that you are here in New York and your request for six house seats for my play. It is over forty years since we last met. It would be easy for me to just send you the house seats, but I'm not going to. And here's the reason.

When we were undergraduates at Oxford, we were great friends. Three months before we graduated, I informed my parents and Helene, my girlfriend, that I would not continue onto law school to study for the bar. I had been seen by a scout from the Royal Academy of Dramatic Art in a college produc-tion of Hamlet. *They offered me a full scholarship, which I accepted with great excitement and gratitude. I never wanted to be a lawyer anyway. My decision more than rocked the boat. It created havoc. My parents were livid. Helene ditched me. Her parents wouldn't have me over their doorstep. Friends and family turned against me. I was alone. The scholarship covered tuition, but barely made a dent in my living expenses. I had to take an assortment of part-time jobs. But they were difficult to maintain, as drama school was intensive. Lines had to be learned and I had rehearsals and classes to attend, but I did what I had to do to stay alive. Dishwashing and car wash jobs were easiest to come by. But I had one skill to fall back on. Thanks to all those years of piano and vocal lessons from age seven on, I was used to performing in public, and I had devel-oped an adequate repertoire. I was able to find two or three nights work most weeks performing at private parties and small clubs. Thank God for the Great American Song Book.*

Cole Porter, Gershwin, Irving Berlin, and all the others. It was a struggle to return home in the wee small hours to my filthy, two-room, fourth-floor walk-up that I shared with a couple of other drama students, wearing my ill-fitting secondhand tuxedo, and then to flop onto a sofa that stank of cat piss before having to be at school three hours later to rehearse for a part in an Ibsen play or some such.

Meanwhile, my family and all my old friends continued to shun me. The only thing that sustained me was my ambition to succeed in doing what I loved most. Defying convention and family expectations was almost an insurmountable challenge, but I never allowed myself to give up.

Then one day, about forty years ago, as I walked down Piccadilly on my way to an interview with an agent, I bumped into you. It was awkward. You didn't know whether to acknowledge me, stop for a chat, or just walk on. I put you on the spot. I blocked your way and I forced you to say hello. We chatted for a couple minutes. After all, we had been close friends at university. And then, out of the blue, you invited me to lunch. I was overjoyed. The ice had been broken.

You led the way to a small, intimate, wood-paneled seafood restaurant you favored in St. James. It was the first time I'd been inside a decent restaurant in years. I let you do the ordering. We had gin and tonics, oysters, Dover sole and champagne. I even became tipsy, not being used to drinking anymore, certainly never at lunchtime. When the bill came, you put down your credit card and asked me to put down mine. My share of the bill would have been equal to my month's rent. I had no credit card. I had barely two pounds in my pocket and not much more in my bank account. You were shocked. I don't know why you should have been. The way I was dressed should have enlightened you as to my circumstances. And this is what you said. I remember the words as if it were yesterday.

"In these circumstances, you'd better leave now. I'll take care of the bill. I never thought, Max, that you would turn out to be a leech."

I fled the restaurant, ashamed and humiliated. I felt tears running down my face. I walked into the church close by and sat in a pew and buried my head in my hands, my body trembling with hurt.

And now you write to me for house seats. You, Michael, who by all accounts is now a multimillionaire, knighted by the queen of England for philanthropy, no less. How much did that knighthood set you back?

A year or so later, I was hired to play at a posh private party. I was well into my second or third number when I felt a tap on my shoulder. It was my hostess, who instructed me to join her in the butler's pantry, adjacent to the kitchen, as soon as I finished my song. She looked uncomfortable. I was worried I may have done something wrong. It appeared that you and your then wife—Helene, I must add, my former girlfriend— had spotted me behind the piano from the doorway when you arrived. You took the hostess aside and told her that as long as I was there, you could not possibly remain as there was "bad history" between us.

Just like that, the hostess told me to leave by the service door. She graciously opened her purse and thrust some money into my fist. It was less than I would have been paid for the full night's work, but it was better than nothing.

And now forty years later, I, like you, have been knighted. I have two Best Acting Oscars, a Golden Globe, two Tony's, and a work schedule that's going to keep me busy for the next three years. Now you write to me, identifying me as an old friend.

When I didn't have a penny to my name or a decent shirt on my back, and wore shoes that needed new soles and heels, you didn't want to know me. You can go to hell and buy your own bloody theater tickets.

And one other thing. After that night when you forced the hostess to get rid of me, Helene called me the next morning to apologize. We began an affair. You didn't know that, did you? And that son you had, who tragically died when he was barely a year old, wasn't your son. He was my son. I have letters from Helene to prove it. It wasn't really a surprise when I read in the paper that she'd taken her own life. She never had a day's happiness when she was married to you. The next sting was that within six weeks of her death you remarried. You and your house seats!

He signed the letter and stuffed it in an envelope.

An hour later, he awoke from his nap, startled by his assistant's return.

"Did you sign those photographs I left for you, Sir Max?"

"Yes, I did. They're over there."

"And what about those six house seats?"

He shook his head, stood, and then walked toward the writing desk. He picked up the letter he'd written, tore it in half, and tossed it into the waste basket.

"To hell with him. Send them."

CHAPTER EIGHTEEN

The First Laugh

Alex Butler had never before welcomed Christmas vacation in Florida with such enthusiasm. He hadn't planned on leaving New York until Friday, but then business at the investment bank had come to a grinding halt. When his managing director had announced he was leaving for Barbados that day and recommended Alex take off early as well, he'd managed to switch flights with surprisingly little hassle—at least for LaGuardia around the holidays. He'd decided not to tell Charlotte; he would surprise her and Tim, their two-year-old son.

He needed to see her. She could be a sympathetic ear—or a shoulder to cry on, depending on whether he managed to iron out his mussed emotions during the flight—even if she had clearly grown weary of his whole situation at work. All the hours and energy he'd spent on what she called his "options scheme" over the past two years. His nights and weekends of sitting at the desk in their bedroom, in front of the computer, calculator at his side, newspapers and financial reports and old financial journals strewn at his feet. All the times she'd emptied trash containers overflowing with his discarded scribbled calculations. Alex knew it wasn't Charlotte's idea of how a young married woman should spend time with her husband.

To tell the truth, it wasn't how *he* thought they should spend their time either; sometimes an idea was just so powerful that it prioritized itself. "Good ol' Alex," the dependable equities desk manager, had long been liked but dismissed by coworkers who considered him too cautious to ever hit the big time. In his work with stocks listed in the Dow Jones Industrial Index, he turned in consistently good revenues, just not good enough, so far, to propel him to managing director status. For years he'd taken succor in the fact that he could sleep at night—as well as smile and even laugh—whereas those on volatile dealing desks suffered mood swings, panic attacks, and Prozac dependency.

Then something even better than that comfort came along. From his painstaking study of the options market, he came up with an idea. A design for a revolutionary program capable of generating considerable profits.

It had been Alex's managing director who suggested that Alex should present it to the firm's executive committee at their next meeting. This committee was comprised of five of the most senior partners, all universally respected as well as feared for rising through the ranks without having so much as earning a high school diploma. Facial details may have varied from one multimillionaire to the next, but they were all balding, navy-suited, rough-around-the-edges ruthless and foul-mouthed workaholics. Not the sort of man Alex wanted to become, but certainly the sort he wanted to impress.

Alex had just begun laying out the numerical component of his presentation on a blackboard he'd wheeled into the conference room for this purpose when the chairman spoke up. "I don't believe in options."

Alex had eked out all of two sentences from his well-prepared speech.

"If we believe a stock is good, we'll buy it. If we think it's lousy, we'll sell it. Why mess about with options, for Christ's sake?"

Alex gulped.

"Butler, don't waste our time or yours on this cockamamie scheme. You've got a job. Just focus on that and make sure you bring us more profits this year. Your last quarter's results weren't so good. Plenty of room for improvement."

His first wave of relief over the impending holiday was a direct response to this moment: he could break what Charlotte would surely consider the good news that his "options scheme" was done for. A second wave of relief quickly followed. A different sort of relief. He needed the time to really think. In two weeks, he had a hefty annual bonus coming, and he wasn't without savings. If he really believed in this system, perhaps it was time to put his money where his mouth and his brains were and set up his own company.

He didn't know what Charlotte would say, but he knew how she would feel.

She would be scared. After all, even if they were far from destitute, they had significant expenditures: their apartment on the Upper East Side, their house in Florida, a full-time nanny. And Charlotte's own earnings as an art dealer, even as a successful one with worldwide recognition, were erratic. That coupled with the high overheads of maintaining galleries in New York as well as Berlin made art dealing a constant situation of feast or famine.

It was midnight when his plane finally landed at Fort Myers after a long delay in New York. He hoped the presents he'd picked out for Charlotte, now packed safely in the trunk of his rental car, would help the news go down easier. He'd also brought gifts for Tim; Anna, the nanny; and Dexter, the German shepherd that had recently been trained by a Naples police officer. He'd bought nothing, however, for Marie. His mother-in-law's Christmas was Charlotte's prerogative.

In their case, the natural friction between son- and mother-in-law was compounded by a language barrier. His German was barely adequate, her English, nonexistent. Spending three extra days with her was the only drawback of coming to Florida early.

By one in the morning, he was finally on the road to Naples and to the house that Charlotte had inherited years before.

He knew the code at the entrance to the gated complex and drove at barely five miles an hour around the well-lit but deserted road and avoided the speed bumps past the manicured lawns and identical single-story white stucco villas. Kitschy, faux Victorian gas lights—electrified, of course—lit the way. At this hour, it was no surprise that every house he passed was dark.

The complex was designed with one single road that encircled the entire lush, green hundred-acre development with cul-de-sacs springing off where the more desirable and private homes had been built. Each cul-de-sac was named after a flower.

He took a right onto Primrose, a cul-de-sac of three empty lots and just four homes. His and Charlotte's was at the end. He didn't see his wife's car, but that was no surprise; she always parked in the garage. It was built to accommodate two vehicles, but the way Charlotte parked left space sufficient only for a golf cart. Alex had expected to see one car in the driveway; it must have been Marie's rental. And she had a cousin in Sarasota who sometimes visited—maybe his was the second car in the driveway?

Not wanting to block either car, he reversed onto the roadway and parked alongside the sidewalk. He took from the trunk his smaller suitcase filled with clothes and work and his larger suitcase filled with the presents. While he had a key, he guessed correctly that the door would not be locked.

He tiptoed into the house, through the small tiled lobby and into the living room. The light was adequate for him to maneuver to the master bedroom, off the living room, as the door was open and Charlotte had not turned off the lamp on her nightstand. He dared hope she was still awake reading—the look on her face when he walked through the door would be a treat.

Before his eyes had adjusted, he heard the separate strands of breath. The tame wheezy snoring of the dog, which always slept near the bed, and Charlotte's own breathing, thickened by slumber. But a third source of breath cluttered the space.

Then he saw them.

Two naked bodies, asleep, arms wrapped around each other. His lips on her tanned shoulder, her hair against his cheek. His leg between hers.

Alex's muscles tightened. He clenched his fists and his mouth opened and closed without producing words. For a moment, he afforded himself the kindness of disbelief: it had to be an illusion brought on by stress and sleeplessness and the sudden jump from darkness to light.

Then the dog stirred from its deep sleep. Seeing Alex, and not recognizing in the poor light that the interloper was its owner, the German shepherd charged toward him.

"Honey—?" Even in the chaos and cacophony, Alex processed that this was the first word his wife said upon waking with such a start. A term directed toward the man in bed beside her—not him. Not her husband. Not Alex.

She blinked furiously until her eyes landed on the dog. "Dexter, what is it? Oh my God—Alex? Alex, what are you *doing* here? Get out. Get out! Get out!" Charlotte screamed.

The man sat up. "You heard her, get out!" he shouted.

But Alex could no more move than he could speak.

The dog's barks blended with the lovers' shouts.

In nearby rooms, Marie and the nanny woke to Charlotte's earsplitting chant. "Get out! Get out! Get out!"

When it became clear that no matter how many people joined in the shouting—the communal effort to expel him from his own house—Alex wasn't going to move, Charlotte jumped from the bed, ran into the bathroom and put on her robe. The man similarly found he could move as well as scream. He sprung from the bed and lunged at Alex.

"You heard her. Get out of here!"

This man—this stranger—in his face. The nanny and Marie shuffling and observing from behind him. The dog staring up at him, surely recognizing him by now but incensed by the whirlwind of noise—still barking, barking, barking. Charlotte wearing the ivory-color silk robe he'd bought her weeks before, standing in the bathroom door, angry arms folded tight. "Get out! Get out! GET OUT."

They formed a cruel receiving line he had to make his way through before he could leave. The dog, his wife, her lover, his mother-in-law, the nanny. Loud. Staring. Waiting for Alex to react.

And react he finally did.

He fainted.

He fell to the floor, and as he did, his head crashed against the round glass-topped table. Blood swelled across the white carpet. The sight of it shook the room quiet.

Three days later, Alex woke up. He rubbed his blurred eyes. Standing at the foot of his hospital bed was Charlotte, a nurse, and a white-coated doctor with a beard.

"Where am I?" he stuttered.

Charlotte was first to speak. "You're in hospital here in Naples. You fainted and banged your head and suffered a concussion," she said stiffly.

He lifted his hands to his head and felt the bandage.

The man with the beard answered. "The MRI showed there was no brain damage, thankfully, but we did have to stitch you up and remove some glass from your scalp." He spoke so softly Alex wondered if he'd failed to notice some sleeping roommate; he attempted turning his head to look, but a sharp discomfort spiked through his neck.

"Am I okay?" Alex asked feebly.

"Yes, you're okay. Your wife has been very candid about what happened. We're concerned you may suffer from depression and perhaps even a nervous breakdown. You're going to stay here for another few days while we keep a check on you." It seemed the man's formative manners returned to him then. "I'm sorry, I haven't introduced myself. I'm Dr. Stewart, and I'm a psychiatrist."

Then it was Charlotte's turn again. "I've telephoned your boss. He knows you're here and you won't be going back to the office for a while. I've also called Avis—they've collected the rental car."

If he could have turned his head from her without further injuring himself, he would have.

"And when you're discharged from here, I'm sure they will want to keep an eye on you before you fly back to New York? Isn't that right, doctor?"

"Yes. Absolutely. You should be able to fly back on your own after a week. You must give me the name of your doctor in New York." And turning to Charlotte, "Once he is discharged from here, will he be returning to your house?"

"Given the circumstance, I don't think that would be best. I'll make a reservation for him at the Marriott. Perhaps you could see that a social worker can get him there." She hesitated. "I have to leave town tomorrow."

Alex said nothing. He would have at least nodded, but the slightest movement of his head sent soreness roaring down through his shoulders. It amazed him that an act so routine could court such searing pain.

Two weeks later, he arrived back in New York. The doorman gave him an odd look as he helped him out of the cab with his luggage. When Alex walked in his apartment, he immediately understood why. Charlotte had been there and stripped the place of its artwork, all the framed photographs, and, of course, her clothes. The safe where she kept her jewelry had been opened and emptied, its door left wide open. He almost ignored her letter on the dining room table. What could it say that he didn't already know?

But still he read it, before he took his coat off. No surprises. He threw it back onto the table and then dragged his two suitcases into the bedroom to unpack.

From the first words Dr. Korbel spoke, Alex knew today's theme would mirror so many from sessions past. A long, ragged pseudo-patient sigh from the doctor followed by the words, "I must ask myself—are we getting anywhere?"

Here's what he meant: He meant *after three weekly, hour-plus-long sessions for so long.* He meant *after at least two thousand three hundred sessions. And after diagnoses of anthropophobia (fear of people), and gynophobia (fear of women), philophobia (fear of love), claustrophobia, and all means of social anxieties and depression. And after the prescriptions for Xanax and Prozac and God knows what else. The in-house treatment at clinics in New Hampshire and Arizona and Utah.* And, perhaps most to the point, he meant *after fifteen years.*

Fifteen years—that's how long it had been since Alex had returned to New York, depressed and shell-shocked and had followed up on his Florida psychiatrist's recommendation of Dr. Korbel.

Educated by the dream teams of Columbia, Harvard, and Zurich, he'd been practicing on Park Avenue for more than thirty years. If you asked ten people what they thought of Dr. Korbel, five would call him God and the other five, a shameless quack. If you asked Alex Butler what he thought of the man, he'd point out that even after he'd paid him probably half a million dollars over the years, Dr. Korbel had never once offered him a cup of coffee, even though the coffee machine was right there and Alex would have appreciated having one.

As it was, he watched the doctor sip his own coffee as he took the soft-shoe approach to berating Alex. It didn't worry him; he doubted Dr. Korbel would fire him as a patient, what with him now being paid fifteen hundred a week.

He tried, at least, to humor the doctor with a nod, but he was called out for it.

"This is what you do, Alex," the doctor said and then sipped. Some days he got quite the rhythm going: dispense nuggets of psychiatrist wisdom and sip the coffee he hoarded for himself, dispense and sip, dispense and sip. "You nod, you listen, and you keep your eyes on the clock. I know you're just thinking of how you need to be at the office." And sip. "I do my part, Alex. Why do you come to me?"

Without waiting for an answer, Dr. Korbel continued.

"When you first came here, your marriage had ended, you had the first of your nervous breakdowns, and you were out of a job and you were in the throes of setting up a new business."

Dr. Korbel took an especially long sip, and Alex confirmed what he hadn't been asked to.

"Yes, that's correct."

"Well, look at what you have accomplished since then. I saw that article in the *Wall Street Journal* about you a couple weeks ago—that one that implied you're a billionaire now. You know how most people would feel if their business succeeded beyond their wildest dreams and they were living in a luxury townhouse on East 63rd? And on top it all, they were in great physical health? They'd be on top of the world." Those who appraised Dr. Korbel as God rather than quack valued his blunt demeanor, his habit of saying what you would expect a psychiatrist to phrase more *diplomatically*. Such as what he now said to Alex Butler: "So what the hell is the matter with you?"

At this point, Alex knew a reply—other than nodding or confirming obvious information—was expected of him. Briefly he considered pointing out that he would share and emote more often if he were offered coffee; it would give him a prop for punctuating his long therapeutic soliloquys. Instead he said, with honesty, that he didn't know. "But that's why I'm here so often."

"It's not enough," Dr. Korbel pointed out. He had long encouraged Alex to make friends and go out to restaurants, plays, movies, concerts. To associate with someone outside his four-person pool of employees—none of whom he talked with unless it was necessary.

"After you leave me, you go straight back to your home office and work, work, work. You've figured out how to live on a desert island right here in Manhattan. Work, visits to me and meals that never vary—canned soup, tinned sardines, and cheese and crackers. What sort of life is it?"

"But you know I suffer from this thing about being with people, especially women. What do you call it—anthropophobia?"

"I can't cure you of that if you yourself don't make greater effort." Dr. Korbel paused. "Tell me, Alex, a simple question. When was the last time you laughed at a joke? A movie? A cartoon in a newspaper? For God's sake, when was the last time you smiled?"

Alex didn't move a muscle. He watched as the psychiatrist took a sip of coffee and wished he could do the same. They stared at each other. "When did you last laugh? Alex? Tell me."

Finally Alex shrugged. "Before that night, I suppose." And how could anyone laugh after coming face to face with a scenario like that one? His lack of recovery—or at least lack of laughter—made perfect sense to him. "It ruined my whole life. Not just because I lost her—I lost my son."

"And it's been fifteen years. Do you understand you're not going to get better as long as you're telling yourself it's impossible?"

"I can't."

"Well, I'm not going to give up on you yet. And I'm giving you homework to complete before I see you next. I want you to try to find some way to laugh."

"Same time on Wednesday, doctor?"

Once again, the doctor issued his impatiently patient sigh. "Sure, Alex. Same time Wednesday."

The walk from Dr. Korbel's office to his townhouse took only seven minutes. He paused at the office on the first floor to collect from his bookkeeper a printout of the most volatile stocks from the previous trading day. With the information tucked under his arm, Alex took the elevator to his apartment on the upper floors. He grunted as he passed the kitchen and saw Vilma, his housekeeper, who told him that she would bring in his coffee with the newspapers momentarily.

He studied the list at his dining room table. This was the key, he'd discovered, to making good money on options: studying only the most volatile stocks. He had built his considerable fortune over recent years by analyzing the three "Vs"—value, volume, and volatility—better than most traders.

His other business philosophy was not to waste time attracting any clients. It cost money to get them and more to keep them loyal. Clients meant socializing and sales patter, travel and entertainment expenses. He was self-capitalized and determined to keep it that way. In addition, he had no partners or shareholders or bank debt. No need for internal memos, meetings, reports. He was the sole decision-maker and the single signatory on checks. And how many businesses could claim a staff with zero deadweight?

At two, Vilma brought in the mail. Quite a pile. One of the letters bore vaguely familiar handwriting. It was written on letterhead of the St. Regis Hotel on East 55th.

"It can't be," he mumbled. Not now—not after fifteen years.

He ripped open the envelope.

Alex,

I'm in New York for a week. I'd like to see you, as I have a few things to discuss.

When would be convenient? Please let me know.

Charlotte

He reached for the telephone. He had Dr. Korbel's private number on speed dial. His heart raced as he read the brief missive and continued racing as he waited for a reaction.

"Well, you have no alternative but to see her. Listen to what she has to say. Just stay calm."

"How can you expect me to see her now?" *After fifteen years. After fifteen years of not one single direct communication from her—only from her attorney. After she turned me into a hermit who's afraid of the whole world.*

"See her, Alex. You can tell me about it on Wednesday morning." Dr. Korbel put down the phone.

The more he looked at Charlotte's note, the angrier he grew. What could she possibly want now? To attack the only area in which he wasn't a total failure—his business?

He swallowed a Prozac and dialed the St. Regis.

"Alex, they've arrived." It was Bill, the business manager, whom Alex had asked to keep an eye out for his ex-wife, escort her to the elevator, and call him when she was on her way up. But that wasn't exactly what Bill was saying. He was saying they. "They're on their way."

They.

Should he call Korbel again? Take another Prozac? Maybe Tim had come with her. He'd be seventeen now. Alex hadn't seen him since that night. Would the boy even recognize him? With a German mother and a Chilean stepfather, would he even speak English?

He stood by the elevator that opened directly into his foyer. For once he was glad it was the slowest elevator in the city of New York.

The doors opened. Alex stared into it. Charlotte, her mother and father, her husband and her brother. Just as Alex stared into the elevator, they all stared out, making no move to leave it. The door started to close, one of them stopped it and they walked into the foyer.

Seeing how they'd all aged helped him work past the shock of seeing them at all. Charlotte's blondeness hadn't exactly changed but now appeared aided by a bottle. The locale of her elegance had shifted from the high cheekbones and sleek, model-like skin of her youth to her attire: her black dress with raspberry piping was clearly expensive, though probably only half as pricey as her shoes.

Her mother, Marie, was similarly draped in costly fabric and flashy finery. She wore her makeup so thick that it bunched in the creases of her skin, accentuating the wrinkles she meant to hide.

Alex didn't immediately hone in on how her father had aged, but it was only because his outfit—or rather, his costume—demanded attention. Fit and rugged, he gave the impression of a hybrid lumberjack, cowboy, and *Oktoberfest* carnival barker: he wore jeans and boots and a Bavarian hat with a feather.

Her brother had aged better than any other member of the family. His always-delicate features had apparently been well-preserved, though whether with lotions alone or also surgery, Alex couldn't guess.

And then her new husband. Good looking. Superficially elegant to match Charlotte herself. Tanned. Oozing sleaze.

For a few seconds, no one spoke. Charlotte broke the silence as she looked past Alex into the living room and dining room, probably to see what artwork he had acquired over the years.

"You have a fabulous townhouse, Alex. So close to Central Park, and everything else. For heaven's sake, though, couldn't you have furnished it better? It looks as if every stick of furniture came from IKEA or a thrift store. This could be a showplace. Look at that fireplace! And then look what you put on the mantle. What is that—a two-dollar plastic clock you found on the curb? With all your money, you couldn't hang up some art? You couldn't hire an interior designer? You couldn't do *something*?"

He breathed in deeply. He had done it: he'd survived her first rant in fifteen years. "I like it the way it is. Don't try to sell me any art."

"I wouldn't try."

"Look, you asked for this meeting. I thought you were coming alone. I didn't expect a gathering. Especially this group."

"Well, now that we have got off to such a good start, maybe we could all sit down?" New Husband suggested. The barrier of accents made it difficult to determine exactly how insincere he was.

Alex led the way into the living room, where casement windows overlooked the busy street. Wooden parquet floor, bare white walls, hole in the ceiling where once no doubt a chandelier hung. Three inexpensive floor lamps placed randomly around the room. Four blue director's chairs and a red bean bag seat. The day's newspapers spread loosely on the floor. It could have been a college freshman's dorm.

He looked straight across at Charlotte, deliberately avoiding eye contact with the others.

"Are you going to offer us a drink?" Charlotte asked.

"My housekeeper is out at the market. What would you like her to fix you when she returns? Tea or coffee?"

She looked at her husband. "Actually, a glass of wine would be nice."

"There's no wine here. I don't entertain and I don't drink. Alcohol would interfere with my medications. Would you like a diet Coke?"

"Forget the drinks. Why are you taking medicine anyway? What's wrong with you?"

"I found my wife in bed with another man."

"Oh my God, Alex. It's been fifteen—"

"What did you want to discuss with me? Does it have anything to do with Tim? My son? The one you've prevented me from seeing?"

"No, Pedro is doing well. He may be coming to college in the States next year."

"Pedro?"

"After Jose adopted him, we all thought it would be best if he had a name that was more Spanish."

"That explains it."

"What do you mean?"

Alex got up from his chair and walked across the room to the large cabinet that held his television. He opened the doors of the cabinet and pointed to the two shelves inside which were packed with boxes and letters.

"Fifteen years of letters, presents, checks, cash, birthday cards, Christmas cards and cards sent for no other reason than a father just needed to have contact with his only child." He was now shouting. "Every last one of them returned 'Addressee unknown' . . . because I sent them to *Timothy Butler*. How the fuck was I to know that he was now Pedro whatever-the-hell-his-last-name-is-now? Did you ever bother to tell me? No."

Alex pointed at New Husband. "You bastard. You stole my wife and helped the bitch steal my son." And now pointing to the bitch herself, "And you have the gall to come to my home, criticize my furniture, and expect me to entertain you with drinks?" He returned to his chair—his college-dorm-chic chair, the sort of décor she would criticize him for owning as though it were more gauche than robbing a man of his son—and he waited. But none of them dared say a word. "Say something. Why have you come to see me?"

Finally New Husband began to speak, not to Alex but to his wife, softly, in Spanish. Her parents then spoke to each other, in German, and then to their daughter, also in German.

"Okay, Alex. Let's start again. Let's calm down and try to have a constructive, adult conversation."

He wished for a second Prozac. His pulse thundered. An anxiety attack couldn't be far off. "Go ahead."

"We've all seen how brilliantly you've done. Some write of you as a billionaire. *The Frankfurter Allgemeine* ran a story about you—'the New York millionaire, who no one sees, hears, or even knows.' They referred to you as an eccentric hermit. They sent a reporter to me. He wanted to know about us and our marriage."

"Did you tell him how I caught you in bed with him?"

She ignored the question.

"The reason we're here is to ask you for some help." She hurried on before he could laugh or scream or throw something or act on any of the desperate, incredulous impulses he may have harbored. "Jose has been working as the representative in Munich for an American Bank. We want to move to the United States. I'm an American citizen, and Pedro was born here. Jose is in a special position because of the work he did for the CIA in helping to get rid of Allende."

Alex nodded slowly, keeping his eyes locked on New Husband now. "Yes, I believe he was implicated in the murder or disappearance of over ten thousand Chileans. And that he was a leader of an ultra-rightwing militant group of thugs. Do I have that right?"

New Husband said nothing, not that he could have with his lips pursed so tightly.

"So, let him come to the United States. What's that got to do with me?"

"Why not offer him a job? He'd be a great asset."

Alex closed his eyes. He pinched the bridge of his nose. Maybe he'd taken much more medicine than he realized; maybe inside his brain right now, mismatched pharmaceuticals were uniting in a feverish haze. It would explain this nightmare of a conversation.

"Is there anything else?"

"We've found a farm we'd like to buy in Litchfield County, Connecticut. There are two houses. The idea is that we'd live in one and my parents in the other."

"And what's that got to do with me?"

He looked ahead. The elevator doors had opened. It was Vilma returning from the market. She ventured into the kitchen to unpack her shopping.

"We'd like you to act as guarantor for the mortgage. The bank will lend sixty percent. We're putting down fifteen percent. We need a bank guaranty for the remaining twenty-five percent."

"Very nice. Anything else?"

Charlotte's brother spoke for the first time, his English clipped but capable enough. "I am forming a string quartet that will be based in Berlin. We are looking for sponsors for a world tour. I wonder whether you would be willing to join our group? The tour will be for the German Nature Conservation Society."

"Very noble. Anything else?"

Vilma stood by the threshold of the doorway and waited for a pause in the conversation. "Can I get anyone something?"

"No thank you, Vilma. The party will be over in a moment."

Charlotte's parents had remained silent throughout their visit. Alex looked up at the ceiling, then on the floor, and bent down to collect the newspapers that he had discarded earlier.

"So what's it to be, Alex? Can you help us?"

He closed his eyes and, for the first time since he had opened her letter earlier in the day, felt his chest muscles relax to the point his lungs could properly inflate with fresh oxygen.

"Well, allow me to address the financial demands and expectations on your shopping list individually.

"First, the request that I give this bastard a position. It would be smarter for me just to saw off the hand I write checks with. The first and only qualification of his I'm familiar with is that he's willing to steal a man's family. It's not a quality I look for in a plumber—much less someone to handle money. My money.

"I suppose I could help you with the farm just for the fun of evicting you when you default—and you would default—but on the other hand, rich landlords who evict their tenants always look like swine in the newspapers. No matter if the tenants themselves are the pigs. So, you'll understand if I pass on that generous opportunity as well."

He stopped, avoiding the saucer-wide eyes of everyone except his former brother-in-law. He pointed to him. "Yours is the only request that isn't clearly rooted in the selfishness of a sociopath. How much do you want me to give?"

"Well," he stuttered, "I was hoping you could sponsor us for $50,000."

"I'll give you five hundred."

He watched them squirm in their seats.

"Vilma," he shouted. "They are leaving now. Please show them out."

"And," addressing Charlotte's brother, "send me a letter about your group, and I'll send you a check. Okay?

"And Charlotte, when Tim—excuse me, *Pedro*—comes to college, ask him to look me up. He can collect the presents that I have for him over there."

She nodded. There was nothing else she could do. For the first time in much longer than fifteen years, Charlotte had been rendered speechless.

They stood and left. No handshakes, no goodbyes. They walked to the elevator in silence.

He watched from his chair as the elevator door closed and began its descent. He then burst out with a laugh; an uncontrolled fit of laughter. He rocked in the director's chair from side to side until the chair lost its balance and he fell onto the floor, laughing, holding his ribcage in a loud and raucous laugh.

Vilma ran from the elevator. As she stood over him, she said, "Signor Butler, Signor Butler, what is it? Are you okay?"

He laughed in a way that resembled choking; it was as though whatever had struck him as funny may be an unfamiliar food—something to which he was allergic—and now his body was reacting the only way it could. As if he were battling a dangerous invader. Though at the same time, he did seem to be enjoying himself. Tears of joy streamed down his face.

Vilma ran to the telephone.

"Dr. Korbel, it's Vilma, Signor Butler's housekeeper. Please come quickly. Something is wrong. I haven't seen him this way in all these years."

The doctor rushed over, probably wondering if he would find Alex Butler unresponsive, cowered in his closet clutching his heart, leaning over his balcony contemplating the swift trip to the pavement below. Imagine his surprise then, to find that his most stubborn client had, at long last, followed his advice. Alex was still laughing when he greeted the doctor.

"I think he'll make it, Vilma."

Alex laughed at Dr. Korbel's words; now that it had re-emerged, it was as though his long-caged laughter meant to make up for lost time.

"So what do you think, Alex? Same time on Wednesday?"

With difficulty and through further peals of hilarity, Alex managed to express that he thought—just this once—they could scale it back to twice a week; maybe even he could get by on a single weekly session.

"Whatever you think. I'm glad you seem to be feeling better, Alex. In the meantime, is there anything I can do to help you? Anything you need?"

A few staggered, calming breaths later, Alex was able to convey the only thing he could imagine wanting right now.

"Coffee?" Dr. Korbel echoed him. "You want me to offer you coffee during your sessions? Well, of course. Why ever didn't you ask me before?"

Inside the elevator, even when the ornate door had closed and the cables had been set in motion, the doctor could still hear the sound of his patient's first laugh in fifteen years.

CHAPTER NINETEEN

Fun and Games

A rchie sauntered into work just as the grandfather clock in the marble pillared banking hall struck a quarter-past-ten. No one batted an eyelid at his late arrival. After all, it was Monday morning, and he'd had a busy weekend playing polo, tennis, and a sport of another kind . . . a tad of sexual debauchery with Fiona, made possible by her fiancée's absence on a business trip to the Far East.

Archie was not the sharpest knife in the drawer. Not by any means. He barely scraped through business school and earned a very mediocre undergraduate degree. He'd only been admitted by virtue of the new library that bore his family name. His father, Jock Webster, was chairman and chief executive officer of a Fortune 100 corporation, a global conglomerate whose business practically every major bank pursued. The long-established Wall Street firm, McTavish, Beacon & Farlow's investment in cultivating a connection with Jock Webster was to take on Archie, a twenty-five year old wastrel, with neither ambition, talent nor any interest in acquiring skills, as a trainee to equip him for a serious senior position with the bank.

It didn't take long for Archie to realize that the bank was divided into two distinct groups: "Officers" and "Men." In spite of his lack of knowledge and interest in the activities of the firm, he carried an engraved business card and heads turned at the country clubs he frequented and at the cocktail parties where he worked the rooms whenever he mentioned that he was with McTavish, Beacon & Farlow. That was enough. No one bothered to ask what he did there. If they had, he would have skillfully evaded mentioning that he spent every morning—along with other progeny of either major tycoons or "old money"—studying the sports pages, making dates, planning weekend activities, and exchanging kiss and tell stories, most of which were either highly exaggerated or totally fictitious. While the Men toiled at their desks, the Officers relaxed over leisurely lunches with colleagues in any of the bank's dining rooms on the third floor or with clients at any of the city's exclusive private clubs. It certainly beat the hot dogs or tuna melts that were the usual fodder of the Men who, between bites and swigs of soda, pored over financial reports and balance sheets, and attended to a variety of routine paperwork without ever leaving their desks.

There was an unwritten rule at the Officers' lunches. Business talk was not allowed. Conversations could flow about art openings, concerts, new plays, sporting events, landscape gardening, upcoming sales at Sotheby's and Christies, but God forbid a potential client, honored with an invitation to lunch at McTavish, Beacon & Farlow, would dare to ask about the price of gold, the prospects for the Dow Jones Industrial Average ("DJIA") or whether the United States dollar was vulnerable. Such questions would result in the cold shoulder.

Afternoons were devoted to out-of-office activities. Under the pretense of a business meeting, many an Officer would sly away to visit his tailor, hairdresser, psychiatrist, cigar merchant, vintner or rendezvous with a girlfriend, or mistress, in a convenient pied-à-terre chosen for its convenience for a five minute walk home on the Upper East Side in time to change for dinner or for a night at the opera.

Meanwhile, the "non-commissioned-officers" (NCOs) were the senior managers of the individual departments who kept the bank afloat with their consummate professionalism, high work ethics, and strong senses of loyalty. They put in long hours without receiving any perks and labored hard under such conditions, never complaining; for after all, they were employed by the established, distinguished firm of McTavish, Beacon & Barlow, and that gave them a leg up at home in the suburbs with their neighbors.

Archie didn't leave his desk that afternoon. He was expecting a call from Fiona and he didn't want to miss it. She mentioned that she wanted to go to a gallery opening that evening and hoped he would accompany her. The promise of making arrangements for another night with her was sufficient to keep him at the bank until five o'clock, but he certainly wasn't going to hang around waiting any longer than that.

As he was finishing discussing his new tennis racket with Linc, with whom he shared a double desk, his telephone rang.

Thankfully, before he could ask "Fiona, so what's the plan for tonight?" the person at the other end of the phone said, "Archie, Rex Hastings here. I'd like to have a drink with you this evening. How about six o'clock at The Metropolitan Club?"

Rex Hastings was the chairman of the bank. His father and grandfather were both former chairmen and they each had died in office, a fact that was at the forefront of sixty-five-year-old Rex's mind. Rex and Archie's fathers were friends from Hotchkiss and were members of the same Westchester golf club. This connection contributed to Archie's reaction to the invitation. Any other twenty-five-year-old employee of McTavish, Beacon & Barlow would have been close to a heart attack on being summoned for a drink with the bank's chairman, and would have spent the rest of the day totally intimidated and in panic mode. But Archie did not see this as a summons, but rather as an inconvenience, given that he would have to forsake the one remaining evening with Fiona before her fiancée returned from Hong Kong.

The staff at the Metropolitan knew Archie because his father was a member, so in his usual style he sauntered into the Club, feeling by osmosis that he was also a long-term member. He half-hoped that he would be fired for incompetence. After a predictable family row and a few months of his father's help, he would easily land another position. Most importantly though, was that during those in-between-jobs months, there'd be more opportunities for debauchery and fun.

Rex Hastings was already at the bar. *Bastard,* Archie thought. *He obviously came up from Wall Street in one of the bank's cars, he could have offered me a ride.*

"What are you having?" Rex asked with a smile. "I'm having a Glenlivet."

"Champagne for me," Archie replied.

They spent a pleasant enough hour speaking a lot but saying absolutely nothing of any substance.

Golf, polo, and Rex's Virginia stud.

Archie inelegantly looked at his watch. Seven o'clock. He began to wonder whether he could simply get up and make an excuse to leave when Rex turned to him and said, "I hope you don't have dinner plans, because I've organized a private room here at the club for us. What I need to discuss with you is in absolute confidence and I don't want anyone to hear us. You understand, Archie?"

Oh my God, Archie thought. *Is he going to make a pass? This is bizarre.* "No, I have no plans."

"Good. Let's go upstairs. Drink up."

Archie followed Rex to the elevator and then up to the fourth floor, along a corridor toward one of the private dining rooms that featured a round table that would normally seat six, but was set for just the two of them. A waiter stood by the open door to greet them.

"I've taken the liberty of organizing dinner. It's set up on the table in the corner over there."

"Gazpacho, chilled pheasant, salad and a cheese board. The wine is on the table and there's port and cognac over there."

"Thank you. I'm sure, Rex, you have something important to discuss and I'm eager to hear it." The two glasses of champagne had given him the confidence, not only to address the chairman by his first name but also to display some assertiveness.

"Yes, you're right to be curious and to get me back on track. Let's get some gazpacho and I'll tell you why I wanted to see you, but remember this is strictly confidential."

"Of course."

"The situation is this, Archie. You know my wife, of course, Angelique?"

"Yes, I do. She's a really lovely and very beautiful lady. She and my mother are good friends. They spend a lot of time together both here in the city and in the Hamptons. I believe you've also had my parents stay with you in Virginia, too."

"That's right. We always enjoy spending time with your folks."

Archie paused to eat some bread.

"I'll come straight to the point, Archie. My wife has a crush on you." He looked straight at the young man and waited for his reaction.

Archie twitched and started to stutter. "I really don't know what to say. I have always behaved in a most respectful manner ... "

"Archie, I know that. I'm not casting any blame on you. None at all. But let's face it, you're twenty-five, she's forty-five and I'm sixty-five. You cut quite a dash at the club whether it's on a polo pony, on a tennis court, or on the thirteenth hole. Not to mention on the dance floor. She's smitten. She asks me about you all the time, questions like, how's Archie getting on at the bank? Why don't we have him over for dinner one night? Has he got a girlfriend? Questions like that."

"Honestly, I have done nothing to encourage her, I promise you."

"Archie, I know that." He paused to take a sip from his glass.

"Well, what can I do about it?"

"Do you find my wife attractive?"

"Yes, of course. She's a very beautiful woman."

"Have you ever had a relationship with a much older woman, Archie?"

"Well, no, to tell you the truth."

"It can be very exciting, you know."

"I guess it can be. Yes."

"How's your French?"

"Basic. I've spent summers with a friend at his family homes in Paris and in Beaulieu. Why do you ask?"

"As you know Angelique is French. She wants to spend four months at her house in Antibes. She's pissed as hell that I can't accompany her for at least some of the time. Damn it. I'm chairman of the bank. Two of our clients are embroiled in hostile takeover bids. I'm on two presidential committees with monthly meetings at The White House. How the hell does she expect me to take off for weeks, never mind months." His voice rose. "Plus, I'm not sure that I want to spend a lengthy period with her. When you get to my age, and you've been married for as long as I have, you'll understand."

Archie nodded.

"Plus, and this is between you and me, I do have another interest if you get my meaning?"

Archie nodded again, not too sure whether he did get the older man's meaning.

"So where do I come in?"

"Very simple. My present to Angelique is you. I want you to accompany her to France, stay with her, be her escort, tennis partner, dancing partner and you can, with my blessing, fuck her." He let out an embarrassed guffaw.

Archie paused. "That's quite a perk, along with medical, dental and vision coverage," he giggled.

"I'm being deadly serious, Archie."

"But how can I simply take off for four months? What's the pretext? I can't tell anyone why you're sending me to France, can I?"

"Of course not. You can tell everyone at the bank, and your father, that I'm sending you to Paris to develop relationships with some of the banks there as well as meet with senior executives at Danone, Renault, and L'Oréal."

"But do you actually want me to do that?"

"Of course not. With all due respect, you don't have the knowledge or the skills to represent the bank with overseas potential clients. You lack the maturity. They would be insulted to meet with someone who has only been out of business school for barely six months."

"So how will I spend my days?"

"I've told you. By doing all that is necessary to make my wife, happy, satisfied, and amused."

"I see. Does she know that you're setting her up with me, or me with her?"

"No, not yet. But you'll come over to the house for dinner. Just the three of us. And, I'll announce that you're going to be in France for a few months attending to some business for us and that she's to keep an eye on you."

"I see."

"And I promise you, you won't be disappointed. She'll keep a lot more than an eye on you."

Archie paused.

"Every week, you'll send me a letter outlining how much you've spent and I'll send you by return mail a check to cover your expenses. And not that you need it, I'll give you a handsome float in Euros that will cover you for at least the first month. I need hardly tell you that you'll need to have a bundle of cash. Angelique is not a cheap date. In fact, I'll get you a special credit card for expenses such as these. After all this is HCF business."

"What do you mean, HCF?"

"High Cost of Fucking."

Archie couldn't suppress a smile.

"Now, remember this is between us."

"Absolutely."

"Let's go now. I'll speak to Angelique tonight and I'll get back to you tomorrow morning about dinner next week."

Two weeks later, Archie sat in the first-class Air France lounge at JFK, nervously awaiting the arrival of Angelique Hastings who had insisted that they travel separately to the airport, sit apart on the flight, and make their own ways to her Paris apartment. "He who pays the piper plays the tune," was a fact he simply accepted. It was of no consequence. He was delighted to bid farewell to Wall Street for a few months, his pockets were lined with thousands of euros and he had a new American Express credit card, with unlimited credit, for the specific purpose of keeping the chairman's wife amused while he pursued what he diplomatically described as "his other interest."

The glass sliding doors opened and out stepped Angelique Hastings. Tall, maybe five foot eleven, in tight, tailored black jeans that clung to her long legs that were evidence of her years as a ballerina with The Royal Ballet.

A heavy Chanel link belt hung around her waist and her long blond hair fell down below her shoulders. Her white silk blouse was unbuttoned to show her tanned cleavage and the sapphire and diamond pendant she always wore. As she walked, her Manolo Blahnik shoes clacked loudly against the marble floor and that, together with the jangle of her gold tone Chanel bracelets, caused many of the seated travelers to look up from their newspapers. She walked toward Archie. He hesitated whether he should stand to greet her but held back, knowing that was contrary to the arrangements. She passed him, without so much as a nod or a wink. He shrugged his shoulders and resumed reading an article in *Tennis World*.

Within a few minutes he heard her giggling. He turned around and saw that she had sat down next to a middle-aged gentleman who had obviously amused her with some comment. He turned away back to his article and pondered over his unjustifiable pang of jealousy. *After all, I'm only a well-paid gigolo.*

He had an aisle seat, three rows behind her in the first-class cabin. There was a spare seat next to hers, but he knew better than to take it.

Upon arrival at Charles de Gaulle, he followed her through into the baggage hall where she was met by her driver. He grabbed his two suitcases from the carousel and stood in line for a cab for the ride to her apartment on Avenue Foch, the most prestigious Paris residential address, famed for its grand palaces, its wide expanse and the magnificent chestnut trees that framed both sides of the street.

Angelique's home was on the second floor of the former palace of a White Russian aristocrat who had managed to get out of Russia, his fortune intact, before the First World War. After the Second World War, it had been converted into five spacious apartments.

"Good, morning, sir," the doorman greeted Archie as he helped unload his bags. "Madame is expecting you. She has left the door of her apartment open and you can go straight in. Georges, our elevator man, will take you up now and we'll have the bags brought up to you shortly."

Archie stepped out of the elevator and straight into Angelique's apartment. He marveled at the high ceiling, crystal chandelier and the painting that faced him. He knew it had to be a masterpiece but was unable to guess who the artist was. He didn't know a Michelangelo from a Picasso.

"Is that you, Archie?" Angelique shouted out. "I'm just getting out of the shower. What took you so long? I've been here for almost an hour. I'll be out in a minute. Walk around. Make yourself at home. We have the place to ourselves. My butler and housekeeper are off today. Sunday. It's a nuisance but I'm glad we have the place to ourselves."

He went to the window and looked out onto the Avenue. He rubbed his chin and reckoned that he too could do with a shave and a shower. It had been a long flight with a six-hour time difference. A nap might be a good idea, too.

"There you are," she said with a smile as she came toward him, barefoot and wrapped in a white silk robe. "Now we can talk. We carried it off quite well, don't you think? No one could possibly assume that we were traveling together. Come into the kitchen. Bernice would have left us some pâté, a baguette and Camembert, I'm sure. She knows that's what I like best when I arrive. It's my idea of re-acclimatizing myself to my homeland. The Germans have a word for it, *gemütlichkeit*. Funny . . . I remember the word in German but not in French." She laughed again.

"Yes, but I think we could have sat next to each other on the plane. That was taking it a bit too far, don't you think? What would you have done if I had come over to sit next to you?"

"I'd have called the flight attendant and had you removed."

He couldn't tell whether she was joking or was serious.

"Now be a good boy and open a bottle of champagne."

They sat opposite each other at the kitchen table and after an hour she yawned. "I'm getting tired. I'm going to take a nap. First, I'll show you your room. Why don't you shower, and definitely please shave, and then come and join me so we can . . . at least get to know each other better, let alone see more of each other." She giggled again. It was contagious. "But don't take too long about it. I don't want to fall asleep before you arrive."

He showered and shaved with the speed of an Olympic gold medalist sprinter, wrapped a luxurious white Turkish towel around himself, splashed some cologne on his tanned body and walked down the marble hallway. It was lined with large modern art paintings and he walked toward the open double doors which he assumed—correctly—was her bedroom, from which emanated the soft sounds of a violin concerto.

To his surprise, Angelique was not already in bed. She walked toward the door and untied the belt on her silk robe and let it fall to the floor. Now naked, she sauntered toward him and pulled the towel from off his waist.

"Well, you are a big boy, aren't you?" She grabbed him. "This is going to make me very happy, isn't it?" She stared into his eyes and he wrapped his arms around her and held her tight.

"Yes, it will. Often."

"Promise?"

"Oh yes."

She offered no resistance as he turned to face her and kissed her tenderly. Their lips lingered as he massaged the roof of her mouth with his tongue.

They moved towards the bed. She reached out and pulled him toward her. He stroked her soft silken skin to the point that neither of them had any control.

She reached down to grab him. It had been a month since he had held a naked woman in his arms. And that was Fiona, a young woman his own age. Angelique was certainly a woman, "all woman" and she was as hungry for him as he was eager to be with a woman who was so experienced. He had to admit, he still had a lot to learn. He moaned with delight as she brought him close.

He put his hand on her shoulder to slow her down. She turned over on her back. He put his arms under her, and lifted her a couple inches off the bed to penetrate deeper.

He felt and saw his perspiration as it dripped onto her, followed by sighs of delight. He fell onto his back. She rolled over onto hers. They turned to look at each other and held each other close.

"I've wanted you for a long time, you know," she whispered. "I spent so many weekends, bored stiff, watching those damned polo matches, just to get a glimpse of you galloping down the field. So dashing you looked. And how jealous I was of all those pretty girls who flocked around you afterwards. And you never spared me so much as a glance."

"Well, how could I? You are one of my mother's closest friends and my boss's wife."

"Well don't let either of those reasons interfere with all the fun we are going to have. Right, big boy?"

She turned over and within a couple of minutes she was fast asleep.

He accompanied her the next two days as she visited the couturiers on avenue Montaigne and jewelers on rue du Faubourg Saint-Honoré where she was greeted with enthusiasm by fawning sales associates who toadied to her, knowing her whims and impulsive spending habits. He sat, bored, eyes frequently closed as she flirted with the obsequious men who attended to her. He soon realized that he would have to forego lunches, as nothing ever crossed her lips after her morning brioche until dinner each evening.

She took him from one art gallery to another, where the routine was much the same as at the couturiers. He could not understand what all the fuss was about so many of the paintings that she stood in awe of as she talked enthusiastically with the gallery directors. He watched, amazed, as she studied one particular painting of brightly colored shapes.

"What do you think of this one? Isn't it magnificent?" she asked as she turned around and saw him slumped in an armchair.

"I don't see what's so special about it. It's the sort of thing I did in my kindergarten."

She glowered and said nothing.

The night before they were due to leave for her house in Antibes, she took him to a formal dinner party—a fiftieth birthday party—hosted by friends who lived in an apartment on the Île Saint-Louis. Fortunately, Archie had packed his tuxedo. They joined the four other couples and the host and hostess for cocktails on the balcony overlooking the Seine.

It was certainly a grand occasion but again, Archie was bored. While he had some basic French skills, he was completely outside his element. He had no idea what everyone was discussing. They spoke so quickly. No one made any attempt to draw him into the conversations by speaking English, in which, undoubtedly, they were all fluent. At dinner, he and Angelique were seated apart and to his right, he had the wife of a cabinet minister, and to his left, the wife of the chairman of one of France's leading insurance companies. Neither of them so much as gave him a glance. He stared down in horror as each course was served, unsure whether he could handle such rich cuisine so soon after an equally decadent lunch. He just moved the food around with his fork. As each guest leisurely sipped the Châteaux Margaux, Archie gulped it down and as the butler refilled his glass, Archie felt Angelique's cruel stare from across the table.

They did not make love that night. In fact, conversation was at a minimum. The journey to Cannes in the luxury of the private plane did nothing to improve Archie's spirits. Angelique brought a bundle of French magazines to read, but he only had a copy of *Tennis World* which he'd already read three times.

Angelique's villa had *been in the family* since 1890 when her great-great grandparents had built it. It had acres of well-maintained lawns and had panoramic views of the Mediterranean. A wide pathway, flanked by multicolored rose bushes, led down to the water's edge where, in earlier days, Angelique kept a speedboat until one of her old boyfriends drove it straight into a neighbor's jetty.

After their first night at the villa, she casually said to him over her daily brioche that she was going to look at paintings at Galerie Maeght, and that she doubted he would want to go with her. Her husband kept a set of golf clubs in his study. Perhaps Archie should take them and go to a nearby golf club and play eighteen holes? She'd be back later.

Archie telephoned Philippe, a friend from London, who he knew was staying with his sister in Gassin.

"Take a water taxi to Saint-Tropez, and I'll pick you up," Philippe said. "I'm happy you are here. I need a golf partner."

Thus began Archie's daily routine. Breakfast with Angelique, and then a water taxi to Saint-Tropez, returning to Antibes at the cocktail hour, sometimes by water taxi and more often in a Riva owned by a friend of Philippe's sister. A quick change for dinner with Angelique at home or with friends of hers, either at their villas or at casual bistros along the Riviera.

Things were not the same. Angelique was irritable, bored, and clearly disenchanted. The sex had lost its excitement and variety. Now it was quick and perfunctory, albeit most nights but no longer in the mornings. Archie had lost interest and Angelique knew that unless she made an effort, he would not be a willing participant, and she too found it difficult to muster up any enthusiasm. Even their nightly activities were driven more by the heavy intake of Dom Pérignon and routine rather than genuine desire.

This situation dragged on for close to three weeks.

And then . . .

Archie was dressed one morning to leave for Saint-Tropez. They'd had too much to drink the night before, and Angelique did not come down for breakfast. Archie left the house to walk the couple of hundred yards to the quay for the boat to Saint-Tropez when he realized that he'd left his wallet behind. He ran back to the house to get it. By the time he had retrieved it, he saw from his watch that he had missed the boat. The next one wouldn't arrive for another forty-five minutes. He sat on the terrace, overlooking the sea. Directly above him was Angelique's bedroom with a wall of windows and two sets of French doors that opened onto a balcony. He heard her speak on the telephone. It was obviously long distance, as she was shouting down the phone. It was clear that she was not in the best of moods.

"Rex, you have to help me. I can't stand it anymore. He bores me. He has no sense of history. No appreciation for art. He has no interest in anything except tennis, golf, and polo. His French is not as good as you suggested. He contributes nothing at dinner parties. He despises French food. He doesn't know a Châteaux Margaux from a Root Beer. He isn't even a good fuck. I'm dying of boredom. Order him back to New York, for God's sake. And to make things even more complicated, I've now got another playmate, but what the hell can I do with this dolt hanging around?"

Archie froze.

Angelique went silent. Obviously, her husband was answering her.

"Okay. I'll tell him. He's left already for golf. I'll leave a note for him. Promise me you'll order him back to New York immediately."

Archie stood, and left in time for the next shuttle to Saint-Tropez. Several hours later as he walked back into the villa, the butler handed him a note.

I'll be home late tonight. Don't wait up for me. It is vital you telephone Rex immediately after you get back. He's waiting for your call. Call him, whatever the hour.

Angelique.

"Thank you, Gaston, I'll have a glass of champagne."

Archie stepped into the drawing room and picked up the telephone and looked at the time. One o'clock in the morning in New York. *Well, she said to call at any time.*

"Archie. Thank you for calling me. Listen to me carefully. Angelique telephoned me this morning. She has gone away for a few days. It's best you leave now. Obviously, it didn't work out. I'm sure you tried your best. Anyway, your father has just appointed Lazard Freres to advise his company on the takeover of a Spanish industrial company. We're very upset at the bank about this. I'm embarrassed because I thought we had that business firmly in the bag. So, Archie,

I'm sorry. There's no rush for you to get back. There's no position at the bank for you anymore, I'm afraid. I'll give you a good reference, of course. And I'll see you at the Club sometime. Stay tonight, of course, but if you can leave after breakfast in the morning, it would be best. Gaston will help you pack and will drive you to Nice airport."

Click.

Archie finished his glass of champagne. Fortunately, Gaston had left the bottle in a bucket of ice on a side table close by. He opened his wallet and took out a piece of paper on which he'd written a telephone number.

"Giovanni, good evening. Is the *Principessa* available, please?"

He waited a minute.

"Darling. It's Archie. Good news. I can come with you to Portofino after all. I can't tell you how much I am looking forward to spending days and nights with you. Please send the Riva to pick me up tomorrow morning. And, tell your boatman to put the Italian flag back on it. No need to hide it anymore. Let it fly proudly in the wind."

CHAPTER TWENTY

I Played for Louis

Jake Baker stood at the door, contemptuous of the couple whose departure he had blocked and of the man behind him who was in a frenzied rush to grab his morning coffee-to-go. He squinted and turned his head from side to side to spot a free table that was halfway clean. It was no easy task during the breakfast hour at this busy diner. There was one table at the back, noisy but at least close to the restroom. He'd taken a water pill just before leaving his apartment.

He shuffled his bulky, ninety-year-old frame—outfitted in a heavy overcoat, a thick woolen scarf, and a fedora—down the narrow path between busy tables. He spotted a used paper napkin on the floor and pushed it aside with the tip of his cane.

"Ce miserable con qui habite dans l'immeuble de Pierre vient de rentrer."

Jake Baker frowned and stared at the young man. He was a regular too, no doubt one of the effete stylists who worked at the salon that just opened on the block. Jake knew when he was being referred to as a miserable bastard, and he didn't care for it.

"Merde," replied his young boyfriend. *"C'est vraiment un vieux connard antipathique. Croisons les doigts qu'il ne s'assoit ici."*

Jake growled. Now they were crossing their fingers that he, "the hostile jerk," didn't claim the table beside theirs. Upon reaching a table at the back, he threw his cane and hat down on the chair closest to him but, before taking his seat, shouted across the room at the two men, "Don't think I don't understand French, you fucking ignorant shithead pansies. I know what you said. I lived in Paris before you were born. Your parents too. Motherfuckers."

The Frenchmen stood, pausing to leave a few dollars on the table, and then hurried out, their wide grins and giggles indicating they were more amused than embarrassed. Theo, the owner, took in the scene from his position by the cash register. The servers and the busboys scurried past Jake's table, all muttering in their assorted native tongues that they hoped they would not be designated Baker's server that day. Hopefully the new kid would suffer that ordeal. He would be lucky if his tip was greater than a grudging fifty cents.

With the arthritis that had spread to his upper arms and shoulders, taking off his overcoat was a painful and laborious process. He placed it on a chair and sat down next to it. His knees now gave him problems too. Standing and sitting took longer and was more painful these days.

A better table had freed up by the front door, but it was too much trouble to move to it. A busboy placed a menu on the table and rushed away, fearful of unfriendly words or commands.

Baker ignored the menu. "Hey kid, bring me that newspaper from over there," he demanded in a tone that made several customers turn their heads. The busboy brought him the *New York Post*, its crumpled pages dampened by coffee spills.

"Jesus Christ. Hasn't anyone left a *Times*?"

The boy shook his head.

"Look over there." Baker pointed to an empty table that hadn't yet been cleared.

Without replying, the busboy reached for the paper.

Jake stroked his heavy, sagging, wrinkled face; the grey pallor of his skin matched the color of his shirt. He hadn't shaved for a few days.

"What will you be sending back to the kitchen this morning, Mr. Baker?"

"Smart ass. If your fucking chef could get it right the first time, I wouldn't need to send anything back, would I?"

"There are other diners, Mr. Baker, that I'm sure would be happy to have your business," Theo replied. To Baker, the eggs were always too soft or too hard, the bagel under- or over-toasted, and his neighbor's omelet larger than his own. The chef peered from behind the rotating steel wheel that held diner's orders to witness this exchange.

"I'll have scrambled eggs, crispy bacon, a toasted bagel, and sliced tomatoes," Baker said without opening the menu. "And bring me some hot coffee. Make a fresh brew, for Christ's sake."

He glanced at the three envelopes peeking from his coat pocket that he had collected from his mailbox a few minutes earlier. He'd open them when he got home.

"Kid, lend me a pen. I want to do the crossword puzzle."

The busboy handed him a pen, terrorized at the thought of the crossword puzzle and endless coffee refills lodging Baker at the table for the next hour or more.

"And while you're at it, I need more napkins."

Theo watched silently as Baker stuffed his coat pocket with paper napkins. He did this every visit. He suspected

Baker never bought toilet tissue or paper towels for his apartment, but he wasn't going to make a stink over it. Everyone had idiosyncrasies, but then again, not everyone was as disagreeable an old bastard as Baker.

Baker stared at the clues and smiled. At first glance, he knew he had the answers to several of them. He was proud that, never having graduated high school, more often than not he was able to complete the daily crossword. Seven down threw him: *Famous composer born in Bonn.* Eleven across too: *Seven down's only opera.*

At the arrival of the scrambled eggs and bacon, he looked down at the plate, picked up a rasher and nodded. Crispy enough. "Where's my bagel?" he shouted to a passing server.

Then back to frowning at the paper. He should have known these answers—since the end of the war, he'd been a professional pianist. Before the war, he had studied hard for his audition at Juilliard. He had failed. The Manhattan School of Music wouldn't have him either. "Adequate but not talented enough," was what the bastard professor had told him after he'd flunked a Chopin piece.

He still believed he could have made it, despite Juilliard, as a great concert pianist, playing in the major concert halls throughout the United States, Europe, and Latin America. He knew he would have cut a dash walking onto the stage to sit down at a concert grand, in immaculate white tie and tails, his thick auburn hair shaking as he pounded the keys to a spellbound audience as he played Rachmaninov, Tchaikovsky, Schumann, and his beloved Chopin. But they said he "lacked sufficient talent," and without a scholarship, there was no way he could afford to attend a school like Julliard anyway.

Instead, he spent the war years playing third-rate swing music with amateurs in a military band in the Philippines, in an unsuccessful attempt to boost the troops' morale. It was a long way from the prestige of Bob Hope's USO touring circus, with all its glamour and celebrities. After the war: gigs here and there, playing corny, predictable Dixieland jazz in smoky bars, basements, and dives throughout the East Coast. In between, Baker gave piano lessons to untalented, spoiled brats whose parents usually fired him because of his language. It took him a long time to understand that shouting, "When are you going to get it fucking right?" at a nine-year-old wasn't the way to cultivate a roster of loyal clients and ensure a steady flow of referrals. And then there was the smell of nicotine on his fingers and alcohol on his breath.

"Fill me up again."

As the boy took the mug from Jake's outstretched hand, he glanced at the man's filthy chewed nails and calloused fingers. Were his colleagues putting him on—telling him Jake had once been a well-known pianist?

Still stuck on seven down.

He turned his thoughts back to the two young Frenchmen from half an hour earlier. Cocky bastards. He had lived in Paris in 1947. His friend, Bob Pollock, a trombonist he'd met during the war in the Philippines, had told him there was a thriving jazz scene in Europe that was rife with opportunities for young, good-looking American musicians. He was considered handsome, once.

That first year in Paris had turned out well. There was no shortage of nightly gigs, a summer on the Riviera as well as a three-week tour with a ramshackle Dutch band to Copenhagen and Amsterdam. They were also booked to go to

London, but the English Musician's Union blocked it. He'd thought it then and he thought it now: *commie bastards*.

Then there had been Juliette.

She was twenty when they met.

And twenty when he left her.

She'd been the house chanteuse at a small club in Montparnasse. She wasn't a particularly good singer—hardly anyone could hear her weak voice over the ruckus of drunks—but she was beautiful. He bought her a drink after her set. His French had improved enough by then for lighthearted conversation, and she spoke adequate English.

She was tall, five-ten, with green eyes and shoulder-length blonde hair. In her black, Chanel-inspired cocktail dress, she held the room's attention as she started crooning prewar hits. However, after just a few bars, she always lost it and the audience resumed its loud, bawdy banter.

Her roommate had left, she told him, and she was struggling with the rent. Within weeks, he had moved in. It was a new experience for him: before the war, he had been too young for relationships, and in the Philippines, he'd followed the customary pattern of bouncing from one sultry inexpensive hooker to another.

Juliette told him that the pianist at the club, an American, was planning to quit at the end of the month and move back to Cleveland. She spoke to her boss and Jake got the job. During the day, they slept, ate, went for long walks, and made love. At night, he played and she sang. They agreed to pool their pay and tips; then one night she confronted him for palming the larger ones. She had asked Philippe, a waiter, to put a marked fifty-franc tip in the glass bowl on the piano. Sure enough, when they emptied the bowl at the end of the night, the bill wasn't there. Still Jake denied it.

She often spoke of their future. Would they remain in Paris or would he take her back to New York? She spoke of having children.

He listened, but as much as he loved her, he couldn't think beyond the next due date for rent on their humble one-bedroom walk-up Montparnasse apartment. When she told him she was pregnant, he gave her the equivalent of $300, keeping only fifty for himself.

"Go get an abortion!" he remembered shouting at her. He was never able to erase from his memory the sight of her standing there, her lips quivering, unable to utter a word, and her hands clenched and propped on the kitchen table to prevent her from collapsing. Within minutes of storming into their bedroom, he had packed his few possessions. Back in the kitchen he found she hadn't moved. Her eyes remained fixed on him as he put the door key down on the kitchen counter.

"I will never forget you," she whispered through her tears. "I love you, Jake."

He had never forgotten her either, in the sixty-five years since. Whenever he thought about the end of their relationship, he admitted that maybe he could have been kinder, but there again, she had no business getting pregnant, but those were the days before the pill, and perhaps he, too, bore some responsibility. But it was so long ago and nothing could be changed. He sometimes wondered what became of her but he didn't dwell on it. She'd be an old woman now, if she were still alive. Nearly as old as him.

Still stuck on seven down.

He turned to the calendar section and, out of habit, checked on who was playing at the jazz clubs he used to frequent before he had to tighten his belt and cut down on any frivolous, unnecessary expenses. His social security checks and paltry savings didn't allow for luxuries. The arthritis prevented him from landing even the occasional gig now. And finding new students for piano lessons wasn't feasible. If Theo didn't offer a breakfast special, he would have to eat at home. He hated to cook just for himself but without Theo's "daily specials" he couldn't afford his daily breakfasts at the diner.

Seven down. Got it. Beethoven. *Of course.* He sipped his coffee. *Beethoven.* Why hadn't he remembered that sooner? Everyone wrongly assumed Beethoven had been born in Vienna. Now, to eleven across.

His brief moment of self-congratulation was interrupted when Theo slapped the check down on his table. Soon it would be the lunch hour and Baker had outstayed his welcome. He had already consumed several free refills and added Sweet'N Low packets to the condiments already amassed in his pockets.

"Kid, come over here. Help me with my coat."

He didn't see the relief on the servers' faces as he shuffled out to go back to his apartment. He had left a dollar tip, double his usual, but he determined that this would not set a precedent for all his daily visits. The boy had been helpful—the newspapers, the pen, and then helping him with his coat and picking up his cane, which had fallen onto the floor. *What the hell . . . it was Christmas week.*

The eleven o'clock midtown traffic was slowed by blustery December showers. A woman was fast approaching him, her umbrella pulled down over her face; he stepped aside to avoid the otherwise inevitable collision. At that moment, a cab sped alongside the curb and into a pool of water that threw a spray onto Jake's trouser leg. "Motherfucker."

He pulled down his hat and tightened his scarf. The store windows had all been populated with festive Christmas decorations and menorahs and he grimaced as he passed one shop from whose open door drifted refrains of "White Christmas." A panhandler, a regular on the corner of 45th and Second, knew better than to approach him. In the thirty years Jake had lived in the neighborhood, not once had he dropped any change in the poor man's upturned old hat.

Christmas would be just like all the other Christmases he'd spent over the last five years. Alone. Trixie was generally off somewhere. And that lady on Park Avenue had dropped him from her list. A pity. She was one of the few women he admired and was one of New York's major socialites. She held a dinner party every year around Christmas and invited twenty or more people who, like him, were not spending the holiday with friends or family.

A woman clutching parcels and corralling two kids bumped into him. "Little bastards," he snarled. She snapped back, "Drop dead."

At those get-togethers, he'd always been expected to sit down at the out-of-tune Steinway and murder a few Christmas carols. But the guests all had to pay their dues. The hostess always asked Ben Norman, one of Ed Sullivan's favorites, to say a few words. He could be relied upon to get the group in peals of laughter pretty quickly. Good food, plenty to drink. Those dinner parties had been grand. The last one ended badly, though. The morning after, the hostess telephoned him and let rip. Apparently, the attractive blonde-haired woman on his right, the former dancer Dolores Arden, had conveyed a litany of complaints about him such as his hand kept roving up her leg, on her knee and on her snatch; that he blew his nose into one of the hostess's grandmother's treasured nineteenth-century Viennese napkins; and that his fingernails were black. The woman on his left, a one-time adagio dancer in Vaudeville, had similar complaints; not to mention she saw him pocket an antique silver coffee spoon.

Bottom line, no family for Christmas and no friends either. Unless he could count on Trixie.

Jake and Trixie had had a mutual love-hate relationship that lasted half a century. She was a few years younger and lived close by in Murray Hill with four overweight cats in a fifth-floor walk-up. The difficulty of navigating five flights after two knee replacements meant she rarely left her apartment, only when she had to. Another reason she stayed home was that her weight fluctuated within a fifty-pound range and was now at an all-time high and none of her clothes fit well. Over the years her hair had been dyed every color of the rainbow, now at rest on a dirty blonde shade with three months' dark brown roots. Her fat, bulbous lips, flabby skin, and multiple chins clearly indicated a lifetime of gluttony and booze.

Trixie was as bad a singer as Jake was a pianist; in fact, they'd met one night when he was playing poorly but she was singing worse. She told him how her father was a juggler who'd vanished before her birth. She told him how her mother had made the inglorious journey from singer to stripper to prostitute, aided by petty theft every step of the way. And there she was. A Mae West acolyte with the cleavage but not the talent to support her ambition.

And then he told her about his life.

Abandoned by a person unknown on a railway platform in Albany, New York, at just a few weeks old, he was raised by the local Catholic orphanage. His strict upbringing, with its heavy focus on ultra-traditional religious dogma, instilled in him a deep-rooted antipathy toward organized religion, especially Catholicism. Around the time he was seven or eight, the nuns recognized his musical talent when they caught him tickling the ivories on an old upright piano in one of the classrooms. They encouraged him, and a local music teacher volunteered to give him weekly lessons.

When he was fifteen, he hitched a ride to New York. He worked various jobs—as a dishwasher, a kitchen helper-turned-waiter, a trainee piano tuner, a sales clerk in a music store in Greenwich Village, and a bellhop at an Upper East Side hotel.

Whenever he could afford it, he would buy the least expensive ticket for a concert at Carnegie Hall and listen to Iturbi, Rubenstein, Paganini, and Horowitz and marvel at their technique and the warmth of the wondrous applause they received. When the music store was quiet, he would listen to classical records and borrow books on harmony, counterpoint, and music theory. There was a Bechstein piano in the store's window and he played it whenever he could, encouraged by the owner, Sol Isaacs, who reckoned that the sound would entice passersby to come inside. One day a customer came in and told him he should apply for Julliard.

Thank God he wasn't "insufficiently" talented for the United States Navy. By February 1942, he had been shipped out to the Philippines, where he spent three years playing with those lousy amateur bands. When he was de-mobbed at war's end, he considered the benefits of his years in the armed services. He was a veteran who had been honorably discharged, and thus was entitled to a modest pension and medical benefits. Jake had enjoyed plenty of spare paid time to hone his piano skills.

He never expected to have the opportunity of spending a couple of years in Paris. After returning to New York, he drifted, but thankfully made a modest living playing for vocalists who needed an inexpensive accompanist—and then with those awful piano lessons. When Bob Pollock wrote to tell him to get his ass over to Paris and take advantage of the State of New York's $250 tax-free bonus for having served in the armed services, he bought a one-way steerage ticket. After the ten-day voyage, he moved into a small apartment that Bob's French girlfriend found for him near the Place Clichy. Nobody today would believe the rent then; he paid about four dollars a month. Post-war Europe spelled rationing. He discovered that an American was entitled to gas coupons whether he owned a car or not. That equated to a black-market income of about forty dollars every month. Within a couple of weeks, he had secured three weekly bookings at different clubs around the city. He had even sat in with the great Sidney Bechet one night; after the set, Bechet had walked off the stage to a standing ovation, never acknowledging any of his musicians. No "thank you," no wave, not even a smile. *Perhaps he thought we were all lousy,* Jake often thought. *Or maybe he was in a rush to get back to Josephine Baker, and who could blame him for that?*

He almost got lucky in his second August in Paris when the city emptied. Bob had been asked to form a band to spend four weeks on the Riviera playing at the Martinez in Cannes and at a couple of parties in Antibes and Grasse. An elderly American woman, the widow of Count Something or other, had befriended Bob at The American Library in Paris and had generously invited the band to stay at her mansion in Le Cannet for the month. Jake woke up one night needing to go to the bathroom. He remembered it was down a corridor and then up a few stairs. Having no idea where the light switch was in that long dark corridor and knowing uneven floor tiles awaited him, Jake turned on the lamp on his nightstand and saw a vase on the dresser across the room. Perfect! He got out of bed and peed in it.

Next morning, he forgot to empty the vase in the bathroom. By midday the temperature was close to one hundred degrees. The room stank. The maid reported it to the Countess, who complained to Bob. Jake was fired and put on the train that same afternoon back to Paris.

Jake shuffled into his apartment building in Tudor City.

Stepping out of the elevator on the seventh floor, he walked slowly to his front door, and passed a neighbor's door where someone had left a gift-wrapped bottle. He glanced left and right, stopped and picked it up and hid it inside his coat for the short walk to his apartment. Once inside, he ripped open the wrapping paper. "Not bad—Mouton Cadet." He tore up the paper and the card, unread, and threw them away before stashing the bottle in the cabinet under the kitchen sink.

Only when he settled at the kitchen table with his mug of leftover morning coffee did Jake remember the mail in his coat pocket. The first was a letter from his landlord stating that in the new year they would begin renovations on his floor and the elevator would be out of use for three days. *Motherfuckers. And I'm on the seventh floor. They say three days. I'll be lucky if it's three weeks. Will I get a discount on next month's rent for this inconvenience? Try getting that from a New York property owner,* he spat. *Bastards.*

The second envelope was a Christmas card from Ken and Darby. He looked at it and sighed. "Love from Kenneth and Darby." *Love . . . that's a joke. Some love!*

He still had a soft spot for Ken, even though that bitch of a wife did everything to poison the relationship. Ken had arrived from Albany fifteen years earlier. The nuns at the orphanage had written to Jake to alert him that Ken would be calling on him and that they would appreciate any help Jake could give the talented, eighteen-year-old pianist. *Hell, I need help too,* he recalled thinking at the time.

Anyway, Ken landed on his doorstep and Jake took a shine to the young man. Tall, polite, good-looking, and raised well by the nuns, the boy certainly had talent. He sure could handle the difficult pieces like Rachmaninov's "Concerto Number 3" and Liszt's "La Campanella." He and Jake hung out a lot together—they went to concerts, shared cheap dinners, and took summer walks in Central Park. Then tragedy struck. Ken was knocked down by an Edison truck on Second Avenue and lost his right arm. It was hard to say who was more heartbroken, him or Jake.

Jake had an idea. Sol Isaacs died years before, and his son, Eddy, had taken over the music shop. Jake persuaded Eddy to take Ken on as an assistant. Eddy and his wife wanted to retire to Florida and sell the business.

Jake loaned Ken $10,000 as a down payment on the business. Ten thousand was exactly half Jake's net worth, but what the hell? Ken was a good kid. Why not?

A few months later, Con Ed settled generously with Ken for the accident and he quickly repaid Jake. Ken took up with Darby, a snotty-nosed Park Avenue bitch, the daughter of a bigshot partner at a prominent white-shoe law firm. She detested Jake and turned Ken against him. Now he only saw Ken once a year and was lucky if he received a Christmas card or an occasional phone call. He put the card aside to open the third envelope.

He pulled out the enclosures. Two tickets for an upcoming concert on January 14th at Carnegie Hall. A yellow Post-it simply read, "Enjoy." Nothing else. He looked at the tickets again. "Alexandre Laurent—Piano Solo."

"Who the hell would send me these? Ken, probably."

Row C—orchestra—center. Arguably the best seats in the house, and usually impossible to get as they are snapped up by board members, donors, and friends of the performers.

"Ken, it's Jake," he said. "Do I have to thank you for the tickets?"

"What tickets?"

"Someone sent me two tickets for some concert at Carnegie Hall on January 14th. Who else would send me tickets for anything, for God's sake?"

"Well, it wasn't me. Who's playing?"

Jake looked again at the tickets. "Alexandre Laurent. Have you ever heard of him?"

"My God. You've got tickets for that concert? Have I *heard* of him? He's the new Horowitz. A genius. French guy, in his twenties, considered the best in the world right now. He specializes in Chopin and Debussy. Schuman too, I think."

"Should I go?"

"You'd be a fool if you didn't."

"I've got two tickets. You want to come with me?"

"What day did you say?"

"January 14th."

"Sorry, I can't. Darby and I will be in Sun Valley staying with her parents."

"Fuck."

He put the phone down and looked at the envelope. No name or return address.

He hadn't been to a concert in a long time and had never had such good tickets. If the kid was as good as Ken suggested, the tickets must be worth a lot. After all the face price was $250.

He was about to turn off the radio when the DJ played Louis Armstrong's "When You're Smiling."

Ah Louis. What a man. Jake closed his eyes and thought back on that night in 1958 when Louis played in Pittsburgh and his pianist was indisposed and they urgently needed a replacement. Someone backstage had suggested Jake, who was playing in the bar at a nearby hotel. The band boy was sent to get him, and thirty minutes later he walked on stage with the All-Stars wearing a borrowed band jacket. He knew the repertoire pretty much—"When It's Sleepy Time Down South," "Indiana," "Basin Street Blues," "Mack the Knife," and "Jubilee"—but he stank. The musicians tried to cover for him. Of course, he couldn't take a solo and he struggled to keep up with the rhythm section. He saw the bass player look at the drummer and shrug his shoulders.

Fortunately, the eyes and ears of the audience were fixed only on Louis; they were oblivious to Jake's playing even if the musicians weren't. At intermission, he followed the musicians into the green room. He sat in a corner while the others chatted among themselves.

The trombonist, James "Trummy" Young, whispered something in Louis's ear. They turned to glance at Jake. "I'll handle it," Louis replied. "I'll call Joe as soon as we're back at the hotel. Billy should be okay tomorrow. The doctor said so."

At the end of the concert, Louis took center stage to introduce the musicians, one by one, and they each stepped forward to take a bow.

"And, on piano, standing in for Billy Kyle, is a Pittsburgh son, a great cat . . ." Louis had forgotten Jake's name. He turned around to face the others to get the prompt but to everyone's embarrassment, no one could recall Jake's name. "Give him a big hand."

Back in the green room, Louis approached Jake to thank him and to apologize for not being able to mention him by name, and to reassure him that he would be receiving a check. Louis gave him a hug and Jake smiled. "I'm sorry if I let you down, Mr. Armstrong."

"You were great. Thank you for filling in for Billy."

Jake smiled and left the room. The other musicians waved. One of them said, "Take it easy, fella."

He stepped into the street. He had played with the great Louis Armstrong! And even though Jake knew Louis had been aware of his subpar skills, the legend had treated him as though he were the greatest. Louis was a beautiful man!

There was no point inviting Trixie to accompany him to Carnegie Hall. She would kvetch about having nothing to wear, disliking classical music, and being out in the freezing cold. To hell with her. She'd become a pain in the ass anyway.

As the days rolled by, he lost his curiosity about who had sent the tickets. He decided on wearing his blue suit. He tried it on. It still fit. It was the last suit he had bought, maybe twenty years earlier. He picked out a white shirt and navy tie. His black shoes needed a polish. To hell with it. No one would look at his feet.

Concert night arrived. A cold, wet, wintery day in New York. Jake walked onto Second Avenue and wrapped his scarf tight around his neck as he waited for a cab. An extravagance, sure, but it was too far to walk to Carnegie Hall and he couldn't mess with busses and the subway. Doors opened at seven, and as he approached Carnegie Hall, a ticket tout approached him.

"You wanna buy a ticket for tonight's concert?" Jake asked, looking at the young man whose face was barely visible from under his hood. "I've got one to sell. Third row, center orchestra. How much?"

"Let me see it."

Jake pulled the envelope from his pocket and took out one ticket. He held it tight in his hand as the man examined it.

"One fifty," offered the man with the hidden face.

"Go fuck yourself. That's a two-hundred-fifty-dollar ticket."

"Okay, I'll give you two fifty."

"Three fifty or no deal."

"Okay."

The man counted out seven fifty-dollar bills and Jake released the ticket.

He smiled as he stuffed the cash in his trouser pocket. This covered the cabs and a few nights of decent dinners. *Thank you, whoever you are, for tonight.*

Minutes later he was seated in what was definitely one of the best seats in the house. The concert hall was filling up. He waited patiently to see who would be taking the seat next to him and wondered what profit the tout had made on the ticket. He didn't have to wait long. A young man, dressed immaculately, took the seat and ignored Jake's gruff greeting. *Fuck him. I hope the tout made a good deal. Standing out in the freezing cold waiting for some mug to pay him, what, five hundred bucks for a ticket. He deserves his profit.*

The lights dimmed and there was a hush as all conversation came to an abrupt end. From stage left, a young man, maybe in his twenties, stepped on stage in white tie. The audience greeted him with loud applause as he bowed and took his seat behind the magnificent ebony concert grand Steinway. *The kid looked the part, but could've he have taken the trouble to have a haircut before appearing at Carnegie Hall? And what was with the beard?*

Chopin. *Ah Chopin.* Jake closed his eyes as he listened to a piece he had not heard in years. There was a time when he could play that piece, admittedly not well, but here was this kid playing it from memory without sheet music. Indeed, the youngster had talent. Then, Chopin. Rubenstein had always been the maestro when it came to Chopin, but this boy would have given Arturo a run for his money.

Jake stayed in his seat during intermission.

The rest of the program was Debussy. Jake was familiar with Debussy's work, as he had been a big influence on jazz musicians such as Duke Ellington and Bix Beiderbecke.

When the concert ended, the applause was both long and deafening. *The kid's great.* After endless bows and bouquets, the young man left the stage.

The well-dressed gentleman stood to leave. The elderly woman to Jake's left turned to him and simply said, "We were much blessed to have been here tonight. We witnessed a true virtuoso, for sure." Jake nodded.

He remained seated until the concert hall was half empty. No point rushing. He was hungry and with $350 of "found money" in his pocket, he could afford to eat a decent meal. The Carnegie Deli beckoned.

He ordered chicken in the pot and coffee.

That kid. He was special. *If only those bastards at Julliard had given me a scholarship, maybe I could have been like that kid, white tie and tails, Carnegie Hall. But no point wallowing in the past.* That woman was right. They'd witnessed a genius. Genius who needed a shave and a trim.

It was around eleven-thirty when he stepped out of the cab and into the heavy wind blowing from the East River. He walked the few yards into his building.

"A messenger dropped off an envelope for you half an hour ago. The super slipped it under your door."

"Thank you."

He ambled toward the elevator, still thinking about the concert. What a night. Best he'd had in years. He was glad he had gone alone. Ken would have rushed straight home to that bitch of a wife. Trixie would have complained about everything and spoiled the evening.

He opened his door, switched on the light, and stooped to pick up the large envelope that had been dropped off. He took it to the table, threw his coat onto a chair, and sat down on the other. His name and address were written in black ink in large block letters.

Several photographs fell onto the table, together with a handwritten note.

Dear Jake,

I'm glad you came to the concert tonight. I hope you enjoyed it. You looked good. Adele and I were sitting in the row behind, several seats to your left. By the way, Adele is your daughter. She is now sixty-four. We are here in New York for another ten days and are at The Surrey. Please give us a call. I'd like to see you again and Adele would certainly like to meet her father. And, by the way, the pianist you saw tonight, Alexandre, is your grandson.

Aren't you glad I didn't have the abortion? Here's the $300 back and I am enclosing some photographs of Adele and Alexandre.

À Bientôt,

Juliette Monet

Jake felt his heart race and his eyes swell. He could not hold back his tears. In fact, he cried and cried until his face was drenched in tears. Jake Baker had a family.